UNMASKING PAULIE BINGHAM

Anne Carter

A Paulie & Kate Novel
Book 1

Beacon Street Books

Contemporary Alternative Romance

UNMASKING PAULIE BINGHAM

by Anne Carter

Copyright © 2012 by Pamela Ripling
Cover © by Pamela Ripling
Edited by J.R. Turner

ISBN-13 978-0615638409
ISBN-10: 0615638406

Published In the United States of America

July, 2013

Beacon Street Books
Santa Clarita, CA 91355-2026
http://www.beaconstreetbooks.com

Unmasking Paulie Bingham

"I'm here to see Paulie Bingham."

"What makes you think he's here?"

Kate swallowed, narrowed her eyes, and looked past the man into the house. "Because I gave him that leather jacket on the couch there, and he never goes anywhere without it," she lied.

"You expect me to believe that? And who are you?" Arms akimbo, the man squared his stance, tried to block her view.

"I'm his fucking *mother*." Now certain that Paulie was inside, Kate muscled her way in, tossed her bag onto the couch. "Where is he?"

Sullen, the man gestured toward the hallway.

Kate paused. "I suggest you get dressed and leave. *Now*."

"Oh, no way. Dude owes me money. I don't mind giving him a little extra time to get himself together, so I'll just hang out."

The cowboy boots placed neatly beside the wall clearly weren't Paulie's style. Kate picked them up, along with an adjacent stack of folded clothing, and shoved them at the man. "How much?"

"One hundred for the hour. No, wait. Two hundred. Because he's a junkie. Makes it tough."

Kate pulled some bills from the hip pocket of her jeans. "Here's twenty. Be glad I don't bust you, too. Now get the hell out." She flashed a fake movie badge she had pocketed just in case.

The rent boy gave her a wide-eyed stare, then hurried into his pants and carried the rest out the door. Kate sighed, waited until she heard the sports car start up and drive away.

She was hesitant to go into the bedroom, afraid of what she might find. Afraid not to.

She eased the door open. "Paulie?" she beckoned softly, peering into the darkened room. The light from a nightstand clock radio barely illuminated the figure of a man lying on the bed.

"Paul?" she repeated, taking a halting step into the room. "Are you okay? It's Kate." She didn't realize she was holding her breath until she heard him sigh. "Thank you," she whispered, then moved closer to the bed.

"I wish... I wish you were really here," came his softly spoken words, wistful, weak.

"I *am* here."

"You are always here. But you always go 'way."

Kate went to him, sat down on the edge of the bed, found his hand in the darkness. "I won't go away. I promise."

DEDICATION

To Tommy H.

I wish you could be here

to help me get this right.

Miss you.

Chapter 1

Summer, 1983. Greek Theatre, Los Angeles, CA

Kate Newman dabbed at her fingers with a pop-up wipe. While her spot behind the curtains prevented her from seeing him, she could hear Paulie's sweet, mournful ballad as he broke the hearts of thousands watching from the outdoor arena. Tonight, no different than any other, the pop crooner sang from the heart; shared his grief with untold numbers of strangers, some of whom shed tears over the painful words of his number one hit song.

"*...you could have saved me... instead you enslaved me... you were just jokin'... this boy is broken...*"

Kate closed her eyes, seeing Paulie's grey-green, lined & glittered eyes before her. His silk tunic swished as he paced. The artificial dreadlocks, part of the "glam look" made so popular by the androgynous likes of David Bowie and Boy George, swayed as he danced around the stage during the refrain. And aside from the usual shouts of "queer!" and "fag!", tonight's crowd was *one* with the star, murmuring the words and sharing the love.

"You okay?" Buzz Hayes, road manager for the band, drew away from the others watching from the wings and touched Kate on the shoulder. "Not like you ain't heard this sappy number before, eh?"

Kate sat down on the floor, drew her knees up, and wished desperately for a cig. Paulie didn't like girls who smoked. "I'm fine," she muttered, tugging at her short, deep magenta hair. "I'm just a bit whacked tonight."

"We're all whacked. It's the schedule. Too much. I'm worried about Paulie. The pace is tough on him."

"He knows what he's doing."

1

"He thinks he knows what he's doing. I'm not sure he does. He lets people take from him." Buzz stepped back into the shadows beside her and lit a joint.

Kate looked up. "Take? Like what? Money?"

"Money and other things. He's doling out pieces of his life. His soul. Ever since we left the U.K, he's trusted all the wrong people."

"Hmm. Are you including me in that?"

"You're just a kid. You wouldn't know how to screw a big star like Paulie. Not sayin' you're not a pro at what you do. You *make* his look, for them." Buzz took a deep drag, gestured toward the audience beyond the curtain. He grunted, exhaled. "Without you, Paulie would just be Southend Paul Bingham, poor scuff from the crap side of London. You paint the rock star on his face. Beautiful face that it is, mind you, but you give him that glam he needs to go out there and seduce the people with the big bucks."

"So who is screwing him, then?"

Buzz took another toke, eyes shifting left to right. After holding it for several seconds, he blew out the smoke. "Can't say. You don't want that kind of knowledge. It's big-people stuff."

"I'm twenty-two. Well, tomorrow."

"Not talking about age. People in this business are killers. Talk is cheap, careers are ruined, money evaporates faster than this spliff. Paul's got a soft heart, and there are those," Buzz said, lowering his gravelly voice and fishing a roach clip from his pocket, expertly pinching it onto the remaining cigarette stub, "who would steal him blind."

"Don't you think you should tell him? I mean, if you're right, shouldn't somebody warn him?" The thought of someone harming Paulie stirred Kate's blood.

Buzz shrugged. "Problem is, Paul is so fuckin' seduced by his own life he can't see anything that would threaten that life. He's drunk wid it. Ridin' the tide. It's all good. Surrounded by people he thinks love him. If I was to mess with that image, I'd be out on me ear. I'd be the bad guy, lyin' about people he trusts. Yeah?"

Kate stood and went to her makeup dresser, began packing up the foundation, powders and highlighters she'd just used to create Paulie's glitzy show image. Her ears noted the change-up on stage when the band launched into the upbeat "Regrets Only". She imagined Paulie sliding into his seductive dance, his multi-ringed fingers grasping the microphone and bringing it so close to his rose-colored lips.

"...send me your regrets.... on-ly... you don't want me to be... lone-ly..."

"I thought he trusted you."

"Naw. Only so far as the tour goes. He can't think beyond that with me. I'm a player, a piece of his puzzle, and as long as I stay in my place, all's cool."

Kate snapped her multi-compartmented case closed, then turned to face Buzz. "What about me? Do you think he trusts me?"

"Sure he does. To the extent that you make him beautiful. You're a chick, you don't threaten. You're part of his puzzle, too. But you go to him, tell him his lover is out screwin' other guys, or that his manager is dippin' in the till, I guarantee you he'll shut down. Paulie doesn't take well to discord. He may let you paint him, but he won't kiss you or hug you or laugh with you."

Her face burning, Kate eyed a pack of Camels on the dressing table. Buzz's words hurt, on so many levels. How could anyone cheat on Paulie? And who was this mystery lover?

She knew betrayal. Brent had cheated. *Self-centered bastard.* But his unfaithfulness led to her being here, and that wasn't all bad. Touring with the Bingham Boys these past four months had been the best days of her life.

Paulie tried not to frown too much while singing. It creased the makeup between his perfectly drawn eyebrows. But he always forgot, because the emotions were just *there*. He couldn't refrain from expressing his sadness, the seriousness of the loss that bubbled up inside every time he sang the song.

He wallowed in the pain, a constant reminder, and all he had left of his life with Jamie. Keeping the pain fresh was the only thing assuring he was still alive.

3

The crowd rocked it tonight, he noted between songs. Lots of smiles in the front. Dancing in the aisles. He smiled back, gave a little wave. "Hullo, Los Angelees! Do you love my jacket?" He spun for his fans, who roared in approval. "I got it in Shanghai!"

So many faces. So much love. He wished he could just leave with them after the show and descend onto one of the clubs on the Strip. He wanted to party. But singing was good, singing was his life, and it paid the bills. *I'm so lucky to be doing what I love.*

"Thank you all, very much! You're the best!"

Before he knew it, the encore ended, the curtain was drawn, and the clatter of the seats began. His smile fell, and he joined the others off stage. He feigned joy, played to their expectations, but it didn't matter. There was always tomorrow night.

They did party, then. The followers swept Paulie up and pushed him into a long black limo, then back-doored him into the Rainbow Bar and Grill and up the stairs to the private, second-floor club where he planted himself onto a couch. A drink appeared along with an assortment of pills.

"Pass," he said, letting the pills fall through his fingers onto the coffee table and taking a sip of the cocktail. He leaned back, dissolved into the cushions, and eyed the room. Lots of action, lots of people, lots of glam. Adoring chicks, all hoping to get lucky, with big, wistful eyes. Pretty boys, all hoping to get lucky, blowing kisses his way. Straight-looking dudes with uneasy smiles, eyes cast down, afraid to show their lust. Paulie smiled. Bizarre life. His life.

"Why don't our beaches look like that?" Paulie asked, peering out the bus window as the sands of Zuma Beach blew by.

"Southend ain't no bloody Southern California, that's why." His band mate, Turner, adjusted his headphones, closed his eyes.

"I could likely get used to this."

Kate leaned forward, spoke over Paulie's shoulder. "There's a nudie beach just down a ways from here."

4

Paulie turned around in surprise. "Yeah? Is there sex?"

"No. No sex, no booze."

"No fun then."

Kate relaxed, stared at the back of Paulie's head. No wigs today, just collar-length, fine ashen hair. His "travel-day" make-up—what he called minimalist—included subdued shadow, conservative eyebrows, thin liner and no lipstick. No self-respecting glam rocker would be caught dead without some kind of face paint.

"Kate? Be a dear and give my neck some love, will you? I must've slept oddly last night."

"If you even slept," Kate muttered. Still, she was happy to drive her fingertips into Paulie's smooth muscles, comforted somehow by his moan of delight.

"Oh... right there. That's good, darling. Mmm..."

Kate pushed her fingers up the back of his scalp, caressing, massaging, drawing circles. After a bit, Paulie surprised her by drawing one of her hands to his lips, kissing her palm, her wrist, her fingers.

"Thank you, love. You're the best. You're too good to me."

"I know."

"Where are we tonight?" Paulie called out.

"Santa Barbara Bowl," Buzz responded from the front of the bus.

"What's...why is everything "bowl" here? Hollywood Bowl, Saint Barbara Bowl, Rose Bowl, what's next, the Toilet Bowl?"

"Better hope not."

The performance went off much the same as the night before, but Kate was morose. She couldn't listen to Paulie's songs tonight. Something had changed with the knowledge of his girlfriend's betrayal. It hurt to know that the painful lyrics actually meant something. Now, instead of her own grief over Brent's unfaithfulness, she felt Paulie's hurt as well. Worse, it was her birthday.

She'd called Albuquerque from the hotel, tried to get past her mother's pleading for her to come home. Just wanted a simple "happy birthday" or "I love you, Katrina" but there were too many admonitions and tears.

The encore was a welcome sound. Bags packed, Kate waited near the door.

"You look glum, chum. Wanna go with us tonight? They say there's a little club down the road," Paulie asked, taking one of her cases from her on the way to the bus.

"Naw. Just dump me at the hotel. I don't feel like partying."

As they boarded, Buzz pulled Paulie aside and whispered something. Paulie nodded, climbed onto the bus and took the seat beside Kate.

Despite the rest of the troupe's vocal chaos, Paulie remained quiet on the ride, and followed Kate and the others off the bus at the hotel. After a brief exchange with Turner, he caught up with Kate at the entrance.

"Aren't you going out?" she asked in surprise.

"No. Not tonight. Too much partying makes Paul a crazy boy. You wanna hang out, maybe just have a meal and unwind?"

Kate slowed, turned to look at Paulie. "You want to hang out with *me*?"

"Sure, why not? Tell you what. Give me a bit to change and then come up... no, wait. I'll come over to your room. What number is it, then?"

Chapter 2

K ate rushed to tidy up the disaster she'd created before the show. Literally running from closet to bed to bathroom, she tore off her clothes as she put things to right and started the shower. She refused to stop and think about why Paulie wanted to spend time with her, or what might or could happen. She just wanted to be fresh and relaxed. Fat chance on the latter.

He called her room first. Kate whipped open the honor bar, perused the tiny bottles of alcoholic beverages with names she'd never heard, and then slammed it closed. While she needed, badly, to calm down, she wasn't certain she could stomach anything stronger than water. And then he knocked.

"Hello, my darling!" He rushed her with an affectionate hug, lifting her small frame easily in a brief swing. Kate was reluctant to let him go, but pulled back to give him a smile.

"You did it yourself. It looks…lovely!"

Paulie raised his carefully etched eyebrows. "Yeah? It looks okay? You know, Kate, I've been doin' me own face for near t' six years now."

Kate blushed. "Of course. I knew that." She turned. "Well, uh, sit down. Make yourself comfortable. Would you like a drink?"

"I've ordered us up some dinner and champers. That okay by you?"

Champagne! Oh, man. "Wow. That's…that's great. I—" Kate pressed her fingertips together, nodded. "Thanks. That was nice of you. Really."

"That …what do you call it? Is it a dress, or a kimono thing? It looks really smashing on you."

"Oh. Uh, this. It's a kimono, yeah. Just comfortable, you know."

"And matching knickers. Absolutely divine."

7

The knock on the door saved her from further concern over her garments. The room service waiter rolled a dinner cart into the room and uncorked the champagne.

Paulie pulled a wallet from his hip pocket, and Kate noticed for the first time that he wore blue jeans and a t-shirt, a rarity. He handed the waiter a ten-spot and walked him to the door.

"There. Now, shall we eat? I'm starved!"

He poured them each a flute of champagne, lifted his glass. "Here's to my good friend Katrina, who is celebrating her best birthday yet!"

Kate blushed, lifted her glass, smiled. "Okay, thanks." It tasted good, and she drank down more than half the glass. Paulie gave her a sweet smile, lifted the lids from their plates. "I hope you don't mind, I'm a vegetarian, and I think you should be, too."

She would have eaten old shoe leather. She nodded vigorously. "It looks great."

"Doesn't it?" He picked an asparagus spear from her plate and poked it into her mouth. "We're nearly the same age, you know. Mine's next week. Twenty-two, going on forty. Or eighteen."

Paulie excelled at chitchat, which put Kate at ease while they dined. He made her laugh time and again with anecdotes about his first visit to America, his childhood in England. "I've changed my mind about a lot of things after coming here."

"Like what?"

"I think you have to pay attention more. You grow up, in your home country, you just sort of trust things, trust that your life is going the right way, that the government is taking care of things, you know, long live the Queen and all that rubbish. Here, I don't feel that safe. Things have gotten very complicated. Oh, it's not all just the U.S. It's mostly just me; I think I'm growing up some. I don't know."

Kate took an emotional breath, remembering Buzz's warning.

"Do you...do you have anyone you can trust, Paulie? Truly?"

Paulie didn't react with the surprise she thought he would. Instead, he emptied his champagne glass and refilled it. "Sadly, I'm not sure anymore. People you think will always be there, are not. People you think have your back, they don't. The only thing that's for certain is your enemies. They are unflinchingly *there*."

Her heart thudded. A chord was struck. She wanted—needed—to reach out to him. Instead, she swigged her drink and then sat on her hands.

"I know how you feel." *And how I feel*. Especially with the "champers" quieting her inhibitions, her fear of intimacy. "It's heartbreaking to be…betrayed."

"You've heard about Jamie, then."

Eyes wide, Kate clamped a hand over her mouth momentarily. "I'm sorry. No, not really. But I think—I think I would punch her lights out if she was here."

Again, her hand covered her lips as she heard her own words. Paulie looked surprised, then grinned.

"You would, eh? Knock those lights right out, would ya?"

Kate bristled, straightened. "Paul. I, I can't lie. I can't bear the thought of her hurting you. How can anyone be so cruel? You wrote those songs for her, didn't you? I didn't know. All I could think of was my own selfish pain."

Paulie's smile faded. "What pain would that be, darling? Please don't tell me someone has stomped on your heart, too?"

She felt tears gathering in the corners of her eyes, took another gulp of champagne. "It doesn't matter. I mean, it does matter, that you ask, that you care. You're an old soul, Paulie. Don't ever let anyone or anything change you."

Paulie reached out, stroked her cheek. "You don't know me, love. But thank you."

She did know him. How could he say that? She looked to her lap as the tears began to fall.

Paulie pushed away their dinner cart, then reached down to take Kate's hand. "Here. Come. We have some things to sort out." She stood, allowed him to lead her to the bed, where they got comfortable facing one another. He again took her hand, examined it while composing his thoughts.

9

"Maybe there is someone I can trust. But first, there are some things you need to know about Paulie Bingham. And Jamie Pritchard. Can you handle difficult topics?"

She watched his lips form the words. She wanted to kiss him, feel his long, slender body against hers.

"What could be so difficult?"

"Well, for starters, Jamie is a *he*, not a she."

Kate pulled her eyes away from his seductive mouth to meet his expectant stare. She swallowed, colored. "So... you're gay."

Paulie drew in a breath. "Well, mostly, yeah. It shocks me that you didn't know."

She knew. A part of her had known all along. Had denied it. Because acknowledging that she wanted a gay man was something she couldn't wrap her mind around.

"So, okay, what does it matter? So you like men. Big deal." Kate shrugged. "It doesn't mean...it doesn't mean..."

"It matters if you and I are to be close. It matters if your motives are for more than friendship, and hugs."

She didn't answer. Motives? Did she have them? Several moments passed before Kate reached up, carefully placed her hand on his cheek. He mirrored her action, passed his thumb beneath her eye to catch a tear.

"Maybe we'll table that for a bit, eh? Tell me about the bloke who broke your heart."

She did, and didn't, want to talk about Brent. "He was so sweet, at first. Really a thoughtful, nice guy. Soft. Compassionate. He didn't want to hurt me. I think I was just too strong. I was too tough on him. He met someone else. He never told me anything about her. Just that they were better suited."

Paulie nodded, gently stroking Kate's hair away from her face.

"He was a big fan of yours, by the way," Kate told him, smiling through her tears. "We saw you last year in Albuquerque, at the Kiva. He somehow got backstage passes."

"And where the hell is Albacricky?"

"Al-bu-cur-key. My hometown. It's in New Mexico."

"Not old Mexico."

Kate punched him.

10

"Ouch! Sorry. So, you got backstage with we gentle boys?"

"I stayed behind. I wasn't feeling well."

"Really? We were that bad? Likely Jamie's fault."

Kate recalled the night. "He was so incredibly high afterward. Couldn't stop talking about the band, and all the cool people he met. Not long after that, the drift began. At first, I think it was a long-distance affair. He had secret phone calls, even a telegram or two. She may have been out of the country."

"Wow. He never let her name slip? Nothing like that?"

"No. Brent really went out of his way to stay transparent. He actually… cried when we broke up. But he still broke my heart."

Paulie frowned. "His name was Brent?"

"Yeah, why?"

Paulie sighed, licked his lips. "Stay put. This calls for more champers."

He poured, they clinked. "Here's to Brent and Jamie. May they have all that they deserve."

Kate wiped her face with her sleeve, sniffed, and tilted her head. "You say that like they're a couple."

"They are, my darling."

"You're joking, right?"

"Wish that I were. Unless I've missed my mark, your bloody ex just came out of the closet and seduced mine."

Maybe he shouldn't have blurted it out, but she deserved to know. She deserved the truth, as did he. And they needed each other's trust. Withholding his suspicions would have been akin to lying. He liked Kate too much to do that. At least she'd stopped crying.

She was lying on her back, staring at the ceiling. He lay on his side, an arm comfortably draped across her belly.

"So now what do we do." Her voice, sad and disillusioned, tore at his heart, prompting long dormant feelings to surface. With the flat of his hand, he began to caress her stomach, her chest. She worked out, this one; firm muscles, small breasts, strong shoulders. She turned suddenly to face him.

"Why me? Do I have a thing for gay men? This is crazy! I'm going to be alone for-*ever."*

"No, no, that's not true," he cooed, threading his hand around her neck and cupping the back of her head. "You are a strong, remarkable girl. And you're bloody gorgeous."

"Yeah, but to who? Look, I can't...I shouldn't..." she tried to get up, but he held her back. They tousled on the bed, with Paulie ending up on top of her. She struggled, he held her wrists.

"Please let me go. I'm so embarrassed. Can we just forget about this? I've had too much champagne, and you probably think—"

"Shh. Shh. Stop this rubbish, will you?"

Kate thrust out her lower lip. "I'm sorry. I didn't mean to unload on you. You've been very nice to me, Paulie Bingham. Too nice, I think."

His green eyes darkened. He wet his lips. "Would it help to tell you that if I was ever to love a woman, it would be you?"

When she didn't respond, he stumbled on. "I meant to say, I do care about you, Kate. Tonight especially, you've opened me up—I haven't talked like this to anyone in ages. Your sweetness, your honesty brings wholeness back to my life. This may sound stupid, but even letting you touch my face took a lot of trust."

She stared back at him.

"I'm sorry that Jamie took your lover away. I would change that if I could. Don't blame yourself. And, sad to say, you likely can't blame Brent, either. I don't know what makes us different. We just are. I've had to learn to live with it."

Kate moved beneath him, and he loosened his grip on her. The look in her eyes changed as she slowly lifted her arms to wrap around his neck. "Have you ever been with a woman?"

Paulie couldn't hold back a smile. "Of course I have. Quite a few, actually."

"And?"

"And what? Are you teasing me, Kate? I've been round this block before."

"What was it like? What did you feel?"

He drew in a deep breath, peered into her brown eyes, intent on expressing the truth. His truth. "Okay. Here's the deal. Recreationally, I prefer men. Long-term commitments, I guess I prefer men. When expressing love, deep, gut-felt devotion—I don't think gender is all that important."

Her hands moved down his back, pressing hard, showing surprising strength. She tilted her hips beneath his, arched just a little. Paulie chuckled. "What do you want from me, sweetness?"

"Make love to me."

"Ah, Kate. I don't know. I've not—"

"It's my birthday, Paulie. And you... you're so beautiful. So incredibly sexy. I can feel it. You could want me."

She was right about the feeling part. As her hands traveled over his bum, Paulie felt aroused. But she was female. It had been a while, a long while, since he'd had sex with a girl.

"It's not that simple."

"Love can be simple." She rolled him off of her, put herself on top, and straddled his hips. "Why would you come here, lay on my bed with me if you didn't want to have sex?"

Maybe he would try. She was so sweet, so needy. *And, come to think of it, so am I.*

"I suppose—"

"No. No supposition. I *love* you, Paul. Let me show you. We can do this; we can feel whole again and damn Jamie and Brent all to hell. Just now, tonight, no barriers between us. It doesn't matter if we are men or women or whatever." She untied the obi holding her kimono closed, slipped the silken robe off and tossed it away. Reaching behind her, she started to unhook her bra. Paulie watched in awe.

"Wait." Kate reached to the nightstand, retrieved a small travel packet of moist towelettes. She withdrew one and pressed it to Paulie's face, carefully wiping his skin free of the makeup.

"What do you think you're doing?" He grasped her wrist.

"Taking off your mask. This isn't about glam, or Paulie Bingham's fetish with Ziggy Stardust. This is about Paul Phillip Bingham coming out from behind the mask and getting real."

He wasn't sure if it was her words, her motions, or her unconditional love, but Paulie's reaction startled even himself as

13

he tentatively pressed his lips to her mouth and offered his tongue. Suddenly, he did want her, needed her love, her acceptance, her lust. Desperate, nimble fingers found and undid hooks, snaps and zippers—even found a condom; and soon Paulie was locked onto Kate in a motion as old as mankind.

He didn't stop to marvel at the change in his role. Didn't seem to matter, for the moment, that they mutually shared in the seduction. Kate clearly adored him, made him feel loved and coveted. She was good with her hands and even better with her mouth. He returned her efforts with halting but affectionate moves that expressed his feelings. What he didn't know, she taught him, and play-by-play, she was his match. Nearly an hour passed before they came up for air.

"Amazing," Paulie murmured.

"I could use a smoke," Kate said, toying with Paulie's damp hair as he laid his head upon her chest.

"Me, too."

"I thought you didn't?"

"It was ruining my voice. I had to stop."

She kissed the top of his head. "I stopped because you stopped."

"My work is done, then," he said with a chuckle.

He hadn't felt so complete, so contented in ages. She had done this for him. *A woman.* It almost made him wish he wasn't gay. He rose up, looked into Kate's face. "Thank you."

"For what?"

"For reminding me. For renewing me." He kissed her again. "You are exquisite."

"So are you. Your trust means everything to me."

"Just so you know, I've never let anyone, ever, take off my makeup before."

He slept, for a time. Kate watched with eyes she wished weren't so clouded with obsession. She touched his hair, a wispy touch, fearful of waking him. For as long as he slept, she could pretend that he belonged to her. That he wasn't gay, that he was a real boyfriend who would stay and cherish her and commit.

Paulie opened his eyes, looked around.

"Is it morning? Are we late?"

"No. We're not late."

He stroked her bare shoulder, ran his hand down her arm. "You're very soft."

"I'll be leaving now."

"What?" Paulie adjusted the pillow so that he was eye-to-eye with Kate. "It's your room, remember?"

"Not the room. The tour. Can you do your own makeup for the rest of the shows? It's only four nights."

Paulie sat up, his face twisted into a worry. "Why? Because of this, tonight?"

"Partly."

"But, no. You can't. Not now."

"What happened tonight changes everything, and nothing. I will always love you, Paulie. Always. You gave me something tonight that I'll cherish forever. But if I continue on, if I'm forced to keep my hands off you and pretend that this just didn't happen… it'll make me bitter."

"Surely we can work something out."

Kate ignored his plea. "If you ever need me, you find me, understand?"

"What if I need you right now? Tomorrow? A week from Friday?"

She laughed. "You won't. You're a big boy with lots of people, millions of people feeding you attention. Lovers at the snap of your fingers. You're on a path. A very different path from mine."

Paulie looked away, and Kate reached for his chin, gently turning him back toward her. She saw the tears. "Dammit Paul, you can't have it both ways."

"I know it. It's just something I can't change. And—and I don't want to change, really. I like who I am. What I am. It's just sad, you know?"

"Of course I know. That's why I have to go. You understand, right?"

He nodded, offered a weak smile. "I love you, too, Kate. More than I want to, right now. Don't ever forget about me, okay? Oh, shit. This is breaking my fucking heart."

Kate reached for her silver case, opened it up beside her on the bed. Choosing his favorite azure blue, she steadied his

15

face with her left hand, began drawing with her right. "Hold still, Paulie."

⚜ I don't know what possessed me that night. Coming on to Paulie was the craziest, boldest thing I'd ever done. I do, however, remember the first time I saw him on stage, back in Albuquerque. I was 21 going on 17. Brent and I had seats in the second section back. I had binoculars, and once trained on Paulie's face, I couldn't tear them away. Yeah, looking back, he did look like a guy with a girl's face. But I saw more than that. Sensitivity, vulnerability, a precious sort of sexuality.

We didn't make assumptions, back then. A lot of heterosexual performers wore makeup and frills. Still, I knew he was wearing a mask.

Brent and I broke up a few weeks later. I was furious, mostly because I had let him into my heart in the first place, and here he'd gone and spoiled things. I was mad at him, mad at myself, mad at my mother. Yeah. She'd warned me about Brent, told me to look for someone else. Someone stronger, a protector, a hero type. I said awful things to her, packed a bag and went to a girlfriend's house across town. Her brother was a promoter, and he said he could get me on with a touring band if I wanted. It was a rough life, he told me, and I'd have to get myself to Phoenix overnight. I didn't care. I borrowed money and got on a bus. Little did I know that the next band leaving the Southwest was the Bingham Boys.

I started as a roadie. I think they gave me the job as a joke, because I'm only a hair over five feet tall. The guys were always tossing things at me they thought I couldn't carry, but I surprised them more often than not. I worked hard, mostly because I needed to keep busy. I watched from the sidelines as Paulie had his face made up before the shows. Not just watched, I studied-I practiced on myself with dime store makeup in motel bathrooms, then wiped it all off before anyone else saw.

The girl who painted him was a complete bitch, and she and Paul fought all the time. One night, he threw her out after a loud and nasty exchange of foul language.

I went immediately to Buzz, told him I could do Paul's face. He didn't believe me, but I persisted. I was like a terrier on a peanut-butter covered rat. I lied all over the place about my training and experience. He finally gave in, sure I would be terrible at it.

Paulie was in a pissy mood, and I thought, Oh, great. Why now? My hands were shaking, and I was embarrassed because my fingers were still stained pink from dying my hair the night before. He stared at me, made it difficult by rolling his eyes, fluttering his eyelashes. I was about to cry. Finally, I pinched his chin and said, "If you hold still, I will make you beautiful. If you keep pissing me off, you will look like fucking Joan Rivers."

He looked me in the eye, as if to see if I was serious. Defiant, I stared back. I will forever believe that this was the exact moment that we fell in love. — Kate

Chapter 3

Spring, 1987. Hollywood, CA

Kate rejoiced when the director called it a day. She'd been on the set since 5:45 a.m., hadn't slept much the night before. Swiping the keys from her dressing table, she shouldered her bag and made tracks for the parking lot.

"G'night Ray," she called over her shoulder to one of the boom camera operators just packing up his gear. Her mind was already going over her options.

A nap? A hot bath? These, of course, would have to wait until she'd stopped at the market. She could do without bread, but she'd been out of coffee for two days. That wasn't going to work much longer.

As Liz bagged her loot, Kate perused the scandal rags at the checkout. She felt the color drain from her face and reached for the closest one.

"Poor Paulie: Pill Popping Poof Plummets" headed a terrible likeness of Paul Bingham.

"That's a good look for you, Kate."

Kate turned her attention back to the cashier, who smiled.

"Your hair. I like that color. Did you cut it, too? It wasn't that spiky before."

"Uh, yeah. Got tired of it again."

She looked back at the magazine cover. Paulie looked ill. They'd kept in touch, for a while, but it had been nearly four years since her momentous birthday connection with the flamboyant glam boy. She couldn't pull her attention away from the pleading in his newsprint eyes.

"Is it black noir? Is that what it's called? I've been thinking of doing mine that color."

"Ebony."

19

"You want me to ring up the magazine, too? Shame about that boy. My daughter has all of his records. He's a homo, you know."

Kate glanced up. "So I've heard. Thanks, Liz. Gotta run."

The article said he still kept a home in Los Angeles, and one in London. Kate had no idea where he was now. The photo, taken outside an L.A. club, made her nauseous every time she looked at it.

Two sleepless nights later, her phone rang at one a.m. She sat up, answered, waited. No one spoke.

"Hello... is anyone there? Who is this?" She could hear music playing in the background. The connection ended.

Kate swung her legs out of bed and sat up. "Damn. *Damn, damn, damn.*" While she couldn't be sure, she suspected Paulie had made the call. Hadn't she told him to find her? She'd done her share of drugs, socially, but didn't know the first thing about real addiction.

She wracked her brain to figure out how to find him. Crossing to her desk, she pulled a dog-eared address book from the drawer and flipped to "C". *Crawford, Brent.* She dialed.

"Kate, it's the middle of the freakin' night. What's the matter?"

"I need to find Paulie Bingham. It's important."

"So? Why are you calling me?"

"Because Jamie will know where he is."

A moment passed when Brent's phone was muffled, then he came back on the line. "I haven't seen Pritchard for three years. And what makes you think he would know?"

Kate sighed. *Brent the bonehead.* Why had she shed so many tears? "Trust me. He will know. Can't you just call him? You must have his number."

Brent paused, groaned. "You would make me call him, after everything?"

"It's not my fault he wasn't good to you, Brent. *I* was good to you, though, so you can feel good about doing this for me. Just—do it. Call him. Find out where Paulie is, then call me back. I'll be waiting."

She didn't remember Palm Springs being so far away. The hastily scribbled address on the scrap of paper in her hand was almost illegible. She hadn't expected the emotional tide that had reared at the thought of Paulie being in trouble. The article implied heroin abuse.

At ten p.m. she pulled up in front of a single story casita at the end of a private drive. A small sports car was nested beneath a tree, and she parked beside it.

The house windows were dark. She knocked, waited. Hoped. It was a long-shot, she knew. Jamie Pritchard had "heard" that Paulie was holed up, trying to battle his addictions alone. She shook her head slowly, knocked again. Paul didn't do drugs. Not the Paulie she knew.

The door opened.

"Yes?" A young man wearing a red silk robe stared at her. "This is a private residence. Are you lost?"

"I'm here to see Paulie Bingham."

"What makes you think he's here?"

Kate swallowed, narrowed her eyes, and looked past the man into the house. "Because I gave him that leather jacket on the couch there, and he never goes anywhere without it," she lied.

"You expect me to believe that? And who are you?" Arms akimbo, the man squared his stance, tried to block her view.

"I'm his fucking *mother*." Now certain that Paulie was inside, Kate muscled her way in, tossed her bag onto the couch. "Where is he?"

Sullen, the man gestured toward the hallway.

Kate paused. "I suggest you get dressed and leave. *Now*."

"Oh, no way. Dude owes me money. I don't mind giving him a little extra time to get himself together, so I'll just hang out."

The cowboy boots placed neatly beside the wall clearly weren't Paulie's style. Kate picked them up, along with an adjacent stack of folded clothing, and shoved them at the man. "How much?"

21

"One hundred for the hour. No, wait. Two hundred. Because he's a junkie. Makes it tough."

Kate pulled some bills from the hip pocket of her jeans. "Here's twenty. Be glad I don't bust you, too. Now get the hell out." She flashed a fake movie badge she had pocketed just in case.

The rent boy gave her a wide-eyed stare, then hurried into his pants and carried the rest out the door. Kate sighed, waited until she heard the sports car start up and drive away.

She was hesitant to go into the bedroom, afraid of what she might find. Afraid not to.

She eased the door open. "Paulie?" she beckoned softly, peering into the darkened room. The light from a nightstand clock radio barely illuminated the figure of a man lying on the bed.

"Paul?" she repeated, took a halting step into the room. "Are you okay? It's Kate." She didn't realize she was holding her breath until she heard him sigh. "Thank you," she whispered, then moved closer to the bed.

"I wish… I wish you were really here," came his softly spoken words, wistful, weak.

"I *am* here."

"You are always here. But you always go 'way."

Kate went to him, sat down on the edge of the bed, found his hand in the darkness. "I won't go away. I promise."

"I'm… I'm really sick, love."

"I know. I'm going to take care of you." Her eyes adjusting, Kate looked around the room. It wasn't like Paulie to live in chaos, and even in the dark this room looked like the spoils of a weeklong party. She turned back to him, strained to see his face.

"Don't—don't look at me, Kate. I'm not pretty. I'm terribly ill. I've really fucked up."

"Shh. Don't worry about that now."

"I'm so sorry. I didn't want you… to see…" His voice drifted, his eyes closed.

"Paulie, don't go to sleep. I need to know something." She touched his face, found it wet with perspiration. His eyes fluttered open. "When was the last time? Did that guy inject you?" He hardly looked capable of mainlining himself, but Kate wasn't sure. "Are you slamming or smoking?"

"It was, last night, I think," he said softly.

"Did you run out of dope? Is there heroin in this house?"

"I don't know. Trying to stop. Oh, Kate. I'm so bloody cold. Is he…is he gone?"

"Oh, yes. Took his gun and hit the trail." She pulled the bedclothes over him.

"I'm sorry. I never wanted this. I thought I could stop."

"I know. Try to rest. I won't leave you."

He slept off and on, with Kate holding vigil. In her bag was the methadone Jamie had sent with a snarky looking courier. It made her uneasy, having illegal drugs in her possession. But for Paulie, she would do anything.

She woke to the sound of Paulie retching in the bathroom. She rushed to the door and found it locked.

"Are you all right?"

"Oh, Christ! Fucking goddam son of a bitch!"

She could hear him thrashing about, kicking at the cabinets.

"Paulie, open the door."

He turned the knob, and Kate got her first look at him in the light. Her words caught in her throat. Paulie's hair was cropped short, his cheeks sunken. He was thinner, drawn, possibly emaciated. Skin pale, eyebrows shaved, and his red-rimmed eyes bore no trace of makeup.

Kate drew herself up. "Come on, babe. I'll help you get a shower. Doesn't that sound good?"

"I'm hurting. It's bad. I think I'm dying."

Despite the difference in their height, Kate reached up and pulled him close. Paulie slid to his knees and began to sob.

Kate wept too, pressing his head against her belly. "You aren't going to die. It might feel like it, you might wish you could, but I won't let you."

Somehow, she got him stripped. He told her he couldn't stand in the shower, so she drew him a bath and helped him settle into the hot water. She swallowed down her shock at his appearance. He clearly hadn't kept any food down for some time. In a clearer moment, he told her it had been three days since he'd shot heroin. His withdrawal was peaking.

Kate knelt beside the tub. "So...how... did... this happen?" she asked quietly.

Paulie closed his eyes, slid down into the water, then reemerged until his chin was above the surface.

"It's a nasty, horrifying story. Someday I'll tell you." He sighed. "If you're unlucky enough to still be of my acquaintance."

A basket of toiletries had been placed beside the tub. Kate snatched up a sample-sized bottle of shampoo and poured out a dollop into her hand. She knew how sensitive he was to touch, so started gently, swirling her fingers against his scalp and neck.

"How's that?" she whispered.

"I don't know how this is possible. People like you don't happen to me."

Kate found him some clean clothes, helped him dress, then deposited him on the couch while she changed the bedding and tidied up the bedroom. She perused the kitchenette for any kind of sustenance. There was tea, of course, and bread.

"Maybe this isn't worth it," he muttered, wrapping an Aztec blanket around him. "It really hurts, Kate. I don't know if I can do this."

"Oh, you can do it, all right. And you will. Here, take another bite of toast."

"I'll be sick. Look. Maybe just one more bang. I mean, can't it be more gradual? Just a bit, I promise. Then, no more."

Kate looked at Paulie, watched him shiver, saw the mask of pain on his face. She went to her bag and brought out a small bottle. "No more smack. No. But I—I got this. It should help you get over this part."

"What is that? Shit. You got methadone? Where the hell did you get that?"

"It doesn't matter. I want you to take this." She went to the kitchenette and returned with a spoon.

"Christ. Like cough meds, is it?" He looked away. "I'm so fucked. From one drug to another. Why won't God give me a bloody break? This is just too hard."

Kate squared her stance, slammed the spoon down on the table. "All right. Would you like me to invite anyone else to your little pity party? Do you want me to call your sister? Some of your fans? How about your little red silk friend I sent packing?"

Paulie stared, wounded. He swallowed hard, then picked up the spoon and held it out to her. "I'm not myself, Kate."

After swallowing the methadone, he dabbed at his eyes with his shirt cuff. "If I...when I feel better, if I'm good, will you do my face?"

Kate sank to the floor and laid her head in his lap.

She aimed the controller at the TV, cycling through the channels without really seeing the programs. Paulie was sleeping again, thank God. He'd managed not to hurl the methadone, and if he felt well enough, she would take him back to L.A. in the morning. She didn't have enough of the alternate drug to last past tomorrow afternoon. Jamie would just have to get her more. Somehow, she would then ease him off the methadone, would help him heal.

Kate rubbed her eyes, thought about the last two days. She'd caught a break at work; a friend had subbed for her on the last day of the shoot. She didn't have another job lined up for at least a week or two and had planned to take the time off. Some vacation! Never in her wildest imaginings would she have thought she'd be helping someone break a date with Judas. Especially Paulie. The tracks on his arms nearly caused her to faint when she first saw them.

"Kate?"

He was awake. Kate tossed the remote and hurried to the bedroom. "How are you feeling?"

"Like I've been run down by a cavalcade of lorries. Am I allowed something like aspirin?"

He sat up in bed, hands bracing his head. "It's like—it's like the worst hangover you've ever had, times twenty. *Thousand.* Times twenty-thousand. And I can't stay out of the loo."

"Do you think you can watch TV with me?"

He grimaced.

25

"Are you hungry?"

Shook his head. "Still feel buggered."

"Go for a walk?"

Paulie merely stared back at her.

"Come on. Let's at least sit outside for a little while. It's a beautiful day. Do you have a hat?"

"Do I have a hat? Things haven't changed *that* much," he said with a brief smile.

There were two chairs and a small table overlooking a pristine pool, surrounded by classic palms. She gave him a glass of watered down lemonade. Neither spoke for a while, as Kate felt herself begin to relax for the first time since seeing the magazine cover.

Paulie placed his hand over hers and squeezed. He was wearing sunglasses and a beret, but she could see his lips quivering slightly before he spoke.

"I'm sorry I haven't been in touch. How, how are things with you? You still working for the studios?"

"Yeah. I'm actually doing pretty well. I worked on that new Lucas film. Big bucks and an Oscar nomination last year. Can you believe it?"

"Of course I can. You're the best. I never found anyone to replace you."

Kate smiled. Paulie kept tight hold of her hand.

"My sister sent me some money. I used it to rent this place for a month. I came out here intent on drying out. Didn't work out well, did it?"

"You can stop now. I give you permission to stop beating yourself up. Everyone makes mistakes."

"And one of mine was losing touch with you. But then, you all but booted me out of your life."

It hadn't been easy. One of the most difficult things she'd ever had to do.

"As I recall, the last I saw of you was your sexy little bum sashaying away from my tour bus."

"I did not sashay."

"Hmm. I guess my vision was blurred." He took a beat. "So. Anyone special?"

Kate looked toward the pool, where a small bird was dive bombing for a quick drink. "Nope. Haven't met any corruptible or convertible gay men lately."

Paulie actually chuckled, and the sound made her smile. He nodded at her. "I think that makes me somewhat happy. I still can't believe I let you seduce me."

Now Kate laughed. "You couldn't have been seduced unless you wanted to be seduced, Paulie Bingham."

"You might be right." He laced his fingers with hers, brought them to his lips. "It was…one of the most extraordinary nights of my life."

"Blame the champagne."

"Ah, yes. That, and all that mumbo-jumbo about getting even with Jamie and Brent. Nothing whatsoever to do with any kind of affection or kindred spirit."

"Is that what we are? Kindred spirits?" She tried that on in her mind, the notion that she and Paulie really did have a link of sorts. It sounded good, was probably as good as it would get. "Why didn't you say anything when you called me the other night?"

"Didn't I?" Paulie looked away. "I wasn't even sure until now that I actually called you. We dropped some acid. I was in this box. This black, refrigerator-sized box, and I couldn't find the opening. I was really scared. I thought maybe I had died, and I wanted to tell you. Even though I haven't called, I had your number nearby. I don't know what I was expecting to happen, but I knew it wasn't good." He turned to her now. "If I didn't say anything, how did you know it was me?"

Kate shook her head. "I don't know. I saw this awful gossip rag, you know the type. I knew something was wrong. I couldn't get you out of my mind."

At the mention of the tabloid, Paulie let go of her hand. "I need to lie down for a bit, love."

She lay down beside him after drawing the heavy drapes. She ran her hand over his head and onto his back, kissed his forehead. "Don't think about anything else but getting well. We can work on damage control later."

He pulled her against him, brushed her with a return kiss. "You always know just what to say, what to touch, how to make me feel like I matter. If I somehow survive all this crap, I'm going to make it up to you."

Kate pressed a finger to his lips. "Don't be ridiculous. There is nothing to make up."

"You'll see. I mean this. Because I am who I am, *what* I am, I can't really be that person who makes all your dreams come true. And I regret that," he said, his voice growing softer.

So do I.

"But when all is said and done, if this broken down, has-been rock star junkie has anything left, I want to share it with you."

It's the drugs talking, but I'll listen anyway.

"You don't have to believe me. Just don't give up on me yet."

She couldn't prevent the small smile that turned the corners of her mouth. Encouraged, Paulie pressed his lips to hers with a tentative, but devoted, kiss.

If she'd forgotten the feel of his lips, it came back to her in a rush that caused her to warm at the memory of their carefree, sexual escapade of years before. The bond they forged that night still existed—it wasn't her imagination.

He pulled back a little. "I'd do more if I could, especially since we already know it works between us... it just doesn't work *right now*, you know, but it's nothing to do with you."

The smack, she knew, had rendered him temporarily impotent. She also knew that's why he'd called the male escort, hoping for a sexual miracle. He confused sex with love, and always had, she suspected. But then, hadn't she been guilty of that same confusion?

He guided her head to his shoulder. He would sleep now, but above his rapid heartbeat she heard him whisper. It was as if he'd heard her thoughts.

"Lovers don't always have to have sex."

☙ *Kate had no idea what she was in for when she came to the desert to rescue me. She had little experience with drugs, aside from the occasional weed that circulated at Hollywood parties. She avoided everything else. And here was*

I, junkie-first-class, hooked on heroin for more than a year. I was living from dose to dose, sometimes shooting, sometimes snorting. In between, I popped whatever I could get my hands—and money—on. Ecstasy, LSD, cocaine. `Ludes, Valium, even morphine a few times.

I thought I could quit anytime I wanted. But I just didn't want to, right? I had all the friends in the world, happy to sell to me, happy to trip with me, score with me. Happy happy happy until I ran out of money. Then I couldn`t get a fucking cigarette much less a gram of H.

I`d tried to quit a few times. But the sickness was so horrible I couldn`t stand it. I`ve never been strong that way. I was a walking, falling down nightmare. The dark specter was just waiting for me round every corner. Once out of cash, I traded sex for drugs when I could. But really, no one -- man or woman -- wanted to have sex with a filthy addict with vomit in his hair.

Sometimes I thought I fancied Kate because she was rather boy-like when we met. The short, spiky hair, trim but hard little body, street-wise mouth. But more, she stood up to— and for—me. She packed a load of strength in that pint-sized package. Otherwise, she wouldn`t have been able to do what she did.

We both thought, or hoped, that the worst was over when we left Palm Springs behind. We were fooled. Back in L.A., in her small apartment, I went wild. Went on a mad, obsessed search for smack. She once put a little bell on the door so she`d know when I tried to sneak out during the night. She handcuffed me to a towel rack so that she could take a shower without worry. (Did she really think that thin piece of chromed plastic could hold a maniac who'd gone off his nut?)

I`d never been so sick in my life. What didn`t come out one end came out the other. I paced, I shook, I sweated. I spent more time in the loo that first week than I had in the whole first year of primary school.

And yet, she stayed. She calmed me. She nurtured me. She spoon-fed me porridge, soup, and love. –Paulie Bingham

Chapter 4

August, 1988. Hollywood Palladium, Hollywood, CA

"Sound check. One, two."

Three black girls chattered happily at the back of the stage as microphones were moved into place. An intent young man ran his fingers up and down the scales of a gleaming, Yamaha baby grand. Paulie straightened his gold and black, hip length tunic a third time, bent to glance into a small mirror. First rehearsal, first night. First time singing his new hit single live. First time sober on stage in years.

"Want to go over the steps again?" he asked a woman who was studying a piece of paper nearby.

"If you want to, sure. But you know you've got it, honey."

He gave a nervous laugh and looked into the mirror again. No braids, no dreads. Spiked hair, all his own. Make up in natural tones. One diamond stud in his ear.

"Yeah, you're right. I'm just a bit crazed, you know." He giggled. "Can we do a run-through of the opening?"

"We have time, if you want. Let's do it."

The seats were still empty; outside, the sun was setting. Early arriving fans lined the street in front of the auditorium, and when the beginning notes wafted from the stage, a distant roar of delight emanated. It settled him. The love was still there.

He remained on the stage until they opened the front doors and he hurried off to await introduction. Somebody offered him a joint. He held up his hand.

"You've no idea how much I want that. Please, take it away." He drank water, looked around. Someone was missing, someone important.

There was no warm up band. His manager thought it inappropriate, that it would dilute the impact of his big return. He didn't mind either way. A local deejay made some announcements while Paulie paced. A teenage boy approached and handed him a small white envelope.

"For me? Ta."

Why were his fingers shaking so? He'd done this a million times. But it never seemed to get any easier, especially without alcohol or drugs.

He carefully peeled open the flap, withdrew a folded note.

"Hey you, can't tell you how thrilled I am for you tonight! I'm so sorry I can't be there. Just a conflict in plans. Ray has this thing we have to go to. Don't be mad. I will call you soon! Love, Kate."

Ray. The man Kate had eloped with two months ago, barely a year after she'd picked Paulie up from the gutter and literally saved his life. Paulie frowned, slipped the note into the pocket of his trousers. The crowd was going mad. People were beckoning; they must have introduced him.

The anxiety ebbed. Thoughts of Kate calmed yet troubled him. But he smiled and raised both hands in the air, showing his adoring fans twin signs of victory. Or, perhaps, peace.

"I'm baaaack!" He threw kisses, waved, smiled. The fans were on their feet and he hadn't sung a note. He grasped the microphone, pulled it off its stand, and brought it close to his lips. The band was ready; the backup singers were in place. "I'm going to do a number from my new record, please, sing with me if you choose; this song is for someone very dear to my heart." His left hand signaled the band and he closed his eyes.

"Do you even know, what you've done? Taken this broken boy, so undone-

"Do you even know, what it's like to be free again? I'm me again..."

He managed to get through the song without tearing up, and progressed through his repertoire with relative ease. Couldn't quite hit all the high notes, but that's what the girl singers were for. It would get better. The fans had him back for two encores.

Paulie left the stage in good spirits, going straight to his dressing room and closing the door. Outside, there were reporters, VIPs, old friends, new hangers-on. There were flowers everywhere, stuffed animals, bottles of champagne and wine. Personal notes of congratulations, proposals of marriage and telegrams, one from Jamie. It could all wait.

He pulled Kate's note from his pocket, sat down, re-read it. This time, he allowed the sadness. He wanted her, needed her here. He'd never met Ray; Kate had run off with him to Vegas, over a weekend shoot for a new television show. It had shocked the daylights out of him.

Paulie caught his reflection in the dressing table mirror. He'd gained back some of his weight, was nearly back to good health. He still experienced backlashes of withdrawal, still had the cravings. It was Kate who'd defended him against the demons for three months while he convalesced in her townhome. Kate, who'd made sure he got out of bed, ate and dressed every day, who pulled him up out of despair. Held him to the floor when he'd gone wild tearing his own clothes apart, madly searching for even the smallest leftover bit of heroin; held him to her breast as he cried for hours in hopeless misery.

Kate had found his band mates. Contacted his agent. Hired him a new publicist. Took him shopping, bought his clothes. She didn't flinch when he told her he was broke, that he'd shot up, smoked, swallowed and snorted over a million dollars in one year. Then she took up with a stranger and stopped calling.

Of course, they traveled in different circles and didn't share friends. When she'd settled him into his new, hillside retreat home in West L.A., she warned that she had to get back to her life. He agreed, but never expected the new man, the abrupt disconnect. And despite all, he thought she'd be here tonight, to share in their mutual success at having saved his bloody life.

November, 1988.

It was a short tour. A toe in the water, so to speak. Paulie was not at all positive that he could maintain the rigors of a full schedule and stay clean. So they did the So Cal venues and then scheduled a break.

The thing about Kate bothered, then worried him. Like a boil he didn't want to touch, but festered. He couldn't disrupt her life. He was afraid to call, but needed to know.

"Such a wuss," he said aloud. The tour had been a smashing success, and he had a little money now. He considered going home. But leaving without seeing her was out of the question, and he couldn't see her if he couldn't call. It depressed him.

The rain, a cold wintry drizzle that reminded him of London, fell steadily. He paced, picked up, and then put down the phone. He went to his bathroom, washed his face, picked up his eyeliner and drew a thin line along his lashes; darkened his natural brows only a little, brushed on some mascara. Left the rest bare.

"This is me. She knows this me." It took him fifteen minutes to find his keys, but he'd embarked on a mission. A friend at the *Reporter* knew where to find her, and he was off.

He strolled onto the set, keeping his distance, observing the action from beneath a black umbrella. Someone approached, a young man hunched over a clipboard. "I'm sorry, this is a closed set."

Paulie reluctantly removed his sunglasses. "I'm here to see Katrina Newman."

"Holy shit, you're Paulie Bingham!"

Paulie smiled, pressed a finger to his lips. "Shall we make that our little secret, then?"

"Um, sure! Wow. I'll get Kate. Just…just stay right here. I'll make sure nobody bothers you."

"Brilliant. Thank you."

She came straight out. He felt a stir, watching her approach. Her hair was back to auburn, cut in long, ragged layers. She was trim, confident and surprisingly sexy, for a woman. She held out her hand. Paulie didn't know whether to feel hurt or to laugh, but he shook her hand and looked past her to the crew setting up the next scene beneath a massive canopy.

"He's over there, is he?"

Kate nodded.

"Can we get a quick bite? Have a chat?"

She glanced back, too, at the cameraman looking her way.

"Sure. Let me just go get my purse."

"Don't. Don't go back in there. Come with me right now." Paulie was surprised at his own demand, but gently took her elbow and urged her along to the car parked nearby.

They settled at a coffee shop a few blocks from the studio. Paulie gave her a long, level stare. She looked away.

"Tell me."

"I'm so sorry. Ray had a pre-Emmy awards dinner that night. It just couldn't be helped. There would've been no living with him if I'd missed it."

Paulie shook his head. "I don't care about that. How did this whole thing happen?"

"There's nothing to tell, Paul. I met Ray, we went out several times, nearly a year, I think. He's a good, honest man. He's kind, stable…"

"And conveniently straight." Paulie dumped a sugar packet into his tea.

"Why are you being so hostile?"

"Why are you fucking with me? You can't love this guy, nor he you."

"How can you say that? You are *so* over-reacting. You don't even know him."

"I know you. And I know that any man who truly loved you wouldn't make you feel like you had to ignore your best friend." Paulie shook his head.

Kate colored. "It's not like that. Am I not allowed to have a life? Surely you're not jealous." She lowered her voice. "You're the one who had to be gay."

"Jealous? No. Disturbed, yes."

"You'd rather I be alone?"

"I'd rather you be with someone you love. Someone who loves you back. You, more than anyone else I know except perhaps me, need love in your life. This doesn't cut it. It's a sham."

"Do you know how much you're hurting me, Paul?" Her eyes darkened with building fury. "Is this how you feel? You *are* my best friend. And you're cutting me down, here. I'm trying, trying to do something healthy and, and fulfilling and right..."

"Oh, *healthy* rears its ugly head, eh? Yeah, I guess hanging out with a poof like me isn't quite the status quo, is it now? Best friend, indeed."

People were staring. Kate took a breath, tried to regroup. Tried to take his hand.

"You know that's not true. Shame on you for even saying that."

Paulie slowly pulled his hand away.

"What do you want me to do, Paul? I didn't realize I needed your approval."

Hollowness spread within him. He drank down his tea, put on his sunglasses. "You don't. Of course. Let's go. I have a rehearsal to get to."

He didn't say another word until they reached the studio.

"Please don't leave mad," Kate said, grasping the door handle.

Because he couldn't help himself, he looked away. "I hope he won his fucking Emmy."

She barely got through the rest of the day. The damp weather played havoc with the makeup, and the talent complained that she wasn't focused. Paulie's diva tantrum she could handle, but Ray's stares unnerved her, and she knew there would be an inquisition when they got home.

And there was. First, the cold shoulder, the passive-aggressive comments. At last, the bomb.

"I thought you were through with that faggot. How mortifying for me to watch my woman walk off with some broken down, drugged-out drag queen. Are you crazy?"

Kate bristled. "Don't call him that. He's a good friend of mine, and he's clean, by the way. You knew that going in. I don't force you to socialize with him or any of my other friends. We just had a quick chat over coffee. Is that so bad?"

"Frankly, yes. Don't do that again."

Stunned by his tone, Kate turned away, her thoughts pained and confused. What did Paulie call her relationship? A sham?

❧ It was inexcusably stupid of me to miss Paul's concert that night. Stage left was the only place I wanted to be. And I knew he was still fragile. I never meant to hurt him.

I told myself it was dangerous to let him become dependent upon me. Sure, I'd helped him get his life back. He deserved better than to die in some dark and dirty world where he never belonged in the first place. But he was well now. Clean, with all the potential in the world to get back on top.

We'd lived together for months while he recovered. We slept in the same bed, at first because I couldn't trust him not to escape, and then because it became a comforting habit. We experimented a few times with sex. Paulie was insecure, afraid, preoccupied with getting it right. It didn't matter to me; I loved just being naked with him. Some nights we just shared thoughts and dreams, and ice cream. But a point came when I knew my fantasy was over. He made comments, from time to time, about other men. I foresaw that my colorful, precious bird was about to fly away, so I kicked him out of the nest.

Ray had been good to me. But only if you measured "good" against the way Brent had treated me. Or Jim or Ronny before him. Ray, at least, stayed, and professed to care. We had fun, laughed together, and worked in the same industry. He coaxed me out of the cocoon I'd built around me, the sheath that kept me from acknowledging that I still wanted Paulie.

If "C" is tolerate, "B" is like, and "A" is love, I'd give my feelings for Ray a "C-plus."

—Kate

Chapter 5

December, 1988

A soft rain fell. Paulie walked slowly down Haymarket, breathing in the sights and sounds of his hometown. Though names like Piccadilly and St. James were not the streets of his childhood, they still belonged to him.

He wore no hat. Rain trickled down his scalp and neck, dampening his shirt collar beneath his raincoat. Hands thrust deep into his pockets, he wandered the day away, recounting his life thus far and trying hard not to think about Kate or even Jamie. The two people, aside from his mum, that had meant the most to him. Two that had failed him. Or did he fail them?

He vacillated between self-pity and self-recrimination. He hadn't even called her to say he was going. Her deep brown eyes, so dark with hurt, were his *new* last vision of Kate. He'd been incredibly rude. Had lashed out from his own bed of pain, unwilling to even try to accept that maybe, just possibly, she did know what she was doing.

Lots of people, straight people especially, married for the wrong reasons. Or, he thought, reasons other than love. Who was he to say they were wrong?

Paulie didn't think for one minute that his own parents had married for love. His angry, brooding father never showed affection, only disappointment toward his dear mother.

I would marry for love, he thought. *Sex would be good. But you can get sex anywhere. Love is... rare. Difficult to come by.* He'd believed, for a time, that he and Jamie would marry one day. There were places where gays and lesbians could have their unions sanctified. In retrospect, marrying Jamie would likely have been a disaster.

Maybe he would call her, later. After he'd walked a few more miles.

39

It's only because of her that I can walk at all. He was considering that fact when a passerby bumped his shoulder.

"Oh, sorry," a man said, pausing to grasp Paulie's arm. "Pardon me. What the devil? Paulie Bingham?"

Paulie brightened. "Ian Flynn! Fancy that. Walked right into each other. Wow. What's it been, like ten years? Twelve?"

Ian embraced Paulie and kissed his cheek. "Ah, who knows? Man it's good to see you! I was just on my way to a little soiree, given by Kevin Davenport. You remember Kev, don't ya?"

"How could I forget? We ditched school together on many occasions. He got me my first high."

"You really ought to come. The gang would love to see you, Paul. You look great. Nothing like we were all led to believe, you know, the papers have a lark with you 'round here."

Paulie nodded. "They have a lark with me everywhere."

"So you'll come?"

"For a bit. Yeah. I'd like that." He followed Ian another block to a second-story flat and inside, where dance music blared. He didn't recognize all of the faces, male couples mainly, but the few he did know all dropped their jaws.

"Well, if it isn't our famous mascot!"

"Oh, no. Don't make me out to be any kind of role model."

"You must be joking, Paulie! You've done more for gay pride than any other, never afraid to be who you are. Hats off to you, boy!"

Somebody thrust a beer into his hand. He started to protest, thought better of it. He put the mug on the table beside him. The smell of marijuana permeated the air, and yellow flags appeared in his head. His brain began to salivate.

"I hear you have a new record," someone said.

"I've heard it. It's first rate," said another. "You must have a new boy in your life to write such sweet songs. Are you in love?"

Paulie grinned. "Aren't we all?" he quipped.

"Here, here! Here's to Bingham! Raise a glass," Ian called out.

Paulie put the beer stein to his lips, fought the urge to drink it down. A vision came before him, the sight of the toilet bowl swirling below him, Kate's arms around him, her soothing words. Then, the doctor's warning; *one drink could start the whole cycle going again, and you won't be able to stop. Trust me.*

That stupid word again. Trust.

He stuck it out for another hour, during which time no less than three of the boys gave him their numbers, then pulled his new cellular phone from his pocket.

"Crap. I've got to run, chaps. It's been a thrill to see you all, my lovelies. Kev, Ian—thanks, and let's keep in touch, shall we?"

The rain hadn't changed. It was like that, here. A gentle patter that cloaked you. He resumed his leisurely pace, gave up trying not to let Kate back into his head.

Eventually finding his way back to the corner at Green Park where he'd started, he sat down on a bench and reached for his phone. Before he could change his mind, he dialed. He'd chosen the cute one with the dark hair and sharp blue eyes. The one that looked most like Jamie.

Kate dropped her keys on the sideboard and kicked off her shoes, then grabbed the unopened mail and carried it to the kitchen to browse while she poured herself a glass of wine. Ads, bills, junk mail.

Ray was still at work, so she relaxed in her solitude, sipping her Chardonnay and thinking about the weekend ahead. They needed, badly, to talk things out. She refused go on feeling like she couldn't even call Paulie, much less maintain their friendship. Ray needed to understand.

Worse, she needed to understand. Was it just about Paulie, or was Ray a homophobic hater? If the latter, she'd missed the signs. Before they'd settled together, Ray had wined and dined her, impressed her as a confident, caring man. Gifts, small greeting cards and whispered endearments made her feel special for the first time she could remember.

Sex was perfunctory and conventional; Ray initiated and controlled what went on between their sheets. Most of Kate's

41

bedroom experience had been with Brent, who'd more often than not encouraged her to take the lead. Knowing what she now understood about Brent, Kate decided that her inexperience with hetero men must be behind her occasional discomfort with Ray's macho behavior. She'd privately vowed to adjust.

But Ray's dressing down of her best friend—and yes, she still considered Paulie her closest confidante—brought new worries. If forced to decide between them, what would she do? She hadn't talked to Paulie since their disastrous coffee break, but she missed him dreadfully.

Kate's dismal thoughts took a decidedly negative turn. She carried the bills to the second bedroom, which doubled as an office, and attempted to file them into the proper desk drawer. She nearly spilled her wine as she tugged on the drawer handle, surprised to find that it wouldn't budge. It was locked.

"Well, now." Where might the key be? She put down the wine and the envelopes, and went to the bedroom she shared with Ray to peruse the dresser and the nightstand where Ray often dropped his coins and keys at night. Now on a mission, she felt around inside the top drawer of the highboy containing his clothes. In the back corner, a key lay hidden. A small key.

In the drawer she found more mail, as expected. She dropped the bills inside and started to push the drawer closed when she spotted two open envelopes pushed sideways toward the back. They were from her bank. She took them out and sat down in the desk chair.

As she unfolded the first bank statement, she frowned. There had to be some kind of mistake. The balance showing in the money market account, the one into which she transferred the bulk of her substantial income, was under a thousand dollars. Quickly she tore open the second envelope, bearing the checking account statement. $568.02.

Kate's face hardened. Ninety thousand dollars had evaporated. She scanned the details, seeing four withdrawals of over $20,000.00 each. Incredulous, she took a gulp of wine.

My money. All my money. Gone.

She looked again, to make sure she'd read the statements correctly.

He has access to my accounts. Did he think I wouldn't find out? How stupid does he think I am?

I am stupid. I apparently shacked up with a thief.

She took the statements and locked up the rest of the mail. Went to refill her glass. Waited. She had to handle this carefully. Maybe there'd been a simple mistake.

He didn't come home until the wee hours and she feigned sleep. It was noon before he wandered out of their bedroom the next day.

"One of the girls last night said I look like Clooney. You think I do?"

Kate looked up from a magazine, considered. He did. "Not really."

"Yeah, I'm better lookin'. Is there coffee?"

"Nope."

"You got a hair up your ass about something?"

"No. But there is something I want to talk to you about. I'm taking a trip."

Ray pawed through the cupboard, pulling out a jar of instant coffee. "Yeah? Where to?"

"There's a pilot being shot in Vancouver. I have it if I want it."

"How much?"

"Don't know. But it will be good. It's a new sci-fi series. Greenburg is behind it."

"Do they need a steady-cam?"

"I think they've already got a full crew lined up."

"When would you go?"

"Tomorrow."

Ray stopped, his cup poised before the microwave oven door. "Tomorrow? Uh uh. Not a good idea."

Kate stood up, crossed her arms. "And why not?"

"Because I don't want you to, that's why not. You think I'm going to let you gallivant all the way to Canada alone? I need to get the time off to go with you."

"You're kidding, right? Like I can't handle this myself?"

"Forget about it. If they gotta start now, they can get someone else."

Kate hesitated. While Ray may have looked like George Clooney, he had at least three inches and forty pounds on the actor. At her adolescent height, Kate was no match for the ex-wrestler-turned-camera operator.

Be careful. Must be careful. "Let me see how soon they actually need me. Maybe you're right."

"That's a good girl."

The fog had cleared. Kate could now see plainly and knew what she had to do.

Paulie trotted down the steps of the brownstone house on Wentworth Road and hailed a cab. Sated, and yet wanting. The boy was good—experienced. Erotic, but not too rough. Generous with endearments and compliments. Paulie could tell he was looking for a regular. He shook his head. He needed a shower.

It was forty miles to Southend-On-Sea. His sister Peg stood at the sink, drying dishes. "We missed you at dinner, Paul. We had bangers. There's some left."

"Thanks, love. I had some old friends to meet. What time is it?"

"9 p.m. The children are sleeping, so keep it quiet, there's a good boy."

He picked around at the sausage, made it look like he'd eaten some, then checked his phone. Must be around 1 p.m. at home. Home? Since when had Los Angeles become his home?

He went back outside to sit on the porch and watch the rain, the cars, their headlights on the slickened streets. Some of the flats had put out Christmas lights already.

Flipping open the phone again, he wondered what he expected it to do. Kate didn't even have his number because of his stubbornness. But he had hers. While he'd never dialed it, it was there, under "speed dial one".

Paulie sighed. He'd been in Britain a week and was already hankering to get back. His life here lacked something. He wasn't the same boy who'd left home ten years ago in search of fame and fortune. He'd gained, and lost, both; had it all, gambled it away. Now, he'd likely lost Kate, too.

44

He sat in the dark, aimlessly opening and closing the phone. He'd wear it out, for sure. Didn't matter. He was getting a good mad on. Mad at himself, mostly, and his anger caused him to fumble the phone. Reacting quickly, he swiped at it before it could tumble down the concrete steps to the sidewalk below. And in the process, he accidentally pressed the '1' key.

He started to hang it up, to slap it closed before it could ring on the other end. Instead, he stared at the device in his hand, watching the little arrows that indicated the call was attempting to connect. And then he heard a voice. Her voice.

"Hey," he said at last, pressing the phone to his ear.

"Um… hi. What's up?"

"I, uh, thought that since we're officially broken up, I'd ask you to give back all my things."

"Excuse me?"

"Yeah, you know, the toaster, the cassette deck, the good china… my heart…"

"Hold on, please. Let me get my appointment book."

"Sorry?"

There were sounds of travel, muffled comments, then quiet. Finally, she returned, her voice barely above a whisper.

"Paul?"

"Yes, darling."

"Where are you?"

"Essex. Southchurch, at the moment. Where are you?"

"In my garage. What are you doing in England?"

"This is where I'm from. What are you doing in your garage?"

"I only a have a minute. And no, you can't have your stupid heart back. Oh, Paulie… things are just…"

Paulie stood up. "Just, what? Has the glow worn off of dear old Ray?"

Was it a sob? A gasp? Or just a long-distance phone sound? "Katrina. What's going on there?"

"It's okay. I'm okay. It's just that… I think he's taken my money. I don't know why. I'm—I'm afraid to ask him. But—" she paused, and Paulie heard the soft sound again. "I'll work this out. Please, don't worry. Are you there for good?"

"Just on holiday. Back soon. Needed to see my family, some old chums. Can I wire you some money?"

"No, of course not. I'm okay. I'm just in a bit of shock right now. Look, I have to go. Let's get in touch after you get back."

"Wait. Give me your address."

"Why?"

"Maybe I want to send you a fucking Christmas card, for God's sake."

"1107 Lewiston Road. L.A. Crap, I don't know the zip. I might not even be here."

"Got it. Listen, Kate…"

"Yes?"

"I miss you, darling. Take care, will you?"

"December 6th. Got it. Thanks."

Paulie's next call was to British Airways.

Chapter 6

"Why aren't you eating?" Ray asked across the table.

"I am eating. I'm just not that hungry."

"You're getting skinny."

"You're imagining it. By the way, do you need anything at Costco? I'm heading out there tomorrow."

"Yeah. Get me a fifty-five gallon drum of ketchup."

"Funny. Let me know if you think of anything."

Kate knew he was working the next day, and if she didn't do anything to arouse his suspicion, she'd be long gone by the time he realized it. It was hard to admit she'd made a mistake, a mistake that had cost her $90,000 and almost the love of the most important person in her life.

When Friday morning came and Ray had gone, Kate packed a bag and put it in her trunk. She cleaned out her desk, removing all personal documents, including the offensive bank statements and her credit cards. She drove first to the bank, where she verified that Ray had made the withdrawals, then she closed both her accounts. An investigation was opened, but they needed more information on Raymond Goff. She had his social security number at home, so took the risk of returning to grab it.

It proved to be her undoing. Ray parked his car behind hers, blocking her in before raging into the house.

"Kate! Where the hell are you?"

"Ray? What are you doing home?"

"I just stopped at the ATM on Westwood. It said the account is closed."

"Must be some kind of mistake."

"No mistake. I went inside. They said another branch, our branch, verified that you had closed it."

Kate took a step backward. Ray advanced.

"What does this mean? Are you trying to dump me?"

"What about my money, Ray? What about the $90,000 you stole from me?" she shouted, her own anger rising.

"Let's call it community property, babe. What's yours is mine, and what's mine is mine. I needed that money. Needed to pay off a few debts. And what's the big deal, anyway, you'll make that back in the next few months!"

"Are you crazy? Community property? That's bullshit. That was my money! You forged my name, and I already turned you in. It's grand theft, and you know it. A felony."

Ray paused, then approached, raised his hand. "You bitch. You think you can get to me? I'll show you what happens to women who cross me!"

Kate's eyes widened and she backed against the wall. There was movement behind Ray; he'd left the front door swinging open, but Kate was afraid to tear her eyes from his murderous face. "Don't touch me," she uttered. "Just leave me alone!"

She saw the movement again and realized that Paulie was standing behind Ray. Weaponless. He pressed a finger to his lips, then pointed to the counter beside Kate, where a meat tenderizer was propped in the dish drainer. He then made a circular motion with his finger. Kate hoped she understood. But before she could react, Ray's fist came across hard against her cheek. He raised it again.

"Hold right there, you smarmy git!" Paulie called out, and Ray spun around, giving Kate the freedom to grab the mallet and bring it down on him. His height, however, prevented her from hitting him squarely on the head. He stumbled, let out a roar and lurched at Paulie.

Kate jumped onto his back, and Paulie swung his fist as hard as he could, connecting with Ray's jaw and sending Ray, and Kate, sprawling to the floor. Ray lay still.

"Oh my God! Did you kill him?"

"The way my luck's been going, probably not. Damn! That hurts. Do you have any rope, wire, anything? Quick before he comes to."

Kate got to her feet, rushed to a kitchen drawer and retrieved a roll of duct tape, then helped Paulie bind Ray's wrists and ankles. They stood staring down at him, chests heaving. Paulie turned to Kate, took her into his arms.

"Traffic was a bitch," he said.

It was 8 p.m. before the police let them go. An attorney told Kate that she had a good chance at restitution, and that Ray would likely be forced to sell his camera gear in order to pay her. Criminal charges were optional.

Paulie took her to his house.

"I think it's broken," he said, holding out his left hand for Kate.

"I'm sorry, Paul. I didn't want you to have to get mixed up in this." Kate carefully wound the Ace bandage around his hand and secured it, then closed the first aid kit and carried it to the bar. Her own cheek still smarted.

"You just didn't want to admit that I was right. Come here." He patted his lap and she crawled onto it. He planted a gentle kiss on her bruised face, then lay back on the couch. "I almost didn't make the flight," he murmured.

"I still can't believe you came."

"I left before you were out of your garage."

When Kate woke, she was still nestled in Paulie's arms. He held her close, even in sleep. Nothing had ever felt this good, nor would likely ever again. His touch nourished her. She knew, now, why she'd stuck with Ray. Because if she couldn't have Paulie, it didn't really matter who she was with, did it? No one evoked feelings in her like Paulie did.

"You awake?" he said softly.

"I am."

"What's going to happen now?"

"I remember asking you that question once upon a time."

"May I be frank, Katie my love?"

"Always."

"I don't want to lose you again. Not ever."

His words warmed her to the core. He stroked her hair.

"Would you consider staying?"

"Staying?"

"Here. With me."

She adjusted her position, looked into his eyes. They were moist with devotion. Pressing her check against his, she whispered in his ear.

"I'm scared, Paulie."

"Of what?"

"What if it doesn't work out?"

"What if it does? I'm willing to try. Are you?"

"I never thought you would even consider something like that. I just don't know."

"Have I misinterpreted your feelings?"

His question startled her. She'd never really felt he understood how much she cared. Now, he seemed determined to make his own feelings clear.

"I thought a lot about this, Kate. Yeah, I was jealous of that guy. And yeah, I was hurt when you dropped out, for the second time. I realized that I'm wretched without you. I felt stupid, walking all 'round London, not seeing anything. Questioning myself about what was real and what was play. And this whole thing about being gay. Five years ago, you set me on my ear. It was a lark, I thought. I was quite pleased with myself. Look at me, boy wonder. I'm actually bi."

He paused, gathered more thoughts. "But after you left, I was troubled. Didn't know how much so. I met Mark. We had a terrible relationship from the start. About two years, it was. I let him get really physical with me. He had me convinced I deserved it. He was doing coke—and as much as I detested drugs, I used it, too. To be cool. He led me around by the nose— literally. We fought all the time. He blackened my eyes. He broke one of my fucking ribs. I celebrated our last breakup with my first shot of the poison."

"I've always wondered."

"The band fell apart. I had thought things were bad with Mark. I had no idea what I was about to fall into. I wandered around L.A., then things started to heat up so I went to New York, spending money like it was grains of rice. I went from one connection to the next, going inside when I was high, slinking out onto the streets when I needed more. One day I woke up, back in Hollywood, didn't have the faintest idea how I got there.

50

I was being passed around between these big boys. I was so loaded I could barely stand up, but I managed to kick one of them in the 'nads. Next thing I know, there were cops. I literally crawled out the back door of this apartment house and rolled into the bushes. I was afraid to come out for like hours."

"It must have been horrible."

"The next thing I knew, Jamie was there, stuffing me into his car. He took me to his flat, threw me into a cold shower. I slept, and the next day I told him I was okay. He made me call my sister Peg, and she wired some money into my account. He knew about this place in the desert where I could hole up. He hired some guy to take me out there, because I was too fucked up to drive. Of course, I made the driver stop off at one of my old connections in Studio City."

Kate shook her head. "Why are you telling me all this now?"

"Because I want you to know who I am. When you showed up out there, I was just, like, you know, waiting to die. I knew I couldn't beat the monster. It had such a strong hold on me. I had nothing left. Nothing. My hallucinations were terrifying. I imagined my brain was being torn apart, bit by bit. And yet, now and again I'd get an image of you. As if… as if you were thinking about me, sending me a message or something."

"And I was lying in bed for nights, worrying about you, wondering where you were."

"I won't pretend that I'm a strong person. I'm obsessive, I'm compulsive, I'm selfish. I'm insecure and co-dependent. I'm moody and bitchy sometimes. But I'm also loving and compassionate and loyal. I could make a good life—we could make a good life together. I'm clean; I'm healthier than I've been in years. Once you are legally free of Ray, maybe we can start fresh. See where life takes us."

"Ray and I weren't really married. It was a lie. He had a prior that wasn't ended."

"Why doesn't that surprise me? Look, darling. What could I do to make you feel more secure? Would it be humiliating for you to shack up with a queer?"

51

"Not any more so than for you to be seen with a woman."

"It *could* damage my reputation. I'm an icon, you know." He chuckled. "But you're dodging the point."

"You aren't proposing monogamy."

"I would try. For you, I would honestly try. The way I look at it, as long as we stay honest with each other, what do we really have to lose except eons of loneliness?" He gave her a peck. "I'm going all mushy and maudlin. It's been years and I'm still searching for that feeling you gave me. So yeah, I'm asking for exclusivity. Stay with me."

She didn't know what to say, felt her eyes welling with tears.

"I've made you cry. That makes me worry." He hugged her, whispered, his voice hoarse with emotion. "I know it's asking a lot. You've been through so much. But I promise you this, good or bad, no one will ever love you like I do."

"Are you sure? Because you'd better not be messing with me."

"I know better than to do that."

Kate paused, watched his face; cherished the moment. "Then if you want me here, well… it looks like I need a place to stay anyway, and I can't think of any place I'd rather be than with you."

They moved the rest of her possessions into his house the next day. Kate didn't know what to expect, but she didn't care. The very thought of having Paulie beside her gave her new reason to live.

Paulie encouraged her to make whatever changes she felt best in their home. He took her out, introduced her to some of his friends, as did she. By month's end, Ray had paid her back most of the money he'd stolen, and she dropped the charges against him.

In the bedroom, they took it slow. Paulie was uninhibited, and he taught Kate how to share her intense love for him, how to best arouse him. Ever so gently, he coaxed her to teach him the same. The question, "How does that feel?" became a joke between them, a private innuendo he would drop in a restaurant, at a party, over the phone. Together, they learned to channel their love and their lust, bonding them in a profound intimacy neither understood nor cared to worry about.

In late December, they made a trip to New Mexico, and Kate introduced Paulie to her mother and father, who treated him with respect, admiration and just a touch of curiosity. He opted to leave his face mostly naked, hoping to lessen the oddity of their relationship to her parents. From Albuquerque they flew on to Heathrow. Peg cried when he introduced Kate as his "significant other."

"Where is your house, here?" Kate wanted to know.

Paulie tapped the side of his head, then his nose.

"Oh. I see."

They went shopping at Harrod's, where Paulie bought a trunk full of pricey garments and accessories for them both. Chocolate truffles for his nieces and nephews. He took her to the cemetery where his parents were buried, then marched her onto a double-decker bus headed for Buckingham Palace.

"Sir Paul of Bingham House to see Her Royal Majesty, please," he told the guard on duty.

"The queen is not in residence today, Sir Paul. But I will be certain to give her your regards. I'm certain she will regret having missed your untimely visit."

Kate almost choked on her withheld laughter. They strolled through Regents Park, and Paulie fascinated her with stories of his meeting with Princess Diana.

"Oh, she's a charming lady. Open minded, too. I'll have to introduce you, darling. You two will get on famously."

"Have you really been knighted?"

"Many times. Never by *this* queen, however."

Christmas was spent visiting with extended family and hunkering down in a small stone cottage in Bath, owned by Paulie's great uncle. It was there that he proposed.

"I thought it was for Peg's sake," Kate teased, toying with the small, velvet bag he'd just handed her. "You weren't serious."

"As serious as a heartbeat. Go on, open it."

The ring was simple, romantic, but still different. Like Paulie himself. "It belonged to me mum. Fortunately, Peg had it, else I'd have sold it by now. I had it refashioned. What do you think?"

Kate gave him a whimsical look. "What do I think about the ring? Or that you haven't formally asked me yet?"

Paulie dropped to his knees, took her hand. "Marry me, Katrina. Or forever lament my broken heart."

She giggled, tried the ring on. It wasn't quite a perfect fit. *It can be adjusted. Like everything else.*

They weren't in a hurry. Paulie decided that Kate liked being engaged, and was trying out the arrangements to make sure they fit, too. By January's end, she seemed comfortable. She understood the makings of his gay friends, the ones that would stop by and give him a hug, or cry about their lost loves. He dutifully listened when one of her girlfriends did the same. They joked about whom would be Mother Teresa next.

In February, Paulie came home to find Kate sitting outside on the patio, alone, solemn. She looked up when he came out.

"Do you still want to?" she asked, her face carefully screened of emotion.

He squatted down beside her. "More than anything."

"Then let's."

"The tour starts in May."

"Then how about April?"

"Grand."

"Here, or there?"

"Here. At the beach?"

"Perfect."

They made plans. Peg and her family would fly over for the wedding, as would Kate's parents. They were discussing food one night when the doorbell rang. Kate got up to answer it, leaving Paulie on the floor surrounded by menus.

The man at the door was darkly, severely handsome. Muscled, as masculine a guy as she'd seen. His voice, however, was surprisingly soft. "You must be Katrina."

Before she could respond, Paulie was behind her, and she found herself sandwiched between the two, who'd locked stares. Paulie recovered first.

54

"Darling, this is James T. Pritchard. I believe you've met, over the telephone?"

"You're Jamie?" Kate blurted out. A chill ran down her spine. Paulie wrapped a demonstrative arm around her, and she reciprocated. "Well, it's nice to finally meet you. Please, come in."

"I can only stay a minute. I just wanted to…to offer my congratulations."

"More like see if it was true," Paulie accused lightheartedly. "Yes, it's true. You're coming, I hope?"

Jamie grinned, and Kate could see why anyone—man or woman—would succumb to his intoxicating looks.

"I wouldn't miss it for anything. Your happiness means a lot to me."

"Trying something new, are you?"

"Go on, turn the knife. I can take it."

"Well it's your knife, after all, isn't it?"

Kate pulled away from Paulie, planted her hands on her hips. "Do you want me to get out the dueling pistols, boys? Twenty steps?"

Jamie laughed. "I like her. She's spunky. She's just what you need, Paulie-boy."

"And how is it that you suddenly know just what I need?"

Jamie went to Paulie, grasped both his shoulders, and looked him in the eye. "In light of all this happiness, do you think you can muster up some forgiveness, Paul? I did, after all, pluck your bony arse from beneath a malnourished rose bush and save you from untold torture at the hands of our oh-so-benevolent media."

Kate could see that Paulie was struggling, but felt she could only make things worse by opening her mouth again. She was a midget among giants.

Jamie, fueled by Paulie's silence, amped up his plea. "Look, old chap. We were kids. We didn't know what was happening. I didn't, anyway. You were ready to settle, I wasn't. I'm still not, you still are. It's all working out for the best. Can't we just… get past it all?"

Paulie slowly lifted his hands, hung them on Jamie's arms. He nodded. "Yes. Of course. I've been bitter so long, I'd forgotten I no longer have a reason." He reached for Kate then, embraced her fully and firmly. And then he said something that surprised them all.

"Would you stand up for me, Jamie? At the wedding?"

The shock on Jamie's face was evident. "You want me in your wedding? *Me*?"

"I think that's ample punishment, don't you?"

"Christ, Paul. I'd be honored. Wow. This is a turnabout. Can I bring a girlfriend?"

"Don't push me. I'm mustering up forgiveness here."

"Okay. Look, I've gotta run. Kate, it's been a pleasure. You will make a charming, beautiful bride. Unless, of course, Paulie is planning to be the bride?"

"Bugger off, plonker," Paulie said, giving Jamie a gentle push.

They were in bed. She wanted lovemaking, he stared at the ceiling. She started to pout, to turn away, then she remembered the vow of honesty.

"What's spinning you out?"

Paulie shrugged, then turned toward her. "It's him, of course."

"Should I be worried?"

"No. I've just got a lot of stuff to sort out. Like why he came here."

"He said—"

"I know what he said. There's always another agenda with him."

"So why did you invite him to be in the wedding party?"

"I dunno. Maybe something about keeping your friends close—"

"And your enemies closer. Second thoughts?"

"No. Not really. I think I was trying to convince myself that I'm okay with what he did. But it's just not that easy."

"You've never shared what he did."

"Maybe someday."

"So he has a girlfriend?"

Paulie smiled. "Code. He has a new boy. Always, a new boy. He finds ways of letting me know. Like I said, it's not easy."

"I'm sure it isn't. Give yourself a break. Like you said, it's been a long time since you've had to have him in your face. There was no closure. Maybe now there will be."

"And you? How would you feel if Brent came knocking?"

"I think a swift kick to the balls would do it."

"Ahh. Now there's true forgiveness."

Kate punched him and he tackled her in a fit of tickles. They ended up in a passionate mating that rendered them both wasted, sweating, mellow.

"This is working for you, right?" she whispered in the dark.

"If you mean do I enjoy being the man, I haven't really thought about it. That's a good thing, yeah?"

The following day, they went shopping for her gown, his attire, and sex toys. She took him to a little shop on Melrose that sold devices of pleasure and they left the store giggling and anticipatory.

She did his face before the wedding. His hair, now shoulder length, was tied into a queue. She wore a simple white cotton dress, he, white cotton pants and a knee length, white Nehru tunic. In addition to their friends, they allowed a small band of devoted fans who'd congregated early on the beach to watch. One of Paulie's gay friends, a minister, performed the ceremony. They each recited their own, personally written vows.

"There is a reason why," Paulie began, holding both of Kate's hands in his, "a reason why our paths crossed, and continued to cross, time after time. It was a message that took us both awhile to grasp. But I have never been more convinced than I am right now that we were meant to be together, meant to stay together, to grow old together."

"There is a reason why," Kate continued," that I never felt complete until I met you. We were the missing pieces in each other's puzzle."

"I'm jealous," Jamie whispered behind Paulie's back.

They were in bed. She wanted lovemaking, he stared at the ceiling. She started to pout, to turn away, then she remembered the vow of honesty.

"What's spinning you out?"

Paulie shrugged, then turned toward her. "It's him, of course."

"Should I be worried?"

"No. I've just got a lot of stuff to sort out. Like why he came here."

"He said—"

"I know what he said. There's always another agenda with him."

"So why did you invite him to be in the wedding party?"

"I dunno. Maybe something about keeping your friends close—"

"And your enemies closer. Second thoughts?"

"No. Not really. I think I was trying to convince myself that I'm okay with what he did. But it's just not that easy."

"You've never shared what he did."

"Maybe someday."

"So he has a girlfriend?"

Paulie smiled. "Code. He has a new boy. Always, a new boy. He finds ways of letting me know. Like I said, it's not easy."

"I'm sure it isn't. Give yourself a break. Like you said, it's been a long time since you've had to have him in your face. There was no closure. Maybe now there will be."

"And you? How would you feel if Brent came knocking?"

"I think a swift kick to the balls would do it."

"Ahh. Now there's true forgiveness."

Kate punched him and he tackled her in a fit of tickles. They ended up in a passionate mating that rendered them both wasted, sweating, mellow.

"This is working for you, right?" she whispered in the dark.

"If you mean do I enjoy being the man, I haven't really thought about it. That's a good thing, yeah?"

The following day, they went shopping for her gown, his attire, and sex toys. She took him to a little shop on Melrose that sold devices of pleasure and they left the store giggling and anticipatory.

She did his face before the wedding. His hair, now shoulder length, was tied into a queue. She wore a simple white cotton dress, he, white cotton pants and a knee length, white Nehru tunic. In addition to their friends, they allowed a small band of devoted fans that'd congregated early on the beach to watch. One of Paulie's gay friends, a minister, performed the ceremony. They each recited their own, personally written vows.

"There is a reason why," Paulie began, holding both of Kate's hands in his, "a reason why our paths crossed, and continued to cross, time after time. It was a message that took us both awhile to grasp. But I have never been more convinced than I am right now that we were meant to be together, meant to stay together, to grow old together."

"There is a reason why," Kate continued," that I never felt complete until I met you. We were the missing pieces in each other's puzzle."

"I'm jealous," Jamie whispered behind Paulie's back.

☞ *When I was a little boy, I had a fascination with weddings. I loved getting dressed up. Weddings were like fairy tales. I always thought it was criminal the way the bride got the best clothes; the flowing white gown, sparkles all, the veil and such. Once, when I was, you know, about seven, my auntie thought it would be a lark to put my cousin's veil on me. I strutted about like a bloody peacock in that gauzy confection. I wedding-marched back and forth across the room, eyes partially closed, imagining what it would be like to actually be in a real wedding.*

On the beach that day in Malibu, Kate walked straight out of one of those fairy tales. The ocean breeze tugged at her veil, her dress, ruffled the gardenia petals in her bouquet. I thought at first of my childhood disappointments. I might be jealous, I thought, of her getting to wear that gorgeous gown. But something mystical happened, and I felt like I was in that gown with her. Stupid, right? I felt the rustle of the cotton, the crisp, silky taffeta underskirt, the toile veil brushing against her face, my face.

That's the kind of connection we have. It's weird. I know. But then, I've grown accustomed to weird.

—Paulie, who knows the true meaning of bride/groom.

Chapter 7

May, 1990. Television City, Los Angeles, CA

"So how long's it been now?"

Paulie smiled, cocked his head. In full dress makeup, two or three braids, and a hat, he looked very much like the boy glam pop star of seven years before.

He leaned toward the microphone. "Just over a year. And we're unbelievably happy."

"Are you no longer gay, then?" the interviewer asked.

Her guest considered. "Well I guess that depends on who you ask." The studio audience laughed, and Paulie giggled. "I don't like labels, you know. Never have. We are inexplicably in love, we have a child on the way, we've been touring, you know, things like that."

"A baby? Well, congratulations! Are you hoping for a boy or a girl?"

"Well, hope has nothing to do with it, actually. She's a girl, and she's coming to us from Kazakhstan."

"You'll be able to coach her on makeup, then, when she's older."

Paulie narrowed his eyes, pursed his lips.

"Now. About Mrs. Bingham. How does she deal with your...fame? Your unusual image?"

"Kate helped design my look today. Does that answer your question?"

"Does she do glam?"

"Only on me."

"Does she get jealous of the attention you garner? It would take a pretty special woman to not feel like she has to compete with such a...a beautiful husband."

"I can't hold a candle to her beauty. She saved my life, you know."

"And I'm surprised to hear you talk about that. You're very candid."

"I have nothing to hide. My life has been played out on the covers of newspapers, magazines and websites since I was sixteen. Heroin nearly killed me. Kate brought me back from the dead."

"So is it more of a *gratitude* you feel for her?"

Paulie's smile froze, the audience groaned. "You just don't get it, do you? Clearly, Mrs. Tibbitts, you've never been in love."

The fans cheered and Paulie stood, took a bow, sat back down.

"All right. Point taken. So you don't do drugs, you don't drink, you don't smoke. You're in a monogamous relationship with a woman, you are becoming a father, and what else could make you more saintly?"

"I'm a vegetarian, and I've forgiven Jamie Pritchard."

"Forgiven him."

"Yes. Go on then, feel free to ask me about my past relationship with Jamie. Everyone else does, and has been, for ten years."

"I think it's common knowledge that you were hurt very deeply by Mr. Pritchard. But you say you've made up. What does he think about your marriage? To a woman, at that?"

"I think he's jealous. He's said as much."

"He wants you back?"

"No. He wants what I have."

"Kate?"

"He wants to love and be loved. Isn't that what we all want, in the end?"

They both believed whole-heartedly in the power of their love. A love that was to be tested, Kate soon found out.

Paulie's arrest in June put the kibosh on the adoption. He could barely look at Kate as she drove him home after bailing him out, worse when the edict came down from the Kazakhstan authorities. No daughter would be forthcoming.

"I don't know what to say. I'm sorry. I'll do better."

She wouldn't look at him, either, for several days.

Until the morning she awoke and remembered with startling clarity that Paulie was human. That he had suffered addictions all his life. He obsessed. He craved everything that was good—and bad—for him. Sex, drugs, rock and roll. Men, food, publicity. Bright lights, anything shiny, anything that would stimulate, brighten, bring him higher.

She watched him sleeping beside her. A golden boy, put into a cage by a needy woman. How could she have possibly thought she could keep him satisfied?

He'd been faithful for fifteen months. She knew it to be true, because he almost never left her side. Even in absence, she would have known. He never lied, because he was so terrible at it. So when he called and said he'd been discovered in a compromising position with a young musician at a West L.A. club, she knew how difficult it was for him to tell her. There were drugs, too, although he swore he didn't use them himself. And she believed him.

Paulie opened his eyes, eyes that had been filled with sorrow for a week. Kate ran her fingers through his hair, rested her hand behind his head.

"It's okay, Paul."

"Are you going to leave me?"

She considered. The thought had come to mind several times. "Do you want me to?"

"No. Not unless I continue to make you unhappy."

"And might you?"

"I have never been more disappointed in myself. I don't know how it happened. He was just there, he was so... he was begging for it. He waited until we were alone in the loo, then he just sort of took his clothes off, and—"

"It's more than I need to know. You are like a moth to a flame."

"For what it's worth, I didn't go through with it. Not completely." Paulie colored. "I'll go if you want me to. But I'd rather not. If you can give me another chance."

Kate swallowed, blinked back tears. "I don't want to have to give you chances. I don't want you to have to battle to stay faithful. It's not fair to either of us. But I don't... I don't want to lose you."

Paulie pulled her against his chest, held her while she sobbed. She cried hard, feeling as if her heart was dying. He was the only thing she'd ever really wanted. She didn't know if she could survive without him, or share him.

"I'm so sorry, Kate. I'll do anything to make this up to you."

She tried to calm herself down. Dried her tears on the bed sheet, but the sobs wouldn't subside. His voice was rough with barely restrained emotion.

"It was only sex. Do you get that? Not saying it was right. But it's you I love, if that still matters. It's you."

She looked him in the eyes. "And if I had sex with someone else? Would you say that it was only sex, then?"

"No. I wouldn't." He wiped another tear from her cheek. "Because that's where we differ, darling. You don't have sex for sex's sake."

"I didn't think you did, either, anymore."

"Well, maybe I'm just a sick bastard, then." He pulled away, got out of bed. She watched while he got dressed.

"Where are you going?"

"Don't know." He leaned down, kissed her on the mouth. "But I will be back, later. Please be here. Please."

She was there. She'd made a platter of sautéed tofu, vegetables and homemade scones. She was also drinking wine, but quickly put it away when he walked in.

"No, don't. Have all you want. It doesn't bother me."

"Are you hungry?"

He ignored her question, took her by the wrist and urged her toward him while leaning back against the sink counter. "I did a lot of thinking today."

"So did I."

"Me first, because I'm the offensive party here."

"Only if you're not going to say you're leaving, because I couldn't bear that."

He smiled, for the first time in a week. "Dammit, Kate, you went first." He paused, trying to remember how he'd formulated the words earlier in his head. It was important to get it right. "Just listen, please, until I've finished. I know I let us down. I asked you into this relationship. You were hesitant. I haven't forgotten that I was the one who encouraged us both to try to make it work.

"For eighteen months, there's been no one but you. There have been many, many opportunities. I'll admit, some took more effort to pass up than others. Jamie once accused me of being a zebra who's tried to whitewash his stripes. I like to think he's wrong, and that I'm a man of honor. I took a vow. I broke it, I blew it."

"Paul, you don't have to do this."

"The question is, will I do it again? Can I promise that I won't do it again? I'm scared now."

Kate shook her head. "Don't be. We can work this out."

"Do you know that boys at my school started calling me a poofter when I was nine years old? They knew it before I did. It's almost like it was preordained. By the time I was sixteen, I'd resigned myself to the fact. I let go. It was so much easier being gay, despite the fact that I was regularly roughed up by the homophobes and gangs.

"The last thing I expected was to fall in love with a woman. I ignored it at first. A friend told me I was in love with the image of being straight. Another told me you were a mother figure. Still another glorious mate said I'd eventually go mad. But I thought of you all the time. And, I'll admit, it wasn't in a sexual way, at first. That night on the road, in the hotel, I didn't think I could make it with you. And guess what? You seduced me in a big way. The way you spoke, the way you touched. The kissing. The willingness. It was unbelievably sexy to me."

Kate was rapt, her hips against his, the warmth and shape of her arousing him along with the memories. She was doing it again.

"And then you left. I went on a rampage. Different lovers every night. Selfish louts, most of them, they thought bonking a pop star was cool. Their particular claim to fame. Cheap shits."

He took a breath. He hadn't meant to go there. To get angry. It wouldn't help.

"You pretty much know what happened next. Parties, drugs, strangers. More drugs. Smack hell. And then, an angel came and rescued me from that hell. How you ever found me..."

"Is it my turn yet?" she asked softly, the affection in her eyes further melting him down.

"I would get to the point if I had one. If I had an answer. I'm still scared. I didn't think it would happen, and I lost control. One slip up and I've cascaded."

"Does my opinion still matter?"

"More than anything. Truly."

"I think we may have to alter things a bit and take it one day at a time. I'm not willing to let this tear us apart. But I have to ask you something very personal."

"Okay, I'll try to answer truthfully."

"Was this...encounter, was it really spontaneous, or did you sort of feel it coming? I mean, were you having thoughts about being with someone...else?"

"If you mean did I go looking for it, no, not at all."

"Not missing it?"

"Being with another man? No. Not consciously, anyway. I love being with you. You're all I need."

"Or so you thought."

Paulie looked down. She had him there. "What do you mean by alter things? You're my wife. You shouldn't have to do that."

"I decided today, while you were gone, that we're fooling ourselves if we think we have a normal, everyday relationship. We don't. So maybe we have to try a little harder to make it work. If you need a night out, now and again, you tell me, you go. And you don't get arrested or bring home germs."

"Are you fucking crazy?"

"And if I need a night out once in a while, I tell you, and I go. And I'll try, too, not to get arrested."

Paulie's see-saw suddenly tilted. The thought of Kate going out on him rocked him, made him dizzy with fear. He'd never considered the possibility. She was more beautiful than ever, her auburn hair trailing down her back, her small waist, tight bum. A compact dynamo of sexual power and nurturing adoration. She went out of her way to pleasure him in ways unimaginable by most girls. Images of her in another's arms took his breath away. Did she know what she was doing? Did she really intend to see other men, or was it her way of chaining him down?

He cleared his throat, couldn't find words.

"Are you okay, husband?" she asked. "You look upset."

"I am *seriously* upset. Can we sleep on this?"

She had expected to be the instigator tonight. But Paulie was in a rare, dominating mood. His touch was firm, masculine, driven. No toys tonight, no artificial aids; just pure, unadulterated passion that had them all over the bed and all over each other. She clawed at his back, he pulled her hair. Frantic kisses left their mouths raw. They slept, at last, tangled, spent, and more in love than ever.

☙ **Our relationship is incredibly complicated. Convoluted, some might say. Torturous, at times. Why didn't I leave him then? Can anybody really answer a question like that? I loved Paulie more than anything imaginable. Life without him would have been more torturous.**

I was selfish, and stupid. So was he. We were so addicted, so utterly dependent upon each other, we feared the potential withdrawal like death.

And yet . . . something was clearly missing from Paulie's life. And mine, tho I was unable to face it. I was so focused on Paulie's misplacement that I completely ignored the fact that I, too, treaded dark waters.

We were good at pretending, but terribly devoted.

I knew, even then, that he was suppressing his needs.

— Kate

Chapter 8

August, 1990. Brentwood, CA

Kate's flight from Vancouver was delayed, so she called Paulie and said she'd take a cab home. No sense in his fighting the LAX traffic during rush hour. She came home to a darkened house, found Paulie on the couch with only the television on. He was holding a can of beer.

"I'm glad that gig is over. So, what's up? I heard the album moved to number ten today."

"I went to see Jamie today."

"Oh, really? What's going on with him?" Worried, she sat down beside him. He never watched television and wasn't watching it now, although his eyes seemed focused on the screen. And she hadn't seen him with a beer in years.

"He's dying."

Kate went cold. She immediately reached for Paulie's hand. "Oh my God. What happened?"

"AIDS. He's got bloody AIDS."

"Sweet Jesus. Where is he, Paul?"

"At a hospital in the Marina. I can't believe it. He never told anyone. He would prefer to die alone."

Kate sat stunned. "How did you find out?"

"He called me. He wanted me to know," Paulie's voice broke, so he cleared his throat. "He wanted to tell me that he contracted HIV after. After...us. Didn't want me to worry. He apparently knew where, or at least when, he got it."

"Do you want me to take you there? You want to spend some time with him?"

"Ah, Kate. He looks terrible. He has lesions, his eyes are all yellow. Such a waste. He was so beautiful. We said our goodbyes today. Is it okay if I drink this?"

"I'm surprised you haven't drunk a whole case by now."

He did drink, then. Kate sat beside him on the couch, sympathetic, listening as he debriefed himself.

"We were together for over three years. He was the first real relationship. The first to ever really...love me. We had great sex. He's a bit older, and he taught me everything about being gay and being in love. He followed the band for a while. My first manager thought it was best that I not go public about my sexuality, so we made light of it. It was okay to wear makeup and long hair; lots of bands were doing it. Bowie, Culture Club, Mark Bolan, you know. So they started rumors about me and this girl, she was cute, I guess, I never had much use for her, nor she me. The press was always talking us up. Her name was Alison."

"I remember."

"Jamie didn't like the rumors. Even though I never even saw Alison. He got very jealous of her. So he blew her cover."

"How so?"

"He set her up with this bloke from Glasgow. Made sure the paparazzi found them together. It was a very mean thing to do."

"Why?"

"Because Ally really fancied this chap, and it was all a sham. The wanker dumped her as soon as it was all finished up. I was really angry with Jamie. So immature. We fought, and Jamie started hanging around this other boy." Paulie took a moment to gather his memories. "He eventually apologized, and I stupidly accepted. You think I'm needy now? You should have seen me at twenty. Anyway, I went crazy with jealousy, I sent Alison on her way, I went public with my homosexuality and Jamie's too, hoping to scare off the straight girls that were always hanging around. The press was damaging, for a while. Jamie got angry and left. That was it. Next thing I hear, he's shacked up with some *convertee* named Brent."

"How long before we met?"

Paulie took another swallow of beer, considered. "Weeks, perhaps. You probably remember what a bitch I was on that tour."

"You scared the hell outta me the first time I put slap on your face."

"Yeah, well you scared me, too, talking back like you did. Trash mouth."

The morning of the funeral, Kate couldn't stop vomiting.

"Maybe you shouldn't go, sweet love. You're very upset."

"Just give me a few minutes. I'll be fine. Must've been the sushi last night."

She was green, but she stood with Paulie as they buried his first love. He didn't cry; he'd cried the whole night when they got the news two days before. Now, he held tight to her hand, a slight frown on his face. He'd surprised her by wearing a conventional, dark suit. His hair was again cropped short, and his eyes were shadowed dark.

He and Jamie still had several mutual friends, many of whom stopped to pay their respects to him at the graveside. Kate watched as a stout man with a shaved head and goatee approached. He embraced Paulie.

"Kate, this is David Stanton, keyboardist extraordinaire, from the early days of Bingham Boys. I think he'd already left the band when you signed on. From the good side of London."

"A pleasure, Mrs. Bingham."

Kate nodded, smiled briefly. David walked with them to their car.

"I was surprised to see you here, Paulie. After everything," David said.

"You know what I feel the worst about?" Paulie stared back toward the gravesite. "He never achieved real love. Never allowed it, I should say. Love just wasn't enough somehow."

"I don't like to speak ill of the dead," David commented, "but he was a fool. No offense to you, Mrs. Bingham."

There was much to be done when they got home. The newly formed Paul Bingham Band would leave on tour in two days, and Kate hadn't even begun to pack. "I swear, I don't know what's wrong with me. I'm usually much more organized than this."

"Do you not want to go?"

71

"I do want to go, are you kidding? I love touring. You know that. I guess with the funeral and all, I'm not moving too fast. Are you going to be okay to go?"

"Yeah. I'm fine. I've written a song. Here, let me get that." He reached a suitcase from the closet shelf for her and put it on the bed.

"You have? That's really nice. I can't wait to hear it."

"It's sad."

"Of course. It's a sad time. He did care, you know that, right?"

"Yeah, I suppose."

The tour kicked off in Salt Lake City, stopped in Phoenix, then passed through Albuquerque. They'd purposely left a night free to visit her parents. Evelyn Newman embraced Paulie warmly.

"How's my favorite son-in-law?" she quipped.

"Your *only* son-in-law is just fine, Mum. And I've brought you a tour shirt. Wear it in good health."

Evelyn insisted they stay at the Newman home, rather than the hotel booked for the band. Paulie giggled at the squeaks made by the hide-a-bed on which they slept in the tiny guest room. Kate, too, couldn't control her laughter at his silly comments. After a few moments of quiet, Kate turned over.

"Could you refrain from movement, my darling?" Paulie asked, sending them both into more fits of giggles. Kate never tired of hearing his lilting, south London accent, his over-the-top charm.

She rose early to have coffee with her mother.

"You seem very happy," Evelyn said, pouring a cup for her daughter. "Paul's a sweetie."

"We've had our challenges, Mom. But I wouldn't trade him."

"Will you try again to adopt?"

Kate sighed. "I don't know. I'm not sure children are in the cards for us. We're both a bit selfish."

"You do lose some of that selfishness when you have kids."

"I guess you would have to. But it may not be up to us." She took a sip of coffee. "We could go private. There are options. We haven't talked about it. Maybe after the tour, which will make us a lot of money."

"No chance you'll have one on your own."

"Paul has some fears about his drug use."

"I see. That's very prudent of him."

Kate nodded. "Do you think I could have some tea instead? This coffee is kind of strong on my stomach."

"You look a little pale." Her mother peered closely into Kate's eyes.

"What are you doing? Jesus, Mom, you're freaking me out."

"Never mind. I have some herb tea that will settle your stomach."

October, 1990. On Tour

Three weeks had passed when the Bingham troupe landed in Miami. Paulie felt better every night, singing his heart out, raking in the ticket dough and delighting a whole new faction of fans. Kate, however, was tired. He took her to Walt Disney World between venues, and despite her fatigue, the day of tramping around the park with Paulie at her side lifted her spirits.

The concert in Orlando exceeded expectations. Paulie was in his element, doing his new songs during the first half, then returning as the formerly flamboyant, dreadlocked glam rocker during the second, when he pounded out his early hits. It meant that Kate had to duplicate his facial artwork from the old days during intermission, put on his wigs and help dress him.

"You look smashing!" she announced, knowing that he still needed pumping up before going on, even now. "Go get 'em, *boy*!" she teased, trying to hide the fact that she was beyond exhaustion.

She smiled at the sound of the crowd when he skipped onto the stage in his silk kimono and leggings. Buzz stood beside her, his hair now a grizzled grey.

"Glad I din't miss this," he muttered. "Din't think for a minute, all those years ago, that you'n him would end up together. I'm glad, though. He's never been happier."

Kate nodded. From the wings, she felt pride as she watched Paulie sing, alternately pointing at the crowd, dancing, thrusting a hip in exaggerated mimicry of his early days. Then the stage lights grew dimmer and dimmer, the sound of Paulie's voice faded away as she collapsed into Buzz's arms.

When she came to, they'd already called the on-site medic. Paulie was halfway into "No Regrets".

"Don't tell him. Not yet. Let him get through this show, please," she pleaded with Buzz and the others, who'd gathered around her. "I'm fine, really. I just want to rest."

She lay down in Paulie's dressing room. He tore into the room after the first encore.

"Kate! Are you all right? They said you fainted!"

"I'm just fine. You get back out there before they turn the house lights up. Go on! Get!"

"Are you sure?"

She nodded vigorously and waved him out. She forced herself to sit up before he got back.

"You scared me," he told her later, as they dressed for bed. "I want you to see a doctor first thing tomorrow."

"But I'm fine."

"But I'm telling you. Please. I don't ask that much of you, Kate. I'll go with you if you want."

He got a recommendation from a woman at the front desk and hired a cab to take them the next morning.

"I don't like to go to strangers. I don't like this at all," Kate complained as Paulie pulled her from the taxi.

"Let me be the overbearing husband for once, will you?"

Dr. Janine Landon was delighted to see Mrs. Paulie Bingham.

"You're kidding. I love him! Is he here?"

Kate nodded, trying to keep the paper gown around her.

"I'm sorry. Let's see what we can find out."

Kate felt sick. Sick with worry about the kinds of test Dr. Landon was running. EKG's, blood work, ultrasounds. A pelvic exam, respiratory tests. Finally, she told Kate to get dressed.

"Do you want your husband here?"

"Is it that bad?"

"It will affect him."

Kate considered, knowing that Paulie was pacing outside the doctor's door.

"I guess he can come in. Unless I'm going to die. That, I would need to tell him myself."

"Not necessary." Dr. Landon got out of her chair and opened her door. "Mr. Bingham? Could you please join us?"

"Yes, yes. Thank you. Thank you. What, uh, what's happening? Hello, darling." He took Kate's hand.

"I don't know how to prepare you for this news." The doctor turned to look out the window. "I don't normally get involved in patients' personal lives, but I read that you recently suffered a failed adoption."

Paulie turned to Kate, silently questioning. Kate stared back, confused, then looked to Dr. Landon, who'd come back to her desk.

"What has that got to do with anything?"

"You're pregnant, kiddos. Three months, give or take."

Kate started to protest.

"I know, you're going to tell me you're still having monthly cycles. That's because you are bleeding."

Paulie opened his mouth, but no words came.

Kate shook her head. "I don't understand. Is something wrong?"

"Not necessarily. Some women just do. I don't see anything unusual. Sometimes, an embryo implants more than once. There are various reasons, the worst of which is impending miscarriage. You have no other symptoms. I think you're safe to start planning for your family."

Kate felt as if the wind had been knocked out of her. Paulie was still holding her hand, but he hadn't spoken a word. She dared a glance at his face.

"I think I'm going to pass out," he murmured.

"Touring can be really tough. You are starting your second trimester. I'd advise you to take it easy, if you can. We'll get you on some prenatals and you should see your regular doctor as soon as you get home."

"Really. I'm *really* dizzy."

75

Dr. Landon chuckled, helped Paulie to a fainting couch against the wall.

"I have to assume you both wanted children. Is this not a welcome surprise?"

Paulie closed his eyes. "Wake me up in six months, will you?"

Chapter 9

She refused to go home. There was a part of her that needed him with her and a part of her that she hated. The part that said she couldn't trust him on the road without her. The bleeding stopped, she got some of her strength back, and she began to balloon out in the front.

Despite his initial reaction, Paulie became the perfect expectant father. The tabloids went wild with speculation that he wasn't the baby's father. Certainly, Kate had been with a *real* man. Although charges had been dropped, his recent arrest didn't help. Kate wanted to sue; Paulie blew it off.

"I learned a long time ago, you can't fight that stuff. It makes me laugh, now. Besides, they won't be able to say a thing when he's born with my eyes,"

"Or she."

"Or she. Yeah."

Because of his past drug use, they opted for genetic testing. Their child passed muster, and the tour ended just two months before her due date. They were finally able to go home together.

It tickled her that Paulie's gay friends threw a baby shower for her, filling her nursery with bottles and baths, diapers and dribble bibs, blankets and booties. She delighted, as did Paulie, in every tiny garment and accessory. They went to child birthing classes together, bought baby books, set up a nursery. They fought over names while Paulie painted the bedroom.

"What's wrong with Wendall?" Paulie asked, giving her his best raised eyebrows.

"I'm thinking Pandora."

"Aphrodite?"

"Derwood."

"How 'bout it's a girl, I pick. A boy, you choose."

Kate smoothed her maternity shirt over her growing belly as she rocked in her new glider. "Okay. But we must have veto rights."

"Agreed."

"I'm still bothered."

"'Bout what?"

"Those ugly papers. I can't let them get away with what they said about us. As if I would ever cheat on you."

Paulie put down his paintbrush, gave her a thoughtful look. "Have you changed your philosophy on limited marital fidelity?"

Kate tilted her head, considered Paulie. "What I said, dear husband, is that if I ever wanted to seek the company of another, I would tell you first."

Paulie pressed his hands together, rested his chin on his fingertips.

"Were that to occur, would I have veto power?"

Kate tried, but failed, to keep a straight face. He was just too adorable for words. "That would depend, I think, on what promises came with the veto. Diamonds, furs, fancy cars, marathon sex…"

"Ah. I think I'm catching on. It's called coercion, darling. Yes, I do believe that's the term."

Kate lifted herself out of the rocker and went to him, wrapping her arms around him and giving him a forceful, passion-filled kiss.

"You're insatiable, you know that?" he murmured, returning her kisses. "It's those hormones. You are perpetually horny."

As Kate neared the end of her eighth month, Paulie grew edgy. He fussed incessantly over her, coddled and waited on her, but refused her advances in bed.

"Paulie… what's wrong?" she asked him one night. "Is it because I'm such a whale?"

"No, no, nothing like that, sweet love. I'm just afraid. It seems wrong. I don't want to hurt you."

"You know the doctor said it was okay."

"I do. But—I… what if…"

"You're crazy. But if that's how you feel, then we need to come up with alternatives."

"Ah, Kate."

"I'm going to take a quick shower while you think about what you know I can do to you."

"I'll be right here."

But in a matter of minutes, she was calling out to him from the bathroom. The nature of her call alarmed Paulie, and he rushed in to find her slightly bent and grasping a towel.

"Something's wrong. I'm cramping. Could you grab my robe? It's hanging on the back of the door."

Wide eyed, he helped her into the bathrobe. "Can you walk? We need to get you into the car. Or should I call an ambulance?"

"I think I can walk. Wow, I felt something earlier, but I thought it was nothing."

Kate sat down on the bed while Paulie hurried into a pair of jeans and shirt. He carefully ushered her to the car in the garage and fastened the seatbelt around her.

She was taking deep breaths. "It's too soon. This can't be good."

"Try to relax, darling. It's not too soon, not necessarily. Just breathe, there's a good girl. We'll be there in no time."

He maneuvered in and out of traffic, cursing the cars that got in his way. "Doesn't Los Angeles know it's fucking 2 a.m.? Where do people have to be at this time? Ridiculous."

"I'm okay. Don't stress."

But she clearly wasn't okay, as the pink robe showed signs that she was bleeding. The ER couldn't get her a wheelchair fast enough for Paulie. His fear made him irritable.

They took her away from him, and he paced. He called David, who came straight away to sit with him.

"Big night, eh?" David asked, handing Paulie a paper cup of tea.

"Thanks, mate. Never would have thought this would be happening."

"I was a bit surprised myself. Would you like to pop out for a drink somewhere?"

"No. I need to stay here, you know…"

David nodded. They sat for ten or fifteen minutes, chatting about Paulie's imminent fatherhood. His friend seemed unimpressed.

"I thought you'd opt to get rid of it."

Before Paulie could register his surprise at David's comment, a nurse appeared.

"Mr. Bingham?"

Paulie handed his cup to his older friend. "Well, here goes."

"I'll stick around, mate. Come update me," David said, and Paulie nodded, then followed the nurse into the ward.

"Your wife is in labor, as if you didn't already know that."

"No, I wasn't really sure. It's early, isn't it? A month?"

"Possibly three weeks. Not too bad. She wants to see you."

Kate reached out to him, tears on her face. "Oh, Paulie," she moaned, locking her arms around his neck.

"I'm here, darling. I'm here. We're going to have our baby, Kate. This is a good thing." He pulled back a little, looked into her eyes. "Remember the breathing we learned? Now would be a good time for that. C'mon. Start with the deep, cleansing breath…"

"Fuck the cleansing breath! It hurts. Bad! Tell them to give me something!"

"Now, Kate, my love, we talked about this. You wanted to go without drugs, remember? You made me promise…"

"Well now I'm promising you hell if you don't get me something. You have no idea how this feels! They didn't tell it all in that stupid class. They didn't tell me my guts would be splitting apart!"

"I've called Evelyn and Pop. They're getting on a plane right now."

"I don't care unless they're packing something strong."

The nurse handed him a damp towel, and he mopped Kate's brow. "Was I this bad?" he whispered to her, just as her contraction passed.

She rolled her eyes. "You were far worse."

"I'm not convinced," he muttered, kissing her forehead.

A doctor came in for a quick check.

"Not progressing," she noted to the nurse.

An hour passed, then another. They took x-rays, while Paulie sat with David in the waiting room.

"I'm not prepared for this," Paulie confessed, rubbing his eyes. "She's always been the strong one."

"Is she the man?" David asked, his voice whimsical.

Unfazed by the question, Paulie shook his head. "We're a-typical. We don't fit into any neat box, David. She is soft, feminine and then tough. A lion. She takes care of me, I take care of her. We put our love above all else, and we still fight like cats and dogs sometimes."

"Sounds pretty status quo to me, except for your being gay. Unless you've abandoned yourself."

"I can't examine that right now. Please."

It was almost dawn. The doctor returned.

"Paulie, she's back in the birthing room."

"I'm on my way. Is everything going as planned?"

"Not exactly. The baby isn't particularly large, but Kate's built, well, small. Her pelvis is not moving much. We're going to watch for a few more minutes to see if she progresses."

Paulie frowned, touched David on the shoulder. "I'll be back."

A nurse gave him a plastic cup filled with ice chips and a spoon. "She could use these."

He offered Kate a spoonful, which she accepted gratefully.

"Am I going to die?" she managed, looking up at him through what he knew was the dark haze of intense pain.

"No." He gave her another bit of ice, which she knocked from his hand. The cup went flying, spraying ice everywhere and sending the spoon clattering to the floor.

Paulie issued a shaky sigh, cupped her cheeks with his hands. "You need to settle down, girl. This is hard work, to be sure, but that's no call for throwing things at me."

He made her cry, felt like a lout and tried to apologize.

Suddenly, there was a lot of activity around them. People moving about, rolling in carts, constructing a device over Kate.

"What—what's going on?" Paulie asked, pulling away from his wife to talk to the doctor.

"The baby is in distress. We need to take it."

"Take it? What does that mean?"

"Caesarian section."

"You're going to cut it out? Cut into Kate? Oh God."

Just when he felt his legs might give way, someone pushed a stool under him, then rolled him close to Kate. The thought of them cutting into her sickened him, but when he looked into her face, he found strength.

"I'm sorry about the ice," she panted. "To borrow a phrase, I'm not myself."

"Yes, you are," he teased, relocating a tendril of hair from her cheek. "Listen, darling, they are going to have to...to... uh, take the baby out."

Kate looked alarmed. "C-section? Oh, crap. Okay. Whatever. Just—just let's get it over with!"

They turned her on her side, prepared an epidural block with a needle to her spine. Paulie blew out a breath, averted his eyes.

Within about ten moments, her pain subsided.

"That's what I'm talkin' about," she said, forcing a smile. "Paulie, remind the doctor I want a bikini cut."

"Heard ya, Kate," the doctor called.

The "construction" they built was a surgery curtain, draped across her midsection. Paulie peeked over to watch as they swabbed her abdomen with some brownish liquid. The doctor raised a scalpel, and Paulie swallowed hard. Quickly he returned his eyes to Kate's face. Clearly, she felt nothing, and he relaxed a little. He continued to wipe her face, kiss her forehead, whisper endearments. It occurred to him that this might very well be the most important day of his life.

"How's it going?" Kate asked softly. "Can you see?"

Scared, reluctant, Paulie peered over the curtain just as the doctor withdrew her hands, holding the tiniest human being he'd ever seen. The baby was placed into a waiting towel, and the doctor grinned.

"You want the honors of telling Mom, Dad?"

Paulie smiled, turned back to Kate. "*I* get to pick her name."

She reached for him, began to cry.

"You did great, little mum. You are a real trooper."

"Can I see her?"

"In a moment," the doctor called. The baby gave out a healthy cry. "Right now, I need Dad front and center. You're going to cut the umbilical cord."

"I don't think I can do this..." he moaned, but with shaking hands managed anyway. He was then guided to gently dip the baby in a bath of warm water. Mesmerized, he stared in wonder at the tiny fingers, toes, lips. The water quieted her some, but she continued to thrash and fuss.

"What should I do?" Paulie asked, fearing he'd do the wrong thing.

"Perhaps something you do best. How about a song?"

"You're joking," he said softly, but then drew closer to the bassinet and began to sing. His rich tenor, softened for tiny ears, caused everyone in the room to pause. Including Bonny Mae Bingham, who opened her grey-green eyes and stared at her father for the first time.

"Hush little baby, don't say a word,
Papa's gonna buy you a mockingbird..."

☞ *There are times in your life when you're scared, most of the time it's for yourself. That night, I was scared for us both. Kate laboured in serious pain, and I sat powerless to help her.*

How had this happened in the first place? Me, a gay man, impregnating a woman? No matter that she was my wife, no matter that we participated in some crazy version of hetero-sex from time to time. I'd never considered myself to have viable seed. Conception occurred for macho, straight men. It never entered my mind even once that our intense, whacked-out lovemaking would result in a real live baby girl.

So yes, I was surprised when Kate became pregnant, but I was completely, utterly blown away when Bonny was actually born.

How in the world could I be a father? I was terrified.

83

Even more terrifying was the possibility that Kate would discover just how terrified I was. — Paulie

Chapter 10

Winter, 1991. Brentwood, CA

The cover photo selected for May's *People Magazine* depicted the Bingham family at home, with a seated Paulie cradling Bonny and Kate standing behind. The message was clear: Paulie Bingham had become a mother. And while he shrugged it off, Kate stewed. Still, for the first six months of Bonny's life, the household routine couldn't have been better orchestrated. With her devoted parents taking turns, round the clock, caring for her needs, the infant wanted for nothing. Paulie was tireless in his support of Kate, her recovery, and their new daughter.

He marveled, from time to time, that they had even conceived a child, something he had never expected nor dared to dream about. He wished that his mother had lived to see his beautiful girl.

Friends and well-wishers frequented their home, bringing food, gifts and news of the outside world. David, especially, spent time helping, dashing off to the market or post office, picking up laundry or dinner. Both Paulie and Kate were immensely grateful.

On the day Bonny turned six months old, the Paul Bingham Band returned to the recording studio with Paulie packing eight new tunes inspired by his roller coaster life. Days alone with her daughter began to drag for Kate, with Paulie slipping into bed just before she needed to get up. Sex dropped off in favor of sleep.

The sessions continued into January, long past Paulie's estimate of eight weeks to complete the album. Changes, he said. He'd had to make changes. Then, a new keyboardist had come in, and they'd had to re-record some tracks.

85

"New? What happened to Lyle?"

"Lyle had some issues to deal with. I asked David to sit in. He's really the best. Did all my early stuff. The difference is phenomenal."

David was a great guy, one who treated Kate with the respect she craved as Paulie's wife. He was a loving uncle to Bonny and Kate was glad that Paulie had a good friend beside herself.

She awoke one morning at 3 a.m. to the sound of laughter coming from the living room. Then, Paulie's voice, shushing the other. Was it David? After some brief, whispered dialog, she heard Paulie saying goodbye.

He fell into bed fifteen minutes later. As Kate rolled toward him, he turned his back.

"Tired?" she asked softly, threading her arms around his waist.

"Yeah."

"Okay." She tried again. "Even for a kiss goodnight?"

He made a kissing sound over his shoulder. The alcohol on his breath made its way to her nose, and she lay back. She didn't sleep again that night.

Suspicion crept into her life, hour by hour, day by day, as Paulie spent more and more time away, usually with David Stanton.

"How's the recording coming?" she ventured one evening, when Paulie happened to be home for dinner.

"Almost done. One more track to lay down. It's really going great. I can't wait for you to hear it."

"Good. I miss you."

"Miss you, too, darling."

Intimacy was token. Kate felt confused and lonely, reluctant to confront him. Until the night Bonny became ill.

What later turned out to be a routine ear infection seemed much worse this night. Bonny cried constantly unless Kate held her. By 2:30 a.m., Kate was worn through, and when Paulie came in the door, she took Bonny upstairs to the nursery and closed the door.

He followed. "What's wrong? Is she okay?"

"She is not okay. I can't put her down. Here, you take her for a while. Unless you are too drunk."

"Bloody hell?"

She peered into his face while patting Bonny against her shoulder.

"Your eyes are red."

"People were smoking at the club. Yeah, I was at the club with David. We were celebrating because we finished. Christ, Kate." He ran a hand over his head. "Here. Give her to me. Looks like you could use a break. Do you think we need to take her to emergency?"

"I'm waiting for a call back from her doctor."

He took the baby and sat down in the rocking chair, started singing softly. In moments, Bonny was asleep. Kate went to the kitchen and poured herself a glass of wine. She needed to calm down before she lit into him. Fortunately, the phone rang before she could pour herself a second glass.

Armed with a dropperful of baby Tylenol and an appointment for later that morning, Kate returned to the nursery. Paulie was still rocking, still humming.

"Why are you so mad at me? The record's done; it's in the can, so to speak. I'll be home more, now, I promise. I'm sorry about the booze. I only had a little."

Kate lost the wind in her sails, sat down in the window seat.

"I'm just exhausted. He thinks it's either her teeth or her ears."

Paulie drove them to the doctor's office at 10:30.

"We must look like death warmed over," he murmured in the waiting room.

"At least you can get away with dark glasses inside."

They stopped for a prescription on the way home, then Paulie took a shower. "Will you be all right? I have that meeting at Epic."

Kate nodded through her fatigue. "Good luck. See you later."

Bonny seemed to improve with the first dose of antibiotics. Despite her lack of sleep, Kate felt a little better, and spent some quality time primping while the baby slept. Around 4 p.m., the doorbell rang.

"Why, David, I thought you'd be with Paulie at the record company."

"No, no, my part is done. Just stopped by to see the little angel. And you, of course. How are things?"

"Well, she's sleeping. Would you like something to drink? I have Coke, Sprite, the usuals."

"No, but water would be great."

They sat on the patio, with the door open enough to hear Bonny if she woke.

"Sorry about last night. It was my fault. I ordered us all a round to toast our new album."

"He told you I was upset, did he?"

"Didn't have to. I know how things are."

"What do you mean by that?"

David took a sip of water. He blinked his ice-blue eyes several times before giving her a chilly gaze. "Oh, nothing, really. Just that, you and Paulie have a rather... unusual relationship. He's often concerned about what you'll think about this, or that, you know."

"I don't see anything unusual about that. Husbands and wives should show concern for each other's conduct. Paulie has a history of self-destructive ways."

"I hardly call a bottle of beer destructive."

Kate tilted her head, stared at this new side of David. "Not for most people. Surely you agree that alcohol could lead him right back down the path to heroin."

David shrugged. "Sometimes it's impossible to change a person's true path."

Kate felt her face coloring. "And you think that Paulie's path is set in stone?"

"Kate, dear, I'm just saying there are some things that shouldn't be meddled with."

"Right. Are you going to bring up the zebra's stripes to me? I don't buy it."

"Hate to mention it, but why do you think he's doing the club scene again? Without you?"

She had no answer because she didn't know he was doing the club scene. David continued.

"I only bring this up because I know how much you... you care about him. How you'd rather he be happy and contented with his natural persuasion."

His natural persuasion. Now he was bringing Paulie's sexuality into it. Had she a gun in her hand, she would have fired it at David. Fired several times. In the face.

Instead, she nodded. "I see you also care a lot about my husband." She stood up. "I appreciate your concern."

David took a moment to absorb his dismissal, then finished his water and took his time getting to the front door. "I know you'll do what's right by Paul. It's been nice chatting. Thanks for the water."

Kate spent two days ruminating, watching Paulie's behavior. David's words echoed in her head. She'd worried about one stinking bottle of beer, but now she worried that he was missing his gay bedfellows.

I need to get away. Let him be for a while.

She made phone calls. Paid all the bills. Had the house cleaned, the laundry delivered. When Paulie came home on Friday night, she was waiting for him.

"You've been a bit off all week, darling. What's up?" He sat down on the couch, picked up the remote to the television. Thought better of it after looking again at Kate's face. "Is it Bonny? Is she worse?"

"No." *How can I tell him this?* Her heart raced.

"I thought I might take Bonny out to New Mexico for...awhile."

He was too perceptive. He knew her too well, was dissecting her comment already.

"What's the matter, Kate?"

She shook back her hair, walked past and kept her back to him. She couldn't bear to see the look on his face. Because it would either confirm her suspicions, or reflect his disappointment in them. Either way it would break her heart. "I'm letting you out of the contract. No more veto power."

"What the hell does that mean? Look, I'm not up to games."

"Neither am I. So I think you need some time to do whatever you want, without me hanging on your back."

She heard him sigh. "Is that what you want?"

"There comes a point when what I want doesn't matter as much as what you need."

Now he stood, approached, turned her to face him. He searched her eyes, but she looked away. "What brought this on? Shit. I know what it is. It's my fault. The late nights. My going to the club. I brought this on myself, didn't I? Look at me, dammit!"

She did look, allowed him to see the hurt. He dropped his hands, turned away.

"I can't let you go."

"You're going to have to. I'm leaving in the morning."

"What did you tell Mum?"

"That we were coming for a little holiday. Nothing more."

Paulie groaned, pressed a fist to his forehead. "Don't go. Please. I can fix this, really I can. You know you're all I need."

"No, I don't know that. I don't think you really know that either. You're like a butterfly in a cage, and I put you there. We've both tried to believe that this is working."

"We had a deal. I would tell you if I felt ... like stepping out. Have I told you that? No. Because I haven't felt it."

"Are you certain? Absolutely sure?"

"I thought we were all about trust. I swear to you, I've been completely faithful. God's honest truth."

"I know that. I do. But you might be trying too hard."

Paulie looked suddenly weary. He rubbed his eyes. "Can we give this a few days?"

"I already have my tickets."

"Dammit, Kate." He dropped back onto the couch. "You don't even realize how unfair you're being. You've pushed me into a corner. You've handled it all, haven't you? Had the whole fucking dialog between us. Is there anything else about me that I need to know?"

She sat down, touched his arm. For the first time she could remember, he pushed her away.

ANNE CARTER

Chapter 11

January, 1992; Albuquerque, New Mexico

E velyn eyed her daughter suspiciously over dinner.

"You might as well tell us the truth, girl. You know you will eventually anyway, so why not get it off your chest early before it festers."

Kate took a napkin and dabbed at Bonny's chin.

"Okay. I'm putting some space between us. Paulie needs to decide how he wants to be."

Her mother shook her head, started to speak, but her father opened his mouth, spoke in his soft, level way.

"Seems to me, the boy already made that decision when he married you, and again when he fathered that little sweet pea. Why are you reopening that can of worms?"

Evelyn raised her eyebrows.

Kate sighed. "You don't understand. Paulie is... gay. He's always been gay. For him to give up men, entirely for me... what was I thinking?"

"Did he cheat?"

Kate stared at her mother's frankness. "Not sure that's any of your business."

"Oh, come on. You've already let the cat out. No sense in trying to stuff it back in."

"No. He hasn't. Not in a technical sense."

"And anyway, by virtue of the fact that you and he have had such a...a healthy sex life, don't you think the term is actually *bi*sexual? You certainly aren't a man."

Kate chewed her lower lip. How in the world had she gotten into this conversation? "Can we talk about something else?"

Evelyn scooped up more mashed potatoes. "Cheryl's coming in a few days."

"Really? For how long?"

"For good. She's finished in New Orleans, so she might set up her photography studio here for a while. In between jobs. Marta says she's looking forward to seeing us."

"Aunt Marta doing okay?"

"Well enough. Says Cheryl is particularly glad you'll be here while she is. You two cousins need to catch up."

Paulie moved all the furniture around in every room of the house. When he finished, he took all of the food and dishes out of the kitchen cabinets and cleaned the shelves, then put everything back. And by Monday night, there was nothing left to do. So he called David Stanton.

A new club had opened in Santa Monica that David wanted to try. He chattered during the cab ride, about all sorts of nonsense that Paulie couldn't care less about. Just before they exited the taxi, David kissed him.

It was a quick buss on the corner of his mouth, but the eye contact that came with it said a lot more. Paulie felt dizzy.

Inside the club, colored lights swirled, dance music pounded from a quasi-*Wall of Sound* à la the 1960s. David found them a small table at the edge of the dance floor, where boys danced with boys and a few fruit fly girls joined in the fray.

David ordered them shooters. Paulie stared at the line of shot glasses on the table.

"I'd rather have a beer," he called over the music.

"Aw, come *on*. You've nothing to worry about. Go on, be a man!"

The joke was not lost on Paulie. "Oh, hell. Why not?"

He was well saturated when David walked him up to his front door hours later. Clearly too inebriated to do any good.

He awoke on the couch the next day, his head pounding and his stomach lurching. He didn't remember much about the night before. But he did remember the kiss.

At first, he called Kate every night on her cell phone. Until she told him to stop.

"The idea here is for a break. Call me this weekend. Or I'll call you."

"Right." *Wrong.*

For the next few weeks, he alternated between going out, getting plastered, and staying in. Once word got out at the club that their newest patron was none other than Paulie Bingham, the boys passed by his table nightly, flirting, winking, hugging him. David became possessive, and one night talked Paulie into leaving early. He asked the cabbie to drive to his place at the beach.

Paulie had been to David's before. When asked to describe it to Kate at the time, he'd said, "early bondage, with a smattering of chrome and glass." Tonight, he stared out at the Pacific, sipping a glass of hard lemonade.

"I miss Kate," he said. David, coming up behind him with a tray of crackers and cheese, groaned.

"Miss her, or the idea of her?"

"Not sure I get your drift."

"You like having a straight woman around. She's your link to what the status quo calls normal. But why do you even care about that? It never bothered you before."

Paulie narrowed his eyes. "Bothered? You think I'm bothered by what I am?"

"She makes you feel that way, doesn't she?"

"No. Not at all."

"That surprises me. I always get the feeling that she is bothered. She wants to forget that you ever had sex with men. But—we don't need to go there. Let's have some nosh, shall we?"

Plied with vodka, then cognac, Paulie spent the night getting familiar with David's various leather straps, buckles and restraints. What seemed like a lark at first soon turned into a date with the Marquis de Sade. Artifacts Paulie had assumed were merely antiques turned out to be elements of David's carnal playground. He lost count of the times David came at him with what he later deemed as actions bordering on assault. At some point, he lost consciousness, waking only briefly as David dressed his wounds. He was so sick the next day that David had to help him into the car.

At home, he vomited repeatedly, then took to his bed.

Why had he allowed the abuse? Had he even protested David's perverted advances? It was all a bad nightmare, touched off by his inability to hold on to the only things that mattered: his wife and daughter. He was unworthy, and so likely deserved the cruelty.

Paulie stopped picking up the phone, letting his calls go to the answering machine. Avoiding further contact with David, he forced the incident from his mind. His face began to itch; he hadn't shaved in days, and he absolutely detested hair on his face. Finding an old beret in the closet, he donned it, put on his dark glasses and took a walk. He was reminded of his days in London, walking around, missing Kate. Always missing Kate. She'd left him a third time.

"This sucks," he said out loud, startling an elderly lady on the corner waiting for a break in the traffic. "Do you need some help, love?" he asked graciously, gently touching her elbow.

"I'm just trying to get home."

"Where do you live, sweetheart?"

"Just there, across the street."

"Walk with me, then."

Halfway through the intersection, she turned and smiled up at him. "I know you," she said.

"Is that so?"

"You're that musician fellow on the cover of *People*. You just had a baby." She seemed so delighted with herself that he had to nod.

"I did, at that."

"Well, congratulations to you and your beautiful wife."

"Why thank you, dear heart." Her love buoyed him. "I was just about to ring her up. I'll share your message."

"My name is Ruby. R-U-B-Y. Ruby."

Because it made him feel stronger, he sat down on Ruby's porch swing to make the call.

"I'm coming out there on Saturday."

"I don't encourage it." Kate sounded distant, cool.

He didn't want to do it, but he pulled the ace he was saving. "You can't keep me from seeing my daughter."

Kate backed off, and the next day Paulie boarded a plane for Albuquerque.

They had a family dinner, as if nothing had changed in the time that had passed since their last visit. Cheryl, tall, blonde and spirited, kept up a lively stream of appropriately neutral conversation; Bonny kept up a clatter with a tiny spoon.

"I can't get over how she's grown," Paulie commented, watching his daughter, who now smeared applesauce into her hair. "She eats just like her mother."

"She's neater," Evelyn said, earning a frown from Kate.

"So when's the new album coming out?" Pop asked.

"Hopefully by the end of summer."

"Then another tour?"

"None planned at the moment. I've just recently lost my keyboard player, so need to replace him before any live performances. Won't be difficult, but I'm not in the mood to go looking right now."

Kate looked up. "Again? What happened to David? You are talking about David, right?"

"One and the same. No longer with Paul Bingham Band."

"What happened?"

Paul looked at her briefly, then back to Bonny. "Let's just say we had different...agendas."

After dinner, Paulie and Kate went outside to watch the sunset.

"We—Bonny and I—we're staying with Cheryl. She got an apartment not far from here, and she has an extra bedroom. It seemed better than, you know, Mom's spare room. And she helps with Bon."

Paulie didn't comment.

Kate sat on the porch step. "How long are you planning to stay?"

"Just tonight. Flight's out tomorrow evening."

"Would you like to take Bonny somewhere tomorrow?"

"Home. I'd like to take her home."

Kate's stomach clenched. Cold. Aloof. Not her Paulie.

Further speculation was put on hold when Cheryl came out, carrying Bonny. "Do you want me to take her on back to the apartment?"

Kate looked to Paulie, who shrugged.

Cheryl took up the gauntlet. "Tell you what. Let's all go to my place, I'm sure Paulie would like to see where we're living, and I have ice cream..." she emphasized the last four words, then trotted down the porch steps to put Bonny into her car seat.

"Do you want me to come?" Paulie asked.

Kate almost smiled at the decided pout in his voice. "Sure. I can give you a ride back for your car later. It's only a few blocks."

The ice cream social was more strained than dinner. Cheryl disappeared into her studio soon after, leaving Paulie, Kate and their daughter alone.

Paulie sat Bonny up in the middle of the living room floor. She immediately leaned over, got onto all fours and crawled toward the couch.

"Well, look at that. Crawling! Amazing."

"That's nothing. Wait until she gets there."

After a couple of false starts, Bonny pulled herself into a standing position. Paulie was delighted and clapped his hands. Bonny giggled, then crawled back to her father and into his lap. "Why, you smart little bugger."

Kate found a ball and rolled it to them. Paulie helped the child roll it back. They played the game until Bonny tired of it.

Soon, the tot was rubbing her eyes. Kate handed her to Paulie for a kiss and he tucked her into her portable crib in the bedroom. She settled quickly.

Kate sat down at the end of her bed, and Paulie sat beside her.

"Do you want me to drive you back to Mom's now?"

"No. Not really. Although," he said quietly, "I am looking forward to her guest bed."

Kate pressed her lips together tightly, hoping not to laugh.

"I'm sorry," she said at last, "but I have it on good authority that Cheryl's couch is not entirely competent, either."

"Competent? Did you say *competent?*"

"So what do you want to do, then?" Kate asked.

He put his hand on her thigh. "If I told you, you would slap me silly."

"Don't even go there, Paul Bingham."

"Okay." He got up, leaned across the bed and drew his finger down the middle of the bedspread. Kate shook her head. He drew another, giving her two-thirds of the bed.

"Paulie, I don't..."

"Three fourths and I keep my hands to myself. Final offer. Deal?"

He laced his fingers behind his neck. "I can hear her soft baby breaths."

"Mmm."

"Does she cry at all anymore?"

"Not much."

"I can't believe how much she's changed. I don't like missing that." He turned on his side, propped his head. "When are you coming home?"

"I was hoping you weren't going to start that."

"Don't you think I deserve to know? I mean, is it next week, next month or never? I'm completely in the dark here. You don't want to see me, you don't want to talk on the phone, and you don't want to talk now. You don't even want me to touch you."

She did want him to touch her. More than anything. But how would she ever be sure?

His words, so softly spoken in the dark, surprised her.

"You know, sometimes I've felt so close to you, I could barely tell where I ended and you began. Yeah, it's cliché, but it's true. The weeks since you left have been hellacious. How many women tell their husbands to go out and decide if they're gay or not? Should be simple enough, eh?"

"Paulie, I didn't say that."

"I know what you said, and what you meant. You somehow got the idea in your head that I was unhappy living a straight life. I'd like to know who made you the expert. I'm tired of people telling me what I am and am not. What I should be and shouldn't be. I feel like some kind of experiment that everyone is waiting to see explode. Waiting for me fail."

A three-quarter moon shone through the open window, illuminating the bed. Kate placed her hand in the middle, on the first imaginary line Paulie had drawn. A moment later, he placed his hand over hers, squeezing tightly before releasing her and turning away.

Cheryl was making Bonny's oatmeal when Kate wandered out of her room. "Where's Paul?"

"He's not in with you?"

"No."

"He must have left early. I've been up since seven."

"Damn. God dammit."

"What, no makeup sex?"

"Cheryl. Not funny."

Cheryl grinned. "What with the tension and vibes last night, I thought you guys would be all over each other the minute Bonny conked out."

"Nothing happened."

"Because you wouldn't let it."

"I need some coffee."

"Prude."

Kate loved Cheryl. They had become like sisters in the weeks since moving in together. Unfortunately, Cheryl homed in on Kate's every emotion, sometimes even before Kate knew what she was thinking.

"You hurt his pride. He's trying to be a man and you're questioning him."

Kate stared. "Do you really think I hurt him that way?"

"Wouldn't you be hurt if he questioned your femininity? I think we're all different levels of sexual beings. I think women's breasts are sexy. Does that make me a lesbian? My ex-boyfriend and I used to watch art films—good name, huh?—with girls on girls all the time. It aroused us both. It doesn't make us any more right or wrong. Paulie's in a very tough spot." Her cousin turned off the stove and poured the oatmeal into a bowl. "One thing's for sure, though, he loves you with all his heart."

"Hit me some more."

"Okay. How's this? Even I can tell that he's not the type of guy who can be alone for very long. So if you don't do something soon, this could end up a self-fulfilling prophecy for you. Being with *someone* might be better than being alone."

Slam. Weren't those her own words? When she took up with Ray Goff? *Oh, Jesus.*

"In fact...now that you have him so trained, maybe I should head out to California. He'd make an excellent model. I think he's incredibly sexy. For a beta-boy type."

Kate showed her cousin her middle finger and headed back to the bedroom.

Bonny was calling.

• **Paulie's leaving shifted my whole sphere. Yes, I knew he'd also come to see Bonny, but the reality was that he wanted to make amends. Trying to get something like healing started. I, on the other hand, was as dense and cold as a lump of grey clay.**

I was back in that cocoon. Severely hurting, as much so as if someone had torn off one of my limbs. He affected me like that, so much a part of me that when we were apart, I could barely balance to walk. To function. Always aching, scared, dark and spinning. When we fought, my future disappeared like the snap of a shutter.

Why was I so frozen? There he was, my life blood, lying inches away from me. All I would have had to do was touch him with one weak finger and he would have instantly enveloped me, rewound time, made everything whole and pure and perfect again.

I held tight to the fact, however, that things would never really be pure and perfect. We were far from pure- we were imperfectly human and humanly imperfect.

So instead of bathing in the warmth of Paulie's love, I sat still, letting the cold waves of depression wash over me.

–Kate

Chapter 12

March, 1992. Albuquerque, New Mexico

Three weeks came and went. Kate took a couple of bridal makeup jobs in order to pass the time. She'd called a truce with her cousin: no more lambasting her about Paulie. She broke her own edict one evening while cooking dinner.

"He hasn't called, Cher."

"He's not gonna call. You told him not to, remember?"

"It's almost Bonny's birthday. And it didn't stop him before."

"He has bigger balls than you give him credit for. He's sucking it up, giving you space."

"Or has given up on us. On me."

Cheryl didn't answer. When another Friday passed and Paulie hadn't phoned, Kate put his CD on and danced around the living room with Bonny in her arms. That night she did not sleep.

Saturday, at noon, she called Cheryl, who was getting a manicure.

"Can you give us a ride to the airport?"

"Hallelujah. But leave Bon Bon with me. I'll bring her to L.A. in a day or two. You and Paul need some time."

He was sitting at the piano, a stack of lined paper in front of him, and a pencil in his teeth. Writing songs. It's what he did when life began to swallow him whole. He didn't like the song he was composing, couldn't finish it. Maybe if he could understand what had happened, he could get on with things. Just eleven months had passed since Kate had given him the best gift of his life. Now, she'd taken Bonny, and her love, away. He'd run out of ideas for getting her back. Frustrated, he slammed his fingers down on the ivory keys.

He thought about how far he'd come. Just surviving his childhood was monumental, with his oppressive, judgmental father and long-suffering mother. School, one nightmare after another. Years of struggling for identity, both on stage and off. Always feeling his way; always expecting the floor to drop out beneath him. The friends, the users; the highs, lows, disappointments. The stream of partners, all promising love but delivering emptiness. The dark and toxic world of drugs, the poisons heaped on him by his life.

And then Kate happened.

So deeply entrenched in his memories, he nearly fell off the piano stool when the phone rang. He thought, fleetingly, that it might be her. His spirit soared at the sound of her voice, but he clutched at his stomach. Too terrified to expect good news.

"Where are you?" he asked, noting the sound of a public address system in the background.

"At the airport. My flight's leaving. Can you pick me up?"

His response was automatic; he didn't want to stop and analyze. "Burbank or Los Angeles?"

"Burbank. 7:00 p.m. "

Paulie closed his eyes, drew in a quiet breath. "I guess I can cancel my appointment with Her Royal Majesty."

Although he'd showered just hours before, he got back in, letting the hot spray pummel his face, his chest. Hoping the water would empower him, dispel his natural fears. Could he begin to believe that this was a positive thing? How far into his own court was the ball?

Her tone had been guarded; she made a much better poker face than he. Paulie was always six feet out in front of himself. She'd only asked him to pick her up, after all.

He went to his closet, barely able to recognize his own clothing. Randomly grabbing a grey dress shirt, he slid it on amid visions of Kate walking toward him at the terminal. A pair of black Dockers followed. Shoes and socks. In his dressing room, he stared into the mirror. His hair had grown out over the summer, just to his jaw, a ragged part to one side. He opened a drawer, absently reached for an aqua eye crayon. Paused, put it back down and grabbed his watch instead. At the door, he put on his vintage, round "Lennon" shades, swept up the keys to the Audi and headed out.

As she stepped off the jet stairs onto the tarmac, Kate wasn't at all sure she was doing the right thing. She shouldered her purse, took a deep breath. It was now or never...and so cliché.

Just be cool. Don't make demands. Let him talk first. The voices in her head were driving her mad. Turning the corner outside security, she scanned the waiting area. Where was he? She looked again, subconsciously seeking the odd man out, the attention-getter, the joker among the masses. He wasn't there.

But someone did approach. Tall, slender, subtle, casually walking her way, he paused to take off his glasses.

"Need a lift?"

"I think I do."

"Where's our little one?"

"Thought she'd catch a later flight with Auntie Cheryl. Said Mommy and Daddy might need to talk alone."

"Bags?"

"No. Not a premeditated trip."

As they walked to the car, she couldn't stop staring, trying to decide what was so different. It was the makeup, of course—or rather, the lack of it. His face was naked. Paulie Bingham never left home without some kind of color, flair, adornment painted on his eyes. And here he walked beside her, more beautiful than ever, his skin clean and free of any remnant of the mask he'd worn nearly all his life.

"You seem a bit edgy," he said, maneuvering the car out of the parking lot.

"I'm just afraid someone might see us together...and tell my husband."

His eyes were on the road, but his lips curved just enough to reward her joke.

"Any place you need to stop?"

"No. Let's just go home."

Clipped, idle chit-chat filled the drive. Once in the house, Kate thought she would burst with emotion. Paulie wasn't giving her any signs. No touch, no intimate smile, no innuendo. No anger, either. He was never so carefully controlled.

"Something to drink?"

"No. Don't feel like that right now."

"And what do you feel like?"

Kate shrugged, feeling more locked up as the minutes passed. She didn't know what she'd expected, but this wasn't it.

"Did our daughter say what it is that we're supposed to talk about?" Paulie asked. He went to the CD player and pressed some buttons, then slipped out of his shoes and sat on the living room floor. Kate followed suit, sat facing him, leaned back against the raised fireplace hearth.

"She wants... us to decide what is happening."

"You can only decide to change what *will* happen. What *is* happening is a result of... possibly... previous decisions. Poor ones, at that."

"You are always about semantics."

"It only sounds that way because I'm British."

"Of course." Kate stared at the carpet, wishing she could will the words that needed to be said. She'd never had difficulty talking to Paulie before.

"If you're not going to talk, may I have the floor, Madame Chairman?"

"Please."

"Maybe you can answer some questions. I assume you came home for a reason?"

"Yes."

"Point. Does the reason have to do with us?"

"Yes."

"Point. Have you made some kind of decision, as related to previously, about the future?"

"This is silly."

"No point. Are you still distrusting of your husband, you know, the one who's never misrepresented the truth even once?"

Kate swallowed, picked at the carpet fibers beneath her toes.

"I wasn't distrusting, exactly, I..."

"Just answer the question, Mrs. Bingham. Why did you come back?" He lifted his chin, gave her a chilly air. "I could've sent you your things."

Kate got to her feet. He was beginning to really piss her off. Something switched on.

"Okay. Here's the deal. My deal. I came home because I was completely, utterly miserable without you. I've thought about this so long and hard my brain is hurting. It's all just too much, Paul. Too much. All that bullshit about letting something you love fly away, and if it comes back, well, that's all crap. I never wanted to let you fly away. I'm scared to freakin' death. If that asshole David Stanton hadn't let on that you were out looking, I never would have known. So you see, I don't really know about you never ... what the hell did you call it? Misrepresenting the truth? For all I knew, you might have been out shagging half the guys in West Hollywood."

Paulie, too, stood from the floor, eyes blazing. "David told you I was... *out looking?*"

"Not only that, he intimated that I was meddling with your natural fucking persuasion! Oh, that's a funny choice of words, isn't it? He said that if I cared about you, I'd step aside."

Her words had clearly stunned him. He turned a quarter turn away, frowning, breathing hard. Kate sat down on the hearth.

"So that's it. All of it. I was, I am, stuck between my own selfish desires and your happiness. What else was I to do?"

He turned back to her. "Tell me, I guess."

"It wasn't that simple."

"How could it be simpler? *'Paulie, darling, that nasty old cur Stanton was 'round here today. He said some stupid, completely unrealistic things about you, which I, naturally, already know can't be true, but I thought you might like the opportunity to explain what is going on, because, really, you have been coming home quite late sometimes.'* How might that have gone, then?"

Kate hung her head. "I had thoughts of killing him."

"I think *I* still might."

She looked up. "He's a thug. Best leave him be."

107

"You don't know the half of it." Paul lifted his chin. "I took down Goff, if you recall."

"What don't I know the half of?"

"Forget it."

"Don't withhold. This is important. Did David purposely lead me down the path?"

"He told *me* that you were bothered by my background, my sexuality. That I was really unhappy because of your expectations."

"It's not true!"

"I agree, a load of crap. David is an old troll looking for a new boy Friday. He thought I was that boy."

"And you fired him?"

Paulie nodded. "It all makes perfect sense, now. I'd no idea he'd come to see you. And why? Because you didn't bloody tell me, Kate. All this misery for naught."

Silence hung between them like frozen air. Kate stood, wrung her hands.

"I'm sorry. He was... so convincing."

Paulie looked to ceiling, shook his head slowly. "I know. I misjudged him, and I brought him into our home. He's a disgusting pervert who will never walk through that door again."

Paulie needed to regroup. The revelations about David Stanton threw a whole new slant on his issues with Kate. Coupled with his mortification at the memory of the night spent with Stanton, he felt mildly nauseous. He unbuttoned the uppermost button on his shirt.

"I move that we vote Stanton out of our lives, and our memories, for good."

"I second," Kate murmured.

"Let's order Chinese. I can't deal with this now."

Kate nodded. "But I need to take a quick break." She went to the bedroom, leaving Paulie to order their dinner. When she rejoined him, she wore a black velour robe, her hair tumbling, uncombed and dripping with curls. She enchanted him. Here was a Kate that he hadn't seen in a very long while – since before her shocking fainting spell. Not pregnant, not bleeding, not swollen with child. Not in pain, not nursing, not haggard from being up all night with a sick infant. It occurred to him, the toll having Bonny had taken on them was steep. He was thrown back to the weeks just before the break up, when he'd been out clubbing while Kate held down both mother and father roles. No wonder David's words had cut her so deeply.

Over dinner, they edged back toward normalcy, allowing themselves a little time to reconnect. Paulie reveled in the sound of her voice, her candor and wit.

"So Cheryl walked around *behind* the car, and… are you even listening to me?" she asked, throwing a cello-wrapped fortune cookie at him.

"No, actually. I was thinking about how incredibly wonderful you are."

"Hoping to get laid, are you?"

"Planning to."

"We'll see about that."

Paulie smiled. "Yeah. We will. When will Bon be here?"

"Most likely, Monday."

"She's good with Cheryl, eh?"

"They are like peas in a pod."

"That's great. That makes me feel good. How are Mum and Pop? Do they hate me now?"

Kate rolled her eyes. "It's me they hate. You'd think they were *your* parents, the way they treated me."

This made him smile. "See? Shame on you for being such a problem child." He moved a bit closer, touched her bottom lip with his finger. She didn't move away. He traced the outline of her lips, drew his finger down her chin and throat, pausing where the robe crisscrossed on her chest. "Have you any clue how much I want you right now? Would you mind, terribly, being seduced by your husband?"

Chapter 13

May, 1994. Barcelona, Spain -26 months later

Kate stared out the window at tourists lined up before the Barcelona Cathedral in the Barri Gòtic. "What do you think Paul will say?"

Cheryl was trying to wrestle a pair of socks onto Bonny's feet. "He'll be delighted."

"I'm not so sure. Only one way to find out. Where did he go again?"

"Downstairs to see if they have any suitable snacks for a three-year-old vegetarian. You want me and Bon Bon to disappear for a while? Give you guys some time to work up a good fight?"

"We don't fight anymore. You know that."

"That was before you lost your diaphragm. C'mon sweet pea. Auntie Cheryl wants to go for a walk."

"Keep a close eye."

Cheryl frowned at her. "I watch her closer than you do."

She met Paulie just coming in with basket of fruit.

"Look what Daddy brought you. A pear, an apple, and a 'nana!" Paulie bent to hand the banana to Bonny, who beamed up at him with a toothy grin before Cheryl herded her out the door.

Paulie joined Kate at the window. "Beautiful, isn't it?" He embraced her from behind, wrapping his arms around her waist. "Wait until you see Hamburg."

She turned in his arms, stood on tiptoe to kiss him. "Listen," she said, "I have a surprise." She kissed him again.

"This isn't one of those, *honey-I-wrecked-the-car* type surprises, is it?"

She smiled, kissed him again, put her lips to his ear. "It's a far better surprise than that."

"Am I supposed to guess?"

"I doubt you can. But you can try."

He sat down on the bed, pulled her into his lap. Pushing her hair aside, he kissed her neck, her ear, her mouth. Flushed, panting, Kate stopped him.

"You're supposed to be guessing my secret."

He looked her in the eye. "We're preggers again, aren't we?"

She'd never expected him to guess. "Actually, yes. How did you know?"

Gently pushing, he laid her back on the bed. "It's you." He shrugged. "I couldn't be happier, my darling. How is it that we are so blessed?"

"Probably because I left our protection in Amsterdam."

"Ah. As simple as that."

"You're not mad, really?"

"Why should I be mad? It's not like we can't afford another child. It's not like we don't have enough room in our family for another. Enough room in our hearts." He placed a hand on her tummy. "Feeling all right?"

"Fine. But I'm thinking maybe I'll take Bonny home, in a couple of weeks."

"If you think it best. Do stay on until we get to London. Peg's looking forward to seeing you."

"Will you miss me?"

"Like a heartbeat. But I want you to be safe and comfortable. Maybe I should escort you home?"

Kate hopped off his lap. "No. You don't want to do that. There's no reason. Cheryl will be there to help with Bonny."

"Speaking of Little Bee, how do you think a baby will affect her?"

"Well, as you have her so completely spoiled, I imagine she'll have to make some adjustments."

"My daughter? Spoiled? Whatever are you talking about?"

Kate went back to the window. "When do we have to be at the auditorium?"

"Got a couple of hours. I'm knackered. Too late last night. I might fancy a wee nap. You?"

"I think I'll go downstairs and sit a while in the courtyard. I just feel like getting a little air."

Hamburg was everything Paulie had said. So were Vienna, Bern, and Paris. Kate soaked in the beautiful, captivating European landscape, the cultural diversities, and the hospitable people. Paulie's fans were everywhere, it seemed, most of them long time followers from Bingham Boys days. The new band had a bigger presence and a larger entourage that traveled from city to city. Paulie seemed on top of his game, reveling in the limelight despite the fast and furious pace of the tour.

The press, however, dogged them, worse even than the fans. Buzz hired bouncers and bodyguards, and still Paulie, Kate and the band were manhandled and accosted at every turn. Airport security varied from city to city. Plans involving alternate routes, disguises and even doubles failed to bring them peace as they traveled.

The hotels were nearly as bad, as family members of hotel personnel were permitted access to their floors. Fans stowed away in luggage transports and room service carts.

"I didn't think people really did that," Kate commented, after one tearful young girl was removed from their suite in Paris.

"You get numb to it after a while. I know I appear callous, but those girls drive me mad. It's like they never even consider that I have a life, too. It's bloody rude of them."

Kate smiled, laid back against a pillow while watching him wrestle with the plastic sheeting over his dry cleaned costume. "Have you ever just sat down and talked to them?"

"They don't want to be talked to. They just want to touch and jab, and grab and cry. They do nothing but moan and sometimes they beg. For what, I'm not quite sure."

"Doesn't it feel just a little good to be so loved?"

"I have all the love I can handle right in this room." He blew her a kiss. "It's worse now, you know. Since you."

"Since me, what?"

"The girl fans. They moaned before, but they rather accepted that I was unattainable because I was gay."

"News flash to girl fans: Paulie Bingham is still unattainable."

Paulie examined his safety-pin covered jacket, shook it and watched the pins sway and shimmer. "The worst ones are the screamers. They pay full price, maybe twenty-five pounds, to come and scream the whole time. I sing, they scream, nobody hears a bloody word. It's sick."

"You are really in a pissy mood."

"No, I'm not. Not really." He hung the jacket in the closet and sat down on the bed beside her. "I'm just being a bore. I love touring, and I hate it as well. Having you along keeps me sane. But it also presents a problem, because, you know, I'd like to take you and Bonny up the Tower tomorrow. It's gorgeous. You can see all the way to Los Angeles from up there."

Kate gave him a skeptical smile.

"But I don't know how we can manage, out in public like that. I worry for you. I worry for Bonny."

"So, we'll come back sometime when they don't know we're here. On a vacation. Incognito." She poked him in the side, pinched him, grabbed him. "It's the price of success, right? The Eiffel Tower isn't going anywhere."

He leaned down and kissed her. "There's a party tonight. Do you want to go?"

"Who's going to be there?"

"No one important. Some guys from the local Virgin office. Deejays, some people I met years back on my first tour. Lots of glamgloms who want to know us."

"I think I'll pass. But you go. That stuff is important to your career."

"I have my career in place. I don't need to kowtow to every record company exec anymore."

"Okay," Kate said, running her hand along the side of his leg. "But you'll get bored here. You hate French TV, French food, and claustrophobic hotel rooms."

"Sure you don't want to come?"

"I think I have a date with a three year old and a coloring book."

114

"Let me know if you change your mind, darling. It will be drab without you."

The party was in a large hotel suite across the street. His bandmates were there, as were familiar faces from the tour. Celebrities that had attended the concert were treated like royalty.

Paulie perused the food table for anything he could stand to eat. Deviled eggs were okay. Raw vegetables and dip. Stuffed mushrooms.

He talked to the record company people, tried not to be too offensive. Watched his bass player dropping Ecstasy with a beautiful young girl. A cute boy with real dreadlocks approached him with a joint, and Paulie turned away, stuffed a celery stick into his mouth.

Someone turned up the already loud music. Paulie sat down on a barstool and a drink appeared in front of him.

"What is it?" he yelled to the bartender, holding up the amber colored liquid.

"Manhattan," the barman called, then tilted his head at a woman sitting two stools away. Paulie picked up the cocktail and moved to sit beside her.

"Thanks," he said. "I don't know you."

"Jeannette," she said into his ear. "You're welcome."

"What's the occasion?"

The woman tossed her blonde hair, leaned close and whispered, "I want to fuck you."

Paulie took a sip of the drink, smiled. "Oh, no you don't."

Jeannette tilted her head, lowered her eyelashes. "Yes, I do."

"I think you're mistaken. Do you see that lovely little girl over there, by the patio door? The one in the sexy black frock and stilettos? She's chatting up Brendan Frasier at the moment, but if she gets wind of your intentions, she'll likely come round and make a meal of you."

He caught Kate's eye and gave her a little wave, then pushed the drink over in front of the baffled woman. "Can't drink this. Wouldn't be fair, would it? Hope you find someone to screw, Jeannette. Terrible thing to be horny and alone."

Once the band reached London, the tour went on hiatus for a few days. There, they would meet up with popular alternative rock singer Rob Evans, who would share the bill for one night of their three night gig at the Wembley Arena. There had been other warm-up bands in various cities, usually local start-ups looking for a break; American-born Evans, however, was a huge name in both the U.S. and U.K., and Kate couldn't help but wonder how Paulie would respond to sharing the stage, the spotlight, and the t-shirt sales.

Peg was all over Kate from the moment they walked in.

"You might bump out a bit sooner this time, dearie. Oh, I was a bouncing ball with my third. No, wait, it was the fourth. Joshua. I think?"

Kate humored her sister-in-law, trying not to laugh as Cheryl made silly gestures behind Peg's back, holding her hands out below an imaginary belly the size of a medicine ball.

"'Course, you're such a wee slip of a thing, I can't wonder but you'll show sooner. So, is it a boy or a girl this time?"

"I don't have a clue," Kate said, taking a sip of tea. It was too soon to even feel pregnant. She hadn't quite gotten used to the idea yet. "I think Paul would like a boy."

"Don't surprise me none. He likely wants a chance to be a good father to a son. Unlike our own."

"He doesn't talk much about your dad."

"Cold herring, that one. Oh, I suppose he had a hard upbringin' hisself. Our grandfather was wazzocked half the time. Beat seven kinds of shite out of our dad. Bad times, then, during the war."

Kate thought about Pop, at home in New Mexico, reading the morning paper. Defending her flamboyant, bisexual husband. "So Paulie and your father didn't get along?"

"It weren't that they didn't get along, they just didn't... anything. It was like Paul was invisible to him. I had it a little better, I was older, and a girl at that. I was supposed to be, you know, soft and girl-like. But Paulie, well, he gave up early on tryin' to please Dad. Thank God for our mum."

Kate nodded. "He speaks very highly of her. Lots of love, there."

"Aye. Mum was angel in line to be sainted, which I'm quite sure she was when she got to St. Peter's. Now, where is me soddin' brother? It's almost time for supper."

"He's out carousing with one of his friends. Someone called Ian."

Kate liked being around Peg. She slipped right into the role of big sister, lavishing Kate with love, advice and family history. Cheryl, too, enjoyed her company. Peg's youngest, a small girl of nine, took an immediate liking to Bonny, who tottled after her cousin throughout the large flat.

"Well, ring him up, will you? Can't be expected to serve him up separately, can we? Mister high and mighty, he is now. Not eatin' meat. Not eatin' bangers or blood pudding. Why, our mum would be forcin' stew meat down his very throat. It's hardly a wonder he's so slender, is it?"

Kate smiled. Peg didn't know the half of her brother's idiosyncrasies. "Don't try to feed him cheese, either."

Peg turned a shocked face. "What does he eat then? Bowls of oats? Turnip greens?"

Sabotage. A therapist once told me I do it to myself when things are going too well. Things couldn't have been going better that spring. Kate was pregnant again, and I was actually delighted. It wasn't so bad being a parent, I'd discovered. She was a terrific mum and Bonny was the perfect child. The tour turned out to be the best ever; we were pulling in big bucks and seeing the world. Aside from an occasional spliff, maybe some sleeping pills, I was pretty clean. Healthy. Happy. We blew into London with reckless abandon.

Reckless, it turns out, on my part. Because a strange thing was happening. I was beginning to see myself differently. The man in the mirror was becoming decidedly straight. Button-downs and pleated dress slacks began taking a stand in my closet. Kate, in her quiet, loving, subtle way, supported this transformation.

I was leaving myself behind without so much as a bread crumb trail. What was next? Football, Harley-Davidson, and steak?
—*Paulie*

Chapter 14

The waitress brought a second pitcher of ale to the table. Paulie winked at her. "Thanks, love."

Ian shuddered. "Did you just bloody wink at that fish? Man, you really have become a breeder."

Paulie rolled his eyes. "You know, that's what's wrong with you. You are so fucking one-sided about everything." He lifted his stein, took a long draught. "You really need to get out more."

His friend laughed. "I get out plenty. You can't judge me and you know it. Just because you've given up cock for cabbage doesn't mean I have to."

Paulie smiled, tilted his head.

"And worse, you're all full of yourself because your wife is sprogged up. I've got you sussed, Paul."

"You have, have you?"

Ian lit a cigarette, handed it to Paul, who didn't hesitate to take a drag.

"Yep. I have a theory." Ian took a gulp of ale, wiped his mouth on his napkin. "This all goes back to Pritchard, doesn't it?"

Paulie's smile waned.

"He ruined you, pal. He fucking ruined you."

"What happened between Jamie and I is mine. We moved passed it. And it has absolutely no bearing on who I am now." He gave Ian a defined stare. "This may sound odd to a devout pillow-biter like yourself, but I don't see the fact that Kate is female as a threat to my sexuality. There can come a point, dear boy, where gender isn't as important as devotion."

Ian raised his eyebrows, took a puff. "Well then. I guess we've effectively put old Ian in his proper place. Didn't mean to offend you, *chappie*."

Paul shrugged, turned to peruse the room. Two pretty boys were extending invitations from a booth across the pub. He smiled, shook his head. Turned back to Ian. "Still mates?"

"I don't know. 'Pillow-biter' might have cut it for me. I suppose it's up to you. Can we be friends if I don't do women?"

"I wouldn't care if you were out spearing pigs. Just don't dis me for my choices."

"Come back to the house. Chaz is in town, and we're celebrating tonight."

"Peg's expecting me for dinner."

"Just come 'round for a bit, then. Your devoted little ladies will understand, right? Call momma and ask if it's all right to stay out a wee bit."

"I don't have to ask."

"Excellent. It's settled, then. Drink up, sister."

The ale had made him fuzzy. Worse, a black ball was forming in his head, a blurry, growing image that masked his sensibilities. When he thought of Kate, the ball moved into place between them. Memories of his addictions, his battles faded behind it. Had he been sober, he would have recognized the devil's face.

Kate lay in the dark, Bonny nestled against her. She hadn't slept and knew it must be past one or two a.m. when she heard someone stumbling up the bare wooden staircase. He was singing, softly, an old Duran Duran song.

He made a stop at the bathroom, then came to their room, sat down. Wrestled with his shoes, then fell back onto his pillow.

Kate drew in a breath, got out of bed. She lifted Bonny gently and carried her to the adjacent alcove, where Peg had set up a small child's cot, and tucked her sleeping daughter in. She returned to the bedroom and closed the door behind her.

Paulie groaned. Kate turned on the bedside lamp.

"Dammit. Don't do that."

Kate crossed her arms. "Where the *hell* have you been?"

"Out," was his muffled response.

"Out. Great."

"Aw, Kate. Can we talk in the morning?"

"It is morning. What's going on? You said you'd be here for dinner. Peg broke her neck to make a nice meal for you, one you would actually eat, and you blew her off. You didn't even call."

"Sorry."

"Sorry? That's it? Not good enough. Paul, you turned your damned phone off! What if I needed you? What if Bonny needed you? We didn't know where you were, or if something was wrong. How could you do that?"

Paulie sat up, rubbed his eyes. "Slag off, will you?"

"No. I want an explanation. You left at noon! Gone fourteen hours, and all you can say is that you were *out*? Out partying with your little gay friends."

"That's enough. It's not your concern where I was. I came back. So just...fuck off."

Blinded with rage at his insult, Kate took a swing and slapped Paulie so hard he fell over on the bed. Momentarily sobered, he stared up at her in shock.

"You hit me," he murmured. "You fucking hit me."

Kate swallowed, looked away. She *had* hit him! Hard enough to make her hand hurt. But it didn't pain her as much as his words had.

With nothing left to say, she turned off the lamp and lay down, her back to her beloved, clearly confused husband.

Although nearly everyone in the house had heard the early morning discourse, no one said a word at breakfast, not even the strong-willed Peg. She did, however, grace her younger brother with a scornful eye. Paulie decided that silence was golden, and that Kate would eventually forgive him his transgression. She insisted on accompanying him to the Arena for rehearsal. They were to meet Rob Evans and his band there, and work out details with Buzz for the three night gig.

Paulie tried to ignore his misery. Flashes of the night before wafted in and out of his mind. Nasty scenes, with unfamiliar faces. The smell of pot, the thin white lines of coke on a mirror. Laughter, singing. Drag queens lounging about. Bowls filled with wrapped candy and condoms. Ian's voice, chiding him, coaxing him, daring him.

I never was any good at dares.

He was slammed back into the here and now as Rob Evans approached.

"Paul. Good to see you, man." The singer held out his hand. Paulie took it.

Still an unmistakably straight, male fox. Too good looking not to be gay. Such a waste.

"Love your new stuff," Paulie said, choking back a wave of dizziness. "This is my wife, Kate."

"For Katherine?" Rob asked, taking Kate's hand.

"Katrina," she said. "For Robert?"

"Robin."

"And Paulie is short for asshole." Paulie turned. "Let's get started, shall we?"

Kate followed Paulie around the Wembley stage, intent on not letting him out of her sight. It was a form of punishment, she realized, but she was unwilling or unable to stop. He'd crushed her last night, and it wasn't over. Not by a long shot.

He'd been unfaithful, there was no doubt in her mind. She would make him confess. Make him suffer for not owning up on his own. She would drop the charges for the comment; he was drunk or worse, and she'd pushed him, hard. But there would be no soft landing for his fall from grace.

The London shows would be different from anything else they'd done. This was Paulie's town, and he was treated as such. Fans camped just outside the Arena's parking lot, waiting for the box office to open, despite the fact that all three shows were sold out. Only twenty-seven hours remained until show time.

"I need to do some shopping." Paulie mumbled. He didn't look at her, but held the backstage door open.

"What for?"

"I need something new to wear tomorrow night."

"What about the green and black thing? I thought that was for the opener."

"I don't like it now. Are you coming along, or should I drop you at the hotel?"

"I'll come."

The shops were in a neighborhood new to Kate, on streets where punk was still very much alive. Paulie tore through rack after rack of designer, androgynous garments. He didn't ask her what she thought of the hunter green velvet riding jacket he took to the cashier. Didn't come out of the dressing room to show off the knee-length, black and silver dressing gown he added to the purchase. Purple drawstring pants and white poet's shirt, with a black lace-up vest.

He's punishing me, now. For hitting him. For the comment about his gay friends. Kate stood from the velveteen couch and walked outside the shop, leaned against the building.

He brought this on himself. How dare he be mad at me?

"Should I get a cab or do you want to walk?" he asked, putting on his shades.

"Whatever you're doing, I'm doing."

"I'm walking."

He looked straight ahead as he walked, ignoring Kate as she tried to keep up and tried to make that look easy.

"You're being awfully rude, Paul."

"I don't take kindly to being abused."

"Neither do I."

He stopped walking, turned to her. "I would never abuse you, Kate. You know that. Look, I'm sorry about last night. Things got late. I was with friends. You're right, I'm wrong, I'm sorry. Okay?"

"No, not okay. It was more than that, wasn't it?" She gave him her best level stare, plucked the sunglasses from his face. "The truth."

"I can't tell you the truth."

Kate's lips parted in surprise. "What's that supposed to mean?"

"Just that…it's more than you need or want to know. You've made that clear in the past."

She swallowed. "So, it's true, then."

He took the glasses from her fingers, slipped them back on and resumed his pace.

The pain was harsh and unexpected. Hearts don't have feeling, she thought. Not really. But the searing ache that burned within her chest was all but debilitating. Paulie stopped, turned back, waited.

"Are you coming?"

They didn't speak another word until they reached their suite at the hotel. Kate picked up the phone and dialed Peg's number.

"Cher? It's me. I have a huge favor to ask you."

"What more can you ask? I've already adopted your munchkin."

"Get Bonny ready to go home."

"Home? L.A.?"

"Yes."

"What's going on, Kate? Does this have something to do with the row you had with Paul last night?"

Kate paused. Paulie was staring at her from across the room.

"Yes."

Paulie came around the bed, sat down, took the phone from her hand. "We'll call you back, love. Ta." He hung up the phone and turned to Kate. "You weren't even going to consult me?"

"You're busy. You have a lot going on."

"You offend me to no end. To suggest that I'm too busy to care whether or not my daughter is going back to the U.S.?"

"I think it's best."

Paulie stood. "I happen to agree. But I loathe it when you make decisions for me."

"I'm sorry about that. But you don't seem to be making good decisions lately."

"I get that." He hesitated, ran a hand through his hair. "Go ahead. But I want to see her before you go."

"*I'm* not going. Not yet. Not like this."

Paulie walked to the window, stared out. "Look, Kate. I know I'm a fuck-up. I know we need to talk this out. I owe you an explanation. Can you, can you see your way clear to putting it off until after the shows? I promise you, we can settle this, one way or another."

Kate considered. He was making nice, asking her to give him a little time. To put a little distance between his offense and his apology. She could do that. For Paulie.

It likely wouldn't change anything anyway.

"Okay. Yeah."

"All right then."

She called Cheryl back and then arranged a flight out the following morning. Paulie sat down beside her again.

"Evans invited us to dinner. You up for something like that? I can tell him no."

"No, I think we should." She wasn't really up to anything. But the distraction would be good. She and Paulie could pretend that everything was fine, the way it was when they'd arrived in London.

"This is my last stop," Rob said, picking up his steak knife. "And I'm ready. I started in Sydney, three months ago."

"You must be really fagged."

"Excuse me?"

Paulie chuckled. "Sorry. *Tired*. I'm feeling it, too. We still have twelve more cities before we finish."

Kate listened to the two men exchange road stories, doing her best to keep up the make believe. Paulie had already shocked her by donning a sport coat and slacks for their dinner with Rob. Was he competing? Doing penance? Whatever the reason, he took on a conservative look that she normally would have liked. Tonight, however, it didn't sit well. She turned to look at their host, who sported a dark leather jacket over an ivory, round necked shirt. His hair, thick, brown, combed at least once earlier in the day, hung just over his collar in the back. Hazel eyes, long lashes, a whisper of a beard. She wondered if Paulie thought he was cute, too.

From the way they talked, Kate realized the men had met and spent time together before. Paulie had never mentioned it.

"You're awfully quiet, Mrs. Bingham," Rob said, pulling her away from her thoughts about Paulie's motives.

"Oh, I'm just enjoying the prattle."

Paulie touched her back, not without obvious affection. "She's exhausted as well. We have a rather rambunctious three-year-old and another on the way."

"Wow. Congratulations. *Wow*. I commend you, being on the road."

"We haven't told anyone yet. Except you, now. I'm going back to Los Angeles on Monday," she blurted. Paulie gave her a brief look, but nodded.

"Some down time will be good for you."

"I think so." Kate agreed.

"We should, uh, get together sometime when you're both back and settled. I have a ranch in Conejo Valley," Rob said.

"Where's that, then?" Paulie asked.

"West of the San Fernando Valley."

Paulie turned to Kate. "Do I know where that is?"

"Yes, you do. It's across the Valley from where you once had friends in Studio City."

"Ah, yes. Friends, indeed."

☞ **It was the beginning of the end. The fabric of our marriage now had more than a small tear. We'd crossed a line somehow, his damaging words, my hitting him. I vacillated between wishing I'd never done it, and wondering if I should have used my fist instead of my open palm. The pain that radiated between us was visible, palpable. People avoided contact with us, except for Rob.**

During dinner, I couldn't help but wish we'd met Rob under different circumstances, or at least, at a different time, when we were more fun to be with. I sensed that he'd be the type of friend we could use. A supportive friend.

The timing of our rift couldn't have been worse, with the thoughts of a new baby still fresh in our hearts and minds. I fell hard, knowing that I'd been building a house of cards for us to live in. Silently, carefully orchestrating Paulie's metamorphosis into the man I wanted him to be. The guilt was enormous. And yet, I still found reasons to love him...and blame him. — KB

Chapter 15

They were in bed. The California king was comfortable, much larger than the small bed they'd shared at Peg's the night before. The soft whir of the hotel air conditioner replaced the groans and creeks of the old house in Essex. Paulie bunched his pillow, fixed Kate with his eyes. Hers were closed.

How could I have messed up so badly? I've really done it now. And for what? Cheap thrills?

And yet he was already fighting the desire to go back. The marijuana had seduced him, the men excited him. Ian had played upon his insecurities, his deeply buried feelings that he had one foot, and one foot only, in a world where he had no business playing.

Kate deserved better. She deserved a man who knew who he was, one confident and secure in being a hero. And despite the fact that she loved him—of this Paulie was absolutely certain—it didn't make their union right. He used to think that love conquered all, but he was no longer sure.

The sex was good. Good enough, made so because he loved her so. They had conceived a baby, a love-child that was an impossibly wonderful gift from God. Twice.

He'd promised Kate that he would tell her if he felt the urge to return to his former lifestyle. It pained him to acknowledge that he did crave what now seemed so simple, his life as a gay man. How could he begin to tell her something like that?

She couldn't be more beautiful, in hetero terms. The punk, almost geeky girl had evolved into a smartly savvy, would-be runway sensation, if pint-sized. More, she was a devoted and competent mother to Bonny. As a partner, she kept him sane, took care of him, put up with his quirks. How could he live without her?

Paulie closed his eyes, realized he was crying. He turned away. He didn't want to wake her.

On Friday morning, Paulie hugged Bonny fervently and presented her with a baby doll she'd pointed to in a shop window. "Happy birthday, sweet Bee. Daddy will be home soon to celebrate," he said, kissing her cheek. "I love you."

He then went into auto-pilot. Once he told Bonny goodbye, he was completely focused on the night's concert, and Kate wished she could also separate herself from the agony.

A few days, and she would be leaving Paulie behind. Again. She wracked her brain, tormented by questions. Was it the right thing to do? As hard as it was to admit, she had lost faith in him. It wasn't so much about what he did, but the way he did it. That he didn't tell her. Instead, he'd gotten defensive and surly. Could things ever be normal between them again?

She sat on a folding chair, watching the action on stage. It would be the biggest show they'd ever done, with lights, animations, extra musicians. Paulie fussed with every detail, crossing the stage and making demands. Kate watched with sad, but adoring, eyes.

Rob was there, too, making certain his band equipment was properly placed. His stage manager talked with Buzz about the movement of Rob's gear during intermission. Kate found it all very fascinating.

A girl rushed past her and dropped a wrapped sandwich in her lap. The sound system was tested. Paulie argued with Buzz about something, and Kate was tempted, as always, to intervene. To make everything right for him. He was a bad negotiator, especially when he let his inner diva come forth. Yet she glued herself to the chair, picked at the sandwich, mentally wishing he could be more... normal. That stupid, horribly inefficient word again.

The day dragged on. Just before dusk, she was asked to move backstage, as the theatre was being readied for the crowd. She went to Paulie's dressing room and waited. When he didn't come, she returned to the stage and watched as Rob's back up musicians took the stage. From the sound of the audience, not everyone in the house was there to see Paulie Bingham.

Someone dashed by, and it took a moment to realize it was Rob himself. Kate watched in fascination as he joined his band mates and picked up a wireless microphone.

"Good evening, Brits!" he shouted, waving broadly. "So glad to be back in London town! What do you say we get this show rockin'? Are you with me?"

Kate was just getting into the song when Paulie tagged her.

"Can you help me, love?"

"Sure. I—I didn't know where you were." She followed him back to the dressing room.

"He's really good, isn't he?" Paulie asked, as Kate tied a cape around his neck.

"Yeah. He is." She sat down on a small, rolling stool, opened her make-up case. "What's your pleasure?"

He gave her a solemn look. "Keep it natural."

"They'll be expecting glam."

"I don't give a flying fuck what they are expecting. I will be who I want to be, when I want to be it."

Kate nodded. "Of course you will," she muttered. Moving in close, she painted his eyes. He peered so deeply into hers, it unnerved her, and she made mistakes. Had to clean off and start again. Those light, grey-green eyes. So filled with pain, so honest, so remorseful.

Kate licked her lips, tried to re-center.

"Take your time."

"I'm not sure I can do this. Maybe you'd better do it."

"Nonsense."

"You're staring at me."

"I love you."

Kate took in a breath, closed her eyes. She wanted to hit him again, wanted to kiss him again. "Please don't talk."

She started again, steeled herself against the emotions that threatened to tear her apart. He looked into the mirror. "Brilliant. As always." He stood then, pulled the cape from his neck. Straightened his trousers. She helped him put on the black and silver dressing robe. He was giving a quick interview before starting his set.

He went to the door, paused, and returned.

"Kate."

She stood, waited as he came to her, and placed his hands on her shoulders. He seemed unable to speak, and Kate

129

stiffened. Slowly, he slid his arms around her, pulling her to him in a warm, needy embrace. He bowed his head, turned his lips close to her ear, whispered thickly.

"I'm sorry."

Despite his near meltdown, Paulie bounded onto the stage with energy and style. Kate, thankful for the wild cheering from an arena filled with Paulie Bingham fans, watched from her customary spot, just stage left; hidden but close enough to see him well. She was reminded of the old days, before Paulie even knew she existed, when she had signed on as a roadie for the Boys. Her boldface lie, the day his makeup artist had walked out. The first time she'd touched his face, her life had changed.

Now, he was alone in the spotlight, and she heard the opening notes to a song he'd written just for her. "Where I Belong" recounted his struggle with identification, and his joy at finding a home with her. She almost smiled before realizing she was not alone.

A man moved in beside her, swaying his hips in time to the music, smiling, mouthing the words to Paulie's song.

"He's awesome, isn't he?" he asked her. His exuberance was comical, but she nodded.

"He's the best."

"He has many talents, actually."

Kate turned to look at the man. He was tall, taller than Paulie, perhaps a bit younger. Short, black hair, combed back; blue eyes, good build.

"How do you mean?" Kate asked, turning her gaze back upon Paulie, who was traversing the stage, microphone in hand.

"It was you, all along...you finished my song..."

The young man grinned. "Well I guess that's for me to know, in't it? I just met him last night. We had a lovely time. Gifted boy, that one."

At thirty-two, Paulie was hardly a *boy*. Kate's stomach tightened, but she held firm to her spot. "Last night. You must be a friend of Ian's?"

"Yeah. Knows how to throw a good party, he does. Loaded with good chang and pot. Anyway, he introduced us. Never thought I'd get lucky with a bloke like Paulie, if you know what I mean. Him bein' who he is, and all. I'm Jon, by the way. How do you know Paulie?"

"When all else is wrong...you're where I belong."

"Jon. Well. I'm his wife."

"Oh. You're the *beard*, right. Ian mentioned you."

Kate stared, but Jon went back to watching Paulie.

"Oh, yeah...you're where...I...belong..."

"Enjoy the show," Kate said, turned to go. By the time she got to the back area, she was running. Blind. Past the stage hands, the roadies, the hangers. Past Rob, Buzz, and the reporters. With the glimmer of sanity she still had left, she rushed into Paulie's dressing room and grabbed her small travel bag. She would need her passport.

Ignoring the security guard, Kate slammed open one of the back stage doors, rushed down the steps, running fast lest the truth catch up with her. Halfway down the stairs, she caught her heel in an imperfection in the concrete and tumbled, head first, down the steps. She landed hard on her hands and her left hip, but got quickly to her feet, hot tears burning her cheeks. Gulping air, she pushed the hair from her face and ran on, through the parking lot, until she got to the row of taxis on the side street bordering the arena.

"The Ritz, on Piccadilly, please."

"You all right, Miss? You've got a spot of blood on your face, just there. Do you need medical attention?"

"No, thank you. The Ritz. Please hurry." The blood was from her hand, she realized. Without a word, the driver handed back a small box of tissue.

Once in her room, she looked at her watch. Paulie would be starting his second set. Wondering where she was.

She quickly cleaned up her hands and face, changed her clothes. Packed. After taking several deep breaths, she was able to dial the phone and call United Airlines. They had nothing until the morning.

She thought about leaving a note. Pictured Paulie rushing into the room, searching, finding her gone. Worrying. *Too bad.*

But what if he called Cheryl? Her mother?

She sat at the desk, took out a sheet of stationery.

"Paul… I've gone home." And because she was still aching inside, because she was so completely humiliated, she wrote, "I am not now, nor have I ever been, your beard."

She would just wait at Heathrow.

He didn't change for his second set. Kate had disappeared, left apparently, according those who'd witnessed her frantic exit. Paulie couldn't begin to understand what had happened, but he finished the show as best he could under the strain of worry. Foregoing the encore, he dashed outside and dived into a waiting limo.

At the Ritz, he tore into their suite, looked quickly around. Her things were gone. He sat down, bewildered, saw her note.

"Oh, God," he managed, covering his mouth after uttering the words. He reread the note, his eyes stumbling over the word. Where had she gotten the idea that he thought her a token bride, meant only to disguise his homosexuality? He remembered explaining to her, years ago, the meaning of the term. Some closeted gays married for convenience, just to protect their "straight" images. They'd laughed about them.

But tonight, she must have talked to someone, seen something, read something… there was no reasonable excuse for her thinking. He thought about going to the airport to try and stop her, but realized it would be a futile effort.

Paulie lay down on the bed, rolled to his side, pulled his knees up to his chin. Kate had gone. Again.

Chapter 16

K ate tried not to doze. The Red Carpet Club room offered a pleasant, private and comfortable respite from the airport at large. When they finally called her flight, she felt tremendous relief. She would no longer have to worry that Paul would rush up and try to get her to stay.

She had only one carry-on. Cheryl had managed to take some of her things ahead the day before. She took her seat in the upstairs, first class cabin of the 747 and kicked off her shoes. Her back ached and her side throbbed from her tumble down the steps. She dug in her bag for two Tylenol.

"I'd like an extra blanket, please," she asked the flight attendant. "And a cup of tea. No, make it coffee. Decaf coffee, with Bailey's."

Kate closed her eyes, leaned back in the cushiony deluxe seat. She was soon startled, however, by a man's voice beside her.

"Why, Mrs. Bingham. Imagine meeting you here."

Her eyes flew open.

"Rob? Oh, wow. You were booked on this flight?"

"For the past month. But I thought you were leaving Monday?"

"Change in plans."

"I see."

The attendant brought her coffee. "Can I get you anything else?"

A rewind button, she wanted to say. Instead, she smiled. "I'm good now, thanks."

"Bring me what she's having," Rob said, then turned back to Kate. "You caused quite a little stir last night."

Kate chose not to answer. Instead, she sipped her coffee.

"Okay. Well. I get that it's a private matter. I just want to say, if you're in need of anything, please, let me know. Shit happens. I know. I invented the term, back when I was married."

She let out a shaky breath, hoping the pain reliever would kick in soon.

"Paul's a really nice guy. He obviously loves you very much."

Kate nodded, wishing Rob would just shut up.

"You know, guys do stupid things sometimes. We don't mean to, hell, we're guys."

"If you're talking about my husband, you are using the term loosely."

Rob sat back in his seat.

"And if you're trying to make me feel better, I might suggest you don't waste your words. I do appreciate it, but my issues with Paulie are...well, private. Complicated. So, thanks anyway."

Rob looked a little wounded, so she continued on.

"If you want to talk about something else, I'd be happy to chat. I could use some diversion."

Rob smiled, and Kate noticed for the first time what a nice smile it was. Boyish, without being feminine. Knowing, but not leering. Genuine.

"So, where are you from?" he ventured.

"New Mexico. My parents still live there. I moved to L.A. twelve years ago. You?"

"I'm from Aiken, South Carolina, originally, but I've managed to evolve into an Angeleno over the past twenty years or so. So we have that in common."

"You said you were married?"

"Yep. But that's been over for, oh, about six years. Ancient history."

"Kids?"

"Nope."

"Girlfriend?"

"Gettin' a little personal, aren't you?" he said, this time showing dimples when he smiled.

"You know about my grand exit of last night, I'd say that was worth girlfriend knowledge."

"Okay. You're right. And no, not dating right now. Writing, singing, recording, touring, selling—and then repeat. No time for romance."

"That's too bad. Romance can be a great inspiration to songwriting."

"Break up songs are even better. Just ask Jackson Browne."

Kate smiled. "Good point. So, are you going to take some time off now?"

"Try to. I get itchy. I try to relax, then I start working again. I need to spend some time outside, on the ranch. Like, ride out and mend some fences. Shit like that."

Kate nodded, noticed that the plane was taking off. She leaned back, closed her eyes, thought about her little girl, so brave on all the flights they'd been on. Paulie had held her hand.

"How about you? What will you do when you get home? File for divorce?"

She turned a startled look in Rob's direction. "Please, don't."

"I'm sorry. Bad joke. I guess I didn't realize."

Kate sighed. "Didn't mean to snap. As I said, it's complicated. We have some unique challenges."

Rob nodded. "I think I understand that. It was rude of me to tease."

"No problem. If you don't mind, I'm going to take a little nap. I was up all night, and I'm—"

"Fagged?"

"Yeah. Whatever."

She went right to sleep, woke two hours later, her back still hurting. She took two more acetaminophen, looked out the window. Rob was reading a magazine.

"Feel better?" he asked.

"No. Not as tired, but I don't feel great."

"I'm sorry." Rob looked down, then took a breath and sighed. "So why don't you tell me about your daughter; what's her name?"

"Bonny. She's at home with my cousin."

"Pretty name. I'll bet she's beautiful."

"She is. She looks a little like me, but with Paulie's amazing eyes."

"Got a picture?"

Kate smiled, pulled her wallet from her bag. Flipped through the photos, then handed the open wallet to Rob.

"Oh, man. She's a heartbreaker. Too bad I'll be too old. Is this your wedding pic?"

"Yeah. We got married at the beach."

"Wow." He looked from the photo to Kate's face, then back. "You've been married how long?"

"Just over five years."

Rob nodded. "Can I say one thing about Paul?"

"Of course."

"He's a truly nice guy. You don't meet many performers on the road like him. I'm sure he has his moments, we all do, but he's just all up front. What you see is what you get. I like that in people."

"Hmm."

They were quiet for a few moments. Rob spoke next.

"So, when's the baby due? You can't be very pregnant."

"Six or seven weeks along."

"Must be exciting."

"It would be, if things were not such a mess." She hadn't meant to say it. Something about Rob's presence made her want to tell it all. "But yeah, I'm happy about it. I mean, how could you not be happy about a baby?"

"I guess I wouldn't exactly know that. Rachel and I, well, we weren't ready for kids, so it worked out that it was better we didn't have them. It would be a nightmare now, trying to juggle them. Especially since she now lives in Israel."

And if Paulie stays in England, will that be our plight?

"Do you think you'll ever marry again?"

Rob looked around the cabin, considering the question. "I don't know. At first, I thought, never again. Never. But as I get older, and I realize that touring won't be forever, I know I'll get lonely. I'm just not sure I'll find someone who's, well, you know, *right*."

"It's hard. I once chose the wrong person, too. Looking back, I don't know what the hell I was thinking. But then Paulie came and rescued me."

"He doesn't really seem the superhero type."

"He's not. But he did it for me. He just got on a plane and showed up at my house and cold-cocked this big jerk I was living with. Laid him out right there on the kitchen floor." She gestured with her hand, demonstrating the prone position of Ray's body. She let go of a little giggle. "He broke his stupid hand."

"He's your champion."

"Odd choice of word."

"You know, your defender."

Her eyes burned with unshed tears that threatened to spill out. She felt her nose turning pink.

Rob unrolled a dinner napkin and offered it.

"Thanks." Kate dabbed at the corners of her eyes.

"Sorry. You already told me to stuff it. I'll shut up now."

"It's not your fault." *It's mine.* She bent over the napkin, unable to hold back the tears any longer.

He hesitated, then reached for her, pulling her against him as she sobbed.

"It's all right. Let it out. Let it go."

Kate cried until she became fully cognizant of Rob's arms around her. She pulled away and dried her face.

"Crap. I'm so sorry. It's just, the hormones. I think. I'm stretched a little too thin right now."

"Don't even… look. Like I said, we all fall into a pile of it now and again. You'll get through this. You will. It takes time to sort things out. What's meant to happen, well, it'll happen."

"I'm sure you're right."

"And think about your little girl. How happy she'll be to see you. And whatever happens, you and Paul will always have her, together. You will always have that link. You'll always be her mother, he'll always be her father."

"Always? Are you sure?" she managed to tease.

"Okay. So I'm not big on vocab. But you get what I'm saying, right?"

Kate nodded. "Thanks, Rob."

She managed to keep the conversation lighter during the balance of the flight. In the terminal, they went through customs together.

"Who's picking you up?"

"I'm taking a cab. I didn't want Bonny back down here again today."

"Good mom. I have a car. I can give you a lift."

"No, really."

"No, really. It's on my way."

"You left a car here for three months?"

Dimples appeared. "I had a friend leave my car here last night. I don't like to be driven places. Makes me nervous. Especially in L.A."

"Well, if you don't mind, that would be great. I live...we live just off Sunset."

A black BMW 3 series convertible waited for them, and the So Cal weather begged for exposure. Kate relished the feel of the wind rushing across her face, through her hair. Rob took the car through its paces winding down Sunset Boulevard.

He pulled into the broad driveway of Paulie's spacious, California ranch house. The sound of the car brought Cheryl out the front door.

"I would have picked you up, girl," she scolded.

"Rob, this is my cousin Cheryl."

"I'm really the hired help. She only pretends we're related so she won't have to pay me. Pleased to meet you."

"Same here. Hey, let me get that bag."

Rob carried Kate's things into the house. Bonny appeared from the hallway.

"Mummy! Mummy! Mummy!"

"There's my girl." Kate lifted Bonny and held her tightly.

"Where's Daddy?"

For reasons she didn't quite understand, Kate looked to Rob.

He touched Bonny on the nose. "Your Daddy's still working back in London, sweetie. Mommy just came home a little early."

"Bon, this is Mommy and Daddy's friend Rob. Can you say hello?"

"Hello."

"Rob, can I get you something cold to drink?" Cheryl asked.

"No, thanks, I gotta run. Just didn't want Kate to ride in some filthy cab."

Cheryl shook her head. "I would have picked her up."

Rob nodded, made a face. "We both know, now, how stubborn she is."

Kate walked him back to his car. "I can't thank you enough for, you know, the chat, the ride, talking me down from the ledge."

"I take it that everything happens for a reason." He got into the car, and Kate closed his door. "Hey. Here…" he began, digging into the console between the seats, "is my card. I use these to pick up girls in bars."

"Yeah, right." Why didn't she believe that for a minute?

"This is my home number. Please don't sell it. But do call it, if you need anything, anything at all. You know if you need to cry, I can make that happen, too. We now know that."

She gave him a light punch on the shoulder.

"Okay?" he prodded.

"Okay."

Her hands were still resting on his door, and he patted one of them. "Take is easy, Mrs. Bingham."

ꙮ **Meeting Rob was like someone handing me a flashlight while navigating a mine field during a new moon. Since the moment Paulie had shown up and decked Ray Goff, I'd had blinders on to all others. Paulie was my whole world, and when that world came to a soul wrenching stop, I guess the blinders fell off. Rob was there, as if waving a hand in front of my face: ""Hello? Kate?"**

When I first met Rob, I had the (probably completely understandable) notion that he might be gay. I mean, why not? Both Paulie Poofter and Bent Brent were on the far side of the gender map. But it didn't take long for me to realize the absurdity of my thoughts, because Rob was anything but a she/male.

I was attracted to his easiness. In direct contrast to Paulie's ADD-like manic moodiness, Rob seemed to pace himself, giving thought to his actions with settling calm. He

exuded strength, both the physical and the character kind. I found myself wanting to stand under his umbrella.

Of course, I had no intention of following up or pursuing anything. I had mountains to scale before I could think about anything as self-serving as a new relationship. Especially since, in my heart of hearts, I hadn't truly given up on Paulie. –Kate

Chapter 17

Kate dragged her suitcase upstairs and dropped it into the corner of her bedroom. She was asleep the moment she lay down, then woke at five p.m. with Bonny sacked out beside her. She quietly got up, started the shower. As steam began to fill the bathroom, Kate looked around at the things that belonged to Paulie. Melancholy began to spread again. She swallowed it down. Her back was worse, her side and now her abdomen was hurting, too. She got into the shower, let the hot water stream down her lower back.

We should have never left. Here, in this house, we were safe. Everything here is the same as it was, but we have changed.

She stood there for some time, eyes closed, rethinking her escape from Britain. Had she been fair, fleeing the way she did? Then the memory of "Jon" came back, and she knew she couldn't have stayed another moment. She opened her eyes now, determined to get back to the reality of her situation. In despair, she discovered that her reality included blood, dripping from her body onto the shower floor.

Not again. Just like the first time.

She founds some pads left over from Bonny's birth, then lay back down beside her sleeping toddler. The cramping in her abdomen intensified. She remembered drinking the Irish cream and chastised herself, afraid to accept that her problems were much bigger than a half ounce of alcohol. She rolled over and woke Bonny.

"Bon Bon, would you go get Auntie Cheri for Mommy? Tell her to come see me."

Bonny slid off the side of the bed and hurried out of the room, returning with Cheryl.

"God, Kate, you look awful. Are you sick?"

"Something's wrong. Can you help me? I need to get to the bathroom."

141

Cheryl turned to Bonny. "Okay, Bonny Bee. You remember the new puzzles we put in your room this morning? How about you go put them together for me and Mommy. You stay in there, and we'll be there in a jiffy. Okay?"

The little girl nodded and left the room. Cheryl immediately took Kate's hands.

"Oh. Oh. Shit. I'm… oh, Cher, it's the baby." Kate tried to stand, but instead doubled over in pain. She slid to the floor. Cheryl got to the floor, too.

"Oh, Kate. Honey, this isn't good. I'm calling the doctor."

She hung up moments later. Kate was grasping at the carpet.

"Kate, listen. He says we should just wait it out here and, well, go in when it's over." She whipped a towel from the rack in the bathroom, then gently tugged it beneath Kate.

"I'm losing our baby. I'm losing our baby! Oh, Cheryl, how can this be happening, now? What have I done to make God so angry? Is it because I messed with His will? Is it?"

"Honey, you don't know what you're saying. You didn't mess with anything. Now put this pillow behind your back. I'm sorry, but this is just like labor. You're going to have to push."

"Are you crazy? Oh, God. This is awful. I fell. Last night. Down the stairs. I was…I was running away. Running from Paulie."

"He was chasing you?"

"No. There was this guy, Jon, he was Paulie's…Paulie's lover. He told me. He, he, oh God! He called me a beard. He might as well have called me a whore! I had to get away from him, from Paul, from that whole sickening mess. I—Oh, dammit." She paused to breathe, to push. She felt a rush of wetness move out of her. She pushed again, and again, until she felt there was nothing left to let go of.

Cheryl made quick work of cleaning her up and following the doctor's instructions on what to bring. "How do you feel?"

"Like bloody hell," Kate muttered, using the words her husband so often spoke. "Just give me a minute. I think I can get up."

Cheryl helped Kate to shower and dress, and then drove her and Bonny to the doctor's office.

"I am so sorry, Kate," Dr. Wright said, after completing his exam. "The good news is, there is nothing remaining in there that we would have to worry about."

"Do you know... can you tell if it was a boy?"

"No, it was too soon to see. You can't really tell until after around nine weeks. I'm sorry. You weren't quite there, yet."

He confirmed it was likely the fall that initiated the miscarriage. Kate went home feeling lower than she had in her entire life. She played with Bonny, faking a smile, encouraging the little girl to laugh and sing. But after Bonny went to bed, Kate lay on the couch, wrapped in her misery.

Cheryl sat with her.

"So, wanna go out dancing?"

"Sure."

"We could play Yahtzee. You used to be really good at that dice rolling stuff."

"I'm no good at it anymore. Everything is a crap shoot."

"I have chocolate chip ice cream."

"A big bowl, please."

She let Cheryl feed it to her. "You can tell me what happened any time, you know. I won't hold you back."

Kate spoke slowly, felt somehow disengaged. "You are the only person on Earth I can tell this too. But you must take it to your grave, Cher."

"At the rate it's taking you to spill it, that could be easy."

"The other night, when Paulie didn't come home?"

"The night you smacked him?"

Kate lifted her eyebrows. "You sure can't keep secrets in Peg's house."

"Even the neighbors across the street heard. Go on."

"He was out with his gay friends. They were getting high and...having sex."

"And this, for some reason, shocked you?"

"Dammit Cheri, he's my husband. MY husband. And it doesn't matter if he's shagging girls or getting...you know, getting it on with guys, it's still cheating. He made a promise to me. And worse, his stupid friends think I'm a wife of convenience. Someone who makes him look straight in the public."

"Well you know that's not true. Whatever he is, he loves you."

"But why would he let them think that? I can't do this anymore. We are just that square peg in a round hole. We keep trying and keep getting bashed."

Cheryl didn't say anything.

"And you know what else? As if the sex stuff wasn't bad enough, he was doing drugs. After the weeks, months we spent getting him back, cleaning him up—Christ! He nearly died out there. I did that for him. I helped him get his life back. And now, he's throwing all that away."

Her cousin sat on the floor.

"For once you have nothing to say? No pearls of wisdom? No admonishments?"

Cheryl looked uncomfortable, shrugged. "Maybe you're right. Maybe you need to let him go."

Kate felt the floor drop open beneath her. It was exactly what she didn't want to hear. "How can I do that? I love him, Cher. We love each other. We have Bonny to raise together."

"It sounds like he's not able to sustain the change. So you have a decision to make. If he can't change, can you? Can you just accept his being a gay man and all that entails? Frankly, I can't see you compromising that way. Sharing a man, as you said, is just not your cup of java."

"This is killing me. He doesn't even know about the baby."

"You have to tell him, babe. You need to call him. What time is it in the U.K.?"

"Six a.m. He'll be sleeping. And Lord knows where."

"I guarantee you, wherever he is, his phone is right beside him."

"Maybe later. I'm not ready to do this yet."

Cheryl nodded, made a rare gesture of affection by stroking Kate's hair and pulling it behind her ear. "So, who was the hottie in the Beamer, anyway?"

"Oh, Rob. Evans. We just happened to be on the same flight. He was our opening act that night."

"He seemed very concerned about you."

"He's a nice guy."

"Is he gay?"

"No. At least I don't think so."

"Hmm."

After Cheryl went to bed, Kate let the darkness, and the sadness, envelope her. She had no strength to ward off the memories, the visions, the imaginings. Jon's words came back to her again and again. Paulie's face, his voice, his touch—*she* wanted to own them. It was all too painful to touch.

The clock over the mantle struck two. Kate threw back the blanket, sat up on the couch. Felt around the coffee table for the telephone, and just as she laid her hand on it, it lit up, began ringing.

"Hello?" she said softly, struggling to get to her feet.

"I'm sorry. I know it's the middle of the night. I had to call, I couldn't wait," Paulie said.

Kate took several wobbly steps toward the French doors leading to the backyard, went outside. A full moon cast an ethereal glow on the shrubs, the pool.

"I wasn't asleep," she said at last, making her way to the chaise lounge and sitting. "Where are you?"

"At the hotel."

Kate nodded, as if Paulie could see her acknowledgement.

"Are you okay?" he asked.

An involuntary, delirious smile passed briefly across her face. "How do you think I would be? I'm…I'm shattered, Paul. I'm afraid for the sun to come up."

"Aw, don't say that."

She didn't know how many more tears she could shed. She was bleeding again, this time from the heart. "You, of all people, would ask me not to share my grief? You have humiliated me. You've lied, cheated, danced on my heart. There's nothing left."

Paulie was quiet.

145

Kate stared up at the stars. "It's not entirely your fault. I take responsibility for this disaster, too. I was a party to this grand experiment, changing the rules, messing with things I shouldn't have touched."

"That's crazy," he murmured. "You are above all that. You and I, we've always believed in our love. I tried, hard, to cover up my flaws, to be the man you wanted me to be, who I thought I wanted to be. I failed. I failed you. But this is not in any way your fault. I just don't understand why you left. We were going to talk, this weekend."

"Oh Paulie, this...man...Jon, do you love him?"

"Who? What are you talking about, darling? You are my *only* love."

Her throat had swelled to the point where she could barely speak. "Never mind."

"No, please. Explain."

Kate took a breath. "Tall, black hair, blue eyes, a tattoo on his right hand."

Paulie groaned audibly. He mumbled obscenities. "Look, whatever he said to you, forget about it, will you? There are some things...you couldn't possibly understand."

"Don't I deserve to understand? Shouldn't we share everything about ourselves? You know everything about me, Paul. I have no secrets from you. I am what I am. I have been devoted, faithful, loyal to you for all these years. If you won't...can't do the same, then I think maybe this isn't going to work."

In her mind, Kate could see the pain in his eyes. She knew she'd hit him again, a virtual slap across the heart.

After a moment, he recovered. "I'm going to finish this tour. Then I'm coming home, and we'll decide, together, what will or won't work."

"And will you continue to partake in those things I couldn't possibly understand? Because if you come home with a nose full of coke, there will be nothing left to decide."

"Christ, Kate! I swear to you, I didn't do coke. I took a hit off a joint or two. I'll admit to it. And it was wrong, because it likely led to my...poor judgment. Please. Don't crucify me unjustly."

"I don't know what to believe anymore. Your friends think I'm a cover."

"Look. I'll cancel the tour. I'll be on the next bloody flight out of here."

"No, don't do that. Do *not* do that. You—you finish the tour. We need the time apart. I need it."

"You know I love you more than anything."

Kate bowed her head, pressed her free hand to her eyes.

"Kate? Do you hear me? I'm a sodding bastard to have hurt you like this. I know I can't ask you for another chance. I'm going to leave it at this. If you feel you can't trust me again, if you think we are better apart, then I'll have to respect that. But please, don't write us off too easily. I'll be home in two weeks. Two weeks. Give me that."

"Goodbye, Paulie."

Cheryl appeared, knelt beside her, took the phone and shut it off. She put her arms around Kate and held her while she sobbed.

☙ **Why didn't I tell Paulie about the baby? Because it was my piece of knowledge to hold onto. Sharing it with him would have been giving up something. I wasn't in the sanest frame of mind, either. My pain was incredibly deep, but it wasn't really about the loss of the child. It was the rest of my life that terrified me.**

Chapter 18

June, 1994. Brentwood, CA

She allowed herself a few days to mourn. But when Monday morning dawned, she left her grief beneath her pillow and squared her shoulders.

"I want you to take a vacation," she told Cheryl in the kitchen. "Anywhere you want, as long as you want, just go."

"I think I'm hurt."

"Be hurt, then, but have fun doing it. You have been practically raising Bonny for us for months. You need a break, and I need to get better acquainted with my daughter."

"But what about when the boy wonder returns? Won't you need some time alone with him?"

Kate touched Cheryl's arm. "I have it on good authority that parents all over the world watch their own children, even while fighting. Isn't it amazing?"

"You'll regret this. You'll see. You'll be begging me to come back, on your knees, crawling over broken glass."

"That could be," Kate murmured. She'd already envisioned throwing every piece of glassware she owned at her husband when he walked in the door.

Cheryl left for New York on Tuesday. Kate took Bonny to Disneyland on Thursday, and the zoo on Friday. Exhausted, on Saturday, she filled a plastic toddler swimming pool and set it up on the patio in the shade. The main pool was cordoned off with temporary fencing until Bonny learned to swim well.

Kate donned a swimsuit and brought a magazine to read. As Bonny splashed happily in her oversized green turtle basin, Kate pulled a chaise lounge and table close by, laden with fruit and snacks for them both. She was well into a story about Matt Damon when the phone rang. Suspecting Cheryl, she immediately answered.

"Kate?" A man's voice. "It's Rob. Evans."

"Rob! Wow, it's nice to hear from you. What's up?"

"I was just going to ask you that. I'm on my way back from West L.A., thought I'd stop by to see you and Paul."

A minor sting. "Um, you're welcome to stop by, but Paulie's not here."

"Oh, I'm sorry. For some reason I thought he'd be back by now. He's still touring?"

"For another week. But like I said, come on by. Bon and I are just sunning. It's such a beautiful day. The gate's unlocked, just come around to the back."

He hadn't been far away, Kate surmised, when Rob walked into the backyard ten minutes later.

"Tea?"

"Sure. That would be great." He sat down at the patio table and Kate joined him, after slipping on her beach cover-up.

"Bonny, come and say hello to Mr. Evans."

The sunny, curly-headed preschooler hurried up to her mother, offered a shy greeting, then returned to the pool.

"She is adorable," Rob said, shaking his head. "You are so lucky."

"Yeah. I am." Kate took a sip of tea.

"Say, I brought you guys this. It's the CD I was telling you about over dinner. Let me know how you like it. It's just a demo; we have a few more tracks to lay down."

Kate picked up the CD and turned it over. "How cool! Thanks so much. I'll listen to it tonight."

"Great." Rob cleared his throat. "So…how's everything?"

Kate shrugged and shook her head slightly.

"You and Paul patch things up?"

She smiled. "Not sure that's the right term."

"I'm sorry. Maybe when he gets back, you two can work things out. What with the new baby coming, time off from the road…"

She glanced up, looked into his eyes. She knew she shouldn't do it, but was unable to hold her tongue. "There is no baby now."

Rob frowned. "I don't understand. Are you saying…?"

"I lost it."

150

The effect of her words was evident. Rob put his glass down, immediately covered her hand with his. "No. I'm so sorry. When did this happen?"

"About, oh, four hours after you dropped me off."

"You must be...devastated. Is there anything I can do?"

She shook her head again. "No, thanks. I'm fine. I mean, someone recently told me that things happen for a reason. Maybe this is one of those times."

Rob was quiet for a moment. "I certainly didn't mean something like this. You're being very brave. Is Paul okay?"

Kate looked to her daughter, who was busy teaching a rubber puppy to swim. "He doesn't know."

"You didn't tell him? Oh, Kate. I don't know about that." Rob also turned his gaze upon Bonny.

Kate sighed. "I appreciate your concern, Rob. I have my reasons. Paulie will be home in five days. It'll be soon enough to tell him the bad news. And I...I needed some time to gain some..."

"Strength?"

She looked at him now. "Yes. Too much has gone down. I think it's time to start caring about me. I know that sounds selfish, but, well, it's just time."

"Not selfish." He stood up, walked over to Bonny, squatted down. "What's your puppy's name?"

"Freddie."

"Freddie. Great name. You and Mommy have a fun time this week, okay?"

Bonny nodded enthusiastically. Rob returned to the table. "I need to shove. You don't have my number listed on eBay yet, do you?"

"No."

"Then the offer stands." He pressed two fingers to his lips, then touched the top of her head. "I hope it all goes well."

Kate watched Rob walk away. She wasn't sure she should have told him so much, but somehow, she felt stronger having done it.

Seattle, Washington.

"You did better tonight," Buzz commented as Paulie carefully dismantled his regalia. The wig went into its plastic bag, the heavy, bejeweled garments onto hangers. "But you still look like you need a stiff drink."

"I'm better because I finally get to board that bloody plane in two days."

"How's Kate?"

His back to Buzz, Paulie grimaced. "She's fine. Just fine."

"You haven't spoken to her, have you, mate?"

Paulie spun around. "What's it to you?"

Buzz held up his hands. "Just askin'. Back off. I care about her, too."

"Aw, crap. No. We haven't talked for…I dunno. Several days. I don't blame her if she never fucking speaks to me again."

"That bad, eh?"

"I'm a walking tragedy, okay?" The two men stared at each other. Paulie eventually turned, sat down at the dressing table. "Do me a favor? Clear all those leeches out of the way so I can get out of here?"

He was walking again. Cool, moist, Seattle air around him. Didn't know the city, didn't know where he was going. Now close to going home, he got scared. Days before, he'd been ready to pack it in. Settle for joint custody. Reprise his *pop star* role, glam up his image some. Talk to Kate once in a while on the phone, wish her well. Hope she found someone more deserving of her devotion.

Now, that didn't sound all that good. He longed for her embrace, her soft lips, her healing hands. He wanted to feel her beside him in bed, know that she was there when the nights were dark. Share the delight of raising their daughter. And now, possibly, a son.

"Face your failures like a man," his father would say. "Learn to rise above your inadequacies."

Thanks, Dad.

The last show was in Portland. But a cancelled flight from Denver delayed his until early Sunday evening.

Kate put down the phone. "Daddy's plane is going to be late, Bee. Let's go ahead and get your spaghetti fixed now. Then you can have your bath, and watch some TV."

"Will I be awake when Daddy comes?"

"I don't know, Sweet Pea. Maybe."

Bonny gave up the ghost at ten p.m., and Kate tucked her in. She poured herself a glass of wine, turned the station to watch a movie. She needed distraction. Thinking about Paulie walking in the door was just too heavy with emotion.

At eleven fifteen, she heard a car door. Her heartbeat quickened. *Should I meet him at the door? Stand here? Stay sitting?* Instead, she took another sip of wine.

His driver carried in his bags, then left as Paulie walked into the living room. He paused, halfway, beckoned to her.

Kate took a moment before rising from the couch. Had it really been only two weeks? The black, silk suit must have been custom made; the charcoal shirt beneath was open at the neck, revealing Paulie's gold chained crucifix. He wore just enough makeup to define his beautiful eyes. Surely he hadn't just walked off an eleven hour flight.

She didn't say anything, but walked to where he stood in the middle of the living room, his hands casually resting in his pockets. Unable to stop herself, Kate moved close, placed her hands on his chest. They stared into one another's eyes for several moments, Kate, at last, slipping her hands inside his jacket around him. She turned her head, pressed her cheek against his breast.

His arms were instantly around her. He bent his head, whispered into her ear.

"I was afraid you might not be here."

They held each other tightly for what seemed like minutes to Kate. She pulled away first. "Do you want something to drink?"

"Sure. Whatever you're having."

"Wine?"

"Red, please."

She poured, and they sat down together on the couch. Paulie reached behind him, withdrew a small plush rabbit. He smiled.

"I didn't think you'd want me to keep her up," Kate said.

"No, of course not. I'll see her in the morning." He took a small sip of wine, put the glass down. Rubbed his hands together. "I can't tell you how badly I wish we didn't have to have this conversation."

Kate nodded, looked briefly away from him.

"You were absolutely right, what you said on the phone, about secrets and that. I behaved despicably, and took my anger at myself out on you. We made promises to each other, and I broke one of mine. An important one. I don't know how I can rectify that."

Kate looked back at him, wishing, too, that they could just forget it happened and go to bed. But she'd done that before.

"I thought maybe it would help if I tell you the truth about what happened that night."

"I think I know enough."

"No, I don't think you do. Ian Flynn and I go way back. We've kept in touch over the years. That day, he invited me out to a pub to lift a brew. I rather fancied that, since it's something that just isn't duplicated around here. You know, we tossed some arrows, ate some really greasy chips. Downed a coupla pitchers of ale. Then he invites me to this party, he says, for one of our mates. I'll just stop in, I say, and off we go to his flat. It all seems right at first, but then I see all these guys staring at me, and they introduce this sweet kid, Jon, to me, and they break out a pile of drugs. Pot, crack, E., reds, bennies—the works."

Kate listened with morbid fascination. She took a gulp of wine.

"Ian sits down on my other side, starts whispering things in my ear. About how Jon fancies me, about how Jon is looking for someone to love, you know, like that, and then he starts in about how I'm denying m'self. Sticks a joint in my mouth. Several times, as a matter of fact. At this point, I was almost too snockered to care. It doesn't take much, these days, to light me up."

Paulie paused, lifted his glass to his lips. "Next thing I know, Ian's leading me into this back room, and Jon's following. I'm lying on this bed, Jon's undressing me. I am laughing hysterically, I'm thinking this must be some wild hallucination, because this guy is looking more and more like Jamie to me. And Jamie is dead, I saw him buried."

Kate began shaking her head as the visual he painted brought realization.

"They set you up."

"Intervention, Ian called it. I was on the wrong path. Heterosexuality is bad for me, you see. So he and my mates decided to remind me of how wonderful gay sex can be." Paulie drew in a shaky breath. "The pot was laced. With what, I don't even want to know."

"I would call that rape."

Paulie gave her a sad smile. "Yes, you would. A girl and boy in a dorm room, he plies her with lots of drinks, maybe spiked, she's half passed out and he sticks her. That might be called rape."

"But this wasn't, for you."

"I have to be honest. I enjoyed it."

Kate closed her eyes, sucked in her upper lip.

"I didn't want to enjoy it. But the fact remains."

"So what does this mean, Paulie? You're telling me that you were tricked into a...a situation, and you took the bait. You didn't tell me about it because really, you *wanted* that boy to...to have sex with you."

"I don't know what I want anymore."

"I think you do."

Paulie shook his head. "Please. Don't go setting off alarms."

"You want me to make the decision, Paul, but I'm not going to do that. This is your issue. You own it. If you tell me that you want to go back to that lifestyle, then I'll have to understand. Don't worry about making me unhappy. I'm already about as unhappy as anyone can be."

"I can't." He hung his head.

"You must. I love you, Paul. With all my heart. I have loved you since the day we met. I will always love you. But I've made *my* decision, and that decision is that I can't share you. I tried to let you go before. I probably should have made that stick. You'd be a lot happier now."

"You are what makes me happy. All this other, just makes me miserable, in the long run. Don't you see that?"

"What am I supposed to do, shackle you? Never leave your side? Keep you on surveillance?"

"I've completely lost your trust."

She hated to confirm it. She reached for his hand. "Some promises are just too hard to keep."

I am not going to cry. I am not *going to cry.* Kate stood, picked up her wine glass and refilled it.

"Do you think that's wise, you know, with the baby?"

She curled the glass against her chest. "There is no baby."

Paulie frowned. "No baby? Really?"

"Nope."

"When did you find out?"

Kate turned away, wandered toward the fireplace. *He misunderstood. All the better.*

"After I got home."

"Oh, darling. I'm sorry. Were you terribly disappointed?"

"Of course."

"I guess mistakes can be made."

"Oh, yes. They sure can."

"Wow. That certainly changes things, doesn't it?"

She went back, sat down again. "Makes it easier, perhaps."

"Makes what easier?"

"You're just not going to make *anything* easier, are you?"

"I don't know what you want me to do, Kate. Consider, please, how stupid I am. Help me out here."

"You want me to say it? You want me to break us up? I've already told you, I won't do that. This is up to you."

He was such a picture of despair that Kate placed her hand on his cheek. "Understand this. If you decide, in your heart of hearts, that you're fighting your natural, inner yearnings, and you want to go back to the way things were before I tried to change you, it doesn't mean that I will love you any less. You and I are soul mates, and I truly believe that. For me to hold you to a standard that's foreign to you is wrong."

"What will happen to us?"

"We'll work things out. Somehow. We have Bonny to raise together. But you need your freedom. And so do I."

"Don't get angry if I start to cry," he murmured, then drew in a deep breath. "All right. I will tell you, right now, these things. I love you, Katie Bingham, like no other. I have enjoyed our marriage, our partnership, every step of the way. Every minute we are together is heaven to me. But as it turns out, I *am* a homosexual man, and I'm having difficulties living in your world indefinitely. There."

Kate felt a cinch had been tightened around her. She nodded her encouragement, despite the fact that her heart was, once again, breaking in two.

"You must understand that it has nothing, nothing whatsoever to do with you, my darling. If there was another way to make this work, I'd be first in line. But in that I respect your desire to…to maintain a monogamous relationship, I'm forced to let you go. I can't go on hurting you, making you so sad." He paused to swallow. "Oh God. This is killing me."

"You're doing fine."

"No I'm not. This is not what I want to say."

"What do you want to say?"

"I want to say, let's go to bed. Let me make love to you, Kate. Let me hold you all night long and well into the day tomorrow."

Kate stood. It was, of course, exactly what she wanted him to say. Loathing her own weakness, she held out her hands to him, helped him to his feet. "Let's go then."

Paulie paused at the bedroom door, turned to Kate. "Once we pass through here, for tonight, no more talk about this nastiness. Deal?"

She nodded, and he led her into the room. They were in bed in minutes, naked and in each other's arms. He stroked her back. She was a picture of femininity. At thirty-two, she looked better than she ever had to his adoring eyes. And despite the rule he'd laid down, he couldn't keep his thoughts away from the worry, the impending loss of the love that had sustained him for over ten years.

Soul mates, she called us. It was something he could latch onto. Soul mates were for a lifetime, weren't they? But what if she took up with another man? The hateful vision of Ray Goff invaded his thoughts. The jealousy and fear that raged within him when Kate had moved on before filled him with fresh grief.

Kate climbed on top of him, took his earlobe between her teeth.

"What's the matter?" she whispered.

"Nothing. Nothing at all."

Her breath in his ear made him shudder. She gave him a quick kiss, and ran her hands down the length of his torso, knowing just how to touch. She was quite the expert, he realized, at coaxing him, enticing him, turning him on. His private seductress. *What man wouldn't want someone like her, 24/7? (A gay man.)*

Testament to her skill was the fact that even now, her hands were bringing him to the verge of erotic destiny, despite his worries. Grasping her hips, he urged her to lift up and engage him.

He let go of worry. Let go of everything. For a brief time, Kate was life, and life was Kate. Being inside her bonded them, and he never wanted to let go.

☞ *She kills me sometimes. She doesn't mean to do it. Kate has to protect herself, and I understand that. She's spent far too much time protecting me from myself.*

I didn't blame her for making me look into the mirror, to confess to my crimes. Looking back, it was bound to happen eventually, but at the time I was still masking my fears.

I lied that night. It wasn't really my goal to make love to her. That was just the feeble remains of the macho-straight-sex machine I'd tried to be. I only really wanted her to hold me.

When Kate puts her arms around me, when she kisses my face, runs her fingers down my back, I feel safe. It's difficult to admit this now. She's absorbed my tears more times than I care to admit. She bandages my wounds. She knows me better than I know myself, which is at the same time a blessing and a curse.

Am I having sex with my mother? Ian thinks I am. It's a disgusting thought and one that I reject. I <u>love</u> Kate; she is my partner for life, regardless of what happens. Despite what I said, I will never really let her go. I lied about that, too, and if she knew I was lying, she didn't call me on it. For once.
—Paulie

Chapter 19

"More, please," Bonny begged, opening her mouth wide as Paulie scooped up another spoonful of cereal. "Thank you," she gurgled, chewing.

"You're welcome, sweetheart. Did you miss me?"

Bonny nodded. "Lots and lots. Mommy took me to the zoo."

"Good thing I didn't go, she likely would have left me there, eh?"

His daughter giggled. "In the monkeys," she told him, amid more laughter.

"Got that right," Kate confirmed. "So what's on the agenda today?"

Paulie shrugged. "Thought I might take a look at a flat in West Hollywood later."

Kate stopped loading the dishwasher and turned. "Really?"

"I think it's wise, don't you? You don't want me underfoot."

"Now?"

"I see no reason to drag it on, darling." Paulie handed Bonny her spoon and stood, walked to Kate and took her hands. "Nothing official? Just separate digs, for now?"

Kate nodded. She hadn't expected this, despite what they'd said the night before. His resolve surprised her. "If that's what you want."

He tilted his head, smiled. "It's what you want as well. Your decision spawned mine, remember?" Paulie stroked her hair. "This way, I won't be far away. Try to keep things semi-consistent for Bonny."

"Right. I understand."

By two p.m. he had a signed lease in his hand; a penthouse, he said, fully furnished with security. He was already packing. He would only need some clothes and a toothbrush.

"You're not staying there, tonight?"

"I thought I might."

"Okay. Okay." Kate drew in a shaky breath. Was this how people broke up? Was it really just a matter of picking up a goddam toothbrush? "I... don't have a car," she managed.

"We'll have to fix that," Paulie said. "It never occurred to me."

Kate shrugged. *It never occurred to me that it would hurt this much.*

When he left that evening, after reading a story to Bonny, Paulie took the Audi and left Kate's brand new BMW in the garage. She kissed him goodbye at the door, felt hollow when he'd gone. Too numb to even cry. It had happened much too quickly.

Cheryl returned four days later. Kate was jogging on the treadmill when her cousin blew in with several bags and suitcases in tow. Bonny ran up and embraced her around the knees, almost toppling the statuesque blonde.

Kate grabbed a hand towel and mopped her face and neck. "You got back just in time. I was just getting ready to stick my head in the oven. As soon as I was done with my workout."

"Bon Bon been a bad baby?"

"No. It's just me. Paulie moved out."

Cheryl stopped moving about and stared at Kate. "Moved out? Like, gone? Whose Beamer is that in the garage?"

"Mine. My break up gift. He moved to an apartment in WeHo. We made an agreement."

Cheryl dug into one of her bags, pulled out a small plush bear dressed in a t-shirt emblazoned with the words, "I Luv New York" in silver. "Bonnie Bee, looky what Auntie Cheryl brought you!" Bonny hugged the bear to her chest and went running from the room. Cheryl went to the refrigerator and took out a beer, then rejoined Kate.

"So what's this big agreement about? He's free to fuck around, and you're here keeping the household together?"

Kate chuckled. "You've always defended him in the past."

"That was before you gave him the keys to the city. What's he doing? What are you doing?"

"We're staying married, for now, but living separate lives. It's a trial. We don't want to disrupt Bonny too much, so he'll come by most nights to visit and tuck her in. It's the best we could come up with."

"Just like that."

"Just like that."

"And you're okay with this? Aside from wanting to asphyxiate yourself?"

Kate sighed. "I don't have a lot of choice."

"You have choices. I don't know about this staying married thing. I guess he does have a boatload of money."

Kate took the beer out of Cheryl's hand and took a swig. "Right. I'm keeping him around for the cash."

"What did he say about the baby?"

Kate colored, handed back the beer. "Um, he was okay with it. A little sad, I guess."

"You did tell him?"

"Yeah. Sorta."

Cheryl finished the beer. "I swear. You and Paul Bingham are the two most dysfunctional people I know." She went back to her bags and found one for Kate, tossed it to her.

"What's this? A gift? You shouldn't have."

"Latest stuff from the Manhattan glamour scene. Brand new colors, compounds. Enjoy."

Kate fawned over the makeup samples. "These are awesome, Cher. How can I thank you?"

"Let's see. How about no mooning over Boy Paul for a week?"

"Unfair."

"Yeah, well life's a crock. What would you like for dinner?"

July, 1994

It was good having Cheryl back. Despite her acid wit and gruff demeanor, Kate needed her cousin's subtle support during the days that followed. Paulie came by, as promised, four or five nights a week to chat and share in Bonny's life. Except for the

fact that they weren't sleeping together, everything else seemed fairly normal.

But the sleeping and sex part was definitely missing.

As she went through some clothes piled on the closet floor, Kate realized that Paulie had been gone for a month. He still had lots of items in the house, having seen no reason to move everything at once and then likely having forgotten. She was reluctant to remind him. These were *him*. The jackets, robes, and sparkly garments smelled of his cologne, told his story. She ran a hand across the rich fabrics, fine tailored outfits.

Chastising herself, she started to leave the closet when she noticed something on the floor. A business card.

Rob Evans, Musician. 805-555-7865

"Hmm." She carried the card to her dresser and stuck it into the mirror frame at eye level.

"Cheri?" She called, hearing her cousin rummaging in the kitchen. "Don't make dinner. I want to go out tonight."

"Good thing since all we have are some expired bean sprouts and hummus."

"Let's splurge."

They dressed up, something Kate hadn't done in forever. Even Bonny happily donned a royal blue velvet dress, trimmed in lace. Kate treated them to the Sentinel House, her favorite Hollywood restaurant.

"Pretty lights!" Bonny exclaimed, sitting in the posh booth between her mother and aunt.

"You like this place, Sweet Bee?"

Bonny nodded, sticking a cracker into her mouth. "Yum!"

"I take it His Royal Majesty isn't coming by tonight?" Cheryl asked, tipping a martini.

"He had plans. He'll be around tomorrow."

"I'll say he has plans."

"What do you mean?" Kate asked.

"He's sitting with a nice looking set of plans about three booths down on the right."

Kate quelled the urge to turn. "Anyone we know?" she said softly.

"I don't know who you know, but I don't know this one. Short wavy brown hair, um…" she shrugged. "Good upper body, nice smile. I'm jealous."

"Paulie doesn't usually like this place. Don't let him see you looking," Kate hissed.

"Too late. They're getting up."

Kate steeled herself. Paulie walked straight up to her, bent and kissed her on the lips.

"Hello, darling."

He leaned across her then, stretched to kiss Bonny's forehead.

"Daddy!" the girl cried, grabbing Paulie around the neck.

"Hello Bon Bon. Having a merry night out with Mummy?"

Bonny nodded. "Sit here."

"Ah, but Daddy's all finished with his meal, Princess." Paulie turned back to his companion. "Alec, this is Katrina, Bonny, and our lovely cousin Cheryl."

The one called Alec leaned in, offered his hand to Cheryl, then Kate. "Kate, ladies, very pleased to meet you all."

British. Of course. Kate smiled. "Nice to meet you, Alec."

"We're on our way to catch a flick in Westwood. Come along?"

Kate diverted her eyes to her daughter, who bounced beside her. Paulie nodded.

"Oh, right. Well then. I'll call you tomorrow; we need to talk about preschool."

"Great," Kate said. "Have fun tonight."

"Will do." Paulie hesitated only a moment before again leaning down and brushing his lips across hers. "Love you," he whispered.

As he started to pull away, Kate touched his chest, prompting him to pause.

"He's hot," she whispered back.

Cheryl barely spoke on the way home.

"I know you're pissed off, and I know why," Kate said, as they got out of the car.

"It's your screwball life."

"You don't understand. I have a plan."

"Your plans are not usually worth the gum on the bottom of my shoe."

Kate only smiled, preceded her cousin into the house.

In the week that followed, Kate and Paulie paid a visit to a preschool Kate had selected, found it to be very private and adequately secure. After a tour, they received enrollment papers and were invited to the summer picnic already in progress on the school's park-like grounds.

Paulie sat beside her on a blanket while she unpacked their lunch. It felt odd, to Kate, for him to slip so easily back into his old role as her partner. And yet, it was a most natural feeling, too. As if they'd never stopped. He took her hand.

"We have new rules, I suppose," he said softly.

"We aren't very good with rules."

"Can't argue with that."

"If you're asking if we should make out, I think maybe not."

"What if I seduce you?"

"You could, but then I would feel like the other woman. Or...man?"

Paulie stared at her, then covered his mouth to stifle a laugh.

She laughed too, and they ended up in a joyful embrace.

"Have I told you today how much I love you, Mrs. Bingham?"

He massaged her hand, laced his fingers with hers. And as good as it felt, it also hurt.

"Did you even ask Alec to come along?"

"I think *not*," Paulie said, with a short laugh.

"He doesn't mind?"

"I told him right up front that you and Bonny are my first priority. That you, my love, are not my ex, but my best friend."

"Is he good to you, Paul?"

"He's a sweetheart. I'm the one who's a downright bitch most of the time."

She didn't have to ask why. He was used to being taken care of, and poor Alec probably wasn't up to speed.

"He seems nice. Is he a decent person?"

"Of course, darling. Why do you ask?"

"I need to know, for Bonny's sake, you know."

"Bonny?"

"For when she stays with you two. I just want to make sure Alec is good with children. Is…discreet. You understand."

"Whoa whoa whoa. Bonny's staying with us? When?"

"Oh, didn't I mention I was going out next Saturday night? I could've sworn—"

"What about Cheryl? She's home to watch her, eh?"

"Actually, Cheri's got a date. Seems silly to hire a sitter, a complete stranger, you know, when you're so close by. She'll have a wonderful time at your place. I'll pack her a little bag, and, what do you think—a sleeping bag? Or do you have a guest bed?"

She watched him from the corner of her eye. He was trying to hide his fluster.

Gum on the bottom of Cheryl's shoe? Hardly.

Chapter 20

July, 1994.

"You're shittin' me. You're unloading Bon on him? You just moved up a rung or two, girl. I didn't think you had the balls to do that." Cheryl gave her a high-five. "And I have a date?"

"Yes, you do. So do I." Kate giggled.

Cheryl gave her a pensive look. "This brings up an interesting thing. When I was in New York, I ran into Richard O'Neill. Do you remember him? Probably not. Anyway, he does portrait stuff, and he's coming out here soon to open a shop in town. He asked me if I'd like to work with him."

"Cheri, that's awesome. Wow."

"But it would mean I won't be here all the time. If you go back to work, too, we'll have to get some kind of day care for Bonny."

"We'll cross that bridge later. Is this Richard fellow date material?"

"Could be," Cheryl said. "Divorced. I was thinking of giving him a call. Maybe the three of us could go out and have a nosh?"

Kate smile, shook her head. "Now who's the nutcase? Call him; you go so I don't have to be a liar."

"And you? You'll sit home and be a liar anyway."

"No, I'll go somewhere. I'll do something."

"Why don't you call Mr. Tight-Butt Hot-Rock-Star Beamer-Guy?"

"Because I'm not looking for a date, or anything else, for that matter. Rob's not interested in me that way."

"Oh, right. He's 'just a nice guy', you said. Who gave you his phone number when he heard that you and Peebo were on the rocks."

169

"He did come by once while you were gone. Brought a demo of his new songs."

"Did you listen?"

"No."

"Fool."

"I can take Bonny to work with me," Kate said. "She's a good girl. I'll just bring her some loot to play with."

"Way to change the subject."

Kate got edgy after Cheryl set up her date with Richard. She pulled Rob's card off the mirror, then put it back. Went back again, took the card and shoved it into the hip pocket of her jeans.

Thursday night, she was dialing when Paulie walked in from the front door. The phone slipped from her fingers.

"Oh, sorry, didn't mean to interrupt."

"Paul! I was, just, um, calling Mom. Line was busy."

He nodded. "I stopped by to tell you that I have the guest room all set up for our little darling. Bed, rail, bouncy horse, pink fuzzy feather fluffy stuffy all over the room. You'd be proud."

"That's great. I'm so happy that you're able to take her. You know," she began, standing and pressing her fingertips together, "maybe you can take her on a regular basis, like a weekend here and there."

"Why not. Splendid idea."

He only stayed long enough to look through his mail and pick up some CD's he wanted. Blew her a kiss on his way out. "See you Saturday, love!"

Kate went straight to her bathroom and filled the tub. His visits still unnerved her. Or rather, his leaving.

By Friday afternoon, she deemed it too late to call Rob. She perused the paper, looking for something to do on Saturday night. A play, perhaps. She was contemplating seeing "Les Miserables" again when Rob called her.

"I know this is really short notice, but I was wondering if you'd be up for dinner tomorrow night."

170

Her faced warmed. "Tomorrow? Saturday? What's the occasion?"

"I believe they used to call it a date, but I could be wrong. Maybe now it's just *hanging out*?"

He must have heard the news. Wow.

She didn't hesitate. "Yeah, why not. Dinner sounds nice. Shall I meet you, or?"

"I'll pick you up. Say, seven?"

"Fancy or jeans?"

"Either. This is L.A."

"Right."

"I'll see you then."

In an instant, everything had changed. All because a man, an attractive, interesting, *straight* man had asked her out.

"Bonny! We're going shopping! Do you have to go potty first?"

Cheryl couldn't resist the tease, which lasted for several hours. It began with a dissection of Kate's garment of choice, the proverbial, black "*come-do-me*-dress" as Cheryl called it, and evolved into questions about the new bubble bath and body cologne.

"Cut it out. Don't ruin this for me. Do you hear me yapping about your date with Richard?"

"Richard isn't my second rock star in the same decade."

Paulie and Alec showed up at six fifteen. Paulie's mouth opened when he saw Kate in the slinky new dress.

"Good lord. And here I thought you were going to a neighborhood potluck."

"No, that would be me," Cheryl muttered, who had decked herself out in designer jeans.

"You always look gorgeous, Auntie Cheryl," Paulie told her.

"And I don't?" Kate asked, with a giggle. She spun around for him.

"Breathtaking, darling. Where *are* you going?"

Bonny emerged from the hallway, dragging a backpack half her size.

"Mummy is going to eat dinner with Rob."

Paulie cocked an eyebrow. "Rob Evans?"

Kate nodded. "Yeah. Just…dinner."

"I see. Didn't know you were seeing Rob."

Behind him, Alec rolled his eyes, and Kate smiled. "Well, I'm not. I mean, I haven't. Not until tonight, that is."

"He just rang you up, out of the blue. He knew about us, I presume? I hope?"

Kate put a hand on her hip. "Of course he did. He wouldn't have called, otherwise. I don't know how he found out. Except for what I said on the plane, but nothing was final yet, then."

"The plane?"

"We sat together on the London-to-L.A. when I came back."

"That so."

"Uh huh."

"So you talked, then. On the plane."

"Yeah. In first class."

"Sat next to you."

"We had coffee and Bailey's. Together."

Cheryl walked between them, swept up her shoulder bag, then turned to Alec at the door. "I don't know about you, but the intellect of these two just goes right under my head. See you tomorrow, Cinderella," she added to Kate, then walked out.

"Tomorrow?" Paulie asked Kate. "Is she not expecting you to come home?"

Kate shrugged. "Maybe *she's* not coming home." She pressed three fingers against Paulie's chest. "Don't you have someplace you gotta be, Sir Paul?"

Clearly distracted, Paulie took Bonny's backpack and handed it to Alec. "Be a love and put Bon in the car, will you, dear?"

Kate squatted down, mindful of her short dress hem. "You be super-duper good for Daddy and Uncle Alec, okay?"

Bonny nodded. "You will get me tomorrow, Mummy?"

"By noon. I promise."

Bonny turned and took Alec's hand. He hesitated, looked to Paulie.

"I'll be out in a moment," Paulie dismissed. When Alec and Bonny had gone, he turned back to Kate. He stared long enough to prompt a sigh from her.

"What."

"Have a wonderful time," he said, leaning down to kiss her cheek. "Be careful, eh?"

"Thank you. I will be fine."

"You look positively ravishing. Not planning to—"

"I'm going to dinner, Paul. Not an orgy."

"I know how you are on first dates."

"*Go.*"

He went to the door, was nearly through it when he turned once more. "You're messing with me, you know that, don't you?" He didn't wait for a response.

Kate was so delighted with herself she did a quick pirouette. While waiting for Rob, she put on his demo CD and listened, loved what she heard. Some of it was edgy, hard. One, Rob solo on the piano, a deep, emotion grabbing ballad. Another, good time guitar, bordering on modern country rock. Kate was amazed at the diversity in the songs, in Rob's talent.

The CD had just finished when the bell rang. Kate took a deep breath, pulled open the door.

He handed her a small bouquet of wildflowers.

She didn't realize how shocked she looked until Rob chuckled. "What? You don't do flowers?"

"No, no, it's not that, it's just…I don't remember the last time…if I ever. These are lovely. Thank you."

She touched the petals, smelled the scent. "I'll just put these in some water. Would you like a glass of wine? Do we have time?"

"We have time and, yes, white, Chardonnay if you have it."

"You got it." *Wow. Flowers.* She dashed into the kitchen, calling over her shoulder, "Just make yourself comfortable in the living room."

She dumped out a vase holding silk ones and neatly arranged the fresh blooms, added water. Held her breath looking into the fridge, hoping she hadn't lied, then nearly spilled the wine as she poured. *Wow. Flowers!* She paused to take a breath.

173

Straightened the straps on her dress. Picked up the wine, shook off her anxiety and joined Rob.

"Here we are." She handed him a glass.

"You, uh, you look amazing in that dress."

"Thanks. I may have forgotten how to blush properly," she said. "I listened to your demo."

"And?"

"Wow. Where have I been?"

"In the land of pop. Not that that's a bad place to be. Paul's music set a new standard in the 80's. He was unique."

"You are unique."

Rob shrugged. "I do what I do because I have to. It's kinda like eating, breathing, you know."

"I do know." Kate began to relax. Music was something she felt comfortable with. "Will all the songs on the demo be on the album?"

"I think so. Plus six or seven others. I've laid down two more since I made that CD. It'll be Christmas before it's done. Maybe Christmas next year. I don't like to rush." He considered his glass of wine. "So, which was your favorite?"

"Definitely *Come By Here*. The piano work is..." she paused, searching for the right word, "haunting. Seductive."

Rob nodded. "Good. Doubly good, coming from you."

He took her to a quietly elegant restaurant in the city. Conversation between them would have been easy, were it not for Kate's fascination with the fact that she was out with someone besides Paulie and immensely focused on every detail. Rob's habits, the way he sometimes gestured with his hands while talking; the only occasional appearance of dimples, the reflection of the table candle in his eyes.

"Let me ask you a question," he said, when the waitperson had delivered their dessert. "If I said, let's go see a film, any film, old or new, what would you say?"

Kate didn't hesitate. "*Somewhere In Time*".

"Good choice. How about, if I said, what's good for breakfast?"

"Eggs. Omelets, bacon, sausage, sourdough toast, Belgian waffles, raw honey, coffee—"

"Whoa. I get the picture. Anything you don't like?"

174

"Don't think I'm horrible, but I've been living without bacon for six years."

Rob laughed out loud. "A woman after my own heart. What's your favorite beach?"

"Malibu. No! Zuma." Now Kate laughed. "What's this all about? I have no problem asserting my desires."

"I like that."

"You now. If I said, if you could go away for a weekend, anywhere you wanted, where would it be?"

"With you?"

Kate paused, looked across the table, and focused on Rob's eyes. "With someone you'd like to be with."

"With you, then. I'd have to say..." he glanced down, dipped his spoon into the tiramisu. "the Boxcar."

"What's that?"

"It's this ramshackle little train car on my ranch. Which reminds me. Where is Bonny tonight?"

"She's with her father. And how does your ranch tie in to my daughter?" Kate shook her head, took a bite of his dessert.

"When you come out, I want you to bring her. I have ponies, dogs and an old barn owl she will just love."

"When I come out?"

"Next Saturday. So she's with Paulie?"

"You're good. You know that? Really good."

He smiled. "How do you feel about that?"

"That you're good at table tennis?"

"That she's with Paul."

"Absolutely comfortable. I have no reason not to."

"He has a...roommate, I hear?"

Kate licked a bit of dessert from the corner of her mouth. "Yeah. How did you know that? And how did you know we'd split up?"

"A not-so-anonymous phone call from a brash, leggy blonde." Now he reached his spoon toward her crème brulee.

"What does that mean? Oh, God. Cheryl called you?"

"Now, I distinctly remember this woman saying, this is not Cheryl Collins, and I am not calling to tell you that Kate Bingham is available."

Kate grasped Rob's wrist before he could get his spoon to his mouth. "She set this up?"

"No. Nothing like that. Don't get all pissed. Believe me, I was most appreciative of her un-thoughtfulness. I'd been wanting to call you. I didn't know how things were going for you and Paul. Now, can I eat this, or what?"

She let go of his arm, smiled, took another bite then put down her fork.

"I think you should know right now, Paulie and I are still married."

"These things take time."

"No, I mean, we haven't taken any steps to end our marriage."

"Yet."

Kate took a moment to compose her words. "We wanted, especially right now, to keep things as normal as possible for Bonny. We sort of didn't say it, but we both know that things could come up that would change what we want. Unless or until that happens, we're just...you know, separated. Bonny likes Uncle Alec. I don't speak ill of Paul. She sees us as one big family that just happens to live in two different places."

"Of course that can't last."

"She's only three."

"Look. I didn't mean to get into that stuff. To be honest, I was really conflicted when I saw you on the plane, Kate. Because I knew if you were there, things hadn't gone well the night before—after you blew out of the arena. I felt guilty all over, because I dig Paul as a person, and I didn't like that I was feeling happy about seeing you."

"Things were already going south. That night, everything just took a turn for the worse." She folded her hands, unsure of how much to say. "When Paulie came home, we had a come-to-Jesus meeting. It wasn't fun for either of us. We had to make some hard decisions."

He touched her hand, a light tap of commiseration. "I appreciate that you told me. I don't have any expectations. Yet." He took a spoonful of his tiramisu and offered it to her. "For the record. I want to be on that list of things that could come up."

176

She took the bite, savored the sweetness. Savored his look. Tried to ignore the slow burn that was building inside her.

After dinner, he asked if she'd like to go dancing. There was a club adjacent to the restaurant, and the band was just heating up.

"I'm rusty," she warned.

"Who isn't?"

There was no chance for a warm-up; the singer had just launched into a torch tune, and Rob held out his arms. Kate felt as if she'd stepped through some kind of magic looking glass.

"Don't be afraid. I'll try not to step on you." He took her hands, wrapping one around his back, pulling her gently closer until they touched. "Coming back to you now?"

Kate nodded, realizing that she hadn't slow-danced, not even with Paulie, since their wedding day.

Rob gave her an extra clinch. He wasn't as tall as her husband, felt solid and taut against her. She couldn't help but conjure the mental image of him mending his fences in the sun. Her forehead came just to his jaw, and she rested against him, closed her eyes as he led her on the dance floor.

She liked the feel of him. Rob exuded a quiet strength, a willingness to be that strength. He smelled good, too. Clean and male, with a hint of a memorable after shave. There was a word she searched for, a word to define the way she felt in his arms. Maybe it was too soon to use the word.

He tilted his chin down, put his lips close to her ear. "This is way more fun than I remember."

The intimacy was overwhelming, intoxicating. A feeling she needed, badly. Craved.

Soon, much too soon for Kate, the band stepped up into a reggae rock and they separated but continued to dance. Minutes later, they left the dance floor warm and pumped up.

"Two Perriers," he told the waitress. "If that's okay with you?"

"Perfect. Wow. I feel like such a cow."

"Moo."

"You aren't supposed to agree."

"I wasn't agreeing. Just communicating. Give me credit. I'm a guy, remember?"

"I noticed that at one point."

She sipped, gazed. It occurred to her that she'd be perfectly content to sit there all night.

They took the long way to the car, window shopping, enjoying the night air. Kate let him take her hand as they walked, felt surprisingly, deliciously connected. He was comfortable, evidenced by his effortless laugh, his familiar way with her. He slowed his pace, pulled her to his other side and took her hand.

"What's the matter? Was I on your bad side?" she asked.

Rob chuckled. "You were on the street side, girl."

"So?"

"So, a gentleman always walks the curb."

"You're kidding."

He laughed again and put his arm around her shoulders, not missing a step.

"Okay, then." Kate nodded, slipped her arm around his waist. They moved as one, unhurried, companionable, and easy.

So different.

Inwardly cursing, Kate wondered if she would ever not look to compare Rob with Paulie.

Like a true-life Cinderella, Kate found herself dreading to say goodnight as Rob pulled into the driveway. On the porch, he drew her close, gave her a lengthy hug.

"What a great night," he said, pulling away.

Kate got out her keys, unlocked and opened the front door. "Would you like—?"

Rob quickly pressed his fingers against her lips. Then, drawing his fingers down, he hooked her chin and gently tilted her head upward. Leaned down, took her mouth, a tentative taste, then another. Kate snaked her arms around his neck, lost herself in the kisses. As his arms tightened around her, Kate felt herself pouring into him, absorbed by the intensity of his passion. He was exploring, feeling his way, discovering how to get inside of her. She welcomed him.

Breathing hard, Kate tried again. "I could just, um," she uttered, then swallowed, steadied herself. "Make some coffee or something…"

Rob smiled, shook his head. "I'll email you directions to the ranch. Make sure Bonny wears shoes."

Kate only nodded, and Rob kissed her again, briefly, turned to go.

☞ Note from Rob: I'm not one to write stuff down, other than songs, but —

What can I say about Kate? That I've been waiting for her all my life? As a songwriter, I would fire myself for writing something so cliché.

I met her over dinner in London. I was already friends with Paul, so had to force myself not to stare at his beautiful wife. I could tell she was troubled. I had no idea the magnitude of the problem, and I still don't. I respect the privacy she gives her husband, her marriage.

I'm in a tough place because I like Paul a lot, and I hate that his misfortune is my, well, quite possibly my chance of a lifetime. What do I love about her? She's strong. She's level-headed, she can make decisions, and she's passionate about her desires. Everything about her is sexy and appealing, even the way she mothers her sweet little daughter.

I have to be honest. I'm looking for a life mate. If things go the way I hope, Kate and I could have an incredible future together.

I just hope Paul can handle it. —Rob Evans

Chapter 21

S omeone was knocking. Kate lifted her head, looked at the clock on the nightstand. Eleven a.m.! "Yeah?" she called out.

"You dead?"

"Yeah."

Cheryl descended on her and sat on the bed. "So?"

"So, what?"

"Did you lose your glass slipper?"

Kate sat up, rubbed her eyes. "Crap. I've gotta go get Bon in an hour."

"Evasion will get you nowhere. Did you jump his bones?"

Kate gave Cheryl a hard look. "No."

Cheryl frowned. "What happened? Does he not do married chicks?"

"You are crass, you know that? And by the way, thanks for setting me up."

"You were taking a month of Sundays to get on the ball."

"We had a wonderful time. He's so…different."'"

"Paulie's different. Rob is decidedly normal."

"He brought me flowers. Can you believe that? He took me dancing at Fresco's. He eats meat. Cheryl! He eats steak! We slowed danced, we—"

"Yawn. Did he at least kiss you?"

Kate paused, smiled. Looked at her hands. "Oh, yeah."

Cheryl lifted her eyebrows. "A little tonsil hockey, maybe?"

"And what about you? You weren't home when I got in at one."

"I had a…very satisfying evening. O'Neill has improved with age."

Kate got out of bed, rummaged in her dresser for underwear. "I've gotta get in the shower. I promised Bee I'd get her by noon."

"Did you talk to her last night at all?"

"Paulie called me twice. Twice! The bugger."

"Jealousy is a mean taskmaster."

"How could he be jealous?"

"He's still laboring under the fantasy that he owns you." Cheryl stood up, primped at her hair in the mirror over the dresser. "He'll get the message eventually that you have your own life. Don't get me wrong, Kate. I still like Paul. I do. I just have trouble with his weakness."

Kate went into the bathroom, started the shower, and then returned to her cousin.

"Men?"

"No. Not that kind of weakness. He's just such a slave to his own addictions. Worse, it makes him unhappy. There are people out there that are co-dependent slobs, but they are happy to be that way. Paulie seems to always be struggling to achieve lofty goals he may not even want."

"What do I owe you for that little gem of advice?"

Cheryl remained serious. "No advice. Just observation. I hope he can be happy."

The words set Kate on edge. She'd wanted Cheryl to be happy about her date. Wanted to share with her the intense excitement of the kissing, the way Rob's arms felt around her. Cheryl had thrown a bucket of water on it all, talking about Paulie.

In the shower, she found herself once again comparing Rob to Paulie. They were clearly from different planets. How could she be attracted to two such polar opposites?

With a quick mental slap, she reminded herself that she didn't really *know* Rob. Had only met him, what, four times? Knew him mostly from his words, not his actions. She'd thought she'd known Ray Goff, too.

Paulie, on the other hand, she had grown up with. She knew him inside and out. Knew every expression and the thought connected to it. Understood his demons, now more than ever, and accepted his faults. Likewise, he knew how to touch her, speak to her sensitivities. He gave her a reason to care, someone to nurture.

She grabbed a towel, began drying off. In her frustration, she reddened her skin. Where was all this crap coming from? Shouldn't she be feeling happy, singing, glowing in the warmth of potential new love?

It was her first visit to Paulie and Alec's flat. Extremely neat, lots of color, contemporary but comfortable. Like anyone else's home. Alec let her in. "They are in the bedroom playing," he told her. "I have to tell you, Bonny is just a delight. We loved having her here."

Kate smiled. "I'm so glad to hear it."

"I'm sorry about the phone calls. He's…well, you know him better than I do, I suppose. He was just being obsessive."

"It's okay. I'm used to it."

She went down the short hallway, following the sounds of Paulie's laughter.

"Mummy!" Bonny disentangled herself from her father and ran into Kate's waiting arms.

Paulie remained on the floor, looked up at her. "Good morning, darling."

"Hey, Paul. It went well?"

Bonny kissed her mother's cheek. "We had veggie burgers last night. And ice cream."

"*Green tea* ice cream," Paulie qualified, getting to his feet. "And how was your night?"

Kate smiled, put Bonny back on her feet. "Get your bag together, there's a good girl."

"Oh no. Was it terrible?" Paulie pushed. "I'm sorry."

"Nothing to be sorry about."

"I left my shoes," Bonny said, before scurrying from the room.

Kate sat down on the bed, and Paulie, naturally, sat beside her. She looked him in the eyes, those familiar, wide-opened windows into his heart. His makeup was a mess, she noted, giving him a sort of off-balance look. But inside those eyes she saw herself.

With an almost palpable bolt of realization, Kate got it. It was Paulie she needed to tell. Paulie who needed to share in her delight. He was, after all, her best friend. And he needed to hear as much as she needed to tell.

"It was…amazing."

Paulie drew in a deep breath. "Yeah?"

"He brought me flowers. Wildflowers, tied together with a bit of raffia. He asked for white wine. We talked about music. We went to dinner at Le Rive."

Paulie nodded, rapt.

"We talked about all sorts of things, including your music, you know, he really likes it, he said you were an icon."

"I am. Go on."

"We went to Fresco's after that, and we danced."

"No shit."

"No shit."

"Wow." Paulie wet his lips, swallowed. "Then what?

"We drank Perrier."

"Good taste."

"Then he took me home."

"And?" He squinted then, cringed maybe.

Kate subtly took his hand, played with his wedding band. "And, then, he left."

"After?"

"After a goodnight kiss. He didn't come in."

Paulie issued a sigh, put his arm around her, and nodded. "Okay."

Kate put her head on his shoulder. "What are you thinking?"

"Don't know, actually. Thank you for sharing." He kissed the top of her head. "What's next, then?"

"He invited Bonny and me out to his ranch for a barbecue."

"Ah."

Bonny called to them, apparently packed and ready to go. Kate stood, but Paulie was reluctant, held onto her hand.

"Am I losing you?"

Kate touched his cheek. "You are so freakin' needy."

"I've never pretended to be otherwise."

"You know how I feel." She bent, took his face between her hands, kissed him on the mouth. "I really, really like Rob. I think maybe something could happen. It would change things, but it can't change the way I feel about you. And because you are a part of me, I'll continue to pamper you and tell you how much you matter."

Paulie nodded. "All right. Just be discreet in front of Bonny, and don't forget your bloody diaphragm."

As quickly as the week passed, it wasn't fast enough for Kate. She interviewed with George Lucas for a new film. "It's another one of those sci-fi space films. He said I can join the crew if I want to," she told Paulie on the phone.

"Just let me know if you need me to take Bonny. So, what are you wearing on Saturday?"

Although he couldn't see her, Kate shook her head. "Why, I'm going naked, of course."

"The raw ground can be murder on your back."

"True, but I don't plan to be one with nature. I'm quite sure there's a...discreet...bedroom in the house."

"Oooh. There you go. The truth comes forth. You're going out there for something quick and dirty."

Kate laughed aloud. "I don't know about the quick part."

"That sounds like you."

He was trying it on for size, this new role, this new phase to their relationship. Although he pretended to in the past, he didn't make changes easily. Kate, too, felt the world was a little off its kilter. "So, you think jeans and a cami, with a snap shirt tied in the front?"

"And boots. Go out and get yourself a pair of sexy little cowboy boots. Perfect."

Kate giggled. "Yeah?"

"With fringe. Do you want me to go shopping with you?"

She laughed harder, partially from relief. "You make me crazy when you shop. I think I can handle this on my own."

"Your loss, darling."

"I know."

Saturday morning found Kate nervously trying to latch Bonny's car seat. Bonny pushed her away, did it herself.

"You look pretty, Mummy," she assured. "Why did you got my jammies? Am I going to Daddy's?"

"Just in case we decide to sleep over at Rob's."

"Does he have a little girl room?"

"I'm not sure, probably not a girly room, but there's likely—just don't worry about that right now."

"Is Daddy and Alec coming?"

"No, Bons. Not this time."

The freeways were crowded, but traffic moved. She exited at Lynn Road and followed the directions in her lap. Her tires crunched over the gravel on the long driveway leading to the "Boxcar" and Rob's ranch. She parked beside his identical, but black, BMW.

He came out of nowhere. "No trouble finding it, I see."

"Directions were good," she said, endeavoring to release Bonny from her confines in the backseat. "Man, I am just all thumbs today," she muttered.

Rob reached around her, unsnapped the latch. Bonny lifted her arms to him.

Kate stood back, cocked an eyebrow.

"Where's the pony?" Bonny asked.

They toured the ranch in an ATV, and Bonny got her pony ride. Kate delighted in watching her auburn curls bobbing as Rob led the pony around a practice ring. She wished Paulie could see her.

In the massive entertainment area behind his house, Rob fired up the grill. Kate watched through the window as he walked back to the house to join her in the kitchen, where she and Bonny chopped summer fruits.

"What are you cooking?" Bonny wanted to know.

"Barbecue stuff."

"I don't eat meat."

"I figured that, small fry. Have you ever had soy hot dogs?"

Behind Bonny's back, Kate made a gagging gesture.

"Yes, Uncle Alec got them. Yummy!"

"Great. Did anyone ever tell you you are a precocious sort of princess?"

"Daddy says I am smart."

"And he's right about that."

It was an easy banter, and Kate liked hearing it. Her daughter *was* precocious, worldly beyond her brief three years. Accepting, giving, passionate. All gifts from her father and mother.

After they ate, Rob took them to the old train car behind the main house. Inside were small, rustic but tasteful sleeping quarters. Used couch cushions formed a small bed in the far corner.

"I've got something in here to show you," he told Bonny, taking her hand. "Just born a couple of weeks ago."

"Puppies!"

Kate almost clapped her own hands at the sight of six retriever-mix pups all scrambling to get at their mother's milk. Bonny squatted to get a closer look.

Rob moved behind Kate, wrapped his arms around her. "Could she have one?" he whispered.

"Oh! I don't know. I need to maybe think about that."

"They won't be fully cooked for another couple of weeks. You can let me know."

He got down beside Bonny then, lifted one of the pups up for her to pet. Showed her how to gently stroke the tiny dog's back.

"The mother won't get upset, will she?" Kate asked.

"Naw. She's a good bitch; she's been through this before. She trusts me."

"You said a bad word." Bonny accused.

"Well now, sometimes it's a bad word. But when you're talking about a mommy dog, it's not a bad word at all."

"Oh. I will tell Uncle Alec."

Rob and Kate exchanged a look, then both laughed.

The sun retired, and Bonny sat at the natural-burl wood coffee table, a myriad of puzzles around her. Rob poured two glasses of wine, handed one to Kate. The night had turned cold, clouds having moved in during the afternoon, so he lit a fire in the broad, fieldstone fireplace.

"This is made to order," Kate murmured. Her daughter yawned.

"Mummy brought my jammies."

Kate's mouth dropped, and Rob chuckled.

"Are you sleepy, Miss Bonny?"

"Can I call my daddy?"

"Daddy's probably out tonight, sweetie."

"He said to."

Kate dug her cell from her pocket. "Okay. I'll dial."

Paulie answered on the first ring. "How's it going, love?"

"Everything is fine. Bon wants to say goodnight." She handed the phone to Bonny, who got up and walked around the room in a lop-sided figure eight as she talked. It was the same habit her father had, Kate noted.

Soon, she brought the phone back to Kate. "Talk to Daddy."

Rob stood. "Now, where are those jammies?"

"In the trunk."

When Rob had left the room with Bonny, Kate resumed her call.

"So, are you staying?" Paulie asked.

"Looks that way."

"All right, then. Don't hesitate to call me, you know, if he turns out to be a brute or something."

"Rob? Don't be crazy."

"I would bring Alec."

Kate smiled. "Thank you, Paul. Everything will be fine."

"You'd best call me in the morning."

"I will call you tomorrow sometime. After I get home. Don't sit on the phone, do you hear me?"

He was quiet. She knew the un-sound of his pout. "Say hi to Alec."

Kate and Rob chatted for a while, sipping wine, enjoying the fire.

"I have one for you. Who would you most like to meet? Name three people," Kate challenged.

"Living or dead?"

"Either."

"Okay. Let's see. First, I know right off, Abe Lincoln."

"Really? Okay, you gotta say why."

"He was the Great Emancipator. And I'm all for emancipation."

"And you're technically from a slave state. Interesting. Who else?"

Rob thought for a moment. "Either Van Gogh or Hemmingway. Why? Because they were both depressed geniuses. Since I'm neither depressed nor am I any kind of genius, maybe I could've helped them. Or learned from them."

"Set them free?"

"Good one." He thought on his third. "I think...Bill Clinton."

Kate chuckled. "Can't wait to hear this one."

"I'd just like to say, what the hell were you thinkin', man, gettin' caught like that!"

Kate clapped her hands together.

"Now you."

"Me. Well, oddly enough, Mr. Clinton is also on my list. But for an entirely different reason," she said, lowering her voice seductively.

"Not sure I want to go there."

"Mae West."

"Like that one. You're almost the same height. You...are sexier, though."

Kate grinned at him, took a last sip of wine.

"Lady Di."

"Excellent choice. She's on my short list, too."

Kate put down her empty glass. Rob sat forward on the couch, leaned his arms on his thighs. "Look, Kate. About tonight. It won't offend me if you want to bunk in with Bonny."

Kate tilted her head. "I think it might offend me that you're suggesting that."

"I'm not suggesting anything. I just didn't want you to think me presumptuous."

"I appreciate that. I guess I was being presumptuous last weekend."

He gave her a soft smile. "I can explain that if you'll come over here and get comfortable with me."

Kate wasted no time moving to the couch. "Okay. I'm here. Explain away."

"You might have figured out already that I'm a bit old-fashioned. It's really hard to be a Southern gentlemen living in the chaos of L.A. My momma taught me that if a guy gets the hots for a girl, he should wait awhile and see if he still wants her. She said a lot of heartache could be avoided. And unwanted children."

"Your momma, huh?"

"My momma. You'd like her. She's a real gentrified lady."

"So what did you decide, after a week of penance for your lustful ways?"

Rob put his arm around her, leaned her back into the deep recesses of the couch. "It only got worse."

"The hots?"

He offered a slight shrug. "That's not the right word. Point is, I do want to have something. With you. Which, I guess, is obvious by now."

She played her fingers on his hair, feeling its texture, its slight silkiness. Peered into his honest, hazel eyes. Wasn't sure what to say, so she nodded.

"I know you've just been though a tough time. And I know it's not all over, yet. But I got a feeling, like maybe we might be...good for each other."

"Good. Yeah." His face was very close to hers, and Kate felt his words against her cheek. "Are you going to get around to kissing me, or what?"

"You gonna be sorry you ast that, girl," Rob drawled. "Just smack me or something if you start to pass out," he added, then laid his lips upon hers, sending them both into a kissing frenzy that swept everything else from Kate's mind.

"Bed," she managed to whisper, and Rob agreed. He led her to his bedroom, a large suite with lots of natural wood on the walls. He turned down the bed, began taking off his shirt. Kate slipped out of her jeans, sat on the bed. Rob fascinated her, everything he did and said. The sight of his muscles surprised her. Not only did he have hair on his chest, he sported a small tattoo on his shoulder. He unbuttoned, then unzipped, his jeans, climbed onto the bed beside Kate, pulled her to him. Reaching above and behind him, he tapped something on the headboard and the lights dimmed.

They finished undressing each other. Rob clearly took lovemaking seriously, slowly. Between the sensuous kisses, the gentle but skilled touches, she never got the chance to perform her usual magic—her partner took his pleasure from arousing her, creating an easy rhythm with her that sent her over the top within moments.

As Kate gave in to the magic, she was remotely aware of a change within her, one that she knew could not be reversed.

Chapter 22

At 2 a.m. the rain began, playing out a staccato on the skylight high above the bed. Kate lay facing Rob, feeling as if she were part of some grand storybook.

"You okay?" he asked, touching the tip of her nose.

"Nothing will ever be the same again," she murmured.

"Is that a good thing, or bad?"

"Good, I think."

"You seem pensive."

"I'm trying to come to grips with what just happened. Maybe—maybe it would help for you to know some things about me. Some things I want you to know."

"I'm a good listener."

Kate drew a breath, took a moment to organize a thought. "In high school, I had two boyfriends. Both of them were sort of the backseat-and-behind-the-bleachers type relationships. It was okay, but not particularly interesting to me. When I should have been going to college, I dropped out and took up with Brent. My parents and I were on the outs. I don't know why, except to say I was generally bitchy. I was a rebel. I should've grown out of it by then, but I hadn't."

"You sound like me."

"After about a year, Brent left me for someone else. I was really devastated. In retrospect, I know it was just the circumstances. I didn't love him. In fact, I'm surprised he stayed with me as long as he did. I could be quite cruel."

Rob frowned. "Cruel? You?"

"He broke my heart, I thought, so I blew out of town. I got a job as a roadie for Paul's band."

"A roadie? Ha!"

"Hey, I was strong. I was tough. I had pink hair, for God's sake."

"And that's when you met Paul."

"Yeah. After a couple of months on the tour, I started painting him. He liked it. We became friends. And one night, I seduced him."

"I can see that about you."

"You don't understand. This wasn't something he was used to doing, in any way, shape or form. Not with girls."

"Then why? How?"

Kate was quiet for a moment. "He did it because...he loved me. I wanted him to be straight. And for six years, he gave it his best shot."

Rob stared at her, clearly at a loss for words.

"It nearly ruined him, trying so hard to be someone he's not. I was kidding myself to think I could change something like that."

Rob shook his head. "Wow. That's...that's just weird."

"I know. And in that whole weird process, I lost sight of who I really was, too. I spent so much time taking care of him, I didn't realize how much I wasn't getting. Don't get me wrong. We had great times. It wasn't all his fault. He was really good to me. He is a very good person; he has a wonderfully warm heart."

"You are a walking miracle, you know that?" Rob stroked her cheek.

"How so?"

"You are absolutely ripe for spoiling."

They cooked up a ranch house breakfast, complete with bacon and country sausage. Curious, Bonny snagged a sausage link from Kate's plate, stuck it in her mouth.

"Bonny! No."

"What's wrong with a little sausage?" Rob asked. "It's good, right Bon?"

She nodded. "Is it meat?"

"She's never had animal meat her entire life. I don't want her to get sick," Kate explained. "Not to mention my catching hell for it."

Rob chuckled. "Get used to it. It's bound to happen now and again. I went through that with Rach."

"Was she a vegetarian?"

"Jewish."

"I see. That could put a different spin on breakfast."

"Not to mention my momma's pork loin roast at Christmas. Two bogeys in one, there."

"What's a bogey?" Bonny asked, stuffing the rest of the sausage in her mouth.

"Bogies are like war missiles that are aimed at your marriage," Rob said. "Let's just say they're problems that happen sometimes that you have to try to fix."

As she drove back to West L.A., Kate thought about the weekend. Saturday had been lots of fun, Saturday night like a fairy tale. This morning was comfortable, easy, and seemed to portend a happy future. How could she explain it to Paulie? Meeting and liking Rob was one thing; coming off of the high of making love with him was quite another. Perhaps this *bogey* would finish her marriage to Paulie. It sent a pang through her.

He expected it, she knew. The comic barbs and innuendo made it clear he would be surprised if she didn't have sex with Rob. Paulie was lately hard to read, however. Maybe because he was living with his own lover. He couldn't very well fault her; his return to the exclusively gay life left her little choice but to find happiness elsewhere. At face value, it all made sense.

But below that face, beneath it all, she knew it hurt him. Selfish boy that he still was, he wanted both. Wanted to keep her and still lead his other life.

"That just ain't gonna happen," she murmured aloud. With Rob, she had a chance. Finally. A chance to be one-half of a balanced relationship. A hetero relationship not crippled by the constant pull of outside forces. Rob had so much to give, as a man, a strong, stable man without the kind of gender challenges Paulie struggled with every day.

Poor Paulie. She thought of all the time they'd been together. Such trying times, fighting the press, fighting the homophobes, the religious zealots. Fighting, it seemed, the very forces of the universe. Fighting each other. Loving each other.

How many times had they fought and made up? Separated, then reunited? But this time was different. There were

195

others—Alec and Rob—and that made it unlike the times before. Paulie had Alec, and she could be happy about that. In time, they would grow into the couple that Paulie needed.

And Rob? She was almost afraid to envision a future with him, so good, so shiny that it blinded her. It would look much better after she told Paulie and gave herself permission to move forward.

Paulie was alone. They'd argued, and Alec had gone out. The rain stopped, but the skies remained cloudy.

He went to his closet, slammed hangers. Picked out his brightest, floor length caftan, slipped it on over his naked body. At his dresser, he sat down and unlatched his makeup box.

He opened his eyes wide, stared hard into the mirror. Still a little red. He picked out a concealer, smeared it gently around his lids. Foundation. Powder. Blush.

Wait. Was he doing it out of order? Did he usually do his eyes first? He groaned, picked up an eye shadow stick.

What had they argued about? He couldn't even remember what started it. Likely his own fault, he'd been a pissant all weekend. No, a bitch. He'd been a flaming bitch to Alec, hounding him about stupid things like the wrinkled throw rug in the kitchen. The radio station he'd chosen to listen to. The wrong tea he'd prepared this morning.

Stupid. Stupid!

He sighed, swept back his hair and put a ponytail in. Found his favorite red wig, auburn actually, the same color as Kate's hair.

Kate.

That was it.

Paulie pulled the wig on, tugging it into place. It comforted him, his female image in the mirror.

She hadn't called. He glanced at the clock, looked away. Four-fucking-thirty and she wasn't back yet from Rob's house. And now that he thought about it, Alec's words came back to slam him anew.

"She's having sex with him, Paulie. Get over it. Let her go, for Christ's sake!"

He'd lashed out at Alec with his harshest words. Alec retaliated, tears had come, and Alec tried to comfort him. Paulie had pushed him away.

Alec went back on the offensive. "You don't get it, do you? Kate's a strong woman, but she's still a woman. Being with you was like her being with another woman. She's not a lesbian, sweetheart." His words had stopped Paulie cold. "Look, I'm not diminishing what you had. You two defied the odds for a long time. But it's time, right? Time for you to stop charading. Get real, dammit, and let Kate be herself."

The memory of the conversation made him tear up again.

"He's wrong," Paulie said to the mirror. "Kate and I have something real. Still." But Alec's words were too strong, painted too vivid a picture in his head. A picture of Kate and Rob on a bed, having passionate, hetero sex. Of Rob being masculine and physical, with an erection like a light sabre. Kate, parting her beautiful legs…

The phone shot a lightning bolt through his vision and he jumped. Took a few breaths before answering.

"I'm home," she said.

"Fine."

"Paulie, what's the matter?"

"Nothing. I'll talk to you tomorrow."

Kate frowned, hung up the phone. She told Bonny to unpack her toys, debated on whether to call Paulie back. He was clearly upset about something.

"Probably me," she muttered. "Damn."

She threw together a boring but adequate dinner of pasta and salad, dishing it out just as Cheryl came in the door. Cheryl got her own plate.

"So how was your weekend? Is his place nice?"

"It's awesome. Huge. Like seven acres, most of it is raw, hilly land. Gorgeous one story ranch house."

"There's giant rooms!" Bonny added.

"Wowie," Cheryl acknowledged.

"And he's gots puppies and horses, too! An I got to touch one puppy!"

After showing Bonny proper enthusiasm, Cheryl turned to her cousin.

"So what's with the gloom? Didn't want to come home?"

Kate shook her head. "I didn't. But that's not it." She put down her fork. "I need to go see a friend."

Cheryl gave her an inquisitive stare. "A friend? Is this friend anyone I know?"

Kate nodded.

"Is this friend ill or something?"

"Possibly. Can you?"

"I was just going to say, I've really been dying to watch *Toy Story* again!"

Kate knocked on Paulie's door a half hour later. She was surprised when he finally responded—in full drag.

"Sorry, I was in the back room. Uh, come in."

Kate couldn't help but stare at him. It had been years since she'd seen him in his regalia. He walked to the liquor cabinet.

"Here. You'll like this. It's peach."

He poured her a cordial glass of a clear liqueur.

"Nice."

"Stop staring at me. You're making me feel awkward."

Kate opened her mouth to speak, retracted before uttering. Instead, she took another sip of the schnapps. "Mm. Not staring. Admiring."

"So why are you here?"

"Where is Alec?"

"Gone."

"*Gone* gone?"

"We had a row. He didn't take his things, so I imagine the wanker will be back."

"Why are you in such a foul mood? Is it the reason for, or the result of, your fight with Alec?"

"Both."

"You wanna talk about it?"

"No."

"I came here because you sounded wretched on the phone. I want you to tell me, Paulie. Is this about me and Rob?"

He wouldn't look at her. He sipped his drink, turned his back. The dress swayed. Kate frowned.

"Oh, boy," she muttered. He was in queen mode. "Turn your ass around and talk to me."

"I can't talk to you."

"Why the hell not?"

"Because you know and I know that I will inherently say the wrong fucking thing."

Kate groaned inwardly, walked around him to speak to his face.

"Okay. Bring it. Say what's on your mind."

He stared at her, and his eyes confirmed her fears. He was not okay with what had happened, despite his playful banter of the day before.

"Dammit, Paul. Don't do this." She paced, gathered random thoughts, tried to piece together a defense. Maybe a little offense. "Listen. We're going to talk this out before it goes any farther."

"Just go home, Kate."

"No way." She was beginning to breathe hard, so great was the emotion building within her. "Take off that ridiculous wig, will you? I can't talk to you like that."

Paulie complied, his expression sour. "That make you happy?"

"No. I'm not happy. We need to have an understanding, Paul. I thought we did, until today." She took a breath, tried to calm herself. "I slept with him. I slept with him and I liked it, okay? I don't understand why that hurts you, and I'm so very sorry that it does. You're the last person I would ever want to hurt. But you need a reality check. Consider that in all the years we've been together, I never once stepped out on you. I never so much as looked at another man. You, on the other hand," she began to accuse. She stopped when he held up his hand.

"I know what I did."

"And what you're doing now. You're living with another man. You've taken a lover. Now you tell me, right here and now,

199

that your relationship with Alec has changed how you feel about me. Inside."

His lips trembled, and he blinked. "It has not." His words were so soft they nearly crippled her. He sat down on the arm of the couch.

Don't do it, Kate. Don't touch him. You will only make this worse.

"Then, if that's true..." she began, swallowing hard. "You'll understand that I *need* you to help me make this change. It might look like it's easy, to you, on the outside, watching me trying to let another man into my life. It's not."

And because he was always honest, because he couldn't hold it inside, she knew what his next words might be. She was right.

"I wish you didn't have to."

Kate sighed. Broke her resolve. Put her arms around him. How she wanted to make everything all right for him! Like she always did. "But I do. I must. We've been through this before. We can't go back to the way it was."

"Is he that good?"

"It's not a matter of good or bad. Don't even go there. It's a matter of what works. Marriage isn't the best thing for you and me, right? We have, maybe, a higher purpose as friends. As confidants." She looked him in the eyes, let some fierceness into her voice. "I made a promise to you. You will always, always be in my heart. Can you get that, Paulie? Always. I just can't sleep with you anymore. And I can't, I can't be married to you anymore."

She took a huge risk. Her last words brought him around like smelling salts.

"You want a *divorce*? Now?"

Kate gave a slight nod.

"Are you going to marry Rob? Has he asked you, already?"

"No. No. Nothing like that. That would be crazy. But it doesn't seem right for us both to be living apart, screwing other people and staying married. I don't think it's fair to Alec, and I'm pretty sure Rob already finds it...awkward."

Paulie turned his eyes away, again. Kate closed hers, leaned against his forehead.

"I didn't expect this," she murmured.

"I'm sorry."

"I know."

"Alec is right. You deserve better. Always have."

"What we had was good, Paulie. What we have now is better. We can transcend all that crap. No more trying so hard to *be*."

He drew in a deep breath.

"Send me the papers. I'll sign them." Blinking back tears, he pulled the band from his hair. "Under extreme duress."

Traffic blurred on the way home. Cheryl was watching TV when she got there, Bonny was in bed.

"How'd it go? Lemme guess. You both cried and kissed and are now completely miserable."

"He agreed to a divorce."

"How did you talk him into that?" Cheryl turned and stared.

"I bullied him."

"And now you're feeling guilty."

"I'm feeling sick. I'll be better. He'll be better, soon. I hope. It was so hard not to help him."

"You've got to stop fixing him. He'll survive. Look at his life so far. He's had nothing but shit thrown at him and he's managed to live through it. He has Alec. He'll be okay."

"I'm not so sure."

"Are you going to tell Rob?"

"Yes. I am. He deserves to know."

"How do you feel about Rob?"

Kate paused. Thought again about their weekend, the lovemaking, the tender, caring way he treated her. "I really like him. He's like no one I've ever been with."

"You've been hanging around gay men and abusers for the last twelve or thirteen years." Cheryl went to her, touched her shoulder. "You went there hoping Paulie would be happy for you. Instead, he shot you down. Maybe you should call Rob. He can make you feel good and right."

"I think I'll just go to bed."

Cheryl nodded. "It'll all work out, kiddo. You'll see. Paul will come around because he wants you to be happy."

"If he can get over his own selfishness."

Kate tossed in bed. Paulie's bizarre behavior troubled her. The drag get up, the depression, the anger. It wasn't healthy for him. Hopefully, Alec had come home and set things to right. Given Paulie some devotion. She wished she had Alec's cell phone number.

She did have Rob's number, however. Her phone was on the nightstand. At around one, she dialed.

"Can't sleep," she complained. "Hope I didn't wake you."

"No. I wasn't sleeping, either. What's on your mind?"

"Just wanted to tell you what a wonderful time I had."

"I'm glad. I'm glad you came out. I wanted you to see my other world. The one I stay in when I'm not working. I love my life here."

Kate sighed. "I like that world."

"You seem quiet. Is everything all right?"

Had she called to tell Rob about Paulie? Would it change anything? "I saw Paul tonight. He's agreed to give me a divorce."

She heard Rob blow out a breath. "Man. That's, that's great. He was okay with it, then?"

"No. Not really."

"So you feel bad."

"Yes."

"I suspect he's in a spot where he doesn't quite know what he wants. Give him time. Don't push him too hard."

"You're very understanding to say that."

"I like Paul. I want this to go down easy. No pressure, okay? This is between you and him."

"I know."

"So when can we get together again?"

Kate smiled in relief. It was just what she needed to hear.

"For you, I will clear my busy social calendar."

"How about we take in a flick on Wednesday night? If you can get a sitter."

"Cool. I'll let you know. I'd like that."

"We can neck in the theater."

"Well that's incentive, isn't it?

⤷ **It was really hard to get excited about seeing Rob when I knew Paulie was so devastated. I felt a bit hollow inside. I was walking on a high wire, waiting for it to snap at any minute. I had bullied him, as only I can. Still, I'd taken an important step. Typical of Paulie-and-Kate, it was me who had to take that step. He would never have suggested we divorce. Cheryl was right about that.**

I was really worried about him when I found him all dragged up. I imagined that he'd cut all his man-clothes to shreds with a razor blade. I guess I should be happy he didn't turn back to heroin.

On top of everything else, getting comfort from Rob guilted me out. I could go and rain all over Paul, then come back to Rob's sheltering arms. Where could Paulie find comfort? I was his confidante, his crying shoulder. I was his shield, his rabbit's foot, his warming blanket. I was his person.

I was also afraid to think too much about what was happening with Rob. One of those, "if it seems too good to be true, it probably is" things. Only it felt entirely real and true. I kept thinking, how is it that this guy isn't already taken? I knew he was married once before, but still. And what could he possibly see in me? I'm not your garden variety petunia.

If I were him, I wouldn't touch me with a ten foot pole.

–Kate

Chapter 23

Cheryl was late getting home from the photo studio on Wednesday. Kate was ready for her date, and Bonny had just eaten dinner.

"I'm sorry. Things just piled up today."

"It's okay. Rob won't be here for fifteen more minutes."

"Yeah but I hate cutting it close." She pulled off her jacket, flipped off her pumps. She went to the cabinet in the kitchen where Kate kept the alcohol, poured herself a small snifter of brandy. Kate followed her to the living room.

"What's the matter?"

Cheryl sat down, swirled her glass. "Rough day."

"I'm all ears. Did you argue with Richard?"

"No. But I did tell him he was a turd for going out with someone else."

Kate cringed. "Really?"

"To be fair, we had a non-exclusive agreement. We both wanted it that way. Originally."

"Friends with benefits?"

"Yeah, sorta."

"So what's the problem?"

Cheryl stared at Kate, gave her a look Kate had never seen before. It was hard, hurt, and yet vulnerable.

"I'm pregnant," she said simply.

Kate lowered herself to the couch. "Oh."

"I cannot believe how stupid I am. Me, of all people."

"How did it happen?"

"The usual way. Lots of groaning and moaning and penetration."

"I mean, how did you not prevent it?"

"The stupid part? Me, stopping the pill two months ago, he, not bothering with a condom, me, stupidly thinking I couldn't possibly be ovulating *that night*, right? He, not

205

worrying a damn bit about it. Two normally clear-headed, responsible adults acting like horny school kids."

"What will you do?"

"What can I do? Get an abortion."

"Oh, no. Are you sure?"

"Kate, what the hell would I do with a baby? I'm a working stiff. I'm not the maternal type. I have no husband, not even a flippin' gay one, to help me. She would grow up screwed up, hate me, leave home and do drugs. I'll be in a rest home and she'll be in prison."

"Won't you tell Richard?"

"What would be the point? He doesn't love me, certainly doesn't want a child tying him down."

"How do you know that? He's the father, he has a right to know."

"Like Paulie had a right to know you lost the baby?"

"That was different."

"Convenient response."

"Look. Think this through, okay? Between us, we can take care of another baby. She could turn out to be the love of your life."

"I need a man for that, first."

"Just don't do anything rash."

Cheryl shrugged. "I just want to not think about it right now. You go on out, have a bang-up time. I've got Ariel, Belle and Buzz Lightyear to keep me company. 'Kay?"

Kate gave her a brief hug just as the doorbell rang.

"Tough week?" he asked, as they drove to Universal Citiwalk.

"Yes. Most definitely. Any moment now, we are bound to have a meteor shower right here on the freeway."

Rob reached over, squeezed her hand. "Just let it all go, for tonight, okay?"

"If I can."

"Paulie giving you more trouble?"

"No. He's laying low. It's Cheri."

"She's not upset about us, too, is she?"

"Nothing to do with us. She just has a problem she needs to address."

"Let me guess. Has to do with a dude."

"Yes."

"He's married."

"Um..."

"He's doing someone else."

"Yes. That's part of it."

"He wants casual sex, she wants a commitment."

"Not exactly. There are extenuating circumstances."

"Shit. She's pregnant?"

"I didn't tell you that. But since she didn't call you and not tell you about me, I guess I can *not* tell you about her."

"Man. That's a bitch. What's she gonna do?"

"I don't know yet. I offered her any kind of help. She's wallowing in it right now, but knowing her, she'll make a decision and move quickly."

Rob shook his head. "My sister got an abortion. We never told Mom, she would've killed us."

"What happened?"

"Shanie got knocked up by this guy from school. Typical scenario. Our folks would have been devastated. I drove her to this free clinic. It was over in no time. I felt sorry for her."

"Did she ever regret it?"

"I know she does, now."

They put on oversized glasses and yarn wigs to enter the blaze of Citiwalk, where every night was Saturday night. In front of the marquee, Rob stared up at the films playing.

"*It Could Happen to You*," he read, and Kate shrugged. "Well, it could," Rob added.

"Great. I love Nick Cage."

They sat through the film, laughing, holding hands, enjoying an occasional "stolen kiss" between bites of popcorn. Afterward, he bought ice cream cones which they ate on the way back to the car.

The mood was comfortable. They talked about things they might do in the weeks to come. A new alternative rock band debuting at the Wiltern. The poppy festival would occur in two weeks. The Getty was bringing a display of Native American art.

Kate marveled at how much they had in common. How easy it was to agree.

Rob drove into the driveway and stopped just behind Paulie's Audi.

"What the devil," Kate said, looking quickly at Rob.

He turned to her. "Should I split? Or do you want me to come in? Your choice."

"Come in with me. The house lights are on, he's probably talking with Cheryl."

"Okay. Let's do it."

Paulie and Cheryl were sitting in the living room. Paulie looked completely different from their last meeting. He was wearing a black beret, the subtle black eye makeup she liked best. A black, loose-fitting suit and a black shirt beneath. He seemed a little nervous, but wide-open. He immediately stood, held out his hand.

"Rob. Good to see you, man." He gave Rob a brief stare, then looked away.

"Paul. Same here."

"Hello, Paulie," Kate said softly, glancing from Paulie to Cheryl, whose expression was non-committal. "What's, uh, what's up?"

"Cheryl and I were just having a spot of tea. I didn't realize how late it was. I should be going."

"No, don't leave. Rob, tea?"

"Sounds good."

Rob sat on the easy chair, across from where Paulie and Cheryl were parked on the couch. Cheryl got up.

"I'll get a fresh pot."

Kate felt a moment of panic. She wanted to follow Cheryl, ask about Paulie, but hesitated to leave the two men alone. She opted for the fifteen seconds it would take Cheryl to brief her.

"He's fine," Cheryl whispered. "Sober, clear-headed. Hear him out, okay?"

"Why wouldn't I?" Kate returned with a frown, then went quickly back to the living room. She sat on the ottoman, which had been pushed aside.

"So, what's up?" she repeated lamely, folding her hands in her lap.

"As a matter of fact, I do have some things I want to run by you."

"Maybe you want to talk in private," Rob said.

"No, no, really. It's nothing you can't hear. All things considered."

Paulie turned back to Kate. "I've leased a home in London. In Hampstead. It's a lovely old estate, three stories, with a garden and a view of the park. It even has a name. *Chanticleer*."

Kate's eyebrows lifted. "You're going back? When?"

"Friday."

"So soon?"

"Wait, there's more." He took a sip of tea. "Peg and the kiddies are moving in, to the second floor. It's a flat all in its own."

"Oh. Wow."

Cheryl returned, put down a pot. "This needs to sit a little."

"I haven't received any papers yet, from your attorney or otherwise," Paulie continued. "But—" he stopped her when Kate opened her mouth to explain. "But, here's the deal. I'm letting the flat go. This house has always been yours, anyway, your car, you know, whatever. I won't need any of it. If and when I return to L.A., there are always places to stay. There's the money, you let me know how much you need on a, you know, regular basis." He paused, folded his hands in his lap. "About Bonny, well, I assume you'll agree to joint custody."

Kate began to quiver inside. She wasn't prepared for this talk, this night, with Rob sitting beside her. She wanted to run. "Of course," she said softly.

"And…and I'd like to take her with me on Friday. For a visit."

"Friday!" Kate blurted. "You're talking about day after tomorrow?"

"Yeah. Her passport's all in order, and I'd love to have her with me for a bit. Say, a couple of weeks. Peg will be there, and the cousins. She'll have a grand time."

"Oh, I don't know, Paul. That's—that's so quick." What was he thinking?

"Her being there would make it...easier."

The silence in the room was palpable. Cheryl picked up the teapot. "Okay. That's probably long enough," she said comically, pouring the weak tea into Rob's cup, then Kate's.

Paulie turned to Rob. "You obviously have spent some time with our daughter. What do you think?"

Rob looked surprised. "It's not for me to say." He glanced at Kate, then back to Paulie. "I don't think it's necessarily a bad idea, though. She's a smart little cookie. From what I hear, she's a great traveler. And," he added, taking a sip of tea, "she certainly adores her father."

Paulie gave a nod, then spoke to Cheryl. "And you, Auntie. Do you think she should go with me?"

"Two weeks? I personally don't think it's any big deal. She could use a dose of Peg's iron hand, if you ask me. Maybe when she comes home she'll actually mind a bit."

Kate's face grew warm. She couldn't believe what she was hearing. She stood up. "Excuse me." She hurried up the stairway and down the hall to her room, closed the door. Sat down on the bed, confused and angry.

He was right behind her, closing the door behind him. She stared up at him. "How could you ambush me like that? No warning. Just out of the blue."

"It wasn't meant to be an ambush."

"Don't take her. You *can't* take her."

Paulie looked down at her, leaned back against the dresser. He looked fearful, fragile. "Please."

"This is because I asked you for the divorce, isn't it? Your way of getting back at me."

"No. It would be your way of helping me to get through this. Look." He approached, stuck his hands in his pockets. "I'm doing my best. I'm honestly trying to make this work. I'm sorry I didn't ask sooner, but it only occurred to me today. You are denying me on principle, not on practicality."

Kate looked on his dear face. The "queen" of the weekend before was away for the night. This was Paulie at his most core.

"If it's too much to ask, then I'll accept that." He turned, picked up the wedding picture from the dresser, stared at it. "If the situation were different, I don't think you'd hesitate. You know I'll take good care of her."

She nodded.

"You have a lot going on here. You have a new love, you have an old entanglement to disconnect. That would be me, of course. Cheryl's gonna need your attention, too. Yeah, she told me. All this and I can't help but think...my leaving will affect you as well. Having Bonny out of your hair for a bit isn't all a bad thing."

He put down the photo, then took Kate's hands, squeezed them. Urged her acceptance.

Having Bonny gone would be worse. But Kate realized that right now, Paulie needed their daughter more than she would. She wet her lips, nodded. "Okay."

"Brilliant," he said softly.

"What about Alec? Is he going?"

"No."

Paulie looked down, hiding his eyes from her. She stood, placed her hands on his cheeks.

"Paulie. Look at me. *Look* at me."

Clearly reluctant, he turned his gaze back upon her.

She saw the unbridled grief. "I'm sorry. I'm so sorry."

"Don't be. It's my lot. I'll live with it." He turned his head, kissed the palm of her hand. "We'd best get back down there before your boyfriend thinks the worst."

He habitually straightened his trousers. Kate walked to the door but did not open it; Paulie was close behind her, and he whispered into her ear. "Happy Birthday, darling."

She walked Rob to his car.

"I'm really sorry about all that," she muttered. "You must think this is dysfunction junction."

"He's like a needle under your skin. But I guess when you've been together as long you two have, it's easy to resort to manipulation."

"You think Paul is manipulating me?"

"He's just scraping the bottom of his barrel of resources. I can't say I blame him."

Kate wasn't sure she understood his tone. "Can I call you Friday after they leave? I might be a little needy."

"Why don't I drive you all to LAX? Then you won't have to call anyone." He put his arms around her, tucking her comfortably against him. "Let me help, Kate. I know this is tough." Without waiting for a response, he kissed her once, twice, then got into his car. She watched from the driveway until his taillights disappeared around the corner.

Kate went back into the house, her emotions churning. Paulie waited just inside the door, his lanky frame leaning against the wall.

"Are you leaving, too?" she asked without enthusiasm.

"I've already worn out my welcome."

She shook her head. "You haven't." She started to follow him out.

"No. Don't. I can still find my car on my own. And if you go outside with me, in the moonlight, I might make you kiss *me* goodnight, too, and I know that's not on your agenda."

Kate stepped back, considered him. "You *are*," she said.

"I am, what?"

"Manipulating me."

"That's absurd. Don't be ridiculous."

She pushed him out the door, shoving him gently all the way to his car.

"What the hell are you doing?"

She advanced on him, until he was pressed backward against the Audi. She looked up; indeed, there was near a full moon.

"How can I let such a little person intimidate me so?" he asked quietly.

"The same way I let my favorite drag queen manipulate me," she responded. Lifting up on tiptoe, she planted a chaste kiss on his lips and then retreated to the house.

Rob made good on his word, arriving at six a.m. to pick them up. Paulie sat in the front seat, Kate in the back with Bonny. She talked quietly to her daughter en route.

212

"You must mind Auntie Peg, understand?"

"Yes, Mummy."

"And Daddy, too. Auntie Cheryl and I won't be there to watch you all the time. You need to be extra good."

"I will. Daddy has a little girl room. Can we get the puppy when I come back?"

"Maybe. Just be a good girl."

Kate looked ahead, at the backs of the two men in her life. It felt incredibly strange to see them sitting side-by-side in the front seats of Rob's BMW.

"British Airways, right?" Rob asked.

"Yeah."

"First or Business class?"

"First. I'm seriously spoiled."

"Why not," Rob said. "I remember the first time I flew my mom out to California in First. She talked about it for days. 'Oh, Robbie! They took such pains to make us all comfortable. Drinks before we even left the airport!'."

Paulie chuckled. "My favorite part, actually. My mum passed before I was able to do the same. Not sure she would've flown anyway; she was a bit of the homebound type."

"Your dad gone, too?" Rob asked.

"Yeah. Heart attack. My mum was run down by a lorry in a goddam crosswalk in Surrey."

"Man, that's tough."

"It's sad, really. I would have liked Bonny to know her grandparents, such as they were. They are her heritage."

Kate listened from the backseat. She realized this was a side of Paulie she'd never known. He rarely spoke of his parents.

Soon, they were at the gate. Kate couldn't let go of Bonny.

"I will miss you lots and lots. If you need to talk to Mommy, you tell Daddy to call me, okay?"

Bonny nodded.

"Auntie Peg will make sure you have everything you need."

Bonny nodded again. "I'm going with Daddy. We'll have lots of fun. I get to see his baby house."

Kate smiled, fighting tears. "That's good."

Because she couldn't let go, Rob pulled Bonny gently away, gave the tot a brief hug. "We'll see you in a couple of weeks, half pint. Enjoy your time with your dad."

Paulie took the opportunity to embrace Kate.

"This is it, then," he murmured.

"Don't go getting all maudlin."

"I was born maudlin."

"Keep in touch. Call me anytime," she said.

"Don't worry. You have the new address?"

"Yes." She looked up at him, unable to hide her grief. "When will I ever see you again?"

He lifted his chin, sighed. "I don't know. Just take care of your own life for a while." He took a moment, swallowed. "Just remember...remember all the things I've said to you. Remember," he paused, pressed his mouth close to her ear, "what we've shared. I may be on the other side of this bloody world, but I'm still here for you. Rob's a good egg. Get him to commit to you, darling. And ignore me when I am being my morose self. I'm the worst kind of bastard sometimes."

Kate heard the loudspeaker calling his flight. She glanced at Rob, who stood nearby, holding Bonny.

"Just a sec," she called. "Take care of yourself, Paulie. Please. I know a lot of nastiness has gone down between us. But I'm still here for you, too. You understand? Don't go off and get all fucked up again. I mean it."

He smiled, rolled his eyes in a way that spoke of his feminine side. "Honestly. You don't think I would do that, do you?"

"I want to be able to trust you."

"Don't lose sleep. "

She hugged him, fiercely. Completely overwhelmed by her feelings of loss. She kissed him, unconcerned about who might be watching. "I love you, Paulie."

After a lingering look, he turned, took Bonny from Rob, and proceeded through the gate.

Chapter 24

She told Rob she wanted to spend time with Cheryl. It wasn't completely a lie, but his expression said he understood her need to be alone for a while. When Cheryl's car was missing from the driveway, he didn't say a word.

"She's probably getting food," Kate mumbled.

"I'll be around," he told her as she started to get out of the car. Kate hesitated, leaned over and kissed his cheek.

"Thanks. And thanks for this morning. Couldn't have done that alone."

"Yes, you could have. But you didn't have to. Call you later."

She paced the house, picking up small toys and moving laundry around. She tidied up Bonny's room and changed her sheets, then closed the bedroom door.

In her own room, she took the framed wedding picture off the highboy and put it inside her top dresser drawer, then took it out again. She sat down, stared at hers and Paulie's smiling faces as they stood in the wet sand of Malibu.

"You cheeky bastard," she whispered, smiling. "I don't regret it, Paulie. I would do it again. I would."

All that serious, grown up talk about divorce, custody, division of property—what was that all about? What was happening? Had she set in motion something she couldn't stop?

She pressed the photo to her breast. No, she didn't want to stop it. She and Paulie had a knack for perpetuating their own misery. Holding each other back, despite their devotion to one another.

Kate didn't know when she dozed off, but she awoke near five p.m., still clutching the photo. Stretching, she realized when she heard the front door that it must have been Cheryl's car in the driveway that woke her. She placed the picture frame on her dresser, then went downstairs.

Cheryl met her in the foyer. They stared at one another, the tall blonde and the short redhead. Cheryl took off her coat and hung it in the closet.

"How'd it go this morning?" she asked, her voice flat.

"About how you'd think. Not too bad. They took off at 8:30 a.m. They'll be flying for a couple more hours still."

"Bonny okay?"

"She was the best of all."

"Of course. Kids are like tanks."

"Have you eaten?"

"Not hungry right now."

Kate nodded, caught herself wringing her hands.

"Yeah, I'm not really hungry either. You in for the night?"

"Yeah, you? You going over to Rob's?"

"No."

Cheryl nodded. "I actually could use a drink. Want one?"

"*Yes.*"

"Looks like rain again. What's that, twice this year?" She went to the bar off the family room. "I got a taste for hot buttered rum."

"Sounds great." Kate sat down on the couch, tried not to fidget. "Have you thought about what you're going to do?"

"Like I can think about anything else," Cheryl called back.

"And?"

"Thought about it, done it."

Kate turned abruptly. "You did it? Today?"

"Yesterday. I'm fine, I'm past it, it won't happen again."

The microwave dinged. Cheryl returned with their drinks.

"And before you launch into twenty-one, you might as well know. No, I didn't tell O'Neill. The man is married. The other squeeze was his wife, in from New York. Contrary to popular belief, they are not getting a divorce. And when they locate Cheryl Collins' brain, we'll shoot you out an email notification."

Kate shook her head, picked up the mug. "Well, that basically sucks."

"And it's over. Cheers."

They both drank the rum quickly and Cheryl made them seconds. "What is it, you think, that makes men such assholes?" Cheryl asked. "Oh, wait. You're in love again. I can't dis Rob."

"You can do whatever you want, and I never said I was in love again."

Cheryl tilted her head. "Okay, that's fair. You like him, don't you?"

"Of course I do. He's...everything a girl could want."

"How was he with Paulie?"

"They continue to act like they are nothing but friends."

"Helpful. But you and Rob...I see real potential there. Don't wait too long."

Kate considered Cheryl's advice. "I don't want to rush into anything. And honestly, I'm still...you know, I'm still..."

"Not over him. Yeah, I get that." Cheryl took a gulp. "Kate. It's okay. I know I've been a complete and utter hag about Paul. But really, truly, there is no one on Earth who can pass judgment on either of you, or the fact that you crossed cultures. He could have been black. He could have been a priest. He could have been a fucking death row inmate. Who you love is nobody's business. It's the quality of the love that counts. It's the devotion, the friendship. Not everybody finds what you found with him."

Kate nodded, drank down her rum. "Right. Now remind me of why I'm divorcing him."

Cheryl fluttered her eyelashes. "It's *so* cliché, cuz. Irreconcilable differences. Oh, and the fact that he needs to have physical relationships with men. There's *that*."

"Right. Now I remember."

"More? Cheryl asked, tapping Kate's empty cup.

"Sure."

Kate could hardly stand up to get the phone when it rang at around 9:30.

"Hi Mummy!" Bonny sang out. "We're in Daddy's new house! It's so big! It's got two upstairses!"

"Bonny, sweetheart. I'm so glad to hear your, your voice. How was the, uh, uh, plane ride?"

"It was fun. Daddy and me took a big nap."

"Good. That's real g'ood."

"Here's Daddy! Bye!"

Kate closed her eyes, waited for Paulie.

"Wanted you to know that we just got in and I haven't managed to lose her yet."

"Mmm. Wonnerful."

"Blasted heat wasn't on, so we're wearing coats until it warms up a bit. The sun isn't even up yet."

"What – what time is it?"

"5:35 a.m. Are you all right, darling?"

"Fine. Jus' a little tired. Me 'n Cheri are drinking, because, basically, the whole world sucks big and it just doesn't matter."

"Good Lord, Katrina."

"What's good for the goose, I say."

"Yes, the gander. I see. Maybe you need to go to bed."

"Ha! The kettle is calling the black pot advice. Look, I got no place to go, no people to see. So don't slag on me or whatever the hell you say."

She could hear Paulie laughing. She refused to let herself like the sound. She wanted to be mad. "Stop laughing, you fuckhead."

Now he was hysterical.

"Don't lose my daughter. You keep her warm, dammit."

Paulie tried to stop laughing. "Is Rob there?"

"No. I sent him away. Just Cheri and me. Poor Cheri, Paulie. I'm so sad for her."

"I know, darling. Take care of her, will you? And yourself. Go to bed."

"Give Bons a smooch for me, okay? And don't tell her that her mother's shit-faced, please?"

"I'll keep your nasty little secret, love."

☞ *In retrospect, I did ambush her. But it was the only way I'd have been able get her to let me take Bonny. She's too*

218

strong for me. Her strength is only an asset when she's on my side.

I needed Bonny to keep me sane and clean. What kind of dad would do smack in front of his three-year-old daughter? Not that I really thought I would, but a little insurance isn't a bad thing. I love spending time with her, anyway. She's just brilliant. So full of joy, her mother's passion and smile. I wanted her to have time with the cousins, too.

Hearing Kate juiced up on the phone made me laugh. She rarely lets herself lose control. It surely didn't do her any harm, and I don't feel guilty about it. I did, once, back when we were in the apartment and I was still on the rattle. We'd had a particularly "trying" day—me trying to escape the flat in search of skag, her trying to keep me inside and alive. She was so overwrought by the day's end she drank a couple of pints of Guinness and then honked up the lot of it. I felt so sorry for her, I was mostly cooperative the next day.—Paulie

Chapter 25

Early December, 1994. Hollywood, CA – Four months later

Kate's hands were rock-steady as she applied the thin, foam prosthetic nose to the alien sitting on the stool in front of her. Using special brushes and adhesives, she smoothed the piece against the actor's skin. She'd already worked on him for nearly an hour. It would be another ninety minutes before he was ready for wardrobe.

She took a break, sipped some coffee. Eyed her silent cell phone, willing it to ring. Bonny's inaugural day at preschool was clearly more difficult on the mother than the child. For the first time in years, she wished she still smoked.

When the phone did ring, she nearly dropped it into a pot of silicone.

"Is this Kate?" A man's voice. British. Not Paulie.

"Yes?"

"It's Alec. Alec Doyle."

Surprised, Kate felt her spirits lift. She found a quiet corner to take the call.

"How's little Bonny?"

"She's all grown up. She's in a pre-kindergarten class now. Today's the first day. I've been a nervous wreck all day."

"Ah, she'll do nicely. You'll see. I've never seen such a charming, articulate child. I miss her."

"She misses you, too. You really should stop by sometime to see her. I mean, if you want to."

"I don't want to confuse her any more than she probably already is." Alec's voice softened, and Kate noted a level of sadness.

"I really don't know what Paulie said to her. He's in Britain, you know."

"Yes, I heard. Oh, sorry. Can you hold the line a moment?" Alec spoke to someone else, and then returned. "Kate, I apologize. Never a moment's peace around here."

"So, what do you do? I don't recall ever hearing it."

"I'm a doctor."

"No kidding? I would never have guessed."

"Mm. It gets worse. I'm a clinical psychologist."

Now Kate paused, her eyes wide. "You're a shrink? Was Paulie your…"

"My patient. Yes. And I've just breached doctor-patient confidentiality."

Thoughts raced through Kate's mind. Paulie hadn't even finished high school. "Wow. This is really a shock."

"I know. I'm sorry. He came to me just after, you know, the incident in London. But let me first tell you, after a couple of meetings, I stopped treating him. It would have been unethical, because I was in love."

"With Paul."

"Yeah."

Kate sighed, then pushed back a lock of hair that repeatedly fell across her eyes. "He does have a way, doesn't he? I don't suppose you've talked to him since he left."

"No. You have, of course?"

"He calls Bonny several times a week."

"Well, that's good, at least."

"He's nothing if not a devoted father."

"One of the things I love about him."

Kate's image of Alec shifted. Strong, but soft-spoken. Didn't quite fit her picture of the kind of man Paulie found attractive. Well, she thought, he looks more like Hugh Grant than Jamie Pritchard. "You miss him, don't you?"

"Deeply." Alec paused, as if searching. "My feelings don't make you uncomfortable, do they?"

"Not at all. In fact, I'm rather happy that you care so much. I hate to think of Paulie getting, you know, hooked up with people who might not really love him." Kate hesitated, wondering if she was saying too much. "He's…he's very lonely. He's been back in London for, what, four months? He hasn't taken a lover, to my knowledge."

222

"Are you certain?"

"I think so, yeah. I think he would tell me."

Alec's silence spoke volumes. The fact that Paulie was alone was clearly significant.

At last he spoke. "Thanks for the chat, Katie. I'm sure I'm keeping you. Don't hesitate to call now and again, eh?"

"Go see him."

"What? I couldn't. He wouldn't want to see me."

"Get yourself a ticket. Today. He lives in Hampstead. I'll give you his address, his number."

"You think?"

"He's living with his sister and her boatload of kids. He would welcome a visit from an old friend."

"But what if...what if he's got someone there?"

"It's a risk. Are you telling me that Paulie Bingham isn't worth a risk?"

She heard Alec chuckle. "I do have friends in Kensington."

He gave her his number, and Kate read off Paulie's home address before hanging up. Kate wondered if Alec had gotten what he called for.

For Christmas, Rob gave her a diamond tennis bracelet. She gave him one of the forty-five, original Indiana Jones fedoras. It saddened her that they would be apart, but her parents and aunt were coming in for the holidays. She couldn't just leave them.

"This airport thing seems to be a recurring theme with us," she observed, standing by as Rob lifted his suitcase out of her trunk.

"A way of life," he lamented. "Wish you were coming with me."

"I know. I just—need to have Christmas here, with my family. You understand."

"Of course I do. It's the same with me. Mom would be heartbroken if I didn't show."

He embraced her, held her much longer than usual. Kate noted LAX police eyeing them, her car parked in the white zone, flashers blinking.

"I'll miss you," he said, stroking her hair away from her cheek, kissing her forehead. "We'll talk."

Kate nodded. "Give your parents my regrets. We'll meet one of these days."

"Bet on it. Merry Christmas." He gave her a brief kiss, then grabbed his bag.

She wept on the way home. Rob's departure for South Carolina had added another layer to the melancholy that began with her feeble attempt to trim her Christmas tree two nights before. The decorations were from her old life. They belonged not to her, but to her and Paulie. Each shining ornament had a history and was a piece of their story. Some were personalized with names and dates. Yet Paulie was 5500 miles away, having Christmas with his sister. Soon, Rob would be 2600 miles gone.

Kate knew she was letting the loneliness swallow her, was powerless to change it. Paulie had called their marriage "an old entanglement to disconnect." She wondered if he had as much difficulty disconnecting as she did. They were deeply entwined. The weekly phone calls were not enough, and yet she knew they had to be. She kept up a brave face for Bonny, a poker face for Cheryl and Rob.

Rob was her star. She saw him most weekends, and he always thrilled her. Yet she knew in her heart she wasn't letting their affair progress. The divorce wasn't even final. Dismantling her life with Paulie consumed too much emotional energy.

Was it more? She wondered if she feared committing to Rob, of letting herself get too close. She'd given so much before, and had failed miserably. She knew she wasn't up to any more mistakes.

"He's not a mistake," she affirmed aloud. *He's anything but*. Rob clearly adored her, and he was being extremely patient. She sensed he wanted to move forward, take another step, but she held back. Kate huffed out a breath. Perhaps *she* was Rob's mistake.

She sat in her car for a few moments once in the garage, mentally preparing herself to go inside and face her expectant family. For she was central to their happiness. She couldn't let them down.

Chapter 26

Christmas Eve, 1994. Hampstead, London

"Open your bleedin' mouth, Paulie." Peg pushed a fork at his face. "You've got to try this. For Mum."

"Mum never forced me to eat anything," Paulie complained, but he opened his mouth and let his sister shove in a bit of mince pie. "Mm. Mm." He swallowed, shook his head. "Frightfully delicious, Pegalicious, actually."

"That's a good chap. Now, help me get the table set. We've not seen the Talbots for ages. On your best behavior, scoundrels," she called to the children, the youngest of which were, as usual, roughhousing on the floor.

"Tell me again. Who are these Talbots?"

"Mum's sister Eleanor's son Edward, his wife Regine, Eleanor's daughter Meg. They're our cousins, so try to be civil, eh?"

"Meg and Ed are coming here? That's amazing. Where do they all live?"

Peg bustled between the stove and the pantry. "Ed and Regine are down from York. Meg lives over in Covent Garden. She's an ar-teest."

"Amazing," Paulie repeated. He'd all but forgotten he had other relatives. Distraction was good.

He checked his watch, waiting for the right time to call Bonny. And Kate. Still too early.

"Get over here, you scurvy dogs!" he shouted at the four children, who obediently lined up in front of him. "All righty, mates. You! Napkins. We'll need nine of each. You! Plate duty." Two of the children scampered to the cupboards. "And you— you're tableware patrol. Got it?"

Only little Ingrid was left.

"I've a very special job for you, Ing. You are to sit beside the window and watch for our guests. When they ring the

225

bell, you open the door and shout, 'Merry Christmas' as loud as you can. Will you do that?"

"Sure, Uncle Paul. I can do it."

"Now, then. Anything else you need me to do?" he asked Peg, who merely grunted.

Meg and Ed were nothing like he remembered them. Of course, he remembered them as nine-year-old thieves. He'd hated them, hated that they were twins, hated that his mother treated them so well when he was banished to do chores.

Ed Talbot was now a stuffed shirt. Paulie wondered where he'd left his bowler, briefcase and umbrella. Regine, his wife, was exotic and quiet, but seemed friendly enough. Meg, on the other hand, was talkative and she exuded a familiar warmth. While Ed spewed forth his Conservative viewpoint, Meg egged him on with her Liberal jibes. Paulie thought it all great fun.

"Thatcher? Terrible sense of style. So bad that my mates and I mimicked her," Paulie said over dinner. "If we liked it, it had to have been horrid."

Ed frowned. "We don't speak ill of the prime minister in our household."

"Didn't speak ill of her, only her dowdy clothing."

Ed regarded Paulie. "I don't see how a man who wears women's clothing could have any valid opinion anyway."

Regine looked up, glanced from Paulie to Ed. "What do you mean?"

Paulie's smile challenged Ed. *Go on, say it.*

"He's bent, dear."

Jacob, Peg's thirteen year old, put down his fork. "Damn right he is, and proud o' it!"

Laughing, Paulie held out a "high five" to his nephew across the table. Peg fussed.

"Don't encourage him, Paulie. Jacob, we'll refrain from profanity at the table. It's Christmas, for Christ's sake."

"Indeed," Paulie mumbled. He caught a shy smile from Regine.

"I say we toast," Meg announced, lifting her wine glass. "Here's to all who are bent, or otherwise blessed with uniqueness."

Paulie looked at Meg, then lifted his glass. "Here, here."

Her brother merely grimaced.

After dishes were done, Paulie put on his mac. "I'm going for a short walk, Peg."

His sister heaved her ample bosom. "You'd best be back for gifts or I'll have your arse m'self."

"No worries. Just a walk round."

"I'll go along. I'll have him back, Aunt Peggy." Meg wrapped her scarf around her neck, put on her raincoat. Paulie held the door for her.

They walked a block before Paulie spoke his mind. "What was that, then, at the table?"

"My toast?"

"Yeah. I wasn't sure, were you poking fun at me?"

"Poking fun, yes, but not at you. It's my homophobic brother who earned that comment."

"Ah. I see."

"He's quite uncomfortable around us both."

"Both?"

"I'm bent too, dear cousin."

Paulie stopped walking, turned toward Meg. "You're a lesbian?"

"Yeah."

"When did you come out?"

"Oh, I'd say it's been about ten years now. It really stews him, since twins normally share so much." They resumed their walk. "We used to be close. Not like identicals, but still— we shared a lot. When I confided that I was gay, he couldn't handle it. Like it's some kind of reflection on him. Sad, really."

"Incredibly sad."

"So it's true you've split from your wife?"

"Yeah."

"How was that, being married to a straight girl? Or is she really straight?"

"Oh, she's arrow straight, all right. But..." he paused, gathering a picture. "She's very tolerant. We had a good life together, most of the time."

"I've often wondered about you."

"So have I," Paulie said, chuckled. "So do you have a partner?"

227

"I do. She's with her family tonight. Shame, eh? It's not easy. My mum's dead, Dad's who-knows-where, and Ed's an arse. It was so nice of Peg to invite us round."

"What's her name?"

"Shannon. And guess what? She's black, too."

Paul laughed. "Double whammy."

"You? Anyone new, since the split?"

"Nah. Well, there was one. Alec. He'll likely never speak to me again. He's…he's great. Very devoted. But typical of me, I blew him off. I miss him, now."

"Maybe you should get in touch."

"We had other problems. Like, he's not out."

"Oh. That's a big problem."

"Yeah. Always sneaking. But he was really a good sport. He loves Bonny." *Bonny*. Paulie looked at his watch. "Which reminds me. I can't forget to call her."

Paulie mused as they walked. He'd never been able to read gay women. Had Meg not confided in him, he wouldn't have guessed at her sexuality. She was pretty, with long, golden curls and green eyes, not unlike his own. Her confession made him feel good. Not so alone.

"Are you and your ex on speaking terms?"

"We've never not been." He slowed, looked at Meg while he strolled. "I love my wife. We're still…very close. She's an incredible person."

"Then why?"

Paulie shrugged. "It's complicated. Or simple, depending on whom you ask. I found out I can't be straight, Kate found out she can't deal with that. It wasn't fair to either. But we hated splitting up." Paulie stopped. They were back in front of his house. "She has a new boyfriend now, and it's…it's difficult."

"I can imagine. But it sounds like you're still friends. That's good, right?"

"Yeah. It's good."

He waited until midnight to call, knowing Kate had planned a four o'clock dinner. She answered on the first ring.

"Merry Christmas, darling."

"Merry Christmas, Paul. It's so good to hear your voice."

"Thinking the same thing. Who all's round there?"

"Mom and Pop, Marta, Cheryl. That's all. And Bonny, of course. How about there?"

"Well, Peggers and brood, and my cousins Meg and Ed, and Ed's lovely wife. We've all just had a fine meal, opened some gifties, and had a rousing round of 'Deck the Halls'."

"Did I know you had cousins?"

"Not likely, since I'd not thought of them myself in ages. Megs is quite nice, no use for Ed, though."

"Let me guess: he's not liberated."

"Do the words 'anal-retentive' conjure a picture?"

"Ugh. I vote to banish him. Do you want to talk to Bonny?"

"Not yet, darling. In a moment. I feel like I haven't talked to you in a decade." He mentally dared her to remind him it had been only five days. She didn't disappoint him.

"I know. It does seem like forever. I was wondering, will you be coming to L.A. anytime soon?"

I could be there tomorrow. He had to bite his tongue.

"No plans right now. Are you…is everything all right?"

"Sure. Everything's fine. I was just wondering, that's all."

"You could come round here."

She didn't respond right away, and Paulie smiled. "There I go, sticking my foot in it again."

"No, you didn't. Maybe…maybe in the spring."

"You're welcome any time."

December 26, 1994. London

Meg and Shannon went with him to Ian's on Boxing Day. After several weeks of turning a cold shoulder, Paulie had forgiven his old friend and looked forward to his annual day-after-Christmas party. Meg was immediately comfortable with his friends, and Paulie tried to relax. He still hesitated when someone handed him a joint. Awash with guilt and fear, he took a quick toke and passed it on. Meg smiled at him, gave him a look that said she'd be the designated responsible party.

229

When the cigarette came around again, he held it up. "Just pot, right?"

"Yeah, yeah, just weed. Seriously. Can't afford anything stronger. But you could," Ian said with a laugh.

"Naw. This is enough. Believe me, mate. You don't want to go there."

He paced himself. Felt the slow buzz, the funniness, the softening edges of his world. Jon appeared, sat beside him.

"Still pissed off?" he asked.

Paulie shrugged, turned to Jon, and lifted his chin. "You didn't mean any harm. But I want to set the record straight. Kate's for real. You got that, right?"

Jon nodded aggressively. "Yeah, I do. I'm so sorry, Paulie. I felt horrible when I found out what I'd done."

"Lose it. It's past."

"Great. So, you want to?" He gestured over his shoulder.

"Maybe later. Stick around?"

Jon put his arm around Paulie and squeezed. "I'm not going anywhere. You say when."

Paulie got the roach when it came around the last time, and he inhaled deeply, closed his eyes.

Spring. She said maybe, in the spring. It was eons away. If she missed him, she hid it well. His warring sides resumed the fight in his head. *Wait for her; don't wait, you bloody fool. It's over. Long over. You lost your chance to keep her.*

Jon, he realized, had his hand on Paulie's thigh. The combination was fully intoxicating, and he handed the now-empty clip to someone else. Wetting his lips, he stood up, held out his hand to Jon.

December 28, 1994. Beverly Hills, CA
"Miss Newman? Dr. Doyle will see you now."

Kate following the receptionist down the hallway and entered an office at the end. By all appearances, the doctor did very well.

Alec stood up, a stunned smile on his face. She'd never taken a lot of notice before, but Alec was quite handsome. Broad shouldered, well proportioned. Clear, blue eyes that crinkled when he laughed. Short, brown hair that he probably hated because it curled. Suit and tie.

"Kate! What a wonderful surprise. Now I realize why I didn't recognize the name. You're incognito." He walked around her, closed the door and gave her a hug. "You needn't have made an appointment to see me."

"Yes, I did. I'm a paying customer, today."

"Oh, dear. Please, sit down. Is something wrong?"

Kate fidgeted with her handbag, gave up a weak smile. "I'm not doing too well."

"How can I help? Is it about Paulie?"

"I'm just not adjusting. I know, it's awkward, for you, but...I thought since you know him, and me, it would be easier, you know."

"Of course. What is it, exactly, you are finding so difficult? Is it the divorce? Second thoughts?"

"No, not really. But I just, I just think about him all the time. I worry about him, wonder about him, I want to see him."

"Good thing he's across the pond, then, isn't it?" Alec gave her a benevolent smile. "And I mean that with the best intentions."

"I know you do."

"First let me say, everything you are going through is completely normal. Mind, I have to separate myself from the situation in order to stay objective, but truthfully, it's all par for the course, so they say. It's normal to process grief. We all go through it when we lose something, or someone, dear to us."

Kate nodded, felt her eyes begin to sting.

Alec snatched a tissue from a box on his desk and handed it to her. "On the subjective side, I might confide that I feel much the same way. We'd do well to be meeting in a pub rather than my office," he quipped.

"I was much stronger when we talked last week. Somehow, I just got mired in emotion the past few days."

"It's Christmas. It happens to hundreds of people every year. We associate Christmas with loved ones, happy memories, joyous times. Did you not spend the holiday with Rob?"

"No." Kate took a breath, sighed. "He needed to be with his family back east. I needed to be with mine, here. He's still back there."

"Did you speak with Paul?"

"Yeah."

"And you felt morose and melancholy afterward."

"Yeah."

"I'm sorry, Kate. I wish there was a magic wand I could wave, for both of us. How did he sound to you?"

"You treated Paulie. You lived with him, loved him. You must know about his inability to hide his feelings. In all the years we've been close, there was only one time when he honestly mistreated me. And it was mainly because he couldn't hide the truth from me, he was angry with himself and he lashed out at me."

"He holds you above all others."

"I've never quite figured it out."

"What caused the break up, if I may ask? We went round and round on it, but he could never quite explain. I've always presumed it had to do with his discomfort with his own sexuality."

"I'll put it simply. He's gay, I'm straight. The emotional parts of us fell in love. Desperately in love. We were both needy, and we locked onto each other like magnets. We figured out how to make the sex work. But his needs were stronger than his will."

Alec nodded slowly. "I understand." He straightened some pencils on his desk. "I'm embarrassed to be in the position I'm in. I know better than all this. But I can't stop thinking about him. He is the sweetest person I've ever met. When he's not being a shrew, of course."

"How was the sex between you?"

When Alec had recovered from her blunt question, he shook his head. "It was… phenomenal."

"For both of you? For Paulie?" To Alec's shocked face, she held up her hand. "Forget I asked that. It's just that…well, sex is very important to him. Like anyone else, he has his…personal quirks."

Alec straightened, cleared his throat. "Yes, I'm well aware of how to satisfy my partner. Paulie, that is."

"Then what happened? You asked *me*, so…"

"He was really bothered by your relationship with Rob Evans. I'd never seen him so upset. His was a dual personality, one-half wanting for your happiness, the other berating himself for not being the man you needed."

Kate felt her own face warm.

"I tried to get him to snap out of it. To realize that you had to move on with your life. It only made him angrier. He accused me of analyzing him. It was a big issue between us. I said some things…some things I shouldn't have, and I immediately regretted them. I hurt him."

"He's very thin skinned."

"And he couldn't understand why I've never…come out. He doesn't comprehend what it would do to my family, my career…"

Kate took note. "Your family and colleagues don't know you're gay?"

Alec shook his head. "I've wanted to come out, forever. But it's so difficult. My father is a regent at the university, a very conservative school full of stuffy old gents who would likely find some way to seek his dismissal, if not just ruin his career. Mum runs a daycare. Fancy me, a perverted, filthy homosexual around her dear little clients."

Kate drew in a breath. "Wow. I can see where that would stick in Paulie's craw. He's almost never *not* been out. He likes public display."

"Yes, I know. And it's not like I'm ashamed of my feelings for him. I'd have shouted it to the world if I could."

"So I'm sure he brought it up when you argued."

"I know I said all the wrong things. Me, a psych. But love has a way of screwing up everything you know. And I knew, I *knew* he was equating me to all those others that have hurt him before. I should have known better than to try to reason with him about you."

"What did you say, exactly?" Kate asked, her curiosity piqued.

"Just that he shouldn't have expected you to deny yourself forever. You're a woman, you naturally have needs."

Kate placed her hands on his desk and leaned slightly forward. "Let me make something perfectly clear, Alec. It was Paulie's needs that broke us up, not mine. The only need of mine not being satisfied was my need to keep him to myself. He came to me. *He* offered exclusivity. He couldn't make that happen." She sighed, felt her shoulders slump as she looked away. "I would have stayed. Forever."

"I'm sorry. I didn't mean it that way. I'm not objective, and I apologize."

"It's okay."

"So how are things going with Rob, by the by?"

Kate gave a slight shrug. "Slow. On purpose. I needed some time, after Paul left. The divorce is...just...hard. You know, I really like Rob. And he likes me. I think, maybe, we could have a chance. But right now, I'm a little scared he'll get tired of my obsession with Paul. He'll move on. I can't blame him. I'm just like a rock in the road."

"Does he want more than you're able to give right now?"

"He wants to take our relationship to another level. I can tell. He's been incredibly patient, but I can't expect him to wait forever."

"You care for him."

"A lot."

"Have you discussed your feelings? Your difficulties with Paul?"

"Touched on. Not too much."

Alec blew out a breath, diverted his eyes for a moment. He stood, walked to his window.

"Are you holding back because of Paul's jealousy?"

"I'm not sure, to be honest. I don't think so. It's easier with him being so far away. But Paul does ask me things, on the phone."

"Has it ever occurred to you that your inability to move forward with Rob could be holding Paulie back, as well?"

"What? How do you mean?"

Alec returned to his desk. "Can you see where you are walking on the top of a narrow fence? Rob on one side, Paulie on the other. Both hoping, possibly, that when you eventually fall off, you will land on his side."

Kate stared at Alec, parted her lips.

"As long as you keep Rob at an arm's length, Paulie has hope that you will return. Now, I could be wrong, very wrong. But when we talked last week, it occurred to me that maybe the reason Paulie hasn't taken up with anyone new is his undying hope that the two of you will reconcile."

Kate began to shake her head. "No. He can't possibly be hoping that. He—he signed the papers. He agreed. He moved away. He's never shown Rob anything but kindness. Acceptance."

"Let me ask you this. What do *you* think is holding you back from committing to Rob? Can you explain that to me, a non-judgmental, neutral third party?"

"You're hardly neutral." Kate let out a shaky breath. "I'm afraid. So many things. What if it doesn't work out, and Rob gets hurt? There's Bonny, to consider. If I let her get used to Rob, and we fall apart, it'll hurt her, again."

"And Paulie? How do you think he would take it if you and Rob were, say, to get married?"

"It would upset him."

"Ah. So here's Kate, worrying about Rob, and Paul, and Bonny all getting hurt. Meanwhile, her own heart is aching without respite. Tell me, dear, when will it be your time? You surprise me."

Kate frowned.

"For all that Paulie told me about you, about what a strong girl you are."

"I—I am strong. Normally. I'm just off-track, that's all. I didn't expect these feelings. It's all so jumbled."

"I suggest you imagine what life would be like if Rob did walk away. What, then, would your choices be? Alone, raising your daughter with a part-time, well-meaning but distant father? Or would you fall easily back in with Paulie, once again struggling with acceptance of his peculiarities? How long would you sentence yourself to such loneliness?"

Kate tried to envision the scenarios he offered. Neither was anything but depressing.

"Now, then. What if you were to allow yourself to enjoy this time with Rob? Can you see yourself, and Rob, having a promising future? Does he care for your daughter? Does he seem to want the same things you want?"

"He adores Bonny. We have so much fun together. He's mellow, he's kind, he's smart…and we *are* really compatible, I think."

"Let's go back, for a moment, to Paulie. The scene where you tell him, 'Paul, I'm in love with Rob. We are committed to spending our lives together. I'd really like your blessing.'"

Kate stiffened. She could already see Paulie's eyes filling with tears.

"He did give his blessing."

"But you didn't believe him."

"No. I didn't."

"Did he not once accuse you of speaking for him when you argue?"

She'd forgotten, for a moment, that Alec had originally counseled Paulie. He knew things.

"When are you going to give him back his responsibility? Look, Kate, I swear, this may sound self-serving, because you know I have feelings, I have wishes and hopes, too. But I promise you, I'm speaking in your best interest. Don't lose Rob. Don't lose your best chance for happiness. If you truly care for Rob, let yourself enjoy him! Open up; move forward, for heaven's sake. I guarantee you, Paulie will survive. He may even prosper, once he understands that you've moved on. Until that time, he's emotionally shackled."

His words stirred her wounds but were also cathartic. She needed a moment to compose herself. Emotionally shackled?

"Take your time, dear. I'll be back in a moment." Alec left the room in response to a blinking light above his door.

Kate took a carefully controlled breath, then stood and perused the books and trinkets on Alec's wall-to-wall shelf unit. A miniaturized copy of a diploma, encased in Lucite, from the University of Birmingham. Pictures of family, pets, sporting events. None of Paulie. But then, there wouldn't be photos of a male lover on the shelf of a closeted doc.

  ℐ When Kate came to my office that day, I almost suggested we not talk about her problems concerning Paulie. I was quite sure I wouldn't be able to remain impartial, as I was going through a rather difficult time myself. I had to ask myself, am I saying what's best for Kate, or for me? Am I being a friend, or an unprofessional doctor?

  For certain, I commiserated. Paulie was never far from my mind, and not a day passed that I didn't regret having hurt him that night we argued. I couldn't hide my jealousy, and it angered me that he still let Kate dominate his life. Theirs is an unhealthy relationship based on obsessive need and co-dependence. But this was one time when I should have been more lover and less therapist. Regardless of whether or not he should love Kate, the fact remains that he does and it was hurtful and irresponsible of me to analyse him in his time of great need and pain.

  I believed what I told her, in any case. She needs to move on and let Paulie go. If he knew what I'd said to her, he'd never forgive me.

  – Dr. Alec Doyle

Chapter 27

Bonny climbed into Kate's lap and laid her head on her mother's chest. Kate ran a hand down the length of her, down to the toe of her footed, fleece sleeper, leaned back on the couch.

"You slept late, sweetie."

Bonny nodded, her eyes closed. "When is Daddy coming home, Mummy?"

"Not sure. Maybe when the weather gets warmer, we'll go see him in England. Would you like that?"

"I want Daddy to come home here."

"I know, Bons. But Daddy has to live in London for right now."

"Why?"

"Because his work is in London. So, he doesn't really live here anymore. But he still loves you, just as much. He wishes he could be here."

Evelyn joined them, put a cup of coffee in front of Kate on the table.

"Here, Bonny. Let Grammy hold you for a while. Mommy needs to have her coffee."

Bonny transferred easily to her grandmother's arms, and Kate took a grateful gulp.

"Thanks, Mom."

"Your father and I wanted to know if you'd like us to stay through New Year's. Just in case you were thinkin' about going somewhere."

Kate pushed her bangs back from her forehead. "Where would I go?"

"We hardly ever get time with our little sweetheart, here. We were thinking of maybe even taking her back home with us for a few days."

"That would be great, you can if you want, but I really don't have any plans. I don't know when Rob is coming back."

"Well, maybe you just oughta find out."

Thoughtful, Kate went into the office, placed her splayed fingers on the fine mahogany desk. It was a huge, heavy, and solid. Paulie had always hated it. She picked up the phone and dialed Rob's number.

"I was just going to call you," he said. His excitement was infectious, and Kate smiled.

"Do you miss me?"

"It's like being without my favorite blankie," was the response. "Hey, I'm going to be staying here a couple of extra days. I'm sorry."

"Really?"

"Jesse needs me to help him with some things. Financial stuff. He's never been any good at taking care of paperwork."

"Jesse?"

"One of my brothers. I need to keep him out of bankruptcy. Or jail."

"Well, I was just going to ask you if you'd be free tomorrow afternoon." Kate spun the massive leather chair as she talked.

"Yeah, but…like I said, I'll still be here."

"Is it a long drive to the airport?"

"Augusta is only fifteen miles from here. Wait—are you—?"

"If it's okay."

"Okay? Are you kidding? Give me the info. I'll be there. Awesome."

Friday, December 30, 1994.

Kate focused 98% of her attention on getting to Rob, after seeing to her parents' comfort with taking on Bonny for a few days. She gave Paulie a call from LAX and announced she was off to meet Rob's people, forcing herself to remain completely neutral to his lukewarm response.

Rob picked her up in Augusta, literally spinning her around in a joyous, kissing embrace. "This is madness," he said into her ear. "I can't believe you're actually here. I've felt like a lost sock."

His every word, every gesture told her she'd made the right decision.

"Are we going to your folks' house?"

"Naw. They'll have to wait 'til tomorrow. I want you all to myself tonight. We have a room in Augusta. Just over that next bridge."

It was *La Maison on Telfair* for dinner. Kate gaped at the chandeliers in the restored Southern mansion, the twinkling lights, the delectable smells. But most of all, she was enamored with Rob. She didn't realize just how much she'd missed him.

"Oh. Look at *that*," he said, pointing at a dessert carried by on a platter. The distraction was just enough for a single red rose, its fragile bud barely open, to appear across her clean china plate.

She picked it up, smelled its heady, intoxicating scent. "You always surprise me."

"It's easy," he replied. "And I want to be the best at it."

"I think I'm out of my league, here," she said, perusing the menu. "Smoked ostrich carpaccio?"

"Ooh, oui, oui, but you must try les Escargots a la Bourguignon, ma chérie."

"Okay, even this hick girl knows that's snails," she said, laughing. "I think I'll stick with the salmon."

"And the filet mignon for me. Merci," he said, handing the menus back to the waiter. He'd ordered them a pricey wine, and the captain appeared to give him a taste. "Excellent. Please."

Kate picked up her glass once it was filled, and watched him chat with the wine captain. Alec's words came swirling through her mind, about what would happen if she said yes to a life with Rob. Even now, when she could barely convince herself that she deserved such a man, he was reaching beneath the table for her hand.

He lifted his glass. "Here's to our first official, East Coast date," he said, flashing her a smile. She joined his toast, took a sip.

"It's good."

"The wine, or the date?"

"Both."

"Hey." He let go of her hand, swung his arm around her. "I want you to know something. I get that this was a big step for you. Don't let all my bullshitting make you think I don't know how important this is."

"I love all your bullshitting."

He kissed her then, a slow, solemn kiss that sealed it for her.

They ordered dessert in their hotel room, then got into bed and watched TV while eating it. When they'd finished, he pulled her close.

"Tired?"

"Sort of."

"Tomorrow night, then."

What? She adjusted her position, cuddled close, drew her finger along his jaw. "Sure?"

"I couldn't sleep last night after you called. I would be content to just hold you all night long."

The television went off, and Kate nestled her back against his chest. He did hold her close, even after his breathing had turned sleep-filled and steady. Still on L.A. time, she laid awake, wishing, hoping and praying that she wouldn't mess up.

Aiken, South Carolina, December 31, 1994

His mom was small and gracious. Jean Evans took off her apron and hung it up before giving Kate a warm embrace.

"Why, I'm so very pleased to meet you. You are just as lovely as Robbie said you were. Daddy's out back, why don't you show Kate around, you'll probably catch him out there somewhere."

Rob was, Kate realized, the spitting image of his dad. Chuck Evans pulled off a pair of work gloves and shook her hand. Over dinner, she marveled at the resemblance to his two brothers and sister, all home for the holidays. Such a large family. She loved it. Aside from Jesse's money woes, sister Shanie's babysitter issues and Dad's dead John Deere battery, the Evans family seemed so together. So solid. And they couldn't have made her feel more welcome.

Kate insisted on helping with the cleanup. Between the washing, rinsing and drying of the dishes (Jean didn't like the new dishwasher Rob had installed), Kate learned that Shanie's husband was in the service. Her two and three-year-olds were all she could handle, so she'd moved home when Doug had been sent overseas. Jesse, too lived at home, but Glen was only in for a few days from his home in Colorado. Glen, she figured out, was divorced, and Jesse, the youngest, never married. The women's chatter painted a finer picture of Rob's life than she ever could have gleaned from him.

To celebrate the holiday, the entire family stayed up, passing around champagne and apple cider. They counted down together as they watched the Times Square ball drop. The first kiss of 1995 lasted well into the new year for Kate and Rob.

Once his brother's affairs were in order, Rob took Kate sightseeing, showing off the lush, green, canopied roads, the verdant horse properties, the lazy, meandering rivers. So different from the deserts of New Mexico, the brushy chaparral of Southern California. Kate was overwhelmed at the sight of stately southern mansions, historical battlefields, the easy, slow lifestyle. No bottlenecked freeways; not one incident of road rage.

Her flight back was on January 2, one day before his. It wasn't as hard to leave him this time, knowing he'd follow the next day. Their parting was tender, intimate and smoochy.

"Call me when you get home," he told her between kisses.

"I will," she promised. "And I'll see you tomorrow."

"Bet on it."

Because of the time difference, Kate arrived home early in the day. Cheryl picked her up, listened patiently to Kate's non-stop chatter about the beauty of South Carolina and her romance-filled days there. Once home, however, Kate realized that Cheryl had barely spoken a word. The house was empty.

"Where's Mom and Pop?"

"They took Bon to the park."

"Oh." Kate rolled her suitcase up against the wall in the entryway. "So what's up? Something's wrong."

Cheryl went to the bar, poured out two fingers of vodka, then splashed in some non-descript mixer. She drank it down, turned back to Kate.

"You got a phone call. About two hours ago. Some guy in London."

Kate felt her throat tighten. "What is it? Is Paulie okay?"

Cheryl walked to her, gently grasped Kate's forearms. "This man, Sheffield, I think, he said he was Paul's solicitor. He said," Cheryl paused, lowered her voice. "He said Paulie's been arrested."

Kate shook her head. "What did he do now, shag the Prime Minister's son?"

"No. You, you don't understand. They're saying he murdered someone."

Kate stared at her cousin in disbelief. "Murder? He killed someone? Oh. No. No, that's, that's just not possible. Not Paulie."

"That's what I told the guy. Look, honey, this is serious. He's in *jail*. There's…evidence."

Horrified, Kate sat down. "Did you talk to Paulie?"

"No. Just this attorney guy. He wanted to talk to you. You better call him back. He said, no matter what time, you were to call."

"Could you make me whatever it was that you just chucked down? Give me the phone number."

Cheryl handed her a note, then went to the bar and mixed. Kate gulped down half the drink while waiting for the overseas connection.

"Yes, this is Mrs.... this is Katrina Bingham. Please, tell me what's going on."

The solicitor briefed her on the events of the previous 48 hours. By the time she hung up, she felt sick to her stomach.

"Tell me everything," Cheryl said, now on her second cocktail.

"Jon Beale is dead. He was last seen with Paul. There's DNA evidence that they were together. The knife in his throat had Paulie's fingerprints on it."

"Holy shit."

"There has to be some mistake. I need to…I need to go. Cheryl, please, help me get a flight out. As soon as possible. I'll just re-pack."

"I'll go with you. Evelyn has already said she'll keep Bonny."

"She knows?"

"Yes. She was here when the call came in."

Kate rushed upstairs and chose a larger suitcase, began slinging clothes into it. Cheryl stopped in moments later, saying she was able to get them two seats out at nine p.m.

"Have you called Rob?" she called over her shoulder on the way to her room.

Rob. Kate froze. After a moment, she remembered to breathe, and again picked up the phone. Artificially calm, she explained the situation, repeated what she'd learned from the attorney.

"That's crazy," he said. "Paul wouldn't hurt a flea. Something's wrong, there."

"I know." Kate propped the phone under her ear and resumed packing.

"What time's your flight?"

"Nine. Four hours, but we have to be at LAX in two. This is just insane." She paused, listened to his mutterings. "Rob? I'm really sorry."

"Look, babe, when you get there, call me with an address. I'll be about twelve, maybe thirteen hours behind you, give or take. I'll probably have to stopover somewhere."

"You—you want to be there?"

"No question. Stay calm. We'll get this straightened out, okay?"

"How can you be so impossibly good to me?"

"Because…because I love you."

☞ **My mind was so numb with shock and apprehension, I almost missed Rob's tender admission. I'd known for some time he had strong feelings for me, but I refused to connect that last dot. I wasn't ready to hear those words. I didn't say them back. But Rob, I'm sure, understood.**

245

That's the thing about Rob. He's always understood everything. He's got more patience than anyone I've ever known.

I had no time to ponder it that day. Paulie was locked up, halfway around the world, alone and likely more terrified than he'd ever been. And I, his closest friend, wouldn't be there for several hours. Who knows what horrors he would experience in jail? Memories of ugly stories came to mind. Soft, gay men in prison with hardened criminals. Paulie's tales of the beatings he suffered growing up, just for preferring the company of boys and painting on his eyebrows.

And murder? What could be more preposterous? In our own home, he balked at killing a spider for me. His liberal leanings abhorred capital punishment. He was swift to blame but even swifter to forgive.

I knew he was conflicted about Jon Beale. Jon's unwitting comment had hurt both of us. But Paulie was quick to remind me that Jon had merely repeated what Ian had told him. Ian had been the true culprit. Paulie always said that Ian was an angry gay man. He resented anyone and anything that challenged the gay lifestyle. Clearly, that included me.

There have been many times when I've had to pump myself up and be strong. Boarding the fight for London was one of the worst. I felt like I'd been sucker-punched. I had little idea of what I could do for Paul, I only knew I had to get to him and wrap my arms around him. —Kate

Chapter 28

January 3, 1995. London

The closer the flight drew to London, the larger the knot in Kate's stomach grew. The jet landed at around four p.m., and Kate called Rob the moment she was out of customs. He sounded tired, but still reminded her that things would get better once they found out the truth.

"I don't know where we'll stay, I've been in touch with Peg and we're going there first." She rattled off Paulie's home address and Rob repeated it back.

"Okay. I'll get there just as soon as I can. I'll call when I leave."

"Thanks, Rob. I feel better knowing you'll be here."

She also called the solicitor from Heathrow. It was too late, he told her, to visit Paulie today, but he'd see to it she got in tomorrow. He'd employed a barrister, and the hearing was set for Friday, just three days away, at the Royal Courts of Justice. He wanted to meet with Kate after she visited with Paulie.

Steeling herself, she hailed a cab and she and Cheryl climbed in. After giving the cabbie the address, he turned around and stared.

"You're his wife," he claimed with a nod. "Rotten luck, eh? No chance he done it. None."

"How do you know? What do you know?"

"I've met Mr. Bingham m'self. Quite the gent, even if queer. I know the address, I've had a few others gone there just today. Fans, journalists."

"Is there a crowd?" Cheryl asked.

"Aye. Eh, perhaps I should get you some help?"

Kate looked at Cheryl, who shrugged. The cabbie turned a corner, then another in quick succession, then pulled to the left curb. He opened his window, hollered out to some men lounging on a bench. "'Ey! You lazy sods, which of you blokes is up to helping a lady in distress?'"

A burly man in a navy pea coat got in beside the driver, and Kate sat back. True enough, a large mob had gathered at the bottom of Paulie's front walk. Kate didn't know which was more surprising—the crowd, or the majestic, three-story Victorian house.

The two men got out first, muscled Kate and Cheryl to the front door, then went back for their bags. Kate gave them each an extra ten pound note.

Peg grabbed her on sight.

"Oh, Kate. I knew you'd come. Wot a livin' nightmare this is!" She hugged Kate so tightly, the latter couldn't breathe. "First you 'n Paulie split, then this terrible thing. The world's gone mad, it has!"

"Where are the children?"

"All except Jacob have gone to Meg's for a time. She come 'n collected the lot this mornin'."

Kate looked around at the grand appointments. They were standing in a room off the entry, a parlor, perhaps. Peg wrestled Kate's coat off her.

"You'll want to get freshened up. I'll make tea, once you get settled. Paul's rooms are on the second floor. You go ahead and take his suite. I know he'd want you in his bed."

Cheryl lifted her eyebrows, and Kate smiled. Peg flushed.

"Oh, dear. There goes me mouth again. Can't say anythin' right since they took him away." She dabbed at a tear.

"It's okay. I'd prefer to take one of the guest rooms. I thought you were on the second floor?"

"He changed his mind. The children were too loud, too noisy on the stairs, and that. I don't blame him a bit. He mostly uses the back stairs and the back door so's we don't even hear him comin' and goin'."

Kate followed Cheryl up the sweeping front staircase. They peeked in at the large suite clearly belonging to Paulie, a grand, expansive room filled with oversized, garish furniture. Kate opted for the second bedroom, and Cheryl landed inside the one across the hall. The décor in the room Kate chose was frilly, fussy and Victorian; she wondered if this was the room Bonny had used.

She didn't take long to change and return downstairs. Peg brought out a plate of tiny sandwiches and three teacups.

"I want to hear it all, down the smallest detail," Kate said. "Don't leave anything out."

"I don't know much, love. Three, no, four days ago, 'twas. Friday last. I took the children down to St. John's for the winter festival. It was to be a sleepover for the children, but I decided I might as well stay, so I rang Paul to tell him I wouldn't be home for supper and not to worry because he wouldn't see me until mornin'. He said he was goin' t' another party at Ian's.

"I got home near half past nine the next mornin', Paulie was quite chipper, in a generous mood, he was. I remember because he was terribly patient with the children, who were all surly and tired from the night before. It was New Year's Eve, o' course. That night, he went out, to celebrate with his mates, I suppose. The next mornin', New Year's Day, there's an awful poundin' on the front door, and there's three bobbies, their faces all harsh and stern-like, and they want Paulie. I say he's still asleep and they'll have to come back later, they will. They get a little harsher and a little sterner and demand that I wake him. Two of them follow me up the stairs. I wake him, and they tell him he's under arrest for the murder of Jonathan Beale."

"What did he say?"

"He just sits up and says, 'you're joking, man. Right?' And the copper says, 'I'm afraid not, sir. If you'll just come with me.' Paulie realizes this bloke is serious, and he says, 'at least let me get my bloody drawers on, mate.' And the copper says, 'make haste.' And I says, 'then give the boy some privacy!' And the copper, he says, 'he ain't no boy, M'am,' so I says, I says, 'I ain't no M'am, either.'"

Peg took a decidedly unladylike gulp of tea. "So Paulie gets up, I help him get himself together, and they put bleedin' handcuffs on 'im. On my baby brother. It was bloody pitiful, it was. They marched him right past the littl' uns, downstairs, their eyes all big with shock."

"Did he say anything else at all?" Cheryl asked, having joined them during Peg's tearful recounting.

"Just, 'I didn't do it. I'm bloody innocent,' he starts yelling. He was crying, too, I think he rather fancied young Jon."

Kate shuddered. As much distaste as she felt for Jon, she'd never have wished him dead. "They're going to let me talk to him tomorrow. I'll also be talking to the barrister. I'm sure there's something they've missed."

"No alibi, they keep sayin' on the news. No one saw Jon Beale after he...spent the evening with Paulie. No one saw Paulie, either. He was alone, here in this house, all night, and no way to prove it! I'm always home...and I couldn't even lie because too many people knew I was at the church!" Peg sobbed.

Kate's cell phone rang. She couldn't answer it fast enough.

"I'm about to board. Any news?" Rob's voice was like a warm blanket around her chill.

"Not really. I can see him tomorrow. You have the address?"

"Yeah. It'll be four a.m. when I land."

"Then I'll see you around five-thirty. Call to make sure I'm awake to let you in. I don't feel like I've slept since I was with you."

"Same here. I'll try to catch some Z's on the plane. Maybe you can get to bed early."

"I'll try."

She slept, but woke several times, disoriented and checking the clock. She dreamed about Bonny, saw her with Jamie Pritchard, then Charles Evans, Rob's father. She dozed, wishing she was dreaming about Paulie. About him being free.

Her phone startled her at six. It was still pitch dark. Kate put on her overcoat and slippers, and tread softly down the backstairs. She unlocked the heavy back door. Rob was shivering on the porch, surrounded not by gawkers but fog.

Kate led him back to her room, where she quietly helped him undress. He slipped into bed beside her.

"The sun won't be up for two more hours," she said softly. "I didn't know how to turn on the heat. But the bed is warm." She wrapped herself around him. "I'm so glad you're here."

"How could I not be here."

She slept now. Safe and secure, at least until sunrise.

Peg eyed Rob with suspicion as he and Kate came down the stairs, hand in hand. Kate gave her a determined smile and introduced him. He won Peg over during breakfast, eating heartily of her fried eggs, black pudding and bangers.

Kate got nowhere fast on the telephone. "He's in some holding cell. His case has been referred to the Crown Prosecution Service. Because of the evidence they think they have, he's been charged. Bail has already been refused."

"When can we see him?"

"At noon."

Her hands were shaking as she signed her name of the visitor's roster. Rob was asked to wait, and Kate followed the clerk to a small, colorless room containing a wooden table and two chairs. A guard stood inside, at the door. Paulie was led in from the opposite side of the room. He was shackled.

Kate rushed to him, threw her arms around him. He lifted his handcuffed wrists, brought them over her head and held onto her. After being with Rob, Paulie felt thinner than she remembered. Ever the chameleon, he'd changed his look again. His hair, now nearly black, was shaped in a boy's bowl cut, with bangs that curled on his forehead. He looked youthful and vulnerable. And very pale.

"I got here as soon as I could." She turned around, spoke to the guard. "Might we have just a few minutes, alone? I promise you he's not dangerous. Not to me or anyone else."

The policeman considered. "Fifteen minutes. I'll be right outside this door."

She got Paulie to sit down, she across from him. "We don't have long. Quickly tell me exactly what happened, Paul."

"Nothing happened. I didn't do it. They think I killed Jon Beale. I swear, I didn't."

"Don't waste time defending yourself to me. When did you last see Jon?"

"It was Friday night. I was at Ian's—a party. Low key, nothing fancy, we were passing a spliff, nothing else, I swear. Jon and I had a little tryst. Afterward, I walked home. He followed me, wanted to come inside. I refused, I was tired. I was starting to get the feeling he wanted to own me. I told him to go home. We had a row out front. It was dark, but the street light was on. My bitchy neighbor from across the way comes by walking her fucking little shit dog, and she sees us shoving each other. Then she went inside."

Kate sighed. "Go on."

"He left then. After cuffing me a couple of times. I went inside. He walked off down the street. That was it. Next I know, the fucking riot squad picks me up out of bed."

"You were all alone in the house?"

"Peg was at some bloody church deal. Yeah, I was alone. All night."

He looked away, and Kate thought she saw a look she recognized. He was lying.

She reached for his face, touched his cheek. He jerked.

"Tell me the truth. You can tell me anything. You know that. Who was with you? Where did you go?"

"I told you the truth. I was alone. I watched some inane stupid program, I was coming down from the pot, and I was pissed off at Jon. I was hungry and pissed off at Peg, too, for not having food ready. I was fucking cold, too, and good company for no one."

"Five minutes, miss."

"Aw, fuck off, will you?" Paulie shouted. Kate got up and pulled her chair around to sit beside him. He was on the verge of a major freak out. She stroked his face, kissed his eyes. Held him close, hoping to calm his fears.

"I will get you out of this. You're innocent. They can't prove something you didn't do."

Paul propped his elbows on the table, leaned against his laced hands as if in prayer.

"Is Rob here?"

"Yes."

"Good. Bonny?"

"No. She's at home with Mom. But Cheryl's here. Look, I'll be back tomorrow. Please, please try to think of anything you may have missed. I'm meeting with your attorney in a half hour."

"It's too tidy. They have my fingerprints."

"Do you think someone set this up?"

"I'm as good as fucked."

"You can't lose hope. Let me see what I can find out."

"I've already told them everything I told you."

Kate gave him one last kiss, stood up. "But they don't know what a poor liar you are. I *will* find out what you're hiding," she said softly.

"Don't waste your time. There's nothing to find."

ANNE CARTER

Chapter 29

Her anger kept her from crying. As long as she could stay good and mad, she could be strong. Rob went in with her to meet the attorney.

"Mrs. Bingham, William Teasdale. I'll be representing Mr. Bingham in court."

"Ms." Kate stared up at the tall, skinny barrister. With thinning hair and a hook nose, he looked more like Mr. Scrooge than someone she wanted fighting for Paulie's life.

"Uh, Ms., uh, Bingham. Did Mr. Bingham divulge any new facts during your discussion this afternoon?"

"No. But you must know he's innocent. He's not capable of such a heinous act."

"Are you fully aware of all the details?"

"We'd like to hear them," Rob interjected.

"And you are?"

"Robin Evans. Kate's..."

"He's my—my partner. And yes, please tell us the details."

"The victim—Mr. Beale—was a 27 year old Caucasian male, believed to be homosexual. From a wealthy family. He lived in St. John's Wood, alone, but was often seen in the company of a group of homosexual men for the purpose of recreational sex and drug use. On the night in question, he attended a party at the home of one Ian Flynn. There, he met Mr. Bingham, and the two left the party in the mid-evening and walked to Mr. Bingham's home in Hampstead."

"They didn't leave together. Jon followed Paulie home."

"Witnesses say the two left the Flynn flat at the same time. Another witness, a Mrs. Finney, deposed that she saw the victim and the accused arguing in front of the Hampstead mansion. There were blows. When next she looked, the gentlemen were no longer on the walk, having allegedly gone inside the home."

"Only Paulie went inside. Jon walked away. She didn't see Jon go inside because he *didn't*."

"Mrs.—Ms. Bingham, believe it or not, I am on your husband's side."

"I'm sorry. Please, continue."

"At approximately 7:30 a.m. the following morning, a Hampstead Heath constable discovered the deceased body of Mr. Beale in the park near the Viaduct. He'd been stabbed multiple times in the throat."

Kate grimaced.

"With what?" Rob asked.

"An ordinary dinner knife. The victim still had his wallet, his watch. In the wallet, I might add, were photos of Mr. Bingham and a hundred or so pounds. His trousers were soiled on the outside, as if he'd crawled a bit on the ground before he succumbed. A Metro police forensics team was able to move quite swiftly, acting on a hunch, since Mr. Bingham was arrested and fingerprinted just minutes away from this very location in the 1970's. There was an immediate match to prints on the silver knife handle."

"That's nonsense. He could have handled any number of knives, in restaurants, events, parties. Were there no other prints on it?" Rob asked, his voice tinged with irritation.

"I understand there was a substantial amount of blood on the knife. I've requested a copy of the report. There was at least one clear print belonging to Mr. Bingham. And the coroner notes that…bodily fluids provided a DNA match, as well."

"So they had sex. So what?" Rob continued. "This whole thing smells."

"Mr. Teasdale, Paulie said that Jon left. He didn't actually go inside. Is there any way we could canvass the neighborhood for more witnesses? If there's a cost involved, we can, of course, accommodate it."

"Police have already gone door-to-door, which is how they turned up Mrs. Finney, who's offered to testify. Apparently, Mrs. Finney and Mr. Bingham have had words in the past, concerning incidents wherein her pet defecated on Mr. Bingham's walk."

Kate nodded. "I can believe that." She paused, considered her next words carefully. "What would you need to clear Paulie? Exactly?"

"My dear, what your ex-husband is lacking is a viable alibi. Because of the forensic evidence, it would take strong direct evidence of his innocence. The testimony, for example, of someone who was with Mr. Bingham at the time of Mr. Beale's death, which was..." Teasdale shuffled some papers, lifted one out of the stack. "Approximately 10:30 p.m. The witness would have to display a modicum of credibility. Inasmuch as Mr. Bingham has already stated, repeatedly, that he was alone, any forthcoming witness, at this point, would likely trigger suspicion of deceit."

Rob looked down. "Damn. This isn't good."

"I'm sorry. I wish there was better news. Now, on Friday next, we must enter a plea. I know he's planning to tell the court he's not guilty. Should he reconsider, we might get a prompt trial. Considering his history of drug abuse, we could use his possibly altered state in our defense."

Horrified, Kate stood up. "Plea bargain? You want to say he murdered Jon in a drug-fueled haze? I thought you were on his side!"

Rob got to his feet, held her gently by the shoulders. "Kate. It's okay. He's just doing his job. We don't have a lot to go on here. We have two more days. Let's—let's get out of here and see if we can come up with anything." He turned back to the barrister. "When can we talk to Paul again?"

"I can arrange a ten o'clock meeting in the morning."

"We'll be there."

There were thirty or more people still gathered at the house. Rob got out of the cab first.

"Listen. I have a statement to make. Those of you who are Paulie Bingham's fans, he sends his thanks for your love and prayers. He's doing okay. He asks that you please, please leave his family some privacy and quiet. This is hard for everybody."

A pushy man stuck a microphone in Rob's face. "Who are you?"

"I'm Rob Evans and I'm a friend of Paul's."

Another came at him. "Is it true that Paul Bingham is back on heroin? That he killed his lover while on a binge?"

"I can't comment on the case, but Paul Bingham does not use heroin. I can't answer any more questions. I am going to escort Ms. Bingham into the house, and I ask that none of you get in my way." He waited. A few people took a step back, then a few more, until the walk leading up to the house was clear. He helped Kate from the car as the cameras began snapping.

Kate held her head up, dared a look at the fans lining the walk. Many of them, she noted, were carrying flowers, photos, and candles. Several were crying. She paused, began collecting the gifts, handing them to Rob when she couldn't hold them all.

"Thank you. Thank you. I will make sure he gets them. Now, please, go home, he's not coming here anytime soon. There will be no more information from here. Perhaps you can gather elsewhere to show your support."

The crowd began to dissipate. Two girls lingered, and one reached out and grasped Kate's arm. Her eyes were filled with misery. Her friend pulled her away.

Kate was shaken, moved. She and Rob entered the house, Kate collapsing onto the parlor settee. "That was just horrible. All those people suffering. I never thought of them that way. They were just an annoyance."

Rob sat. "So. What do we know? You suspect he wasn't alone. How can we determine that? Can we talk to this Flynn character?"

"I suppose that's a start."

Peg came rushing in. "How is he? Is he okay? Is he eating?"

"Of course he's not eating. He barely eats when he's not in jail," Kate mused. "Peg? Did the police search his room?"

"Aye. More than once. Oh, they made a terrible mess. But I've since straightened it all out. I made his bed, tidied up the clothing they tossed out of the drawers. Uncivilized lot of heathens, they are."

"Maybe they missed something."

"They did." Cheryl walked in, held out her hand. "This was in the pocket of his raincoat."

258

Kate took the small cellular phone from Cheryl. "His phone. Of course."

"It should have a history of calls made and received. At least ten or so."

"You want to look into it?" Kate said, handing the device to Rob. "I'm going to go over his room again. I know how he files things. How he hides things. Maybe... maybe, something..."

"Great. I'll call some of these numbers and see who they are," Rob agreed. "I'll need some paper."

Cheryl went back upstairs with Kate, and they entered Paulie's suite of rooms. "The raincoat was downstairs, in the coat closet. He had to have been wearing it that night. They probably missed it because it's a lady's coat. They obvious don't know their perp very well."

"Good work, Sherlock," Kate said. She took a long, panning look around the bedroom. An ornate, brass filigree headboard crowned the king sized bed. Taking a deep breath, she approached the dresser, began calmly digging through the drawers. Cheryl went to the closet, patting down the upper shelves, looking through the clothing.

"What am I looking for?" she called over her shoulder.

"I wish I knew. It'd be much easier to find."

Kate sat down on the bed, turned back the comforter. Freshly laundered grey sheets were tucked so tight they would have passed military muster. Grey?

"Peg?" Kate called down the staircase to her sister-in-law, who was helping Rob notate the results of his phone calling. "Did you say you changed the sheets?"

"They took his. The pretty maroon ones he so loves. Said they had the right to take them. Nasty perverts, you shoulda heard the filthy things they said."

Kate got Teasdale on the phone. "The police took his bed sheets. Can you get a copy of the findings? I want to know if they can prove, in any way, that Jon Beale was here. Ever."

"I'm already working on it, Mrs.—er,"

"Kate. Just Kate. Thank you."

She looked out the window. Only a few of the fans remained. She thought of the day before, the friendly cabbie who'd helped her out. He'd tucked his card into her hand at the door. She remembered his mention that he'd brought others to the house before.

Miraculously, "Dickie" answered his phone, and yes, he remembered her.

"I don't suppose there is any way to know if a cab came or went the night of this horrible murder," she asked.

"I'm sorry, Miss. Only way would be if drivers talk to each other. Like I might spill over a pint that I'd given a ride to Tony Blair. My mates might tell others. News travels fast, as they say. I can surely ask round, but seein' as how there's lit'rally hundreds of cabbies in this town, if someone did drop a fare there on Monday night, you most likely won't hear about it. Lots of 'em keep to themselves."

He took Kate's number, nonetheless, and promised to call if he discovered anything that could help.

She conferred with Rob over tea. "What did you find out?"

Rob smiled. "A lesser man would be in a raging, jealous, rampage."

"Don't finger me. It may be my number, but it's Bonny he calls almost every day." Kate nodded. "Honest. They go on for hours."

"I talked to this Ian Flynn dude. Dodgy. Said he's traumatized, not sure I go for that. We'd better not rely on his testimony for the defense, either. Didn't sound too sure that Paulie was innocent."

"Rat bastard," Kate proclaimed. "He had nothing useful?"

"Went to primary school with Paul. Off and on friendship. Critical of Paul's foray into straightdom. Oh, and he's missing a silver table knife."

"What?" Kate snapped to attention, dismissed her thoughts of how many ways she could disfigure Flynn. "Did he tell the police?"

"He hasn't felt up to cleaning since the murder. Only discovered it missing today. I suggested he call Teasdale." Rob picked up the log he'd written. "Other than that, Paul called home, he called a Miss Megan Talbot, I guess she's his cousin? And that's it."

"Did you talk to Meg?"

"Briefly. There was lots of noise, sounded like kids, said she'd be by later. Now, incoming calls are more difficult. Some are without identification. One came in at 9:25 p.m. Another at 11:30. No number. Talked two minutes the first time, a minute and a half on the later call."

Kate was intrigued. "Do you think the barrister can subpoena the records? See who it is that called?"

"Don't know. When a number is blocked, it might be untraceable."

"He said that Jon left here around 9:30. It might be that he got that first call as he was walking home. Maybe whoever made that call changed his mind about seeing Jon."

"Jon had another lover? A jealous one?" Cheryl suggested.

"Flynn?" Kate asked.

"Could be," Rob agreed. "I get the feeling that as gay men roll, Paulie and Flynn are more alike than, say, this dead dude."

Kate shook her head. "Maybe, but it's not always that cut-and-dried."

"Well...you oughta know," Rob teased, and Kate pushed at his head.

"You're the only person who could get away with that," she said. "Still...Paulie was at Flynn's. The knife is likely the same one that's missing. He must have used it there, and the killer snagged it afterward, meaning this whole thing was premeditated. Paulie *is* being framed."

"But who could he be protecting? Think of it from Paul's point of view. Who matters to him? Besides the obvious."

"I have an alibi. I was with you," Kate said.

Cheryl shook her head. "Maybe he's not protecting anyone. Maybe he's been threatened. Blackmailed, or something. Maybe he's afraid."

◦❥ *Cheryl Collins checking in.*
This whole mess with Paul is surreal. As Kate and I are closer than sisters, Paul has been like a brother to me for

years. *Of course I've made a career of dissing him, but it's all show and he knows it. This murder charge is the biggest load of bullshit I've ever heard. A complete farce.*

Not saying because it's U.K. -crap like this happens at home all the time. Especially to celebs. When you add "gay" into the mix, in snobby blueblood digs like Hampstead, you get lots of press and lots of pressure on local law enforcement. Paul's an easy mark because of his history as a sexual anarchist and prolific drug user. The cops couldn't have picked a better suspect.

I'm worried for him. And for Kate. He's never been in a jam she couldn't get him out of. I feel bad for Rob, too—he's the impotent one here, because he can't fix anything for anybody. Like me. We're helpless bystanders watching the people we love drowning. — Cher

Chapter 30

Paulie sat on the corner of the cot, his knees drawn up to his chin. He'd stopped weeping, had coaxed himself into a state of numbness. Kate would be back today, trying in her obsessive, determined way to chip away at his carefully built wall. He could refuse to see her. They wouldn't force him, right? In truth, however, he did want to see her. Any time, any place.

But she couldn't possibly understand his predicament.

He needed a miracle, but that miracle would not, could not, come from Kate.

She dreaded the visit. She had no reason to expect that he'd be any more approachable today than he'd been yesterday, but she had to try.

"Why are you doing this?" she asked, pretending to be calm. Inside, she was ready to burst, to box his ears.

"I'm not doing anything."

"You're being stubborn. There were times when I thought it was kinda cute, that stubbornness. But now? It's just asinine. Do you get that? Who called you Monday night?"

Paulie looked up for the first time. "What do you mean?"

"You got phone calls that night. Who was it? Did it occur to you that this person might provide an alibi?"

"Have you forgotten that you phoned me that night? To tell me you were off to the east coast to meet your new lover?"

He looked back down. Kate flushed, felt her fingernails biting into her palms.

"I did. I didn't equate the two. But the other call, the earlier one, came while you were still walking. Did this person come to see you?"

"Since when have you joined Scotland Yard? Don't you think I've had enough interrogation and humiliation?"

"I'm not trying to humiliate you. I'm trying to make it so our daughter has a father that's not incarcerated for the rest of his GOD DAMN LIFE!" Kate pounded the table with her last words. Paulie didn't move.

"Go away."

"What did you say to me?"

"I said, go away. Please."

Kate gasped. She couldn't believe his callous words. "Just like that. Go away."

"Send Rob in. *Please*."

"Why should I?" Kate stood firm, crossed her arms. Paulie stood also, placed his hands on the table and leaned forward, his face close to hers.

"I don't need your help. But I do need his. So *go*."

"Why, you...you prick. How can you talk to me like that?"

"I asked nicely."

Calm down. He's acting this way for a reason. You know he would never hurt you.

Kate gulped in some air, turned and walked out. Without speaking, she waived Rob toward the door.

He looked different than Paulie remembered. Not as handsome, not as trim. Muscular, sharp, attractive, but no Adonis. Rob seemed nervous.

"Sit down, mate."

Rob pulled out the chair, sat. "I don't have any good news, Paul."

"Not looking for news. I have questions for you."

"Shoot."

"Do you love Kate? Really love her?"

Rob seemed surprised, tilted his head. Took a moment. "Yes."

"Will you marry her?"

"We're not there yet. Frankly, I'm not sure how she feels. A lot depends on her, obviously."

"You only need to sort it out with her. She might not understand it all, but she loves you. I'm quite certain she would marry you."

"I appreciate your confidence. Where is this going?"

"And Bonny? You'll care for her, too?"

"Look, Paul. This isn't one of those death-bed promise routines, is it? Because it doesn't have to be."

"Just—please; humor me." Paulie bowed his head for a moment, then returned to the conversation. "I don't have great expectations. It's not very likely I'll beat this rap. So, I need to at least know that my family—because she is still my family—that they will be taken care of. Bonny is very fond of you. I'm quite happy about that."

Rob drew in a breath, let it out slowly. "Kate thinks you're hiding something."

"I'm well aware of what the little Sheila thinks. It's true that there are things she doesn't know, but she's way off base. Let her waste her time chasing shadows and hunches. It will keep her busy for a while."

Paulie rubbed his hands together, stared at Rob. "I'm still entering not guilty. It will go to trial. If, by the grace of God, the truth comes to light, I'll go free and everyone will be joyous and forgiven. If not, I'll appeal." He ran fingers through his hair, the handcuffs dragging against his forehead. "I was quite the hag to her. I sent her off in a proper pout. Go give her some affection."

Rob shook his head. "This is just the pits."

"I love her, still. Don't be jealous. If by chance I get through this, and you two marry, I hope you won't lock me out. I'm not a threat, believe me."

"I've never considered you one. I've nothing but respect for the caring you feel for each other. I just hate to see her in such pain."

"I hate it, too. But there it is."

Kate couldn't help but notice the change in Rob's mood when he emerged from the court's holding facility. He was somber, thoughtful. She wasn't sure she liked it.

"Okay. What did he say to you?" she asked.

"He just…just wants to be sure you and Bonny will be okay if he's sent up."

"So he's resigned to a conviction?"

"Not entirely. He's still going to plead innocent. I think he's hoping for some kind of divine intervention."

"Fat chance of that." Kate felt heavy, clouded. She got out of the cab and waited for Rob. He leaned out.

"I'm going to take a run down to Trafalgar. I'm going to meet with my record company agent about the upcoming release. Is it okay?"

"Of course. Good to get your mind on something else for a while. I might take a nap." Kate bent down, gave him a kiss. "See you when you get back."

She waited until the cab was down the block, then turned, noticed two girls still sitting on a blanket at the corner of Paulie's small front garden. She approached them.

"Hello," she said awkwardly. "Are you girls all right?"

They both nodded vigorously. "We're sorry. We'll get off the lawn."

"No, no, I didn't mean you had to go. It's just that you haven't left. Don't you get hungry, or need to use the loo?"

One shook her head, the other shrugged. Kate sighed, thinking they couldn't be over fifteen or sixteen years old. "Come inside. You can use the bathroom and have something to drink."

The girls scrambled to their feet and followed Kate inside.

She met them back in the parlor with a plate of leftover scones and sweetened tea.

"Okay. So tell me about yourselves."

"I'm Missy, she's Regan. We live down in Eltham. My step-dad drives us up here in the mornings, picks us up at night."

"Don't you go to school?"

"We're on holiday, doncha know?" Regan offered, talking through a mouthful of food.

"Oh, right. Have you ever met Paulie?"

"We've seen him plenty, but never got the nerve to talk to him."

Kate nodded. Paulie had never catered much to his young girl fans. Always more interested in the boys. "Well I will be sure to tell him about your...patient waiting here. He'll appreciate your caring so much."

"Is he going to go to the pokey?"

Kate felt her mouth go dry. She swallowed, mustered a smile. "We sure hope not. We don't know yet."

The one called Missy spoke up. "He din't kill that guy. I read in the papers that the bloke died around 10:30 p.m. "

"That's right," Regan agreed. "He'd long gone by then."

"How do you know that?" Kate asked, frowning. "You...weren't... *here*, were you?"

Regan nodded. "We were hiding."

"In the bushes at the corner. We saw Paulie coming, so we rushed to hide."

"Yeah, we almost got ratted out by the neighbor's stinking lit'le mutt."

Kate's eyes grew wide. "You saw Jon Beale?"

"Yeah. What a nasty sort. Punching Paulie in the face, he was. Paulie pushed him back. The only words we could make out was Paulie saying, 'Go home' again and again. Then he went inside and slammed the front door. Jon kicked the door, hard, let out a sort of growl, and then left."

"Which way did he go?"

Both girls pointed, west, the same direction Paulie had indicated.

"I don't believe this," Kate murmured.

"Oh, it's true, all right. My dad was late getting us that night. He came just after, about 9:45, it was. We couldn't sleep the whole night from the excitement of it all."

"Girls, this could be very important information in defending Paulie. Would you be able to re-tell it to the barrister? Could you swear to it in court?"

"Damn straight we could," Regan boasted.

"Would your father testify?"

Missy frowned. "My step-dad says Paulie is a poofter. He'd likely not help."

Kate hunted down a piece of paper and pen. "Write down your names, phone numbers, and addresses. Let your families know that a Mr. Teasdale will be calling you."

Teasdale called Kate that evening.

"I can present at the hearing on Friday. They aren't particularly credible witnesses, as they're underage and fans, at that. One of them was disciplined at school for lying to the headmaster. But it's worth a shot."

Deflated, Kate went upstairs and waited for Rob to come to bed. It wasn't a long wait.

"I'm sorry. Is there anything I can do to help? A back rub, maybe?"

Code for lovemaking. She pulled off her nightgown and turned onto her stomach. The "back rub" was just what she needed.

The hearing was scheduled for eleven a.m. on Friday, January 13th. Kate didn't miss the ominous foreboding of the date. She wore a conservative dress suit and heels, Rob, a suit. Peg, Cheryl and Meg all dressed in their Sunday best. Buzz and Turner arrived, as well as Ian Flynn and some others who considered themselves Paulie's friends. They waited outside the courtroom, dodging reporters and photogs.

At 10:55, Kate's cell went off. It was Dickie.

"I've got a mate here who says he delivered a fare to the corner of Mr. Bingham's street on Friday, December 30th, that is, around 9:45 p.m. "

"Oh my God. Really? Does he have a description, anything?"

"A man. Raincoat and hat. Paid cash, tipped well. Got out on the corner opposite."

Kate sank back down. It wasn't enough. "9:45 is about right. Look, we're just going inside. Will you be able to get this gentleman's information in case we need it later?"

"You got it, Miz Bingham. Wish him well, eh?"

The doors opened, and she hurriedly whispered the details of the conversation to Rob as they entered the courtroom.

She caught her breath when Paulie entered. Someone had brought him a suit. He was showered and combed, and sullen. She cursed herself for not realizing he would need clothes. Meg, sitting beside her, squeezed her hand.

When asked, Paulie spoke up. "Not guilty," he said, soft words Kate barely heard.

She stared hard at the judge, studied his stony attributes. He squinted, his wrinkled face breaking into hundreds of tiny

268

facets. He asked questions, William Teasdale answered, then presented his additional facts. The judge was unimpressed. The whole affair was brief, mundane, depressing, and trial was set to begin in six weeks' time. The barrister complained, asking for a sooner date or that bail be set. Without looking up, the judge denied both. Paulie would be transferred to a local jail to await trial.

The dock officer led Paulie from the room. At the exit he turned, looked directly at Kate, his eyes dark with remorse and fear. As she sank into Rob's arms, the outrage in the room rose to a chaotic roar. Cameras flashed, others broke down. Cheryl helped Peg up, embraced her.

Ian Flynn was waiting at the door.

"I'm very sorry, Mrs. Bingham. Paulie's a good heart and a dear friend. Please call on me if I can be of any service during the trial. We must help him beat this."

Kate nodded, didn't respond.

☙ Paul Bingham was nothing like I'd expected him to be. I've dealt with pop stars before, have found them to be a nasty lot of self-important heathens with inflated egos, who think that throwing pounds at a problem will cause it to evaporate. Paul is a humble sort, a man-child lost amidst hideous accusations of acts he can't bear to think about much less commit.

When Sheffield rang me up, I nearly turned him down straight away. It was Kip's heartfelt request that caused me to reconsider. I found it difficult to interrogate Paul in the manner in which I needed to, especially since he didn't have much fight left in him once we reviewed the evidence.

Can't say I completely understand his relationship with the ex-wife. Katrina Bingham is a puzzle in herself. Clearly a fierce loyalty there, despite the fact that she has another man in tow.

I hope Paul's fans are praying for him, for we will certainly need God's ear in the coming weeks. Yes, I knew the odds were against us when I agreed to take on the case. All I could think about was, "what if this was Kip facing the jury?" Paul's strength of character gives me hope for my own gay son.

—Barrister William R. Teasdale

Chapter 31

Late February, 1995. London

On the Friday before the trial was set to begin, Rob and Kate flew back to London with heavy hearts. The media had amped up the press coverage, and Paulie's Hampstead estate crawled with reporters, friends, fans and complaining neighbors. After the first night, Rob approached Kate with a proposition.

"We need to get out of here. Nothing's happening until Wednesday."

"I can't deal with those people outside."

"I mean, we need to get a room somewhere. This place is a flippin' zoo."

Rob's manager found them a rental flat in Paddington. Quiet neighborhood, bedroom, bath and a kitchenette. Cheap enough not to arouse suspicion. Kate fell back onto the bed with a happy moan.

"Excellent idea, Robbie!"

"That place was making me crazy. It reminded me of when my grandmother was dying, and we all hung around her house for days and days. Damn! Paulie would hate what's going on over there. I mean, there's a point where you show your respect, express your concern, and then go home." Having hung up his damp coat, he laid down beside Kate.

"They don't know what else to do," Kate said softly.

"I know."

"Teasdale says we can see Paul on Tuesday."

"Good. Although I can't say I look forward to being with you afterward."

"I'm sorry. I can't help it. He's like a child. Stubborn, spoiled, immature…"

"And terrified."

For a couple of days, they pretended that nothing was wrong. Stocked the tiny kitchen, shopped for clothes, wrote a song for Paulie. When Kate got through to Alec's office, the receptionist said he was on an extended vacation. A family member was ill, the woman said. Kate still left a message.

When Tuesday came, Kate decided that she would change her approach to her time with Paulie. She brought him a veggie burger and a pile of chips, joined by a bottle of iced green tea. He seemed surprised, a little suspicious.

If possible, he was thinner than ever. Kate wished fervently to take him away.

"This is actually quite good," he said, offering her a bite. She didn't want one, but desperate to connect with him, took a nibble anyway.

"Are you okay? Has it been awful?"

"Worse than awful. At first, they put me in with a group of bad boys. One shouted, 'backs to the wall, gents!' when I came in. Nervy wankers."

"I don't understand."

"Surely you've heard the one about not dropping the soap in a gay men's shower?"

"Oh. I get it. Sorry."

"Shame on you, married to a well and true faggot for how long?"

"The guard said when we're done talking, we can call Bonny."

"Yeah? Brilliant. That's good. You think?"

"She misses you terribly. Mom and Pop just took her back home with them, she's having a good time, but...with us both gone, she's a little sensitive."

He nodded, chewed the burger.

"So..." Kate began, looking to change the subject. "You know they're still saying Kurt Cobain didn't commit suicide."

"So I've heard. Someone besides me must hate that grunge crap. Richey James still missing?"

"I don't know. That song by 69 Boyz is number one."

"It's okay. Right now, I'd listen to about anything. Except Madonna."

"Would they let you have a radio or a CD player?"

He shook his head, took another hungry mouthful. "Although," he managed, between bites, "the one bloke has been very kind. Got me a few cigs."

"I guess that's good," Kate lied.

"Got nothing else to do. I'm going mad."

He finished the meal, drank down the tea. "That was fab. Thanks, darling."

"Sure."

Paulie leaned forward, lowered his voice. "Listen. I had Teasdale draw up some papers. I've assigned my meager assets over to you. We, uh, back-dated them. He contacted your man in L.A., the divorce attorney, who knows some people who will authenticate them."

"Why did you do that?"

"If I'm convicted, we will lose everything. It will all go to Jon's family. That money belongs to Bonny."

Kate ran her hand over his. "And when you walk free, how do you plan to get it back?"

He smiled for the first time since the arrest. Handcuffs jingling, he placed his hands on her cheeks, drew her to him. Kissed her gently, his eyes closed, and held her lips against his for several moments.

"For luck," he whispered. "Pray for me."

The trial began on Thursday morning. The Snaresbrook Crown courtroom was filled to capacity, not a single open seat in the press box, and fans crowded the street outside. Jon Beale's murder was on everyone's wagging tongue.

Opening arguments were difficult to listen to. Kate held tight to Rob's hand, unable to take her eyes off of Paulie's frightened expression. Both prosecuting and defense barristers droned on, their diction as stilted and dry as their steel-grey wigs.

"Not exactly Jack McCoys," Rob whispered.

Jon Beale's family sat behind the prosecution. Their glances her way were stony and even hateful. Kate couldn't begin to deal with their grief and anger.

Ian Flynn was the first witness. The prosecution established Ian and Paulie as schoolyard friends, and Ian

273

recounted their reuniting in recent years. When asked about Jon and Paulie's relationship, Ian described them as occasional lovers. He looked directly at Kate. She stared back.

"I actually introduced them. I thought they'd be perfect for one another."

"And were they?"

"Apparently not."

"Why do you say that?"

"By his own admission, Paulie had tired of Jon. They bickered."

"And when did you witness Mr. Bingham and Mr. Beale arguing?"

"When they came out of my back bedroom, I noticed animosity. Paulie was in a snit."

"I'm sorry, when, *precisely?*"

"Just before they left my flat on the night Jon was killed. Around 9 p.m. , I believe."

Prosecutor Mindon paced, eventually making his way back to the witness stand. "About what, do you think, they bickered?"

"Why, sex, of course. Isn't that what all gay men fight about?" Ian smiled at the laughter coming from the back of the courtroom. The judge hammered.

"Conjecture," Teasdale asserted.

"Sustained. If the witness does not know about which the deceased and the defendant *bickered*, he shall refrain from supposition."

Ian crossed his legs, laid his hand against his cheek. "My apologies."

"Were there drugs being used at this party at your flat?"

The witness fluttered his eyes. "Drugs? Drugs are illegal, sir."

"Let me rephrase. Did you suspect that some of your guests were using drugs or possibly brought them into your home?"

"You know, it does sometimes happen. I can't search everyone that comes through the door. I may have smelled a wee bit of burning cannabis, now that you ask."

"Were Mr. Bingham and Mr. Beale using cannabis that night?"

"They may have been."

"Did you see them using?"

"No, but they *were* giggling a lot, you know, after."

Mindon sighed, picked up a plastic bag from the evidence table. "Item #1, a silver table knife manufactured by Rogers Brothers, pattern, 'First Love'. Found embedded in the throat of the deceased."

"So there it is!"

"You recognize this item?"

"Of course. It's one of eight such weapons I inherited from my dear, departed grandmother."

"Was this utensil part of your meal service on the night in question?"

Ian laid a finger against his lips, looked up at the high courtroom ceiling. "Hmm. Not sure."

Rob turned to Kate, whispered. "This guy is a piece of work."

"No matter. Perhaps another witness will have a better memory," Mindon commented.

"It might have been. Yes, I might have put it down to cut some teacakes. That's entirely possible."

"So it is also entirely possible that Mr. Bingham used this particular knife to cut a teacake?"

"Doubtful. Paulie doesn't like my teacakes. Perhaps some other intent?"

"No further questions."

Rob squeezed Kate's hand. "You can exhale now, babe."

"I just keep thinking of how Paulie feels sitting up there." She stared, hard, at Ian Flynn as he passed her seat. Flynn, however, had his nose in the air.

The prosecution next called Mrs. Finney.

"They were pushing and shoving each other, and using quite foul language," the matronly witness whined.

"Where, exactly, were the gentlemen standing when you observed their disagreement?"

275

"On the walk leading up to Mr. Bingham's house. Near the bottom of his porch steps. The porch light was on."

"Could you hear what they were saying, Mrs. Finney?"

"I tried not to. The color of their words was terribly offensive. The taller one, the one who's now deceased, he was quite upset. Mr. Bingham was sort of quiet, but became more agitated."

"How offensive? Can you repeat any of what you heard?"

The white-haired woman looked across the courtroom. "I used to work in a pub in Blackpool, Sir. I certainly can repeat what was said. He, Mr. Bingham, called Mr. Beale a cocksucking wanker. Mr. Beale then called Mr. Bingham a fucking arsehole, and hit him on the jaw with his fist."

Gasps and titters passed through the room in reaction to the witness' recollection.

"Did Mr. Bingham retaliate?"

"He pushed Mr. Beale off the walk, and told him to leave his property or he'd be callin' the police."

"And what did you do then, Mrs. Finney?"

"Why, I took George and went right inside, I did. George is my pommie poochie. I put him in his bed and rushed right upstairs to look out my bedroom window."

"What did you see, exactly?"

"Well, by that time, they had gone inside."

"Inside Mr. Bingham's house?"

"Yes. The door was closed. I saw the second floor lights come on."

"Thank you, Mrs. Finney. No further questions."

A forensic expert from the London police took the stand. After a long, tediously graphic description of the manner in which Jon Beale was stabbed and subsequently bled out, he testified that the dinner knife did, in fact, contain one-half of one clear fingerprint matching that of Paulie Bingham's right thumb.

"Mr. Teasdale, you may cross-examine. Proceed."

"Thank you, my lord. The defense calls Mr. Ian Flynn."

The usher reminded Flynn that he was still under oath, and Teasdale approached the witness box.

276

"At the time Mr. Bingham and Mr. Beale left your home on the night in question, would you say they were walking together, or separately?"

"Can't say, really. Paulie announced he was going, put on his mac, Jon followed. Once they went outside, I did not see whether they walked side-by-side, arm-in-arm, or cheek-to-cheek. They could have been lock-stepping for all I know." More laughter ensued.

"Bastard," Kate whispered.

"MR. FLYNN," the judge bellowed. "You will refrain from frivolity, or be found in contempt. This is a serious matter concerning the death of your alleged friend, Mr. Beale."

Ian re-crossed his legs, alternating his position. He rolled his eyes.

"Mr. Flynn, this social gathering at your flat, what was the occasion?"

"Nothing special. We started the party on Boxing Day, you see, and found it so enjoyable, we resumed on Friday."

"Was a meal served at your soirée?"

"But of course," Ian replied, patting his chest subtly. "What kind of host would I be without a little nosh? Let's see, there was a crab salad, a lovely tomato bisque, and little toast points. Oh! And a pate. Crackers. What else was there, Paulie?"

The judge pounded with his mallet. "The witness will not address the defendant."

"Sorry."

Teasdale resumed his cross-examination. "You have stated that you recognize the dinner knife that has been entered as evidence. At what point, Mr. Flynn, did you discover that this particular knife was missing from your service?"

"Uh, it was, I believe, a few days later. I was so stricken by the news of poor Jon's murder, I took to my bed. I hadn't yet cleaned up the flat from the party."

"You had not tidied up, nor washed the dishes, for three days?"

"Yes. I mean, no. I had not."

"So, in the meantime, you are not really certain of where the knife was between the time that Mr. Bingham may have used it, prior to his leaving your flat, and the time that it was found imbedded in the victim's neck. Is that true?"

"I don't know what you mean."

"I mean, dear fellow, that the knife may have remained in your possession after Mr. Bingham left until the time that Mr. Beale was stabbed with it. In fact, anyone at the party may have pocketed the knife after Mr. Bingham sampled your unappetizing teacakes."

"Objection!"

"Sustained! Mr. Teasdale, I beg you remember to withhold personal opinion from your comments."

"Sorry, my lord. The defense merely wishes to remind the court that no one witnessed Mr. Bingham removing the knife from Mr. Flynn's home. Now. According to my notes, you told the court earlier that when they, the defendant and the victim, came out of your back bedroom, you noticed animosity. I quote, 'Paulie was in a snit.'"

"That's quite right."

"Yes. However, you later told Prosecutor Mindon that both Mr. Bingham and Mr. Beale were, how did you put it? 'Giggling a lot.' Um, which was it, Mr. Flynn? Snit or giggling?"

A scowl crawled onto Ian's face. "I don't...recall."

The responsive murmur circled the courtroom as Ian Flynn was dismissed.

Kate's eye was drawn to the defendant's dock. Paulie was animated, and Teasdale leaned over, placating. Momentarily, he straightened, called Mrs. Finney back.

"Mrs. Finney. How long would you say it took you to put..." he glanced down at his notes, continued, "George, in his bed and then climb the stairs, cross through your bedroom, open the drapes and peer outside?"

"Why, I don't rightly know, exactly. Not long, surely."

"You're quick up the stairs, are you?"

"Well, no, not quick. Not since I broke my hip this past September."

"When you put your dog down, did you just...sort of...toss him onto his bed and go?"

"Why of course not, Mr. Teasdale. I always give him a right pattin' down, and a little smooch. He's all I've got, now."

"I see. So you carried, or walked, your Pomeranian to his doggie bed, is it in the foyer of your home?"

"No. On the back sun porch."

"Then you had a little affectionate period with him, walked back to your foyer, then climbed the forty-odd steps to the second floor..."

"My lord, what is the point of this tale?" The prosecutor abruptly stood.

"Overruled. Carry on, Barrister."

"I'd say it might have taken you, what, ninety seconds? Two minutes?"

"Objection. Counsel is leading the witness."

"Sustained. Mrs. Finney, how long do you think it was?"

The woman gave a frightened look to the judge. "Why, it might have been as much as two minutes...or a bit longer."

"Long enough," Teasdale continued, "for Mr. Beale to have walked off into the dark night, and Mr. Bingham to have entered his home alone, without your having actually seen either."

"Oh, dear. I was so certain Mr. Beale had gone inside. Now, I'm not—I'm not... oh, my."

The defense had no further questions.

     There I was, being defended against murdering someone, and all I could think about was getting my hands around Flynn's neck. A wee bit of burning cannabis?

If there was ever a time when I needed a good long toke off of a spliff, it was then. It was hard to keep my hands from shaking. I'd been given a cup of tea in the morning, with some sort of nasty crumpet. From where I sat in the defendant's dock, I could see Kate, Rob, Peg all sitting near the front of the public gallery. I could see a few of my mates crammed into the back. The rest were strangers and invisible to me.

I might as well have been wearing a dunce cap, sitting on a stool in the middle of the schoolroom. So many times I nearly shouted out, but Teasdale had warned me that any

ANNE CARTER

mouthing off would have been met with clear disdain from the judge.

The prosecutor looked completely naff in the wig. It was longish and terribly outdated. Teasdale, in contrast, wore a modified, trimmed up version, still archaic but somewhat fashionable as horsehair barrister wigs go. I've become quite the expert.

I wonder if they ever wear them to bed. Kinky.

The jurors stare at me until I look up, then they all find other fascinating sights within the courtroom.

I nearly chucked at the appearance of the knife they say killed Jon. All brown and crusty. How they could lift a print off that mess is beyond me.

Ian's teacakes are poisonously bad. –Defendant Paul Bingham

Chapter 32

Kate hosted all of Paulie's supporters at Chanticleer. Buzz took her into an everlasting bear hug. Unknown friends introduced themselves, offered snippets of how they met or knew Paulie. His agents and managers, some from many years past, filed by. It was more like a funeral than the onset of a trial.

It *felt* like a funeral. People talked as if Paulie had already been sentenced. It sickened her. Confused and angry, Kate wanted to escape, to find someone to talk to that understood her outrage, her fears, her grief. And that's when she realized why she'd felt something so amiss. Someone was missing from the party, and that someone was Paulie's second most ardent supporter. Alec Doyle was not present.

"Excuse me. Please. Excuse me." She gently pushed her way through the people who'd gathered in the great room. She caught Rob's eye and gestured toward the stairs. He met her halfway up.

"I never heard back from Alec. I'm going to call his office again. Maybe he never got the other messages on his cell."

"Or maybe he doesn't want to be involved."

"I highly doubt that. He really cares for Paulie."

Rob nodded, returned to the crowd as Kate continued on to the second floor. Instead of going to her own room, she slipped into Paulie's suite and sat down on the bed. It comforted her somehow. She dialed Alec's number.

There was only a voice responder.

"Alec, it's Kate. I'm sure, I hope you know what's transpiring here in London. Everything is so chaotic, when you get this message, please, please call me on my cell. If you can book a flight you should do it. He's going to need every ounce of support we can give him. Okay? Thanks. Bye."

By nine p.m., Kate was dragging. The day in court might have been a marathon, the way she felt. The gloomy reception only added to her blue mood. Rob ordered a late meal in, and they ate sitting at the coffee table.

"I was ready to ram a butcher knife into that guy's throat myself," she hissed, then bit into a club sandwich. "Some friend, Flynn. He's the one, you know, who started that whole thing with Paulie and Jon. Do you remember the night I went tearing out of Wembley?"

"How could I forget? You knocked me down trying to get out the back door."

"I did not! You liar. I was running because Jon Beale had just so much as told me he was Paul's new lover, and I was nothing more than a beard."

"Whoa. No wonder you took off."

"That ass Flynn set him up with Paulie."

"It *did* occur to you that Paulie could've refused Mr. Beale's amorous advances."

Kate gave Rob a mock-hostile look. "Actually, it did. And that fact is one reason why we are no longer married."

"Remind me never to double date with Ian Flynn."

She was about to counter when her phone rang. Alec's voice on the other end filled her with relief.

"I've been so worried about you!"

"I'm sorry, dear. I've had some rather difficult times."

"Are you coming to London?"

"Yes. How's Paulie? How's he holding up?"

"It's not good, Alec. I don't know if you've read the news, but he doesn't have a very strong case. The only witnesses we have are two teenage girls with a history of lying."

"Girls? What did they see?"

"They saw Jon Beale walk away from Paulie's house. That's it. The prosecutors will say that the girls aren't credible, or that Jon could have returned within the hour. They say at some point Paulie followed or walked with Jon to the nearby park and killed him. And Paul has no real alibi from about 9:35 until Peg came home the next morning. Nearly twelve hours, during which time Beale was murdered and found in that park. It's just terrible."

Alec didn't speak. Kate could imagine his pain at realizing Paulie's true predicament.

282

"When will you be here? Do you want to meet at Paulie's home? Or at your hotel? Just say. Rob and I can do whatever."

"Uh, I will call you when I arrive. I may have to go straight to the court."

"Oh. Well, then, we can have dinner together."

"That would be nice. Thanks, Kate, for getting in touch with me. My heart is aching over this. I can't imagine how he is surviving."

Alec did not show up at the courthouse the next morning. Kate fretted, and left him another message.

Teasdale called each of the girls to the stand, gently asking them how it was they came to be hiding in the bushes on the Bingham property. Each tearfully described the fight between Paulie and Jon, and Jon's subsequent storming off. The prosecutor came right back with school records reflecting disobedience and dishonesty on the part of one of them. Playing on her youthful naiveté, he further got the other to say she'd do anything for Paulie Bingham. *Anything*, she emphasized, staring at Paulie with blatant worship. Kate sank back against her chair.

When they broke for lunch, Peg announced she didn't feel well and needed to get a cab home. Kate insisted on going with her and asked Rob to stay at the court in case she was late getting back. He agreed and she hailed a London cab.

"I'm so sorry, love. It's just so hard to sit there, watchin' those bloody heathens rip into me lit'le brother. I know 'e's not perfect. But you'll not find a more golden heart than his. I just got ill thinkin' about how they're goin' to throw him into a cell and toss the key." Peg sobbed, and Kate comforted her as best she could.

"Why don't you lie down, Peggy? I'll get you a nice cuppa. Just rest."

After putting up the tea, Kate quickly went upstairs to retrieve a sweater she'd left in the guest room. As she passed Paulie's room, something glittered above the bed and caught her eye. A rare sun, just breaking through the clouds, sent an odd beam of light across from the window, reflecting off the intricate brass headboard. Kate went to the bed and sat down.

She was, again, overcome by the feel, the aura of Paulie. She ran her hand over the shiny metal, the curving question marks and commas that made up the design of the fancy headboard. The glitter again reflected, only now she realized it was red, not golden. She reached out, feeling along the cool brass until she touched something that did not belong.

Stuck on to the end of one of the curlicues was a ring with a red gemstone setting. She worked it until it popped off and into her hand.

"How bizarre." She hadn't seen the ring before, a large, heavy, clearly masculine ring with what looked like a ruby in the center, gold and black design work around it. At closer look, she recognized it as a class ring. Quickly turning on the bedside lamp, she peered closely, trying to make out the tiny words. *University of Birmingham.* Beneath that, the Hippocratic staff. Above, the initials, *"A.D."*

As realization dawned, Kate slowly closed her fist, the ring inside. Downstairs, the teakettle was whistling.

She couldn't get back to the courthouse fast enough. Lunch time traffic in London was notoriously bad, and she got out of the cab before it came to a complete stop near the entrance. Panting, she slipped quietly into her seat just as the audience was sitting, the judge having just been seated.

"Are you okay?" Rob asked.

"Yes. I have new information. I don't know what to do."

"You need to talk to Teasdale, then."

"It might be nothing."

Kate tried to calm her breathing. *It might be nothing.* Alec may have given the ring to Paulie in Los Angeles. Paulie probably stuck it on the bed frame as a lark.

"The defense calls Katrina Bingham."

What?

Rob looked at her, frowning. "Did you know about this?"

"No. Absolutely not."

She got up, approached the stand, took her oath and was seated. Her eyes were immediately drawn to Paulie's.

"Ms. Bingham. Will you state your full name and your relationship to the defendant?"

"Katrina Newman Bingham. I am Paul Bingham's former wife."

"You are divorced, then?"

"Yes."

"How long have you known Mr. Bingham?"

"We met on May 16, 1983. Eleven years, eight months."

A shout came from the back. "But who's counting?" Laughter ensued.

Stoic, Teasdale continued. "And during that time, you were married for how long?"

"Five and a half years."

"Would you describe Paul Bingham as a violent person?"

She couldn't help but smile. "No, sir."

"Would you say he has a...spontaneous temper?"

"No. Not at all."

"During that eleven years and change, did he ever strike you, or anyone else, for that matter?"

"No, Mr. Teasdale. Not that I recall." she lied, hopeful that no one in the courtroom knew about Ray Goff. She again glanced at Paulie. "I once smacked him, though."

Paulie smiled back at her, gave her a subtle nod.

"Oh, and how did he respond?"

"He was shocked, and he cried out, 'you fucking hit me!'"

Kate knew her words would cause a stir, and she noted a few smiles amid the jurors.

"I see. Now. You and Mr. Bingham have a daughter, do you not?"

"We do."

"She is...how old?"

Kate felt her nose getting red. *He had to bring up Bonny.*

"She is almost four."

"And how is Mr. Bingham's relationship with his little girl?"

"He is quite smitten with her, actually. They're very attached to one another."

285

"And you share custody, is that right?"

"That's correct. They talk on the phone almost every day, and we arrange family visits periodically."

"Objection. I fail to see the value of the time spent discussing family matters."

"Counsel?"

Teasdale approached the judge. "My lord, I feel it is important that the jury learn the kind of person my client is, to establish his…his strength of character."

"Overruled. Continue."

"Did Mr. Bingham ever discuss his relationship with Mr. Beale, with you, Ms. Bingham?"

Kate felt her stomach clench. She wasn't sure how Teasdale wanted her to answer, so she hesitantly opted for the truth. Sort of.

"Not really. I only know that they did, in fact, have a…an encounter. Paul said that it was nothing, um, serious, although he thought Jon was a nice guy."

She looked to Paulie for confirmation. Again, the almost imperceptible nod.

"Thank you, Ms. Bingham. That's all."

Kate started to rise when the prosecutor stood and approached her.

"Permission to cross-examine the defense witness?"

"Permission granted. Proceed."

"Mrs. Bingham. Is it true that on the night of second June, 1994, you had a conversation with Mr. Beale at a concert here in London? While your husband was on stage?"

Kate blushed. "I-I'm not sure I recall."

"Yes, I believe Mr. Beale spoke to you, and you left Wembley Arena in a great hurry. In your haste, you took a tumble down the backstairs. You were pregnant at the time, and less than thirty-six hours later, you miscarried the child, is that not correct?"

Horrified, Kate stared at the prosecutor. "I—I—"

"Objection! Mrs. Bingham's experiences last summer have no bearing on this trial!"

"Oh, but they do, for whatever Mr. Beale said to Mrs. Bingham could be construed as the cause of the loss, motive enough for the father of that child to seek retribution!"

Chaos broke out amidst the jurors and audience. Kate tearfully looked to Paulie, who stared back in stunned silence.

"Order! The objection is overruled. Mrs. Bingham, please verify the truth of counsel's statement."

Kate took a shuddering breath, cleared her throat. Rob was sending her strength with his trusting eyes.

"Paul and I had argued earlier, over something stupid I can't even remember. I was stewing throughout the concert. I didn't feel well, and I decided to return to the hotel. I don't even recall what Mr. Beale said, other than a comment about how well Paulie sang. The conversation had no bearing on my fall. I simply tripped."

"But you cannot deny—"

"Just a moment, sir. I'm not through talking. As far as the miscarriage being some kind of sick motive, it's not possible. Because Paul didn't know about that miscarriage until you shared that information with this entire courtroom just now."

Flustered, the prosecutor shuffled his notes.

"You did not tell your own husband that you had lost your child?"

"I chose not to share that unhappy news. I allowed him to believe that it was a mistake that I'd thought I was pregnant."

Paulie crossed his arms on the dock, put his head down.

The prosecutor turned away, then returned to the witness stand.

"My apologies, Mrs. Bingham," he murmured. "You may step down."

Kate longed to walk straight to the defendant's dock and face Paulie, but Teasdale's look told her to be happy with the small victory. It was a sympathetic gain for the defense; there were several women on the jury.

She took two steps and then detoured, passing in front of the dock after all. The dock officer looked up, on alert. Kate paused only briefly, took Paulie's hand, subtly pressed Alec's ring into his palm before circling around to sit beside Rob. To those watching, it was only an affectionate gesture from his grieving ex-wife.

Court was continued until the next morning. As an emotionally distraught Kate stood, a page rushed up.

"Miz Bingham, Mr. Teasdale would like to see you in quarters."

She looked at Rob.

"I'll wait."

Kate started to move away, but he stopped her, pulled her back. "I'm sorry they put you through that. Stay calm, okay? This isn't over yet. I think we gained ground today."

She nodded, offered a weak smile. "Thanks for sticking with me."

In the barrister's quarters, Teasdale was arguing with another man. A third, the young page, stood by. Paulie sat staring out the window.

"Kate, this is Mr. Sheffield, Paul's solicitor. I believe you've spoken on the telephone. And Kip, my aide."

"Nice to meet you both."

"Now, we must discuss what just occurred. I need to ask why you didn't tell me about your discussion with Beale. I was disadvantaged out there."

"*You* were disadvantaged? I didn't even know I was being called. That was a complete shock to me."

"I apologize, but I was only informed this morning that they were planning to call you. Given the lateness of the day, I felt it best if I questioned you first, to set a first impression with the jurors. Mindon blindsided us both with his question." Teasdale paused. "Is it true?"

Kate looked around, but Paulie was turned away.

"You may be frank inside this room," Sheffield said.

"Yes. It was all true."

"All things considered, I feel you handled it well. I'm deeply concerned about how he came about that information. Who else knew about your loss?"

"Only Cheryl, Rob, and my doctor."

"Perhaps someone in your doctor's office passed on the information to Mindon. Someone who wants Paulie to be convicted."

Kate shook her head. "I just can't imagine that."

The barrister sighed. "We are rather low on material. We may have to present closing arguments tomorrow."

"No! I mean, something may come up, soon, we don't know..."

"We can't delay the courts for something that may come up, dear."

Kate paced, returned, wet her lips. "I need to talk to Paulie. Now. Alone."

Teasdale shook his head. "Can't be alone. Not in these chambers. But you can have five minutes before they sweep us out, and I'll leave Kip to mind you."

Kate looked at the youth, then back at Teasdale.

"And by the way, Kip is deaf and dumb."

"And blind. Don't forget blind," the youth offered.

The barrister and solicitor left, and Kip sat in a corner chair with a Walkman plugged into his ears.

Kate approached, held her hands out, just short of touching him. She'd never once considered the possibility that he'd find out. Paulie stood up.

"I'm sorry," Kate began. "I just couldn't tell you. I should have."

"No, I'm sorry," he said softly. "It seemed odd to me at the time, but...you're a far better liar than I am. I should have been there. I can't fathom that you went through that alone. The whole blasted thing is my fault."

"No. But now's not the time to debate that. We have a much bigger problem to discuss."

Paulie rubbed his eyes. "You can't do it, Kate. Please, don't."

"I have no choice. I cannot, *will not* stand by while they lock you away, all because of some stupid secret. He was with you, wasn't he? He's your alibi. He's the one you're protecting."

"I can't betray him."

"I can."

"No. He's a good man. You don't understand what that will do to his life."

"I understand what not doing it will do to mine. To Bonny's, let alone yours."

"I'll deny it."

Kate cried out in frustration, grasped his suit labels. "You are SO pissing me off!"

"Go ahead. Hit me again. I rather fancy that."

His quip calmed her somewhat. "You once told me that no one would ever love me like you do."

"It's true. Always."

"Then please, let me do this. He will survive. I don't think I can."

"It has to be his decision. I gave him my word, some time back. I care for him, Kate. He's been better to me than any other man in my life."

"Well he's not returning the favor. He never showed up."

"Have you been in touch?"

"Yes. Finally. He returned my call last night after weeks of leaving messages. When we talked last month, I told him he should come and see you."

"You saw him?"

"Yeah. But I only found the ring today."

The page stood. "Almost time," he muttered.

"Why did you see him?"

"He'd called, and we talked on the phone. It was because he missed you so. He was very troubled, and he wanted news— any news—about you. Then, just after Christmas, I went to see him."

"Because?"

"Because I was so sad."

He swallowed, did the handcuffs-over-the-head routine again, held her close. They were both crying now. Teasdale walked in, but neither of them moved.

"I need to get some waterproof mascara," she told Paulie.

"So do I," he whispered back. They exchanged an affectionate kiss, and then Kate left him and went in search of Rob.

Chapter 33

S he explained it all to Rob over her menu in Chinatown.

"I just don't understand why Alec didn't come. He didn't have to say he'd be there, but he did."

"Second thoughts."

"Maybe. This has got to be killing him."

"Maybe he's just waiting for last-ditch. Hoping something else will preclude him having to give away the farm."

"If I could just talk to him again, I bet I could convince him."

Kate felt edgy, disconnected. While she muddled through her mismatched thoughts, Rob ordered and then snapped his fingers to get her attention.

"All this time we've focused on Paulie's alibi. We haven't even touched on who the murderer might be, why they would frame him. Who are his enemies?"

"I did go over that with Teasdale. I don't think he has any, aside from thinly disguised misogynists like Flynn."

"No one, in his past, that he shot down or insulted? I once sacked a guy for dealing coke to my crew."

"He's insulted a lot of people. It's part of the game. And Ray, of course. But not enough to warrant killing to get to him."

"In your opinion. What about his bad years? You said you lost touch when he was laid out on smack."

Kate nodded slowly. "I suppose there could be. But why now? It doesn't seem likely. That was a long time ago."

"Somebody wants to see him convicted. Somebody with the power to get your doctor's office to give up information illegally, somebody who knew Jon was sweet on him. They even knew you'd talked to Jon that night at Wembley. Can you think of anyone in the Bingham entourage who seems even the slightest bit suspicious?"

Kate sighed, shook her head. Taking a single chopstick, she speared a small shrimp and stuck it in her mouth.

"That same somebody also lifted the knife from Flynn's house after Paulie used it. Who was at both places? The concert and the party?"

"Besides Jon, I can't know that. I obviously wasn't at the party, nor could I possibly know everyone at the concert. Your people were there, too, milling around."

"This person knows you."

Kate put down her chopsticks and stared at Rob. A chill ran down her back.

"How can that be?"

"I don't know. But I got a feeling. This person is more than just a random badass. This was carefully orchestrated. Think about it. They knew you were pregnant, when you and Paul hadn't made it public; they knew you talked to Jon, knew you'd fallen down the steps. Was anyone outside to see you fall?"

"No one close enough. People in the distance, but...no. I'm pretty sure."

"Did you tell the doctor about the fall? Where it happened?"

"Just that I fell down some steps. I never said where."

"But then, you were pretty upset. Someone might have been out there, having a smoke. And really, all these people might be employed by our phantom. He didn't have to be there himself, right?"

"You mean, he could have had spies traveling with us?"

"Or he bought their info later."

Kate digested Rob's suggestion, realized her phone was ringing in her purse. "Maybe it's Alec." She quickly dug it out and answered.

"Kate? William Teasdale. Sorry for the hour. I hope I'm not interrupting."

"No, of course not."

"I need to let you know that Mr. Bingham and I have had a conversation, and we've decided that he will take the stand tomorrow. I thought I'd let you know in advance."

"Oh...do you think that's wise? I mean, of course you do. But, is it risky?"

"We don't have much to lose. I feel that the jury is entitled to experience Paulie's honesty and charm. He deserves the right to tell it from his perspective, because, after all, he is our only real witness, and in England, he is still innocent until proven guilty. The burden still lies on the prosecution."

"I understand."

"And you may want to arrive extra early. I'm alerting the media that Paul will be testifying. Hopefully, there will be fans for miles, camping on the lawn and demanding our boy go free."

"I don't believe it!"

"Believe it, dear. We may go out, but we will go out kicking and screaming. When you arrive, ask Kip to bring you back. Paulie would like to see you, and he asks that you bring your kit, whatever that means. As long as it doesn't contain weapons."

Kate slowly ended the call and dropped the phone into her bag.

"He's putting Paulie on the stand tomorrow."

"No way."

"Way. And we need to go shopping."

Kate turned again, punched up her pillow. Beside her, Rob slept, had been sleeping for nearly two hours. After dinner, they'd gone to Harrod's, where Kate hastily put together a "kit" of all Paulie's favorite makeup. Brushes, foam wedges, tissues rounded it out. Was it a good idea? Maybe it didn't matter.

Now, in the dark, she fretted about the day to come. Tried to imagine Paulie, sitting at the witness stand. Tried to remember the faces of the jurors. Would they sympathize? Realize that the evidence was circumstantial, if somewhat compelling? What would Paulie say? Hopefully, he would be his sweetest self. No diva tantrums, no stubborn, fussy snits.

She could barely see Rob's face. Thought about how devoted he'd been throughout the ordeal. He'd dropped everything to support her in London, canceled meetings and even an interview. They'd been photographed from every which way, and Rob's likeness and name was now intricately woven together with Paulie's. They were both connected to a murder investigation.

Tomorrow, everything would change, one way or another. The trial would end, and they would begin the excruciating wait for a verdict. At home, Bonny knew nothing of her much beloved Daddy living behind bars, possibly forever. Kate purposely put Bonny from her mind, knowing the pain that would eventually result. It was too much to bear right now.

She reached out, touched Rob's face, slid her fingertips into his rich brown hair, and combed through the locks. He made a sound, and she repeated the action.

"Rob?" She moved closer, continued stroking his hair. "Robbie?"

"Hmm?"

"I can't sleep."

He swept an arm around her, pulled her against him. "You okay?"

"Yeah. I just can't stop thinking. I'm stuck on a loop."

"Let me distract you, then."

"Okay."

"Let's see. Mom thinks you are the best thing since automatic ice makers."

Kate smiled. "I like her, too."

"You're not so bad."

"The next few days are going to be tough."

"I know."

"Please don't let my runaway emotions put you off, okay? If he's convicted, I *will* go to pieces."

"I know that, too. I *will* be here to put you back together."

She touched his cheek, his chin. "I don't know what I would do without you now. How I would have gotten through this."

"You're stronger than you think. That's one of your best assets."

"I know I've been missing in action lately. When we get back, when this is all over, things will be better."

"Would you like to go steady?"

294

"You'd ask me that, even with all this drama? Even though I seem attached at the hip to my eccentric ex?"

"Even with all that. Somehow, I understand it. I get that he comes with the package. I'm still buying." He kissed her gently. "We just need to get through this first."

Although they left the apartment at 6:30 a.m., long before sun up, the road leading to Snaresbrook Crown Court was lined with people. It was cold and wet, but the fans were there in droves, after hearing the news on early morning radio and television. It was 7:15 before they were admitted to the barrister's chambers. This time, Rob went with her.

Paulie was waiting, along with the entire defense team. Kate went to him, Rob held back to chat with Teasdale; Kate put the case on the table.

Paulie spread his arms wide: they'd taken off his handcuffs while he dressed. "I could fly away."

"You look sharp. Who's dressing you these days?"

"Young Master Kip has been a tremendous asset. Picked out my threads, moussed my hair. I'd be quite the toast of King's Road."

"Are you all right?"

"Yeah."

"Do you know what you're going to say?"

"Not yet."

"Good. It's better that way. It'll seem more natural and honest." She snapped open the brand new train case. "What would you like today, my darling?"

"Do you remember that show in Amsterdam?"

"It was a bit of this," she recalled, picking up a small, silvery-blue crayon. "And this," she added, finding a charcoal pencil. "Nude foundation, thin cranberry gloss. And I think I have it all."

"Brilliant memory, Kate." He lifted his chin as she tied the black plastic cape around him. Rob stepped up.

"Can I watch?"

"Absolutely. You have to watch her to believe it. Sit a spell, Mr. Evans."

Kate focused, began building the layers. Despite the color, she kept it tasteful and not too pervasive. "Hold still, Bingham. You're moving."

"You'd move too, darling, if you were about to be placed in the crosshairs."

She paused, looked him in the eye. "You have twenty-thousand fans outside. They're sending their collective love and prayers in here, you know."

"It only takes one," he murmured.

Kate nodded. "I know that." *Alec Doyle.*

He beckoned with his fingers. "C'mon. Give us a love before you put on my lipstick."

Kate bent down, kissed his lips twice, then found the gloss. She carefully dabbed on the sheer color, went back to her case.

"Here. Take a look."

"You even brought a mirror? Amazing girl."

She pulled off the cape, gave him the hand mirror. He stood up, primped at his hair. "Excellent. What do you think?" he asked of his counselor.

"Uh, very nice indeed. Quite joyous."

Rob stood, too. "You look great, Paul. Dashing."

"Not too queer?"

"Oh, it's queer, all right," Rob said. "But tastefully queer." He walked up to Paulie and paused, then embraced him. "Be yourself, man. That jury out there, they want to acquit. I can tell."

"From your lips to God's ear," Paulie said, hugging Rob back. "Thank you, Ev."

Seeing Rob with Paulie nearly reduced Kate to a quivering mass. She swallowed, hard, busied herself with repacking her case. The one-half of one-percent doubt she may have had about loving Rob disappeared in its entirety.

☙ **I didn't know how I would get through the day. To me, it felt like they were putting Paulie before a firing squad. He was in no condition to talk about what happened. Had he been properly coached? Would he go to pieces up there, possibly sealing his fate? God forbid he got into a foul-**

mouthed diatribe. His bravado attitude didn't fool me: he was scared.

It was ludicrous to think at the time, but I wished I could speak for him. I didn't trust him as far as I could throw him. He'd never, ever, been any good at defending himself. The street fights had made him defensive and rude. Words were his only weapons, and he used them freely when challenged.

(Please don't mouth off, Paul. This is Kate talking.)

Rob thinks I am overreacting, but he doesn't know Paul like I do. No one does.

Chapter 34

"My name is Paul Philip Bingham. I am 34 years old, I was born in Essex, I now live in London. Some people call me an entertainer."

After swearing in, Paulie sat down, gazed out at the sea of expectant faces. To his left, the twelve jurors stared, and he gave them a polite nod. Ahead sat Teasdale, Sheffield and young Kip. The observers filled the room, with several standing in the rear. Just to his forward right, Prosecutor Mindon and his assistants. Behind Mindon, in the first row, sat a man, a woman and a teenage girl, all wishing Paulie dead with their eyes.

The judge, above and immediate right, adjusted his white, horsehair wig.

In front of Paulie was a microphone, and he almost smiled. Here, at least, a familiar object in a world full of the alien.

Teasdale stood. "Ladies and gentlemen of the jury, Mr. Bingham would like to make a statement. If the court will indulge."

The judge nodded. "You may proceed, Mr. Bingham."

"Thank you, M'lord, Sir." Paulie cleared his throat, adjusted the microphone. What would they do, he wondered fleetingly, if I broke into song? It would certainly be easier than what was expected of him. But what would he sing? "Freebird"?

"I look the way I look today because this is how I am normally. I felt it was fraudulent to appear otherwise, and also, I am more comfortable this way. As has been alluded to, I am, primarily, a homosexual man. I was made aware of that fact by others at the age of nine years, and was regularly punched up because of it. Since I was usually smaller than those doing the punching, I rarely fought back. I mean, what was the point? Anyway, despite what some may think about gay people, I've had two long term, significant, committed relationships in my life. I believe in monogamy.

299

"I know you're all likely asking yourselves, what's an avowed gay man doing with a beautiful, heterosexual woman?" He sought Kate's face in the crowd, smiled briefly. "What I did was, I fell in love, we shared lots of good times, we conceived an angel of a daughter. But there was that gay thing and we decided that we'd be better off friends than spouses. It was around this time that I met Jon Beale."

A hush fell over the room. Paulie noticed a glass of water had been placed in the box, and he took a shaky sip. "Jon was nice enough, but was rather forced upon me by my well-intentioned mates, who thought I needed to be reminded that I preferred men. Jon was a simply joyous chap, always smiling, always cheery. But he was also a man's man, so to speak. We had a brief encounter, but I wasn't terribly interested. I was dealing with the separation from Kate."

She was sending him sunbeams across the courtroom. It buoyed him.

"A couple of weeks ago, Flynn invited me round to his parties. Or perhaps it was one, week-long party following Christmas. Christmas was a lonely time for me, away from the family I loved in the U.S. And as before, Flynn and the others thought it a lark to sic Jon onto me again. They told him I fancied him, and that I was ready to hook up. I was not, but I was also concerned for Jon's feelings. I stayed for a while, had a meal, partook of the libations, you know, and then Jon started asking me to join him in the back room. I made the mistake of indulging him and quite honestly, my own selfish need for attention."

There was a low murmur in response to his confession. From the corner of his eye, he saw Kip rise and leave the courtroom.

More water, clear the throat. I'm making them uncomfortable. Maybe I'll make them so uncomfortable, they'll acquit just to rid themselves of me.

"I was immediately remorseful. Jon clearly wanted more from me, and I wasn't interested."

"May I interrupt?" Teasdale asked.

"By all means. I'm rather bored with my own voice at this point."

One of the jurors, a young woman, stifled a giggle.

"When you say Jon wanted more from you, of what are you speaking?"

"I think he wanted to have a serious relationship."

"And you told him you were not interested?"

"I tried to be gentle. No use in crushing the bloke. He wasn't going along, so I thought to go home. As has been attested to, he started following me. I stopped once or twice to tell him not to waste his time. It was bloody cold out, my house is several blocks away. He ignored me, and we ended on the walk out front of my house. We argued, and yes, Mrs. Finney's account of what I said is true, although I will spare you all from my crude lack of manners."

"And then what happened?"

"He continued to try to convince me that he should come in, he would show me, he said, why we were to be together. I finally told him I couldn't do it because I was still in love with my wife."

Someone in the jury gasped, and Paulie was afraid to look to the audience. He stumbled on. "This revelation enraged him. He told me I was lying, that I was perverted, that I was off my head. When I protested and threatened to call the police, he punched me here," he said, pointed to his chin, then his brow, "and here. It's only just now healing. I pushed him, as hard as I could, which was a chore as Jon was a much bigger person than I. He stumbled backward and lost his footing on the edge of the walk, so I took the opportunity to rush inside and bolt the door. He pounded for a bit, kicked my front door. I was bloody scared, as my sister and her children were not home. I was alone. Then it was quiet, so I peeked out the side window and saw him storming off, back in the direction of the Heath."

"What did you do next?

"I went upstairs, to the second floor, and turned up all the lights. I was shaking. I turned on the telly, held onto my cell phone and got into bed."

"Why did you, uh, hold onto the phone?"

"In case he came banging back on the door. I wanted to be ready to call the police."

301

Teasdale nodded, then turned to listen to a whispered message from Kip, who'd just returned with a small paper bag.

"Mr. Bingham, if you don't mind, I'd like to ask you to participate in a wee exercise. Forgive me for springing this on you, but a bit of information has just been brought to my attention."

Paulie shrugged. Teasdale carried the paper bag to the witness stand and withdrew a silver table knife. He carefully placed it in the center of the wooden ledge before Paulie.

"Now, sir. Imagine, if you will, that you are about to be charged by a raging—let's say it's a bear. How would you defend yourself?"

Mindon, who'd sat quietly throughout Paulie's testimony, stood, but seemed at a loss to formulate an objection.

Paulie smiled briefly. "Are you joking? You think I could stop a bear with *that*?"

"If that's all you had, what would you do?"

"Well then, if I may stand?"

"Of course."

Paulie stood, looked around, embarrassed. "Is the bear taller than me?"

People laughed, Teasdale chuckled. "Let's say he is. But he's coming at you at a rather fast clip."

"All right." Without further thought, Paulie swept up the knife and held it out toward the barrister, its blade at an upward angle.

"Thank you. The court will note the position in which the defendant is holding the knife, and most importantly, that he is holding it with his left hand. You are left-handed, are you not, Mr. Bingham?"

"Yes sir. Another of my minority attributes. May I ask, is there some significance to the way I'm holding this knife? Would the bear have won?"

"Hard to say, Paul. Perhaps had you turned it around..." Teasdale took the dinner knife from Paulie and wrapped his hand around its base with the blade pointing down. He lifted the knife high and sliced the air with a downward stabbing motion. "You know, this way, as was demonstrated by Mr. Jones when he described how the victim was attacked."

302

Eyes wide, Paulie sat back down.

Teasdale returned the knife to the bag. "No further questions at this time. Thank you, Mr. Bingham."

Mindon cleared his throat. "Requesting permission to question the defendant."

Paulie looked to Teasdale, who had already warned Paulie that cross-examination would likely occur. The judge approved, and the prosecutor came forth.

"You said, Mr. Bingham, that you remained inside and alone after Mr. Beale allegedly left your property. It has already been established that you have no proof of same, is that correct?"

"Well there is the matter of my word, sir."

"Your word. Yes."

"Inasmuch as I have not been proven guilty of any crime, there is no reason to doubt my word, is there?" Paulie continued.

"You do have a history of drug use, yes?"

Teasdale threw down the bag he'd been holding. "Objection! Whether or not Mr. Bingham has used drugs in the past is not relevant."

"Sustained. You do not need to answer, Mr. Bingham."

Paulie leaned close to the microphone. "No, actually, it's okay. Yes. I used heroin at one time, but I've been clean for nearly eight years. By now, it's a matter of public record. I've nothing to hide. I'm quite proud because it was the most difficult thing I've ever done in my life."

"Is it not true, that in June of 1990, barely a year after your marriage to Mrs. Bingham, you were arrested in Los Angeles for lewd and lascivious conduct? For having sex with a man in a nightclub loo?"

Paulie's eyes narrowed and his throat closed. "I—"

Teasdale was instantly on his feet. "You do not need to answer that question, Mr. Bingham. My lord, the incident about which my colleague asks did not result in any citation or judgment, as charges were dropped as unsubstantiated."

"Sustained. The jury will disregard."

Yeah, that's likely. Paulie hazarded a look at Kate and Rob. Kate was shaking her head, slowly, her expression grim.

He wasn't sure if it was the memory or Mindon who had garnered her ire.

Mindon, apparently, wasn't finished. "My lord, it is merely my intention to present a more complete picture to the jury. Mr. Bingham has chosen to omit certain aspects of his life that may have a bearing on his true character, thereby having an effect on their opinions."

"Proceed. With caution, sir."

"In January of 1992, your wife left you. Do you recall the nature of your disagreement?"

"No disagreement. She went for a visit to her parents' home."

"Because you were fighting. I ask again, about what did you argue, enough to cause Mrs. Bingham to take your child and flee?"

"Irrelevant!" Teasdale called out.

"Overruled."

"She did not flee. I was working hard on a new album, working round the clock. Our daughter needed lots of care, she was just a wee one then, and Kate needed more support than I could give her. Her parents were a tremendous help. I did go out there for a visit, as well."

"How long was she gone?"

"Two months. I know that because I missed her every one of those sixty days."

"But didn't she storm out in anger, because of your spending time clubbing with your mates?"

"No. Go on, ask her!"

Mindon ignored Paulie's exclamation, walked before the jury and then back to Paulie. "Let's go back to the night of the murder. You said you went upstairs to watch television. At what time did Mr. Beale return?"

Incredulous, Paulie frowned at the prosecutor. "I've already told you, he did not return."

"And just how do we know that, again, Mr. Bingham?"

Paulie felt his face growing hot, his palms perspiring. He tried to calm his breathing, not wanting to appear angry, or worse, guilty. He took a gulp of water, swallowed, and straightened in his seat. The sound of his own heartbeat was deafening. *I'm going to fucking black out. I can't do this.*

"Because I said so," he said quietly.

"Because he was with *me*," came a strong, clear voice from the back of the courtroom. Cacophony erupted in the room, and the judge was forced to pound his gavel. Paulie looked up, squinted to see if the voice belonged to whom he thought it did.

Praise Mary and Jesus. It's Alec.

In an instant, Kip was escorting Alec Doyle to the front, and Teasdale approached the bench.

"My lord, I'd like to request a short recess. Apparently my star witness has just arrived."

Kate's heart was racing so fast she thought she might have to lie down. With Rob in tow, she forced her way through the crowd to where Alec was being led from the room. The dock officer stood close to Paulie. She paused to compliment her ex.

"You were awesome. You had them eating from the palm of your hand until that jerk Mindon stood up."

"I'm sorry he dragged out all that nastiness," Paulie murmured.

"It doesn't matter. Alec is here."

"Yeah. I'm quite amazed."

Kate squeezed his hand.

The recess lasted twenty minutes, and Paulie was allowed to leave the stand, replaced by Alec, called by the defense.

"State your full name and occupation."

"Alec Frederic Doyle. I'm a physician. I'm a native Londoner, but have lived in Los Angeles for the past two years." He took the card from the usher, read aloud. "I swear, by almighty God, that the evidence I shall give shall be the truth, the whole truth, and nothing but the truth."

Kate sat straight and stared directly at Alec. It was all but over now, if Alec told the truth, and it appeared that he was about to.

"Please recount, for the court, the events of December 30, 1994."

"I flew into London from Los Angeles on Thursday, 29 December, and visited with friends in Kensington. On the evening of the 30th, I called Paul Bingham on his cellular phone, at approximately 9:25 p.m. He invited me to his home."

"I'm sorry, please explain your prior relationship to Mr. Bingham?"

"We were partners. Uh, we had a relationship. In Los Angeles, after his separation from Mrs. Bingham. We were flat mates as well."

"I see. Do you know why Mr. Bingham chose to omit this information from his testimony?"

Alec twisted in his chair. "Because I am not known as a homosexual. My sexual orientation has been a secret for all of my adult life. My whole life, that is."

"I see," Teasdale said with a nod. "And Mr. Bingham was respecting your secret?"

"Which is why, I'm quite certain, he did not reveal that I was with him the entire night of the murder."

"At what time did you leave the Hampstead mansion?"

"Around 7:30 a.m. on 31 December, well in advance his sister's return. I didn't want Paulie to have to explain my presence."

"Are there any witnesses to your arrival?"

"I believe the cabbie that dropped me will remember me. I gave him a rather substantial gratuity."

"Can you provide contact information for this cab driver?"

"Well, I'm not sure I—"

"I can," Kate called out. "I can," she repeated, more quietly. The judge frowned but did not lift his gavel.

"Mr. Doyle, if I may ask, why is it that you've gone to such efforts to hide your sexual preference for men?" Teasdale resumed.

Alec coughed a little, moved the microphone. "Personal reasons. My family and my professional colleagues are not particularly liberal when it comes to homosexuality."

Kate looked to Paulie, saw him bow his head.

"What made you decide to come here today, to share this new information with the court?" Teasdale asked, a benevolent expression on his normally chiseled features.

"When I heard about Paul's trial, I knew I had to come. But first, I had to inform my parents. It was only fair, they are both in ill health and I feared the shock might be bad for them."

"You say you had to come. Was this a moral, ethical decision?"

"Partly, yes. But mostly it was because…" Alec faltered, looked to the defendant dock. "Because I care for him. I couldn't let him go to prison for protecting me. I was there, I—I spent the night in his bed, and if forensics want to check it out, I'm quite certain they will find evidence of same. I'd be happy to cooperate with any necessary…corroboration."

Someone in the gallery started clapping, others chuckled, and a loud murmured ensued.

The judge called both counselors to the bench. After a brief exchange, Alec was dismissed.

"This court will adjourn at this time, and reconvene at 9 a.m. tomorrow. Unless the prosecution wishes to cross-examine Mr. Doyle, I'll ask the barristers to prepare closing arguments."

"The prosecution has no further questions at this time, but reserves the right to cross-examine in the morning."

Everyone was talking at once. Kate's spirits lifted as she watched Paulie and Alec exchange looks across the courtroom.

ANNE CARTER

Chapter 35

Kate cherished the feel of Rob's hand as they strolled down Regent Street toward Piccadilly Circus. The bright lights, made fuzzy by the endless misty rain, painted a colorful, bright background. They found an Italian restaurant just off Piccadilly and slipped into a booth.

"So tomorrow's it," Kate said, turning her wine glass by the stem. "They told us to bring an overnight bag to court."

"In case we can't get back?"

"I guess."

Rob shook his head. "They're crazy if they don't acquit."

"I'm scared, though. They could think Alec and Paulie are both lying. Paulie perjured himself."

Rob shrugged. "I think the reason was addressed. Unless something drastic happens, Mindon's not going to cross-examine Alec. It'll be over in no time."

"Thank God Alec showed up."

"Do you think they'll reconcile? That Paul might come back to L.A. if he's let off?"

"I hope so."

"You've missed him a lot."

Kate nodded. "Yeah. I can't deny that."

"I'm still worried about who's collected all this info. The prosecutor, today, questioned Paul about your going to your parents' house. That was, like, over three years ago? Who told him that?"

"Teasdale said it was anonymous tips. Mindon says he got a phone call, or several phone calls, I don't know."

"They must realize by now that this informant is really the killer."

Kate gave Rob a skeptical look. "I don't have high hopes. The Metro Police turned it over to Scotland Yard, but they didn't really get too deeply involved because they thought they had their killer. Apparently, there's a lot of flak from the locals about there being a murder on the Heath. It's not the first, though."

"Won't be the last. It's like Central Park."

"It makes me nervous. Should I be scared?"

Rob gave her a level stare. "Not scared. But cautious. Someone went to a lot of trouble to implicate Paul in a senseless murder. You and Alec are both, well, people he values."

Kate touched her forehead, looked past Rob to the raindrops flowing down the front window of the restaurant. "And Bonny."

Rob reached for her hand. "Talk to your mom tonight. If things go well tomorrow, we'll be on the next flight out."

"Dr. Doyle. You testified that you left the Hampstead mansion at approximately 7:30 a.m. on December 31st. Are there witnesses that will confirm your departure?"

"Not that I'm aware of. Again, only the cab driver."

"So, therefore, if you did, in fact, arrive at Mr. Bingham's estate the prior evening at around 9:45 p.m., you could have left the estate at 10:00 p.m. that same night."

"In theory, yes. But I didn't."

"What did you and Mr. Bingham do during the evening in question?"

Alec smiled. "We watched *Corrie* together for the first time. It was a lark."

"*Corrie*? You're speaking of the television program *Coronation Street*?"

"Yes. Paulie commented that it was about time Bet Lynch did something with her makeup."

"Gilroy!" some shouted from the gallery amid the laughter that erupted at Alec's recollection.

"Yes. Forgive me. Bet *Gilroy*."

Mindon turned to the jury. "Of course, Dr. Doyle, you could have watched the aforementioned program from your hotel room, is that not correct?"

"Could have. But believe me, it was far more enjoyable watching it with Paulie. He's quite the expert on the characters."

More titters from all directions.

Rob leaned into Kate. "This isn't going the way he'd hoped. He's probably wishing he could just get Alec off the stand at this point."

Before Mindon could redirect, Alec continued. "We had green tea ice cream, we lit a fire in the fireplace in Paulie's suite and got into bed. We talked for hours about our relationship. I asked him to come home. Back to Los Angeles."

"And was he anxious to leave Britain?" Mindon asked.

"No. He was reluctant. He had concerns about me. About my not being out. I told him I'd think about it. The longer I stayed with him, the more convinced I was that...that...I didn't want to live my life without him."

"No further questions."

Teasdale stood. "If the court please, may I redirect?"

The judge nodded.

"To reconfirm, Dr. Doyle, you stated that you phoned the defendant at approximately 9:25 p.m. Where were you at that time?"

"I was getting into the taxicab leaving Kensington."

"And what did Mr. Bingham say?"

"He said to come on round. He was nearly home, he said, he was walking home from a party but that he'd be there by the time I could arrive from my friends' home."

"Thank you. The defense wishes to enter into evidence, telephone records for both Dr. Doyle and Mr. Bingham, confirming that a call was made and received at the time stated by Dr. Doyle." Teasdale handed a group of papers to the court clerk.

"One last question. Dr. Doyle, did the defendant ever mention Jon Beale to you?"

"Yes."

"And when, and in what context, was that conversation?"

"The night we've been discussing. He was quite upset about the argument that had transpired, and expressed relief that I was there, in case Mr. Beale returned with more aggression."

"He felt safe in your presence."

"Uh, yes."

311

"And to reconfirm, Mr. Beale did, or did not, return that evening?"

"He most certainly did not."

Alec took a seat beside Kate. Teasdale then called a Mr. John Sylvester, the cab driver who transported Alec from Kensington to Hampstead. The cabbie described and identified Alec, and shared that the doctor had given him a ten pound tip. He further mentioned seeing two teenage girls get into a car parked a several yards away.

"The defense rests."

The prosecutor's closing argument lacked fire. Mindon recalled for the jury the fingerprint, and tried to instill doubt about the credibility of the witnesses, claiming that Dr. Doyle's tardiness in providing an alibi brought question to its validity. Further, not one "reliable" witness had been able to testify to the fact that Jon Beale had left the defendant's property. He charged the jury with the responsibility to see that justice was served, and Beale's murderer be brought to pay.

Teasdale, however, spoke in a candid, impassioned tone with the jurors.

"As you have seen, the prosecution has been unable to show compelling evidence that Paul Bingham had either motive or opportunity to enact the killing of Jon Beale. Mr. Bingham is a man who meets his challenges and deals with them in a peaceful manner. His shortcomings lie mostly with caring too much, not with cruelty or indifference.

"Indeed, it was out of affection and respect for another that Mr. Bingham withheld information that could have immediately cleared him of any and all suspicion, an alibi that could have been provided by his onetime domestic partner, Dr. Alec Doyle. By Dr. Doyle's eventual account, he and Mr. Bingham were together, inside the Hampstead home of Mr. Bingham, prior to, during, and after the time at which Mr. Beale was murdered. DNA evidence taken from Mr. Bingham's suite of rooms will likely place Dr. Doyle there, as does the testimony of..." the barrister paused, glanced down at the note paper in his hand, "Mr. Sylvester, the cab driver who dropped Dr. Doyle at

312

the Hampstead estate at approximately 9:45 p.m. on the night of the murder."

The barrister paused to have a sip of water. "The jury will also recall the evidence that indicated a portion of Mr. Bingham's right thumbprint exists on the murder weapon. However, the defendant has shown that his left hand is the one he habitually uses for a singular action. Eating a teacake, however, might involve both hands, both knife and fork, in which case the fork would be in the hand he favors."

Teasdale wandered past the jury and looked into each face, as if asking for their vote. "Ladies and gentlemen of the jury, I ask you today to recognize and respect the fact that Paul Philip Bingham is not guilty of the crime for which he is charged. Let us do what is right and honorable and allow this young man get on with his life."

News of the impending verdict had doubled the crowd outside Snaresbrook. Fans camped on the lawn, clogged the streets. Media had set up camp. Inside the courtroom, Kate could hardly get a breath. Her chest felt as if she was wearing a tightly laced corset. Rob kept hold of her hand. Even the normally placid Alec was wide-eyed and unable to sit still.

What if? What if they found him guilty? What kind of appeal could they possibly make, having already used every possible angle and testimony? Kate saw Paulie in the kind of orange jumpsuit that American convicts wore. She imagined him wearing an old-fashioned ball-and-chain, lifting a sledge hammer and breaking rocks in a quarry. She thought about him undressing and walking into the prison shower, his slight, trembling form on display to those who knew he was gay, knew he was alone and scared. Her throat swelled and she tried to swallow.

"The defendant will rise."

The jury filed in. Most kept their eyes averted, but one or two looked Kate's way as they took their seats. The clerk asked for the leader's response, a small white card that contained the plan for Paulie's future: freedom or prison.

"Will the foreman please stand? Mr. Foreman, will you please confine yourself to answering my first question either yes or no. Have the jury reached a verdict on Count 1, upon which you are all agreed?"

"Yes, my Lord."

"Do you find the defendant guilty, or not guilty, on Count 1?"

"We find the defendant Paul Philip Bingham...not guilty on Count 1."

There was instantaneous applause from the gallery, jurors smiled openly for the first time. Kate felt her eyes flood with tears as she turned first to Rob, then Alec, hugging them each in succession.

Amid the joyous response, only one sound of discord could be heard, that of a woman crying inconsolably from a seat behind the prosecution desk.

Across the courtroom, Paulie lowered his head into his hands.

How did I feel? So many things. Relief, obviously. Dizzy. Fearful. I wanted to crawl into a hole, disappear. I knew the press would be all over me like flies on shit. I was afraid to face Alec, despaired at what he'd been forced to do on my account. Wondering if Kate had somehow coerced him to confess. I wasn't thinking about the things I should have been considering, like the fact that my daughter still had a free father. That my sister could finally stop moaning. I didn't consider, either, that someone else had actually murdered poor Jon, and that someone was still lurking.

Instead, I turned all of that off. I slipped into that mode that had so often carried me in the past. I sought solace in some form of escape, distraction, substitution for an uncomfortable reality that included all the nastiness that would undoubtedly follow the culmination of the trial.

There would certainly be some price for me to pay for being rescued. There always was.

—Paulie Bingham, Acquitted Pop Star

☙❧

Also from Beacon Street Books!

Part 2 of Paulie & Kate's story:

FOR THE LOVE OF KATRINA BINGHAM
BY
ANNE CARTER

"Don't be desperate. It doesn't become you."

Kate pressed her mouth hard against his, knowing the lips, the tongue, the slight unevenness of his lower teeth. She *was*, suddenly, desperate, and the more he fought her the more she wanted from him. Paulie accepted her kiss, let her probe his mouth, suck on his lower lip. She waited, her breath hot and rapid against his chin.

He pressed a finger to her lips.

Kate swallowed, rolled back onto her pillow. "Oh, God." *He doesn't want me.* It was bound to happen, eventually. He preferred men, had made it perfectly clear. He had a man at home waiting for him. A man that had just offered to take care of him the rest of his life, without the burden of children, or menstrual cycles, or jealous boyfriends. And here she was, still as needy, possibly needier, than the night so long ago when she'd pulled the same stunt. She swallowed again, hoping to stifle a possible sob, then she threw back the blankets and stumbled out of bed to retrieve her t-shirt from the floor.

Paulie was quick to crawl to the edge of the bed and grasp her arm.

"Not so fast. Come back to bed."

"It's okay. I get it."

"No, you don't get it. Come."

315

The neediness forced her to comply. He pulled her back close against him, dragged the covers up to her shoulder.

"Will you talk to me, Kate?"

She shrugged. "Whatever."

"It's important."

"Sure."

"Put aside being pissed off for a moment."

She nodded, let herself pout. It was dark, and he wouldn't see.

"What's going on with you and Rob? Honestly, now."

She wanted to turn her back, tell him it was none of his business.

"I don't know."

"Well now that's really sad."

"I told you. On the phone."

"What I heard was you backing away from a future with him."

"I'm not ready to shack up. I appreciate that he's ready, he wants to know that I'm in, but I'm not really that confident."

"Do you love him?"

"Loving someone isn't enough." She felt his chin against her forehead. "All I can think is, what if it doesn't work out?"

His hand moved to the back of her head. "Seems to me you said that before. To me."

"And look what happened!"

"Ah. I see. Maybe that's where we need to start."

"Start what? Don't be my therapist, Paulie."

"No therapy, just talk. And just so I understand, you're inferring that we failed, is that it?"

"Well, we did."

He adjusted his position, moved a leg over hers so that they were touching all the way down. The intimacy of the move was not lost on her.

316

"Are you comfortable?" he asked, lips close to her ear.

"Of course I am."

"Do you still love me?"

Kate looked up, hoping she could see his eyes in the darkness. They were expectant, but confident. "You know I do."

"And I, you. Are you glad that we had a child, or would you not if you could do it over?"

"Glad? She is the light of my life. I can't imagine life without her."

"Good. Me too. Now, tell me again how you think we failed so badly?"

෧৵

BUY IT FROM BEACON STREET BOOKS!

Dear Reader,

The author hopes you've enjoyed Paulie and Kate's story, and if so, that you will share your thoughts with others. Reviews always appreciated. Thank you!

Beacon Street Books

http://BeaconStreetBooks.com

Meet Anne Carter

Creating fiction gives one the power to design other lives, filled with romance and adventure, intrigue and passion. My own writing career began in middle school creative writing class, inspiring me to later major in literature. All it took was one teacher's encouragement and I was on my way.

I'm the author of nine published novels, including mystery, romance, paranormal, alternative romance and even a middle grade reader. As for the personal stuff, I'm a Virgo, a procrastinator, like warm better than cold and drink neither Coke nor Pepsi. I was born in the Midwest but migrated to California as a child. My hobbies include doll collecting, photo restoration and writing, of course. My favorite sport is ice hockey, my favorite TV shows include Elementary, Person of Interest, NCIS, Downton Abbey, LOST, and Grey's Anatomy. I am married to my hero of 30+ years and have 3 great kids.

As a free-lance writer, I hang out at my website, Facebook, and other fun cyber spots.

.

Visit me at http://www.anne-carter.com.

Also by Anne Carter:

PAULIE & KATE'S STORY:

UNMASKING PAULIE BINGHAM
FOR THE LOVE OF KATRINA BINGHAM

STARCROSSED ROMANCES:

STARCROSSED HEARTS
A HERO'S PROMISE
THE GYSPY IN ME (FALL, 2014)

BEACON POINT ROMANCES:

EVER & ALWAYS (PREQUEL)
POINT SURRENDER
CAPE SEDUCTION
ANGEL'S GATE

ALTERNATIVE ROMANCE NOVELLA:

STARFIRE